MERCEDES LACKEY

The
ELEMENTAL
MASTERS

THE CASE OF THE SPELLBOUND CHILD

TITAN BOOKS

The Case of the Spellbound Child
Paperback edition ISBN: 9781789093735
Ebook edition ISBN: 9781789093742

Published by Titan Books
A division of Titan Publishing Group Ltd
144 Southwark Street, London SE1 0UP.

First Titan edition: January 2020
2 4 6 8 10 9 7 5 3 1

A CIP catalogue record for this title is available from the British Library.

Printed and bound in Great Britain by CPI Group Ltd.

To Leandro Pardini

1

Alf grinned as he pushed open the whorehouse door into the damp London night. Good pay for an easy job had brought him and Reg enough to splash out on a night of it, and he was feeling fine.

Then a blinding flash whited everything out, at the same time that Alf's head erupted in excruciating pain.

Then flailing, then falling, falling.

Then for a moment, nothing.

And a moment later, he found himself standing in a gray fog, though there'd been no fog when he stepped out of the whorehouse. He stared straight into the eyes of his mate, good old Reg, who'd been a few steps behind him.

When had he turned? What had hit him?

Reg held a lead cosh in his right hand, and stared down at the street at his feet.

Wut? Was we. . . .

Reflexively, he stared down too—and saw his own body lying face down in the dirt in front of the whorehouse door, with Reg between the body and the temporarily empty street. Two and two added up to *Reg just bashed me 'ead in. . . .*

Bloody 'Ell!

And at just that moment, when he was torn between blind rage and shock, he felt something he'd never felt before: a cold chill, a *graveyard* chill, and a strong, almost irresistible pull at his back, as if something had just gaped open behind him and was about to suck him in.

Instinct did the rest. So instead of flying at Reg in a fury, he leapt forward, into the street, into the path of a slow-moving, transparent cart, which did not so much as pause for him as it passed right through him. Or he passed through it. . . .

That wasn't what had his attention, as he whirled to see what had been behind him. It was a gaping, swirling hole where the whorehouse door had been, behind where he had been standing, a bottomless hole that drank in what little light there was and let none escape.

That was when he realized, somewhere in his head too deep for thoughts, that he wasn't just hurt, he was *dead*, that his "mate" Reg had just murdered him, and that the hole would have sucked him down to Hell if he hadn't jumped out of its reach. Why it couldn't do so *now*, he had no idea, but he didn't intend to stick around long enough to find out. As Reg stuffed the cosh in his back pocket and bent down to start rifling through Alf's clothes for valuables, Alf turned and ran.

Through the pub on the other side of the street. Without opening the door.

The moving shadows, the transparent figures bellied up to the bar paid him no heed as he sprinted straight across the pub floor and out into the "area" in the back. And straight through the privy. He stopped just short of the next building, not because he was winded—he wasn't—but because shock stopped him.

Everything past the pub wall was lost in the shadows and fog, but he still *felt* that hole to Hell out there. Waiting. Waiting for him to accept his fate and let it take him.

"Ye keep on waitin'!" he shouted, his voice curiously thin and reedy, scarcely more than a whistle. He looked down at himself. He looked exactly as he remembered himself when he'd left the whore's room and come down to wait for Reg. Moleskin trousers, bracers, threadbare shirt, battered tweed jacket, boots badly in need of resoling. But . . . faded, what little color there had been all drained away, leaving everything in shades of gray. Just like everything around him. And other than emotion . . . he didn't feel anything. Not tired. Not in pain. Not hungry, though he'd been famished a moment before, and about to suggest to Reg that they get a meal at the pub. He wasn't cold or hot, and he couldn't smell a thing, and he knew the "area" back here reeked of shit and urine. And he could see through everything except himself.

Instinct, which had served him well until Reg betrayed him, told him that his smartest move was to stay still and quiet until he had a better lay of the land. So wait he did, as pub patrons came and used the privy or just pissed against the nearest wall. And he never felt a moment of fatigue, for what might have been minutes, or might have been hours, until that cold, dark tugging at his insides . . . stopped.

Cautiously, he stepped through the pub wall, feeling something like resistance this time as he forced his way through it. It was—well, he wasn't sure what it was like, only that he didn't much like the feeling, but it was better than waiting for another drunk to come out here to piss and open the door. Through the passage he went, then passed with a shiver right through all the blokes crowded up against the bar, then caught a bit of luck and got through the front door along with a staggering drunk.

The hole in the air was gone. It felt like a victory, and he whooped and shot his fist straight up, then shook it at where the hole had been. "Yew ain't got me, yer barsterd! Yew ain't gonna get me neither! Oi'm too tough fer 'Eaven an' too smart fer 'Ell!"

He stood there, rejoicing in his achievement, for quite some time, as wraiths of people and carts and the occasional cab passed through him. But eventually, as the elation wore off the thought came slowly creeping up upon him.

Now what?

After fruitlessly looking for Reg—though what he was supposed to do if he *found* Reg, he had no idea—he went to stand by his unmoving body and brooded down at it.

He was a ghost now, he supposed. It was clear given the way that the living passed right through him that revenge on Reg was flat out of the question. So what was he to do with himself now?

Ghosts apparently didn't eat, drink, or need shelter; and he didn't *feel* anything at all except emotion. For a very long time he stood there, staring at his body, which lay conveniently out of the way of traffic. A few other people stared at it too, and moved on, as he himself would have done had he encountered—say, good old Reg—in a similar state. Dead bodies on the pavement were not an uncommon sight at night in this part of London, and once they'd been looted were regarded more as an inconvenience than a curiosity, much less a horror.

Just as he began to wonder if anyone was going to do anything about him before dawn, the police "body wagon" showed up to collect it, the loaders picking him up by the shoulders and heels like a bit of old rubbish and unceremoniously heaving him up into the wagon-bed with three others like him, another man, a child, and an old woman.

And the wagon rolled off. He knew what came next: the morgue, someone going through his pockets in a vain attempt to find something to identify him, finding nothing because of course Reg had taken everything, maybe a day before he was either dumped in a common grave with the other unidentified stiffs or (more likely) sold off to medical students. So there was no reason whatsoever to follow that wagon.

In fact, the only thing that really mattered, the thing that made him red hot with anger, was that bloody Reg was going to get away with it all.

And even then, he couldn't sustain the anger. It bled out of him like water in a sieve, leaving him, once again, feeling nothing, and wondering what to do with himself.

One by one he ticked off all the things that used to give him pleasure, and realized they were all things he couldn't do now. Eat, drink, natter with the lads, gamble, whore, sleep in a good soft bed—

Did ghosts sleep? If he could pass through walls and people, a bed probably wouldn't hold him.

He realized he'd been staring at the spot where his body had been all the time he'd been thinking, and raised his eyes as the whorehouse door opened to let out another customer.

Well . . . I can still watch.

When the madam closed the door on the last of the evening's customers, once again, he found himself with nothing to do.

Watching had been . . . exciting at first, but not for very long. He soon realized that without a body to be aroused, watching other people rut was disappointing. In fact, the only interesting thing was watching and listening to the girls when they weren't futtering. He'd always assumed they were getting pleasure out of it all too; after all, they certainly made all the sounds and expressions of someone having a good time.

Except it turned out that they weren't.

He'd never kept to any one house or any one girl; he'd always told himself it was no use having a favorite, because if the girl found out she *was* a favorite, she might start asking things of him, like presents, or for him to keep her. The one he couldn't afford, and the other would be as bad as a wife, and more expensive, with none of the advantages, like putting her to work *for* him, and Hell's own chance of getting her to take a real job after the easy work of lying on her back in bed for her money.

So he'd never caught any of the girls he used at the tricks he caught them at now.

Like, using the *exact same words and actions* on every single man that took them upstairs. It was like watching a play, over and over and over.

This was a house with only four girls, and he had half the night to watch 'em at it. He'd stayed with the Irish gel after she'd sent off a sailor, because he'd been curious enough about what she did between men not to leave for another room. Wash up, it turned out, and wearing an expression of utter weariness while doing so. He'd been about to leave when a second mark came pushing open the door, but her first words to him stuck him in place, because they were *identical* to what she'd said to the first lad he'd watched her with.

"Oh, come in, me foine boyo! Sure, and with such a foine lad as yew at me door, I'll nivver go back to Ireland!"

And after that, every word, every action, was identical to her performance with the sailor, right down to the timing of every sigh and cry.

And when he slipped into the other rooms, he discovered it was the same with the other three girls. The only time they changed their performance—and even then, it was only the "before" and "after," not the act itself—was with someone they'd had before.

By the time the madam closed the door on the heels of the last man, he was thoroughly disenchanted. Not that he'd been *enchanted* by whores before, but a man liked to think he was something special in the way of a stallion, and now he knew he was just one more broken-down old nag at the back end of the stable, getting the same perfunctory rubdown and ration of dusty old hay as the rest.

He was brooding over this as he forced his way out through the closed door and into the street.

And it felt as if he had walked into a gale.

The pressure of something *like* a mighty wind, but not wind, forced him into a crouch, and to his horror, he felt and saw bits of himself flaking off and floating away! It took him a moment to realize that what he was fighting was—

—the morning sunlight, pouring down the street from an unusually cloudless sky.

In a complete and mindless panic he turned and forced his way back in through the closed door of the whorehouse, where he stood just inside the front passageway. He should have been shaking. He felt—lessened, somehow, as if something was missing. Reflexively, he looked down at himself—

—he could see through himself.

Terror engulfed him.

He hadn't just imagined that the sunlight was stripping bits of himself away. He'd been eroded. His mind went blank with shock, and he fell gratefully into the blankness, because blankness was not terror.

He was jarred out of his shock when the madam of the house walked through him to answer a summons at the door. Outside, night had fallen. The sounds of the pub across the street came to his ears as if from a vast distance. And *he* was no longer transparent.

A dull sense of relief came to him. So—whatever the sun had done to him, there must have been a way he had healed himself over the course of the day. Except . . . he didn't remember anything of the day. Nothing at all. What had happened to him wasn't like sleep, and although it had repaired him, it hadn't refreshed him at all. It had been more like he was a kind of clockwork that had run down, and something had just set him going again.

Or actually, more like being blackout drunk, without the fun of getting to that point.

He wasn't sure what made him more uneasy and unhappy, nearly being torn apart and scattered on the wind by sunlight, or going all blank for the day.

And now what was he going to do? The night-time hours stretched before him, and there was not one single item in the entire list of things that used to give him pleasure that he was able to do anymore.

And the one thing he *could* do—spy on people—wasn't any fun if he didn't have anyone to talk to about it. What was the good of knowing secrets about people if you couldn't make use of those secrets?

He stood there in the passage, brooding, while customers came and went. After last night's revelations, he really didn't want to watch the whores anymore.

Someone walked through him on his way upstairs, whistling "You'll Miss Lots of Fun When You're Married," and this time it struck him like another (but pleasant) blow to the head that *now* he could get into any music hall and any theater in the city for free, and stay as long as he liked. In the toff seats, too!

A surge of cheer went through him at the thought, and suddenly everything seemed brighter. *Bloody hell if I can't get into them fancy toff whorehouses too!* He'd heard they had all sorts of goings-on there, music and dancing and orgies, good as a music hall or better, 'cause the girls had less on.

Without actually thinking about going anywhere, he found himself out on the street again, heading in the direction of the Old Mo. That'd be a good place to start!

And to his pleasure he discovered he could stride along as fast as he cared to without his legs tiring a bit. He increased his pace to a trot, then a run, with the same lack of fatigue, and began to laugh as he ran along. *This is more like!* he thought, giddy with the freedom of it.

But just as he thought that, he became aware of a tugging on his insides, as if the guts he no longer had were tethered to something behind him, or the air in front of him was solidifying like curdled milk. He slowed from a run to a trot, within a few paces more from a trot to a walk, and within a few more paces—he couldn't move forward against the pull at all. He strained against the invisible tether to no avail; he just could not move forward another inch.

But he *could* move sideways.

So he did, pushing through building walls, crossing streets at a slight angle, straining as hard as he could. He felt as if he'd been harnessed to a beer-wagon and was trying to pull it. But of course, he didn't break into a sweat. Presumably because he couldn't sweat. He wasn't panting, because he didn't need to breathe.

At one point in the Herculean effort, he wondered *why* he was doing this. But the answer was obvious, really. He was doing it because it was something to do.

He knew this neighborhood like the back of his hand, although he'd never traversed it in quite this way before, literally cutting through shops and private spaces. That was how he recognized what was happening the moment he crossed the same street he had been on before, but facing in the opposite direction. He stopped then, and looked back over his shoulder. He couldn't see the point from which he'd started; that gray fog that hung over everything, even indoors, obscured things beyond about fifty feet. But he knew where he was, and he knew where the whorehouse was from here, and by his best guess he was about five hundred yards from where he'd died. So he'd likely just toiled his way halfway around a circle that was about a thousand yards across, centered on the whorehouse.

Slowly, he began to understand just what this meant. He could not go more than five hundred yards from where he'd died. This, then, was going to be his world. One tiny music hall, three whorehouses, a half dozen pubs and cookshops, some goods shops.

He sat right down in the middle of the street, defeat crushing him to the ground. What was the point then, after all? He'd escaped Hell—but for what? He remained there in a dull, unthinking haze until a growing sense of sick unease roused him, and he felt, without knowing why he felt this, that the unease had a direction.

He looked up, to see that the sky was definitely lighter in the direction of his unease.

There was only one thing he could think of that would account for that. The sun was about to rise.

He got wearily to his feet, and shuffled toward the nearest building, which happened to house a cookshop whose owner was just opening up to catch the dawn risers. With the door wide open, at least he didn't have to shove his way into the building. Without a glance at the waiting food—which he could neither smell nor taste—he passed through another doorway and found himself in the kitchen of the shop. Off to one side was a third doorway whose dark mouth beckoned to him. A cellar.

He plodded his way down into the comforting darkness, sat on the floor, and let the numb nothingness of yesterday engulf him.

When he came back to himself, it was to the sound of footsteps coming down into the cellar. The owner's wife, lantern in hand, was halfway down the steps before he roused himself enough to stand up. He knew her of old; she went out of her way to sell him the oldest of pies, the sandwich with the rind of the cheese instead of a good slice, and the stalest bread. He'd been sick more than once after eating what he'd bought here. He'd accused her of trying to poison him. How she would laugh at him if she could see him now!

The thought made him furious, and he stood in the middle of her cellar, knee-deep in a basket of taties, and snarled at her. "And what're yew comin' down 'ere for, ye old sow?" he snarled. "Spoilt taties t'bake up fer t'pisen summat else?"

And to his astonishment, she looked right at him, and froze.

Her eyes widened in horror; she shook as if she had an ague. Her mouth opened, but nothing came out of it.

She can see me?

He cackled wildly, and snarled at her, making the worst face he knew how to do. Then he reached for her.

She shrieked at the top of her lungs and dropped the lantern, which shattered on the floor, the flame immediately igniting the pool of spilled oil. With another shriek, she whirled, with only purest good luck keeping her from setting her skirts on fire, and raced up the stairs, still screaming.

Leaving him laughing harder than he had ever laughed before in his entire life.

He backed up and tucked himself into a corner as the cookshop owner clattered down the stairs, more concerned about his property burning down than about the hysterics of his spouse, and stamped out the flames with a pair of sturdy hobnailed boots. Once the danger was over, the man left and came back again with a lantern of his own, cleaned up the mess, and then peered in every corner of the cellar, looking right into Alf's eyes more than once—but *he* clearly saw nothing.

"Yew stupid cow!" he called up the stairs. "Yew broke th' good lantern and spilled me good oil an' there ain't naught down 'ere but taties an' turnips!"

The woman cried out something incoherent amid her sobs, which made her husband spit in disgust and stomp his way back up the stairs, shouting abuse the entire time.

Alf couldn't contain his glee, and didn't try. If he'd been at a loss for what to do with himself before, well, he wasn't now! "I'll be a 'aunt, tha's wut!" he proclaimed out loud. "'Er an' 'er ways kep' me awake wit' bellyache many a night, well, I'll be makin' *'er* nights a misery, see if I don'!" Revenge! Now *there* was a pleasure he was still capable of! And if he couldn't revenge himself on Reg, he'd take his pleasure where he could find it.

Up the stairs he went, and peeked into the kitchen. There was the hysterically weeping woman and her impatient, hectoring spouse. She'd pulled up her apron in both hands and buried her face in it. Grinning maliciously, he crept up close to her and waited for her to bring her head up to answer something her husband said.

She found herself staring directly into his eyes. He snarled at her, and made a grab for her. His hand passed right through her and she fainted on the spot.

Chuckling, he glanced out of the open back window and judged it was just past sunset. *I wonder who else can see me?*

No time like the present to find out.

Well, he'd wanted something to do, and haunting people was turning out to be the most entertaining thing he'd ever done in his life that didn't involve a whore. It beat dog-and cock-fighting, that was certain.

Besides the woman at the cookshop, he had a regular little flock of those he was able to terrify on a nightly basis. There was the little Cockney whore who worked on her own and had laughed at him because he wouldn't pay her price. He'd have knocked her sideways if she hadn't had her man with her. Well, now she had to see him stalking her every step she took, and her man didn't believe what she was seeing any more than the cookshop owner had believed his wife. It tickled him no end when her custom fell off because of him, and her man beat her for it.

But he didn't spend the entire night just stalking her, oh no. He knew to the minute from the sounds of the Bow Bells just when the cookshop owner and his wife went to bed, and moments after they pulled up the covers and the old man was snoring, he was *there,* gobbling and grimacing at her. She'd lie there praying silently at him, shivering, tears streaming down her face. She didn't dare wake her husband, so she had to lie there, staring at him, unable to move. Once she even brandished a cross at him, and he laughed at her and lunged for her. She fainted again.

There was a whole family of filthy Dagos living in one room above an old-clothes shop. The parents couldn't see him, but the brats could, and he made sure the whole lot got woke just before dawn with the carrying on and caterwauling when he made his appearance. Haunting them was how he found out that even though his hands passed right through people, they weren't immune to his touch. When he contacted them, they felt a chill. And not like a little shiver either, a deep, bone-chilling cold, icy enough that when their parents woke to their screams after he had touched them, the adults exclaimed over the shivering bodies, and chafed the nippers with their hands or wrapped them in all the meager blankets, trying to get them warm again. At least, he was fairly sure that was what was going on, since he didn't understand their babbling.

Periodically he'd let them alone for a few nights—because there were others who might or might not be able to see him, depending on circumstances. The madam of the whorehouse liked to indulge in absinthe, and when she was in her cups, she got glimpses of him. There were other brats in the neighborhood besides the

Dagos, and the littlest could reliably see him—it seemed as if nine or ten was the cutoff for being able to consistently see ghosts. Some drunks could see him, though their reactions varied—some were terrified, but some just took him as another spirit of drink, rather than an actual spirit. So every so often he'd give his regulars a respite from his presence and go haunt someone else. That only increased the terror and despair when he turned up again.

And the more he frightened people, the stronger he got. He didn't feel thinned out anymore. He didn't have to go into that blank state by day unless he wanted to. He even managed to cross the street just before sunset without having parts of himself evaporate.

It had been in the early spring when Reg murdered him—and Reg hadn't been back to this neighborhood since. But now that he had his haunting and tormenting to do he found himself losing track of time, and only realized it was summer when it dawned on him that the nights were much shorter than they had been. He had decided to give his usual victims a respite, and was prowling part of his domain he usually didn't get to, when he spotted something coming toward him that literally stunned him for a moment.

It was a young man—dressed like a toff, he would have said—but there was something wrong with him.

He was just as solid as Alf himself.

And that was impossible.

Unless—this was another ghost?

In that moment he was terribly torn between two impulses—to hide from this apparition, and to approach him. What if this bloke was hostile? What if he was stronger than Alf? What if he was something *more* than a ghost, what if this bloke had been *sent* by Something—sent to haul him through that door he'd escaped—

But on the other hand, it had been so long since he'd properly heard another human voice, so long since he'd exchanged words with *anyone.* . . .

Loneliness—though he would *never* have admitted he was lonely, even to himself—won out. "'Ere!" he called out, before he could stop himself.

The young man jumped, startled, and turned to stare at him as if surprised to see him. "What?" he replied in tones far more cultured than Alf's. "Who are you? What are you doing here?"

18

Alf puffed out his chest and strode toward him, sure of at least one thing: a lad this nervy was no match for him. "Name's Alf," he said, prepared to be friendly now. "This's *my* place—leastwise—" he faltered. He couldn't say it. "Since Oi . . . since Oi . . ."

"Since you died, you must mean," the young man said, regaining his composure. Up close he was curiously androgynous; very well dressed for this neighborhood, with his neat suit, proper shirt and tie, and an actual hat rather than a soft cap. Alf would've called him a "nancy-boy" at best, and any number of obscene things at worst, and probably kicked him around back when he'd been alive, but now, well, beggars could not be choosers. This was the first time he'd seen anyone to talk to, and until this moment he hadn't realized just how starved he was for another voice that would actually answer his. Besides, there'd be no satisfaction in kicking him about; it wasn't as if this sort of body was able to feel or do much of anything.

The young man stuck out his hand. "The name's Hughs. Peter Hughs. I got knocked over by a runaway cab about five years ago, six blocks that way." He waved vaguely in the direction of the river. Hughs eyed Alf knowingly. "I'd venture to say you popped it within the last couple of months, eh?"

Alf scratched his head; he'd definitely lost all track of time, and the openness of the young man honestly caught him off-guard. "Prolly," he admitted. "Oi'm not sure. . . ."

"It's easy to lose touch with how time passes," said Hughs, with a nod. "Are you keeping to the half-world, or have you gone all the way over to the spirit world yet?"

Alf shook his head. "Yew lost me, mate," he replied, as they both ignored a beer cart that drove right through them.

"This is the half-world, or that's what the other ghosts call it," Hughs explained, waving his hand to indicate everything around them. "But if you let all this fade, you end up in the spirit world. You can't see the living anymore, and the buildings are mostly shadow, though they get more solid the older they are. The spirit world is where most of the ghosts spend the day, if they're living in a part of it that's safe. It's all right *here*, but there's parts of London—" he shivered. "—you wouldn't want to meet up with the things that live in the spirit world there. Fortunately they're as stuck in their parts as we are in ours."

But Alf had fixed on Hughs' first statement. "Other ghosts? Yew mean there's more'n us?"

Hughs shrugged. "Hundreds. Thousands, maybe. London's a big place and people die all the time. A lot of them don't want to leave."

"'Ere," Alf said, uncomfortably aware of the living walking all around and through them. "Le's find someplace we ain't got people walkin' through us. Yew sound loike th' kinda bloke Oi oughter know."

"How about up there?" asked Hughs, pointing to a rooftop, and chuckled at what must have been Alf's expression. "Don't worry, I'll show you how to get up there."

And so Alf learned how to fly, as ghosts were supposed to fly in stories, just by will alone. He was still marveling over that as they settled down on the rooftree like a couple of starlings.

Hughs taught him a lot in the time between when they'd met and dawn. Why strong emotions from the living that connected to ghosts (like fear) made them stronger, how to move completely into the spirit world and out again, what the dangerous things in the spirit world were and how to avoid them, why sunlight was perilous, and who his ghostly "neighbors" besides Hughs were. There were more of them than Alf would have thought, but according to Hughs, most of them were crazed, and spent most of their time brooding in specific places wholly in the spirit world, none of which were within "his" territory.

Somewhat to his surprise, Hughs was easy to like, and Alf found himself telling the young man all about his hauntings. Hughs listened intently but without comment until he had finished. He saved the cookshop shrew for last, and actually laughed for the first time since he'd been murdered as he described how she had waved a crucifix at him. Hughs was a good listener, and Alf had always liked to talk.

"You seem to be enjoying yourself," Hughs said, after a few moments of silence.

He shrugged, and looked down at the shadowy living passing to and fro below them. "There's damn-all else wut makes me 'appy," he replied, a little bitterly, then laughed again. "An' it does make me 'appy."

Hughs nodded, then glanced behind them. "Sun will be up soon," he said. "I need to get back to my part of town. Would you like me to meet you again some time soon?"

Alf hesitated. What he *wanted* was for Hughs to come by tomorrow. And the next day. And the next. He'd had no idea he was so starved for company, but now that Hughs was about to depart, he found himself fighting the impulse to seize the young man's arm and beg him to spend the day *here*.

Which . . . would make him look desperate. He didn't want to look desperate, he wanted to look strong, like his living self, fearless and dependent on nobody. He didn't want Hughs to get the idea that Alf needed him.

So he shrugged. "If yew ain't got nothin' else to do," he replied, trying to appear indifferent.

Hughs hesitated. "I do have a lot more to tell you, but I don't want to impose on you or be a crashing bore."

That made Alf laugh, since the last thing Hughs was was a bore. "Termorrer then," he said genially. "'Ang about the pub, Oi'll meetcher there."

And without waiting for an answer, he drifted down to the ground and sauntered off, trying not to look as if he was hurrying.

2

"...And if there's anyone you want to send a message to, they can do it."

Alf had only been listening to Hughs natter on about "mediums" with half his attention, but he nodded. "On'y bloke I wants ter send a message to is th' one what did me," he replied, a bit bitterly. "An' that message'd be with a cosh loike 'e did me with."

Hughs grimaced.

But Alf ignored his expression, because the idea of actually being able to communicate with the living had sparked something in Alf's mind. "I wunner," he mused. "Mebbe I could get 'im to go somewhere's he'd get coshed regardless." If he could find a medium who could somehow get a message to Reg that he'd hidden some money or valuables somewhere . . . wait, not just Reg, but Reg and a couple of other chancy blokes he knew . . . if they all converged on the same spot at the same time, *someone* was going to end up very dead. Granted, that would not give Alf the same satisfaction as doing the blighter in himself, but it would be revenge.

"So how d'yew find a medium?" he asked.

"Oh, if one's anywhere about, you'll know," Hughs assured him. "You can feel it, here." He tapped his head. "It's like they're costers, calling out in the street, but only we can hear them. There is absolutely no doubt when there's a genuine medium somewhere near enough that you can reach her."

Alf brightened, but only for a moment. "Ah, wut's the chance uv that?" he asked, as his initial excitement faded into the usual dull apathy. "Nobody respek'table'd come 'ere."

"Well, if you keep haunting that cookshop keeper's wife, *she* might become desperate enough to send for one, and I expect she'd have the money for it," Hughs pointed out, then stood up. "Keep your hopes up, Alf. I'm going to go back to my cellar for the day."

Alf waited until Hughs was out of sight before dropping down to the ground and making his way to the pub's cellar. It was a good place to spend the day, especially when he wanted to think. About the only time someone came down there was when one of the barrels upstairs was about to run dry. There was wine down there as well, but not a lot of call for it; beer and gin were the usual tipples in this part of town, and the barkeep liked to have the gin where he could keep an eye on it.

Alf settled down among the kegs in the corner furthest from the door. He didn't actually need to sit, but he found sitting let him concentrate. He kept turning the idea of talking with one of those "mediums" over and over in his mind. The first problem he could see was how to get the message to Reg in the first place. He didn't imagine that these women—Hughs had said they were mostly women—did anything out of the goodness of their hearts. So there would be the matter of finding some way to pay her to get the message to Reg. And if that could be surmounted, there was the question of how she would find Reg to deliver the message, since he hadn't been back to this part of town since he'd murdered Alf.

Then there was the matter of getting him to believe the message. Though that was about the easiest of all the problems to solve. There were quite a number of things only he and Reg knew, not the least of which was that Reg had been his murderer. Better not bring that up, though, or Reg might get the wind up and vanish.

On further thought, he discarded the notion of getting a couple more chancy lads involved as far too complicated. How would he make sure they all arrived at the supposed cache at the same time? Obviously he couldn't give them a time to be there!

So it would have to be a place where Reg would be sure to run into fatal opposition. Now . . . how could he manage that?

Then it struck him, and he grinned, because the idea solved all of his problems at once. He'd tell the medium to get her pay from Reg.

So she had a motive to find Reg and deliver, first the bona fides, then when she'd got her pay, the message. And the message would send good old Reg after money Alf had supposedly cached—straight into the hideout of a gang that Alf had stumbled on quite by accident—and stumbled right out of again once he realized what he'd found.

Now he just had to frame the message in such a way that Reg would believe that he, Alf, had no idea it was Reg who'd done him in. That gave him something to mull over and cogitate on until sunset.

He felt so good about his plans that he took the time to waylay the cookshop woman in a particularly artistic fashion, floating up near the ceiling of the bedroom so that she didn't spot him until she was already in bed. He'd never done that to her before, and she fainted again. Her husband took her faint as sleep, grumbled when he couldn't rouse her, and turned his back to her, disgusted with her lack of response to his efforts at what passed with him as seduction.

And then it occurred to him—terrifying her into fainting was hilarious, but as Hughs had said, if there was *anyone* that would have both the "respectability" and the money to bring a real medium to this neighborhood, it would be her. So he needed to do more than just frighten her into unconsciousness. He had to frighten her into *acting*.

Wait . . . no, what he needed to do was convince the *cookshop owner* that his wife wasn't just being hysterical. The owner was the man holding the purse strings. *He* was the one who had to be convinced that there was a ghost haunting the place.

Fortunately, now he thought he knew how to do just that.

Lessee . . . I gotter notion. . . .

He floated down from the ceiling and right over—and then *into*—both of the unconscious figures. And as he had with the Dago nippers, he concentrated on both of them, on making himself stronger at their expense.

And to his glee, it began to work. They both began to shiver, and both woke up at the same time.

And then something new happened.

As the woman stared at Alf's face, mere inches from hers, her breath puffed out in visible clouds, *and so did her husband's.* The iron bedstead rimed over with frost.

And then her husband's eyes flew open and stared into his in horror.

"*Sweet Jesus!*" the man howled, starting back.

With a cackle, Alf dropped through them and came to rest just under their bed. He had *never* felt so strong, so powerful. It was absolutely intoxicating. He had no idea he could do anything like this!

He listened to the woman sob, but this time, the man was very nearly as hysterical, begging her forgiveness for not believing her. The bed creaked as they both sat up, and he could only imagine what was going through the man's mind at this point.

Finally incoherent babbling on both their parts gave way to silence.

"Wut d'ye s'pose 'e wants?" the man asked, into the darkness. "'E's gotter want *something*, don't 'e?"

The wife just continued to sob, softly. The man cursed. "'Ang it all," he said decisively. "Wutever 'tis, I'll foind out."

Alf smiled to himself, and sank through the floor. Now to see if the madame of the whorehouse was receptive enough to see him tonight. For tonight, he'd concentrate on the victims with money. And find out just how strong he could get.

Oi'd niver hev guessed how inneresrin' this was gonna be.

"Well, you've managed to raise a ruckus," Hughs said, as they met, as usual, outside the pub about two days later.

"'Oo? Me?" Alf chuckled. "Oi dunno wutcher mean."

"Oh, you are the talk of the supernatural neighborhood," Hughs retorted. "You have managed some fairly clever tricks so far, and there are bets on whether you'll learn how to become strong enough to actually affect the physical world."

Alf had not expected that, and his jaw dropped. "Yer meanter say we c'n *do* that?" he gasped.

"You already are," Hughs pointed out, lofting himself up into the air, and picking out a rooftop to settle on, as Alf followed him. "You're pulling energy out of your victims and the air around them. That's what's making things cold when you touch them."

Alf resisted the urge to blurt "*I am?*" and just nodded. "I didn' know we c'ld do more'n that, though." He sat down on the roof ledge overlooking the street where the little music hall was. Oddly, since learning how much fun it was to torment his victims, he hadn't gone back there. *Mebbe Oi should. Ain't there s'posed to be theater 'aunts?*

"The stronger you become, the more you can do, but there are limits," Hughs said casually. "In general, you can't fling anything heavier than a plate about. But it certainly makes a fine show when you break a teacup or two against the wall." He raised an eyebrow at Alf, who felt a surge of great satisfaction. Now, there was a thought, indeed. What would the cookshop owner think if he flung a saucer across the room? Or better still, a knife?

Then his eyes widened at another thought. If his plot to get Reg murdered by proxy didn't work out . . . could he possibly lure Reg *here* and get the job done himself?

Wait—wouldn't that be far more satisfactory?

Well, it clearly *would*. And a lot less complicated. He'd still need the medium to get a message to bring Reg here, but the rest would be up to him. Much more the way he liked it.

Hughs gazed at him speculatively. Alf grinned a little. "Reckon Oi might just get things lively 'ere."

"Well, if you want to lure people to come gawk at the spectacle, regardless of the reputation of this area, that will do it," Hughs replied. "And one or more of them is bound to bring a medium around, if that's what you wanted. Personally I prefer things quieter."

"Wut fun's quiet?" he asked rhetorically. "On'y prollem Oi c'n see's most folks 'round 'ere ain't got a lot uv stuff t'fling."

Hughs laughed as if he had made the best joke in the world. He felt rather proud of his quip.

Well, if he was going to get a lot of attention, he was going to have to make a spectacle of things where more people than just one or two could see it. And the Dagos weren't in the least interested in drawing attention to themselves. Besides, they'd probably just run off to their heathen priest if he began lobbing bits of their property about.

No, after due consideration, he decided that what he needed to do was concentrate on the cookshop. But this time, before it closed, or after it opened.

But he'd need strength, so time to draw on those Dago brats as the easiest source of it.

"Oi'm gonna cause me a bit uv ruckus," he told Hughs, and without a farewell, headed for the Dagos' room.

He had left them alone for quite a few nights while he concentrated on the cookshop, and he could tell by the relatively relaxed atmosphere in the room that once again they had allowed themselves to believe he was gone. He also realized, given that the parents were half clothed, and the nippers less than that, that it must be a very hot night tonight. Well then! He'd be doing them a favor. . . .

By the time he left, he was bursting with strength, and they'd thrown every stitch they owned over their bodies and were huddled in blankets while frost rimed everything metal in the room, and even some of the wood. He'd decided to let them off easy this time; he hadn't actually shown himself. Not that this had lessened their terror. If anything, it had probably made things worse, which was good for him.

The cookshop was just about to close for the night; there was always a last-minute rush of business, as the owner sold the things he couldn't manage to revive the next day at heavily discounted prices. So the stage was perfectly set, as he shoved his way in through the wall and surveyed the little room for things small and light.

He wasn't quite sure where or how to start. Hughs hadn't given him any instructions, and he was damned if he was going to ask for any. But there was a picture of the Queen on the wall, cut from an old newspaper and inexpertly framed with a few sticks of wood. It looked light enough, and hopefully it wasn't nailed *to* the wall rather than hung on it. He drifted over to it, put both hands on the frame, and concentrated with all his might on pushing *against* it, rather than through it.

With a thrill of delight, he saw it move!

Now alight with energy and encouragement, he continued pushing at it, trying to rock it to and fro. The gargantuan effort it took made him feel as if he were trying to push an elephant uphill against its will, but not only did it move, he was able to get it swinging.

And about the time it was rocking back and forth merrily on

its nail, and clattering as it did so, he heard, faintly, from the living world, words that warmed his soul.

"Bloody 'Ell—lookit thet!"

He glanced at the rest of the room. The half dozen or so shadowy customers crowded in here to bargain for sandwiches of three-day-old bread and stale cheese had turned to stare at the wildly swinging portrait of Her Majesty.

Someone screamed just as he managed to shove the picture hard enough to send it clattering to the floor.

Silence, as everyone in the cookshop froze. He took the opportunity to rush through them all, sending their temperature, and that of the shop, plummeting.

That did it. Everyone who was not behind the counter ran for the entrance, jamming it in their panic. More screams. Now bursting with energy, he tried lifting a stale bun left on the counter. And succeeded!

Now nearly blind with elation, he tried throwing it. It bounced off the back of someone's head.

The cookshop owner's wife fainted dead away again. The clot at the door unjammed, and the would-be customers fled into the night.

Alf lifted the bun from the floor, and held it. To the cook-shop owner, it must have looked as if it were floating in mid-air. The man stared at it, paralyzed and numb, his face frozen in an expression of bewildered terror.

Alf flung the bun again.

His aim was perfect.

It struck the cookshop owner right between the eyes, and the man dropped to the ground like a poleaxed steer, although Alf hadn't thrown the thing with any force to speak of.

Cackling with glee, he left the shop, and spent the rest of the night experimenting with pebbles from the street, throwing them at windows to make a racket, and leaving many of the residents of the neighborhood suffering the worst night of their lives.

Hughs' head came up like a rat terrier's on a scent. "Do you feel that?"

It was just after sunset, and they were both sitting on the roof of the whorehouse. Alf had been playing his ghost tricks with increasing success for the last week or more. For the past three days, total strangers had been thronging the neighborhood, hoping to catch a glimpse of the goings-on, but of course they were too timid to venture here by night, and by day the only things that were to be seen were crooked pictures, a single pane of glass he'd allegedly broken, and the actual scenes of his shenanigans. He'd heard that street brats were doing a brisk business in pebbles he'd supposedly thrown—certainly by last night so many of them had been sold to the curious and gullible that he'd been unable to find any to hurl at windows. He'd been forced to look for bits of broken tiles on the roofs.

Alf cocked his head to the side, and consulted his insides—and yes, he *did* feel something. Not like that tugging that the hole to Hell had made on him. More like—more like there was something out there waiting for him, quietly calling out things only he could hear. As if he'd made an appointment, and the other party was patiently biding his time until Alf got there.

Wait—

Not *him. Her.* He was sure of it, although he couldn't have said how he knew.

"Well, you got your wish, Alf. Someone's brought in a medium. A real one." Hughs blinked slowly, and looked down the street, in the direction of—the cookshop. "A good one, too." He glanced over at Alf. "Shall we go see?"

Alf felt a mingled thrill of uncertain emotions. Part fear, part hope, part he couldn't identify. This was what he'd been working toward, wasn't it? Now he'd find out if he could lure Reg here and murder the bastard and get his revenge. But suddenly, and briefly, he wasn't so sure. . . .

But Hughs was already drifting down toward the street. Halfway down the young man looked back over his shoulder at Alf. "Coming?" he asked.

Don't be a bloody coward, he growled at himself, and followed.

There was a small crowd around the cookshop door—all locals, all shabby, so whoever this medium was, she hadn't brought any outsiders along, at least none he could see. Grinning maliciously, he shoved his way through the crowd at the door and window and made a point of passing through them all, drinking in their energy, so they cried out at the cold and some of them scattered. Only then did he enter the shop to find a single person sitting on one of the rickety chairs at the lone table there.

He examined her critically. She wasn't much, in his opinion. Pretty, oh yes, pretty enough—but not impressive. Blond, slim. Dressed in some plain but odd fashion, and with, of all damn things, a parrot on one shoulder. She didn't look nearly as old as he would have thought a "medium" would be, and while her dress was "odd," it wasn't "odd" in the ways he would have expected. She should have been draped in shawls, or done up like a heathen Chinee or Hindoo.

And it was only after he'd been standing there studying her for a good long while that he gradually realized that *she* had been staring straight at *him* ever since he'd entered the shop, her expression appraising and critical.

"So," she said aloud, her voice somehow echoing strongly in *his* world. *"You're the clever lad that's been up to tricks around here."*

He felt immediately put on the defensive. "And wut if Oi am?" he demanded. "Yew gonna stop me?"

"I'm more interested in finding out if you're just desperate for attention, or you actually want something," she said coolly, quite as if she talked to spirits every day. *"Obviously the one thing you don't want is to move on, or you wouldn't be playing the silly brat with stones and buns like a street Arab."*

Now he seethed with resentment. How *dared* this slip of a girl judge him! What could she possibly know, anyway?

"Sez yew, ye gurt cow!" he snapped back, then felt like a complete idiot, because she obviously wasn't a cow, and she was laughing at him. He snarled and crooked his fingers, and advanced on her to give her a good dose of what he could do—

Except the parrot mantled its feathers and growled at him, and suddenly he couldn't move at all.

"I don't think you understand what you're dealing with," she said, calmly, and turned her gaze slightly to the side of him. *"Does he, Peter?"*

Peter Hughs stood where her gaze had fallen, and as she asked that question, the young man laughed. "No, Sarah, he doesn't. And I hate to say this, but absolutely nothing he has told me makes me think there is anything redeemable about him. The opposite, in fact. Every time I gave him a hint about how he could salvage himself, he ignored it, but every time I pointed him in the direction of revenge and intimidation, he could not act on what I told him fast enough. It's time to send him on his way."

"I couldn't agree more," echoed a new, feminine voice. Startled, Alf whipped his head in the other direction to find that there was a new person—to all intents and purposes another ghost—standing beside him.

But this woman was just as outlandish as the medium was ordinary. She had a plain but strong face, but was dressed in plaid trousers of dull brown and yellow, a greenish, thigh-length tunic, a broad leather belt, and strange, wrapped-leather shoes. She also carried a naked, bronze sword in one hand, a small, round shield on the other, and had a raven the size of an eagle on her shoulder.

"We're ready if you are, Sarah," the woman continued, bringing the shield up to hold it between herself and Alf.

And to Alf's horror he felt something hideously familiar open up behind him. The irresistible tugging at his insides. The cold chill at his back. *"No!"* he screamed, and turned to run for the door.

But Peter Hughs suddenly had a stout staff in his hands, barring his way, and the strange woman advanced on him with her shield thrust aggressively at him. "I'm afraid the answer is *yes,* bucko," the woman said evenly as her raven raised its wings and took to the air, hovering above him so his escape was barred on all sides. "Time to go."

But he wasn't prepared to leave without a fight, and he braced himself, gathering all his stolen energy and readying an attack as vicious as anything he'd had planned for Reg.

And that was when a little waist-high cannonball of fury came out of nowhere, caromed into his midsection, and knocked him back.

Right into the gaping maw of the hell-hole that had opened up behind him.

Sarah Lyon-White let out her breath in a sigh of satisfaction and relief, as her friends Nan Killian and Peter Hughs, and her ward Suki, all emerged from the bedroom upstairs. In order to make sure they had all their possible strength in the spirit world, they had been laid out up there on the bed borrowed from the owner of the haunted cookshop, Sam Browne, and his wife Annabelle. "That went well," she greeted them.

"Suki made the difference," Nan observed, patting the little girl's tumble of unruly black curls. "The last thing he was expecting was to have her crashing into his gut and knocking him off balance." She looked over to the young man—who looked very little like the androgynous "Peter Hughs" of the spirit world. This man was an athletic, dark-haired, handsome, and very broad-shouldered and masculine fellow with the subtle details of dress that marked him as a university student of some kind. He looked—and in fact, was—the sort of young man who flung himself into sport *and* his studies with equal enthusiasm. Caro was more than making up for her previous life as a bed-bound invalid. "Any trouble with the Portal, Peter?" Sarah asked, a little anxiously. If Caro's hold on Peter Hughs' body was going to be challenged, she would always be in danger around a Portal.

"None whatsoever," Peter responded, in a pleasant, cultured tenor. "Nothing calling to me, no urge to throw myself into it, and no sense that anything on the other side wanted me there." He flashed both of them a dazzling smile. "I think we are all safe in assuming that the Powers That Be are perfectly satisfied with my tenancy of this body."

It was getting harder and harder for Sarah to think of Peter as "Caro" and not as "Peter Hughs." Which, she supposed, was all to the good, another sign that the spirit that had been born and died female had settled neatly into the male body whose original soul had been cast out of it, too weakened by drugs and despair to care to live anymore. And certainly the fact that a Portal into the next world had no hold over her—him—seemed like the final token that so far as that next world was concerned "Caro" could go right on living as "Peter" until she—he—reached the Biblically promised three-score and ten. And perhaps beyond that.

"I have to conclude you're right," Sarah agreed.

"Well, that makes me as pleased as Punch." Peter shoved both hands in his suit pockets and rocked a little back on his heels, a smile on his face. "Because I've never felt as comfortable in all my days, and not just because I'm not sick all the time anymore.

I know you're skeptical, Sarah, but I tell you, nothing feels quite as *right* now as being a fellow." He dropped his gaze to Suki, who was standing beside him, done up in her Baker Street Irregular disguise as quite the tough little street-lad. "So Suki, have *you* got any desire to be a lad?"

Suki looked up at him and snorted derisively. "Not bloody likely, ye gurt loon," she said rudely.

Sarah giggled behind her hand, and Nan laughed openly. "You'll never get her to give up her velvet, silk, and lace for trousers, Peter," Nan chuckled.

"I like trousers," Suki admitted, meditatively. "But dresses is better." She stuffed her abundant curls up into the flat cap she took out of her back pocket and nodded with decision.

There had been a very interesting effect to all of this, something that Sarah had begun to note now that she had been informed that she was a Spirit Master. Every spirit that she sent to the other side, willing or not, bequeathed to her a burst of magical energy. The more willing they were, the more energy she got. And this had not been an exception.

No wonder I never seem to run out of power.

Sarah turned her attention to the Brownes, who had emerged from the safety of the kitchen and observed all this banter with expressions of utter bewilderment. There could not have been a couple in all of London who would have fit the words "cookshop couple" as well as these two: middle-aged, plump, both enveloped in huge aprons, he going bald and she to gray under her cap. And, for this part of town, astonishingly neat and clean. The late unlamented Alf's complaints of being "pisened" by the food here probably had more to do with the rotgut that he drank than anything he ate. Finally Sam voiced the only thing that he could comprehend. "Is—it gorne?" he croaked.

"*Very* gone," Sarah affirmed. "Isn't it, Annabelle?"

The wife nodded, her face flushed with relief. "It's gorne," she confirmed. "I dunno where it went, but it went *somewheres* what ain't 'ere."

"And it's not coming back," Nan said stoutly, and reverted to the language of the streets and her childhood. "Blimey, if we hain't blowed it clear t' 'Ell, an' the Divil may 'ave it."

"Divil *keep* it!" put in Suki, which at least brought a shaky smile to both the Brownes' faces.

"Now, I'm not guaranteeing what will happen if you don't keep our bargain," Sarah warned, knowing very well that present terror is soon forgotten, and bargains made out of fear forgotten quicker still when the fear is gone. "You've surely heard all the stories from your grannies about what happens if you don't keep a bargain sealed the way we sealed ours."

With John Watson's help, she and Nan had concocted an impressive little ceremony in lieu of actual payment for ridding the neighborhood of the haunt, which had involved pricking of fingers and fingerprints in blood on a most artistically rendered document provided by Peter, who had a vast collection of ornate parchment proclamations and charters in the University College of London's many libraries to use as models. The "bargain" was a complex one, that bound every single person who had come forward as suffering from the hauntings to provide some sort of service to someone else in the group.

The huge Italian family, the Bartilinos, were to provide two children every day to sweep the area at the front of the cookshop and the yard in back, and to help tidy when the shop closed. The Brownes were to provide one plain baked potato for each of the Bartilinos every evening. Mrs. Hardy, who ran the brothel and prided herself on having the cleanest house and girls in this part of London, was adding the Brownes' laundry to hers, and sending clothing to be mended to the Bartilinos, who were to get anything past mending for themselves. And Lottie, the Cockney whore who had been a thorn in Mrs. Hardy's side, was to join the House, and Nan had gotten rid of Lottie's now-ex (and very abusive) pimp-lover by the simple expedient of Peter breaking his jaw. And since Lottie also had clever fingers and had once worked for a milliner, she was to help the Bartilinos by teaching them to make fabric flowers they could sell, from the scraps of the whores' cast-off finery and any other rags of a better sort they could acquire. The Brownes were to supply the House with space in their ovens, since the House had a very unreliable stove. And those other neighbors of the area that had suffered fewer visitations had agreed to take on evening patrols to keep criminal outsiders such as Alf on their better behavior. It wouldn't be possible or even practical to try to keep them out—but a few broken heads would teach troublemakers it wasn't wise to make their trouble *here*.

Peter was highly amused by all these machinations, but Nan in particular was pleased, as they had the side effect of unifying the neighborhood and making it safer and more pleasant for everyone. She and Sarah couldn't do anything about the poverty—but they could make people's lives better by teaching them to help each other.

"Oh nobody's goin' ter be fergettin', Miss," Sam Browne pledged fervently. He mopped his face with his apron. "Not arter what we bin t'rough."

"May I suggest, however," Peter spoke up, "That you continue the *tales* of hauntings, and make them as bloody as you like. That will bring a lot of the curious with money in their pockets here, and that can only help improve things." He winked.

"You shock me, young Marster," Sam said, with a weak grin. "You shock me. An honest feller loike yew, University chap an' all, suggestin' sech a thing!"

Peter shrugged, and grinned back.

After a refusal of the cookshop's hospitality past a cup of tea all around, the party took their leave, as the crowd outside the windows parted to let them past, then thronged into the shop to hear the (undoubtedly much-embellished) tale of exorcising the haunt.

It was late—nearly midnight, in fact—but they were not in the least concerned about walking to a part of London where they were more likely to be able to find a cab. Nor were they concerned about how dark it was, here where the streetlights were very few and far between. Well, other than being careful about placing their feet. This was not a part of London to fall down in, because you'd get back up again smelling rather awful.

But ruffians were not a concern. There were four of them, after all, and although they were relatively well dressed for this neighborhood, they all gave off an air of watchful—and sober—competence that would make would-be thugs think twice about taking them on.

Of course, if any would-be thugs *did* take them on, it would not end well. Sarah, Nan, and Suki had all been trained by a Sikh, a Hindu, and a Muslim who had *all* been military men as well as skilled in their own native weapons and martial styles. And although their weapons were not at the moment visible, they were all armed. As for Peter, he had taken up boxing at University, and was quite competent at it. And enjoyed every moment of it.

"I hope this project didn't interfere with your studies, Peter," Sarah said, since she hadn't apologized for asking him to play "bait" for them these past couple weeks. If it had not been for him leading Alf on, she very much doubted it would have been so easy to be rid of him.

"Not at all, actually. My body gets almost as much rest when I'm spirit-traveling as when I'm actually sleeping. Doesn't yours?" he asked, glancing over at her.

"It does, actually, as long as we aren't fighting anything," Sarah agreed. "I must say, I'm awfully glad you found you were still able to spirit-travel once you settled into Peter Hughs. It's been exceedingly helpful."

"So am I! Otherwise you might have just discarded me like a finished project, and I enjoy helping you and the Watsons far too much!" Peter teased. "I'd have had no excuse to keep looking you up, otherwise! And I enjoy your company almost as much as your adventures!"

"Well, since you decided on medicine instead of law, and John is unofficially a kind of mentor to you, *that's* the biggest lie you've told today," Nan replied, laughing at him.

"Now, I never actually told old Alf a lie," Peter pointed out. "I just never told him the whole truth. And I'm not responsible for where his imagination took him." Then he frowned a little. "I do wish there was a way we could track down this 'Reg' person, though. I'm not pleased that there's still a cold-blooded murderer about."

"Oi," Suki objected. "Wotcher think I been doin'? Oi 'opped 'round to Lestrade, an' give 'im everything yew tol' us. 'E didn't need much asides of 'Alf' an' 'Reg' an' where Alf's body wuz foun'. 'E 'ad that there Reg coolin' 'is 'eels in gaol in no time. An' arf a dozen lads willin' t'swear 'e tol' 'em 'e done for Alf too."

"Lestrade is competent enough on his own ground," came a deep voice from behind them. "Don't ever tell him I said so, however."

Sarah glanced behind her, but couldn't see much but a tall shadow that had moved up to join their group. There was no doubt of who that shadow was, however. "Hello, Sherlock," she replied. "Are you about to resurrect soon? I certainly hope so. We miss you, and passing meetings like this aren't enough."

"Not immediately, no," said Sherlock Holmes. "Not until I am certain that Mary Watson is also safe to be resurrected, and that is not yet possible to say."

Sarah nodded, but she was disappointed, and she was fairly certain that Mary Watson, although she would not complain, was weary of masquerading as a young man. It had been an adventure and an amusing novelty for a while, but Sarah's intuition suggested Mary wanted to move about as herself freely again.

"So what brings us the brief pleasure of your company, Holmes?" asked Peter.

"Partly to ensure your safety, and partly to guide you to the growler driven by a confidant of mine that I secured for you," Holmes replied. "And if you'll look about a block ahead, you'll see it waiting there for you."

"Why thank you, Sherlock!" Sarah exclaimed with gratitude.

But when she looked behind her, he was already gone.

3

The growler would drop Peter off last, allowing him to use as an excuse that a growler was the only cab he could find at this hour. Not that he'd need an excuse, not really. The real Peter Hughs had been an utterly useless, spoiled, wet mess, a disappointment to his parents and to himself, unwilling to actually put in the work to succeed at anything, and so, ended up at failing everything, including life. And he'd come within an inch of so completely betraying everything he should have cared for and fought to protect that he had nearly provided the spirit of Moriarty with a new body.

Only the intervention of the brave ghost of a former invalid named Caro had prevented that—even as Peter abandoned his life and body, Caro took it before Moriarty could, intent on denying the villain a second life, regardless of the costs to herself.

And Caro's sacrifice had been rewarded. She settled into Peter's body, weathered the pain and suffering of being weaned from the opium he had given himself up to without a complaint, and endeared herself to Peter's parents in the process, who thought that the opium withdrawal was a life-threatening disease, and were astounded by the "new" Peter that emerged from his brush with death.

And Caro—now really, truly "Peter"—had rewarded them. He'd—Nan could only think of Caro as "him" and "Peter" now—had gone back to the University course he'd abandoned. After wavering between law and medicine (much to the delight of his parents, who would have been happy with anything at that point), he'd chosen medicine "out of gratitude to Dr. John Watson, who saved me." He had moved back in with his parents, who were very well off, although the new reformed Peter would have given them no qualms at all if he'd insisted on living in his own flat. But this was in no small part because he was very much taken with "his" little sister, who adored the new and reformed big brother that had come home very much the improved prodigal.

Not that Caro had entirely abandoned her original family. She was quietly making certain they were all right . . . but was not unhappy to discover that they had moved on past her death.

"It's not as if I was much more than a pleasant burden," she'd pointed out. "And I do not blame them in the least that they miss me, but are relieved to have that burden gone."

And with that, she moved on herself, into her new family, and the new role of advisor to her new little sister. As Peter, she was determined to make sure that sister grew up to be as strong and capable as Sarah and Nan, and was taking advantage of being the "Golden Child" to get that project well underway.

So as long as Peter could say with truth that he had been undertaking a charitable task in the East End—and, not incidentally, came home sober and smelling of nothing more than a bit of sweat rather than gin—his parents would not care how late he arrived, nor what conveyance he arrived in.

The growler pulled up in front of the girls' flat. Sarah and Nan, birds riding sleepily on their shoulders, talons clenched tightly in the cloth of their gowns, got down first, allowing Suki to jump down after them.

"Good night, Peter!" Sarah said, as their friend poked his head out the door of the growler to make sure they made it safely inside. The long habit of over-caution as Sherlock tracked down the last of Moriarty's extensive gang was going to be a hard one to break . . . and the girls were not certain it was one that *should* be broken. There was nothing to be lost by investing in being alert and careful, after all.

They moved quietly so as not to wake their landlady, Mrs. Horace. She was a treasure, and even Suki understood how much of a treasure she was. There were not many landladies in London who would let two unattached young ladies rent a flat from them. There were fewer who would have allowed those young ladies to adopt an urchin off the street. Fewer still who would tolerate comings and goings at all hours of the day and night without assuming the worst possible things about their virtue and honesty. And never mind tolerating the exceedingly odd pets of a Grey Parrot and a Raven.

Then again, it was Lord Alderscroft who had arranged for this flat to be let to them, so, although the good lady had never implied that she had knowledge of Elemental Magic, or even powers herself, it could certainly be implied that she could, in the words of Kipling's Puck, "see further into a millstone than most."

They tiptoed up the stairs to their flat and let themselves in.

They found a single gaslight turned low, some bottled lemonade, and a nice selection of cheese and biscuits waiting for them on the table in front of their cold fireplace. Mrs. Horace, once again, making sure that they were being cared for. "Oh, bless!" Sarah said aloud. "I'm starving."

It appeared the others were as well. They all sat down without even taking off their bonnets—well, Suki did take off her cap—and even the sleepy birds woke up enough to accept a biscuit or two.

But everyone's clockwork was quickly winding down, now that the elation of a relatively painless "exorcism" of that vexatious spirit Alf was over, and when Nan volunteered to tidy up and put the tray out on the landing, Sarah was only too happy to accept.

She was relieved to get out of her gown and into . . . well, as diaphanous a night-dress as she could sew. *I suppose if I actually had any shame, I'd have been blushing when I bought this fabric,* she thought with a soft laugh to herself. One could easily have used it for tracing paper. It certainly left nothing to the imagination.

But the only other person who had ever seen her in this gown (without the much more opaque wrapper she'd made to cover it) had been Suki, who had seen things in her childhood that would have brought the blush of embarrassment to almost anyone. And even then, it hadn't been Suki "in person," it had been Suki spirit-traveling.

Sarah arranged herself on her bed in a position best suited to catch the least breeze from the open window. In fact, it had been scarcely two months since Suki had startled her by appearing at the foot of her bed in the middle of the night, at a time when Sarah *knew* the child had to be tucked up in her own bed miles away at the Harton School, run by their good friends and mentors, Memsa'b and Sahib Harton. Suki had known *exactly* what she was about, too, for the first words out of her ethereal mouth were, *"Gor blimey! I done it!"* in tones of triumph.

"And you go right back to where you came from too, missy!" Sarah had said. "You are *not* to pop into someone else's bedroom without a by-your-leave!" But her tone had not been *too* harsh, and Suki had giggled, waved goodbye, and vanished.

A breakfast conference with Nan followed, and an unplanned trip to the school later that morning had resulted in the acquisition of the following information: Suki was homesick. And she had been listening very carefully when the adults had been discussing spirit-travel over the course of several nights—a natural subject, since it had played such a large role in Nan and Sarah's latest case with John and Mary Watson. The adults, of course, had had no idea that Suki was paying any attention at all—which, well, they should have known better. Suki was an information sponge, was utterly fearless, and wanted very badly to see her foster mamas.

And on being asked, she had freely admitted she'd been trying for many nights to spirit-travel to see them.

"Well, that djinn is not going back in the bottle," Memsa'b had said with equal parts exasperation and admiration. So Suki was allowed to come home, Beatrice Leek had been sent for, and Suki had been put through a very strict, thorough, and *proper* course of training, right alongside Peter Hughs, and emerged out of it, in Beatrice's words, "a complete natural."

And when the girls had been recruited to lay Alf's ghost, it occurred to both of them that Suki could be their extra weapon— and that it would be an excellent chance for her to work alongside them for the first time. "We might as well let her," Nan had said, practically, "since she's *going* to turn up regardless, no matter how hard we try to keep her out of it. It's not as if she hasn't been doing risky work with the Irregulars all this time. And it's not as if we weren't doing equally risky occult work when we were her age."

Sarah would have liked to point out, one, that they'd had the help of Robin Goodfellow, and two, it wasn't as if they'd been given a choice . . . but she really couldn't, in good conscience. Because once you had talents and began training in them, it seemed that no one ever really had a choice, and trouble would find you, regardless. So Suki might as well get into her trouble under the supervision of adults.

And she really had done very, very well tonight. Sarah was terribly proud of her.

"Suki clever bird," Grey muttered, as if she were reading Sarah's mind. Which, actually, she probably was.

"Yes, Grey," Sarah murmured back, as sleep took her, "Suki is a clever bird indeed."

"Well, that was pleasantly successful," Nan said over breakfast. "I'm glad Beatrice put that particular ghost-laying in our path. It gave us a chance to see how all four of us can work together."

Sarah nodded, mouth full of toast.

"Oi—" Suki began, and blinked at Nan's admonishing glance. "*I* b'lieve I got the hit in just right."

Nan didn't have to remind Suki why her pronunciation was so important. Like Nan, she was going to have to remember to cultivate two kinds of English—"proper" English, the sort you would speak around Lord Alderscroft and the Watsons, and the jargons of the street. The first would ensure middle- and upper-class people took her seriously. The second would cement her as "one of them" with the lower classes. The one and only time Suki had complained about how hard it was, Nan had pointed out, "Sherlock Holmes is a master of not less than thirty or forty English accents and dialects. Surely you can keep track of two or three." Since Suki absolutely idolized Holmes, that had ended that argument right there.

"You did, Suki," Nan agreed. "You took my cue right when I gave it. You hit him just below his hips, as Gupta has shown you. You used just enough force to knock him off his feet and backward, and bounced off him to keep yourself out of his reach, should he have made an attempt to grab for you. It was textbook-perfect."

Suki beamed. She was an exceedingly pretty child; she made a handsome little boy, and an enchanting little girl, with her mop of black curls, enormous brown eyes, and cafe-au-lait complexion. Nan was not really sure *what* nationality or mix of nationalities she was; she had evidently been sold by one of her parents as a sort of slave to a disreputable faux-medium-cum-prostitute at a very young age, and attempts to trace her origin, even by Holmes himself, had failed. Nan and Sarah, to protect her, firmly claimed her to be Italian, and claimed she had been entrusted to their care by an impoverished, widowed gentlewoman of good character. She looked Italian enough for the story to pass, and even if Italians were held in scorn by most English, they were less scorned than other races, or a child of mixed blood. Nan and Sarah didn't personally care if she was Italian, Hottentot, or a Moon Child, and Lord Alderscroft absolutely doted on her and would have spoiled her dreadfully if he'd gotten the chance, but she was going to have to make her way on her own one day, and the more protections that were in place for her, the better off she would be.

Nan privately hoped that one day it would be Suki who would be the headmistress of the Harton School. She had a wonderful mix of empathy and hard-headed practicality that would be very useful in that position. But that would be a long time from now. *And very likely Memsa'b will try to hand over the reins to us, first.* She hoped *that* would be long in coming.

"I want to do another," Suki announced, after finishing her eggs— or rather, making them utterly vanish. "That felt—" She screwed up her little face to think very hard. "Useful. I like being useful."

"Well, I was actually thinking of something you could do partially on your own, Suki," Sarah told her, refilling the child's cup with half tea and half milk. "I was hoping you would befriend the Badger Court Twins and persuade them to go through the Portal for me."

The "Badger Court Twins" were not twins at all; the frail little spirits looked nothing alike and were not even of the same age, though they had perished in the same cholera outbreak. But they had found each other while bewildered by their own deaths, and clung to each other like desperate siblings, appearing only rarely and almost never to adults. The Portals frankly terrified them—Sarah said she suspected they had both been traumatized by awful stories of what happened to "bad little children" and unconsciously associated the fact that they had died with "being disobedient." They were the last haunts of this neighborhood and Sarah had been trying with no success to get them to cross since the girls had moved here.

Suki made a face. "They's—*they're*—a dead bore."

"Ghosts can't all be exciting; in fact, most of them aren't," Sarah pointed out gently, as Grey nodded agreement. "But it's our responsibility to help all the ones we can. And they won't let me near them. They might respond better to you."

Suki heaved a huge sigh. "All right. I c'n try luring 'em."

"Hopscotch, or jacks, or rope-skipping," Nan suggested. "You know how to make things out of nothing in the spirit world, and they don't seem to be able to. If they see you playing in the street, they're likely to come out. You can show them how to make playthings and befriend them that way."

"'Strue I don't have girlfriends what ain't—*aren't*—at the school," Suki admitted, brightening. "The Irregulars is top-hole, but—"

"But as soon as you are in a dress they treat you like a hanger-on," Nan finished for her, having seen that very thing for herself. It was as if the moment Suki donned skirts, she became a nonentity, barely tolerated. Then again, that was the way the boys at the Harton School often treated their female classmates—and generally, the girls *let* them. At the school, Suki wouldn't tolerate that, but the Irregulars were a much more hardened lot. "You can make them feel happy and ready to cross, and have some fun at the same time."

"Right then." The child nodded with decision. "I c'n start ternight."

Nan exchanged a wry look with Sarah. *Oh, to have the energy of a child again!* she thought. While working was certainly far more interesting than not working, she was not eager to jump *immediately* into a new task the way Suki was.

If putting Alf to rest had been an assignment from Lord Alderscroft, or a task shared with the Watsons, the next move for the morning would have been to report their success. But Beatrice Leek had merely passed on the word that the denizens of the East

End neighborhood had been desperately looking for someone to rid them of the pestilent haunt, and said, "And I'll just let you get on with it, dearies," after giving them the name and address of the Brownes. So there really was nothing to do this morning but have a nice, leisurely breakfast and contemplate possible activities involving Suki for the afternoon. Playing in one of the parks? A trip to the British Museum was always fun *and* educational, and Suki considered it a high treat. Not the zoo—it would be crowded with over-stimulated, over-tired children and increasingly cross nannies.

But any plans went flying out the window when the doorbell rang downstairs, and Suki ran to the window and announced "message." "Message" only meant one thing: the Watsons wanted them (and possibly by extension, Lord Alderscroft wanted them), and had sent one of the Irregulars bearing a summons.

Sure enough, Mrs. Horace came tripping up the staircase to tap on the door and open it. "Message from the doctor, ladies," she said cheerfully, handing over the envelope to Sarah, who got up to accept it. "Just leave the breakfast things, I'll clear up for you."

"You know us too well, and spoil us too much, Mrs. Horace, and thank you for last night's treat," Sarah replied with a smile, opening the envelope. Mrs. Horace, far too good-mannered to wait around to hear what was in the message, dimpled, and closed the door, trotting back down the stairs. "Well, this is interesting. It's going to be a bit of an expedition, and John is going to play the distraction while Nan and Peter investigate. His Lordship suspects some double-dealing at a private asylum—and John says the situation is far too complicated to go into in a note. We're all to go—Suki, you'll be up with Brendan as a horse-boy, so go find your livery and put it on. Sarah, we're nurses."

That meant the unusual instance of an actual disguise, and in this case, one neither of them had used before, nursing-sisters' uniforms supplied long ago by Alderscroft.

The note specified that they should come in an hour, which was plenty of time to go by 'bus, so that was what they did, taking the short walk to Baker Street from where the 'bus dropped them. Alderscroft's carriage was already waiting at the front. Suki greeted the coachman, Brendan, like the old friend that he was, but with immense respect, and would have hopped up beside him, but he indicated she should wait in the coach for a moment with Nan and Sarah. Shortly after they seated themselves, John Watson, Peter, and Mary Watson emerged, Mary Watson dressed in a suit as a young man. Nan felt a bit sorry for them; she and Sarah were dressed in white and light blue, cool cotton and linen. John, Peter, and Mary might have been in linen, but it was a sober black, and did not look at all comfortable in this heat.

Once they were all seated, John tapped on the roof with his cane, and Brendan pulled away.

"This is a very odd, and somewhat delicate matter, since it involves a cousin of a friend of Alderscroft's," John said, once the coach got into motion. "The friend is, of course, one of his Hunting Lodge here in London—who it is doesn't matter, except that he daren't meddle in this matter himself without opening himself to some ugly accusations."

"Hmm," Nan said. "That sounds as if there is a lady involved."

"More than one," John said. "He has an underaged female cousin whose father remarried, then suddenly died, leaving his widow in sole control of the fortune."

Nan frowned. "Is the death suspicious?"

"Not at all; I've made some quiet inquiries and it appears the man was in poor health, knew it, and was hoping to provide his minor daughter with a responsible guardian until she came of age. On his death, the girl reacted with predictable grief—then there was some sort of major incident regarding her behavior. I have no details on that incident, only that it was 'distressing.' At that point the widow declared the child was uncontrollable and inconsolable and had her sent to a private asylum for 'her health.'"

"Hmm. We've heard *that* one before," Sarah muttered.

"Here is where things get tricky. The cousin managed to get leave to visit her recently, and he says that the girl is, without a doubt, behaving quite, well, mad. He immediately suspected that either the chief physician of the asylum is medicating her with something that causes strong hallucinations, or that grief has triggered latent Elemental powers and she is seeing Elemental Spirits and has no idea how to cope with the experience." John paused, waiting for the girls to say something.

"Or there is a third or fourth explanation. She is mediumistic and being thronged with haunts—many of these private asylums are in former manor-homes—or grief triggered telepathic powers and she is being overwhelmed with the thoughts of people who *are* genuinely mentally ill." Sarah looked to Nan, who nodded. "So I assume we are to investigate all four possibilities?"

John smiled. "It's almost as if I were working with female Sherlocks. We have an appointment to tour the facility, arranged by Alderscroft, with a view to placing a patient there. Peter and Mary are my assistants. You are my private nurses. Suki, you will keep your senses sharp for anything that might be going on outside on the grounds—it has been noted that the girl sometimes gets worse after being taken out for air."

"What's the complication that prevents the cousin from investigating himself, if he's an Elemental Master?" Nan asked shrewdly.

John flushed a little. "Before her father's death, the girl confided to him in a letter that she was desperately in love with him, and asked him if he would consider marrying her."

"Oho," Nan replied. "And if anyone else has gotten wind of this—"

"Yes," John nodded. "If he tries to interfere, there could be all manner of scandal, since the will stipulates that if she marries, her fortune comes to her immediately. The least of the possible scandals is that he could be accused of seducing an innocent girl in order to get his hands on the money. I know nothing about the stepmother other than the cousin's suspicions, but if he is correct, and she put the girl away in the first place in the hopes of continuing to keep control of the fortune, she'd do anything to add disgrace to the charges of madness."

"Money do seem to be a powerful curse sometimes," Suki observed meditatively. "I does like havin' it, but it do seem to bring its own troubulations."

"Tribulations, dear," Mary corrected automatically. "Other than that, you are quite right."

"Well, what I would like to know is, has this cousin got the obvious ulterior motive?" Nan asked bluntly. "I mean, he can protest all he likes that the girl approached *him,* but there's a fortune at stake here, and a presumably naive girl in her teens who could just as easily be put away again once she's been safely married. He wouldn't even have to put her in an institution! Just manipulate her to keep her a quiet invalid at home, and *he* could go about having as many opera singers and music-hall dancers as he cared to support!"

By now John knew the girls far too well to object to this, or protest that a gentleman would do no such thing. He knew such a protest was gammon, and he knew they knew such a protest was gammon. All he could do was shrug. "Alderscroft seems to believe him," he said. "And the Lion isn't easily gulled. And young people, girls *or* boys, are apt to get pashes on inappropriate objects."

"All right then, we'll go into this with an open mind—assuming nothing," Sarah declared. "With the one object to determine if the girl is being interfered with by anyone or any*thing*. And if we find out the poor creature truly isn't in her right mind . . . perhaps we can determine an exterior cause."

"And if we can't—we report just that to Alderscroft," Mary added. "People *do* go mad all on their own, poor things, and sadly, science and medicine have no answers for it."

"I can go flittin' about lookin' for 'aunts if Brendan keeps 'is eye on me," Suki offered.

"That would be extraordinarily useful, Suki, since in spirit form you can go places in the asylum I cannot. The basement or attic or other dark places, for instance."

"Closets," Suki said wisely. "An' yew'd get inter trouble if yew went about pokin' into closets for no good reason." She stirred a little. "Mebbe I should go up on th' box with Brendan?"

John glanced out the window of the coach; Nan did the same. They were in a very quiet, *nearly* suburban neighborhood, with relatively new houses—they wouldn't impede traffic here if they paused long enough for Suki to scramble up. John evidently felt the same. He knocked on the roof of the coach and Brendan stopped, and looked down through the trap door.

"Suki's ready to come up," Nan said, before Watson could speak, and rather than waste more time, simply stood up while the coach was stopped and boosted the slender child up through the trap. Suki scrambled up into her "proper" place like a little monkey, and they were off again.

"Sherlock made contact last night," Sarah said, once the horses had settled into their slow trot. "Unfortunately, Mary, he doesn't think it's safe to come back yet."

Mary Watson sighed. "Which means it's not safe for me to either. Oh well." She shrugged. "It can't be helped. I just wish my voice was deeper. It's impossible to convincingly impersonate a young man when you are a piping soprano."

Peter laughed. "I'll talk for both of us, you just nod or frown at the right times. We can carry it off for one afternoon, anyway."

As the others chatted, Nan reflected on the setting they were going to—a private "hospital" or "invalid home." It wasn't the first one of these they'd gone to, investigating a situation there, and it probably would not be the last. It was all too common for wealthy people to use such a place to tuck "inconvenient" relatives away, out of the public eye. Physicians often turned a blind eye when enough money exchanged hands, but just as often, the physicians actually *agreed* with "reasons" why some people— especially women—should essentially be incarcerated away where they could be easily forgotten. Rebellious girls who wanted more than to be a father's business deal, followed by becoming a husband's ornament and walking womb for the production of an heir, for instance. . . .

She couldn't help but reflect on how lucky she and Sarah were. They had highly interesting, incredibly adventurous lives, and were valued for their intelligence and other gifts. *And that was luck on top of luck on top of luck. I could have been one of those girls in that brothel. Or married to that Italian lad with a half a dozen nippers. Or . . . well, scraping my way from meal and bed to meal and bed, and never knowing where the next one was coming from.*

She shook herself loose from both thoughts. Better to keep an open mind, and be aware of all possibilities. *That is the original plan,* she reminded herself. *Don't go in with preconceived notions.*

And there was nothing worse for an investigation than preconceived notions.

As the coach pulled into the driveway for this place, she became aware of just how correct *that* thought had been—because the building could not possibly have been older than fifty years. *So much for the notion of ghosts,* she thought—although, to be sure, it was possible for the place to be haunted, just not by centuries of accumulated spirits. It appeared that it was *not* a converted manor, but a purpose-built establishment. But it was not surprising she had never heard of it until now. Most of these places did not advertise and kept themselves very quiet. It was in their interest to keep their business somewhat under the rose, as it were. After all, when you were coddling shattered nerves—and to be fair, that was often the primary business in such an institution—you didn't want fuss and bother upsetting your patients. And when you were confining the "inconvenient," well, you certainly didn't want to draw attention to them.

This place styled itself a "Convalescent Retreat," so the directors intended to perpetuate the appearance that the inmates would eventually get well and go home, even if that was quite impossible.

John Watson had made arrangements for the visit in advance, and they were not kept waiting when they arrived. The entire party was brought straight to the director's spacious office, where John and the director began a coded conversation in which John implied, but did not say, that the patient in question was *not* expected to make a recovery.

But that was where the conversation deviated from what Nan had expected, because the director evidenced concern, and began close questioning as to possible "alternative treatments" with a view to restoring the imaginary patient's mind and sensibility. She sensed John's astonishment, because he had assumed, given what they thought they knew, that the object would have been to keep the patient placid and confined here, not actually attempt to *cure* him.

John swiftly, and skillfully, switched the slant of his inquiries, and it quickly became apparent that this establishment was not what they had assumed it was.

Nan could tell that John badly wanted to regroup and come at this with the new information, but that was going to take some very fancy verbal footwork. So for the next half hour, she watched in growing admiration as John—and Peter, following John's lead—managed to back them out of the predicament they'd almost entangled themselves into. The original plan, that Nan and Sarah should tour the place with one of the establishment's nursing sisters, was clearly now out of the question.

When John finally managed to extricate them all, they went down to the coach to find Suki very much awake and bouncing impatiently on the driver's box. "Brendan, just take us somewhere quiet, please," John asked the coachman, as that worthy raised his whip and his eyebrow simultaneously. "We did not expect what we encountered."

"Well, milor' Alderscroft ordered a luncheon packed into the boot, Doctor," Brendan replied with complete calm. "I suspec' the best answer would be a picnic."

"Make it so, Brendan," Watson replied. "Perhaps lemonade and cold chicken will help us decide what we should do next."

4

Brendan managed to find a nice little spot just off the road, on top of a hill and under a tree, to spread out the rugs and the food. He declined to eat with them, saying, "It's not me place, Doctor," but did not object to having a plate made up that he could eat at his leisure. Resourceful as always, he had brought nose-bags of grain for the horses. He trudged off with the leather bucket from the boot at the back of the coach and came back with water for the horses as well, and they left him to tend the beasts as he saw fit while they ate and worked out what their next move should be.

"There ain't a haunt in that place," Suki declared around a chicken leg. "I was *all* over it, and not a haunt a-tall."

"I don't see how we can go back," Mary Watson observed, peeling a hard-boiled egg. "But I am also reluctant to just go back to Alderscroft and say 'nothing needs be done.' There is *something* suspicious about all of this, but I cannot put my finger on what, precisely."

"I completely agree on both counts," Peter replied. "And this is where I have a proposal." He looked to Nan, Sarah, and Suki. "Is there any reason why we cannot spirit-travel during the daylight hours? I know that sunlight erodes true ghosts, but would it trouble us?"

Nan blinked at him, as Suki clapped her hands, regardless of the chicken leg she still held. "According to Beatrice, the living aren't impeded by daylight," Sarah replied with authority. "She says our link to the living world makes us impervious to the sun. In fact, she has a great many anecdotes about those who have seen far-distant friends and relations by day, often when they are ill, in peril, or have been rendered unconscious or sleeping."

"Well then." Peter smiled. "Here's what I propose. We can either have Mary send her little Air Elementals to find the right patient for us while we enjoy our luncheon, or we can spirit-travel there, split up, and search the place for her ourselves. Once we find her, we lead Nan to her, and Nan can read her mind to see what the devil is going on with her. Now what do you think of that idea?"

"I think it's a capital one, Peter," John enthused.

"Hmm." Nan was not entirely certain about this plan. "There are a lot of things you're blithely assuming I can do that I've never tried before. Reading minds as a spirit, for a start. Reading the mind of someone who is mad is another; I'm not at all sure what will happen if I try."

"We don't *know* that she's mad," Peter pointed out. "All we know is that the cousin said she appeared to be mad."

"True." Nan frowned. Like Mary, she felt as if there was much more going on than there appeared to be. "I suppose we really need to try," she said at last. "I can't in good conscience just walk away from this. I have the strongest feeling that *someone* is being ill-done-by, and I feel as if I need to find out exactly who it is and remedy the situation."

"Since we have no way of actually identifying the girl we are looking for to the Air Elementals, we should probably spirit-travel and search the facility ourselves." Sarah shrugged and smiled. "I very much doubt we'll attract any attention if some of us, overcome with sleepiness after an excellent picnic, fall asleep in the shade."

"In that case, I am very glad that I came providentially equipped with a book," Mary replied. John Watson looked a bit crestfallen, until Sarah offered him the Walter Scott she'd been carrying.

"I have Alexis de Tocqueville if Scott palls," Nan added as he accepted it.

With regret, she gestured to Mary to pack up the delicious-looking cakes and strawberries. It was a bad idea to try spirit-traveling on too full of a stomach.

John went to tell Brendan that they would be here for a while;

Brendan responded by moving the entire carriage into the shade of more trees nearby. Then they all settled down, Mary and John with their books, the rest for their "nap."

"The director's office?" Nan suggested, as a place for them all to meet.

"We've all been there but Suki. . . ." Sarah glanced at their ward.

Suki sniffed with disdain. "I can scarper there quick as quick," she said.

"All right then, it's agreed." Nan and Sarah put their backs against the tree trunk, with Neville and Grey on their shoulders; Suki lay down with her head in Nan's lap, and Peter sprawled out with his hat over his eyes. But a sharp eye would note that all of them were in physical contact. That was because, for efficiency and efficacy, Sarah, as an Elemental Master of Spirit, would be in control of their exits into the spirit plane.

Once she had learned that Sarah was a Spirit Master, Beatrice Leek had been unsurprised, but had added some unexpected information. "Oh, well then," she'd said casually. "You can go anywhere you like."

It had taken a moment for the meaning of that to sink in, and it had been Sarah who had gaped at the self-styled witch, and asked incredulously, "Do you mean . . . anywhere in the world? But that would take for—" And then she had stopped as Beatrice gave her a *look* that suggested Sarah was missing something important, and amended, "—you mean, instantly?"

"Oh aye," Beatrice had replied. "I mean exactly that. As long as you've been there yourself, or know someone there to use as your beacon, you could go to the moon if you chose."

Heretofore they had assumed that to get to any place via spirit-walking, they would actually have to *walk* there, in spirit. But here was Beatrice telling them that since Sarah was a Master, they could simply will themselves there. It had been a revelation.

They'd tried it out at once, of course, opting to travel to Criccieth in Wales, lying down in their flat with great anticipation, and on awaking in the spirit plane, finding themselves immediately at the little guest cottage they'd hired when searching for a new Water Master for Alderscroft.

It was just as well there was no one currently hiring the snug little cottage, or it could have gotten a reputation for being haunted.

Nan envied Suki her ability to compose herself and drop off into the requisite trance almost immediately. For her part, she wished they really *were* just a friendly party out having a picnic in the countryside. It would have been lovely to actually be able to take the nap she was going to feign. Brendan had picked a great spot: enough of a breeze to keep the heat from being oppressive, but enough gentle summer warmth to encourage drowsing. A lark sang in the distance, bees hummed somewhere nearby, and the scent of hot meadow grass was as good as perfume.

She closed her eyes, and chided herself for allowing her mind to wander. She needed to get her thoughts back on the task she was supposed to be doing. Dropping into the proper mental state required being able to relax and concentrate at the same time, and without Sarah to give her the proper nudge, sometimes she had a spot of difficulty—

She felt herself falling into the trance, relaxed a little more, and sharpened her focus on every remembered detail of the director's office—

And then—there she was. There was no transition as there was when she would step "out of her body" into the corresponding space in the spirit plane. Instead, one moment she was in the soft darkness behind her closed eyelids, and the next, standing in the brilliantly sunlit office. She glanced around and noted wryly that Sarah and Peter were already there, Peter absent-mindedly standing in the middle of one of the visitor's chairs. Grey was on Sarah's shoulder, and the comforting weight of Neville was on Nan's. "You're late," Sarah teased. "Suki already let us know she is here and—"

Suki dashed right through the closed office door to slide to a halt next to Nan. "See!" she crowed. "Tol' yew I'd be here!"

Oblivious to all the activity around him, the director continued working at his desk. When Nan concentrated, she heard the scratching of his pen on the paper, and the distant sound of bird calls through the open window. Being in the spirit plane was no longer a novelty, but entering it by daylight was. As usual, the living world around her was not unlike a faded watercolor, but since sunlight flooded everything, it was as if the faded colors had been painted onto glass. It was, she thought, rather lovely.

"Well, I hate to throw cold water on our plans," Peter said, "but I've only just realized that we don't have any way of identifying the girl we're looking for . . . except that she's allegedly mad."

"Actually, we do," Nan corrected, admiring the way beams of light slanted across the books behind Sarah. "She's under eighteen, and from what we know, probably several years younger than eighteen. Most of the patients here are fully adults. She is presumably sound in body, if not in mind. Most of the patients here are suffering from health breakdowns or extreme old age, and many will be bedridden. There can't be too many girls here who fit both criteria."

"Sherlock is rubbing off on you," Peter observed. "All right then, how shall we divide things up?"

"By wing," Sarah decided. "Nan, can you ascertain whether your telepathic abilities still work in the spirit plane before we go searching room to room?"

Certainly, she thought at them.

Sarah nodded. "I heard that," Peter echoed. "Now what about reading the minds around us?"

She bent her attention to the director, who was slowly and deliberately writing in what looked as if it might be a casebook. It took a little more concentration to skim his surface thoughts than it did when she was fully in the material world; but in a minute or two, she had learned it wasn't a casebook after all, it was his betting record! With amusement, she noted that he was a very modest gambler, betting entirely on horse races, and risking not much more than a common day-laborer would have. Many bettors prided themselves on a "system"—but being a man of science, he concentrated on learning as much about the health of the horses in the races he followed as he could, and placing his bets accordingly. The pure pleasure he experienced in recording his modest winnings made her smile.

"I can use my powers," she told them. "You'll just have to use your powers of observation."

"The only thing we need to observe is whether or not we find a possible candidate for Alderscroft's target," Peter said pertly. "Then we find you and *you* tell us what the devil is going on here."

Nan *tsk*ed. "Lazy. I'm sure you could adduce plenty, if you would learn to apply Holmes' methods. All right, let's take to our respective wings. We might as well look for other irregularities while we're at it. More ammunition for Alderscroft's guns will be useful if I do uncover double-dealing."

Nan had the South Wing. The first floor contained only absolute invalids who could not leave their beds—which, when she reflected upon it, was sound management. You didn't want people who could wander off on their own on the first floor. Every room she inspected was clean and cheerful, with a fresh bouquet of fragrant garden flowers near at hand, even when the tenants of the beds clearly were not particularly aware of their surroundings. The couple of aged people who actually were alert, despite their invalid status, had been supplied plentifully with books and at least one other pastime within easy reach. One old lady was happily occupied with crocheting yards of intricate lace with a hook scarcely bigger than a needle, and very fine thread. An old man was engaged in cutting intricate silhouettes out of black paper with nothing more than a tiny pair of scissors. One of the nursing sisters came to check on him, patiently whisked up the scraps, and praised his work so extravagantly that he blushed.

This place was, to be quite honest, something of a revelation. So many establishments like this one were run with the intent of warehousing the sick until they died, or serving as a means of confining inconvenient relatives, that to see one run *properly* gave Nan a bit of pause. And still she could not shake off her cynical suspicions that she was only seeing a pretty veneer over a rotten base.

And yet—no one knew she was there. To achieve a deception of this magnitude seemed impossible. This was not a show concocted for her benefit. The director would have to have known that Watson's crew was coming, and when. He would have had to have known of Nan and Sarah's abilities. And then he would have had to arrange for the entire establishment to erect and maintain this facade, somehow, until he could be certain they were gone.

On the second floor she found genuinely ill people—no few of whom were yellow-faced men who from all appearances had done their level best to destroy their own livers with drink. Most of these were marginally ambulatory, and several of them were sitting in chairs at their windows. Once again, bright, clean, cheerful rooms met her critical gaze. But she found no sign of a young girl.

It was on the third floor that she struck gold.

Two of the nursing sisters were conversing as she passed by them in the hall, evidently discussing a patient. ". . . and if it was me," said one of them crossly, "I'd be slapping her until her cheeks were bruised instead of coddling her with milk diets and poetry books."

The other sniffed, and nodded. "Crying herself into being sick, making ugly messes for us to clean up, and no sooner is she clean and sweet-smelling again but she's in hysterics and starting a new round. I tell you, when *my* old dad went up to Heaven, God bless his honest soul, there was no fainting and wailing and carrying on for *me*! No, it was off to work like any other day, and I might have dropped a tear or two in someone's bath, but never did I dare to let them *see* it."

Well, that sounded promising! It fit all the parameters, especially that the patient had plunged into melancholy on the death of her father. So—*hysterics and tears*—it sounded as if all she needed to do was follow the sound of weeping.

Nan concentrated until she heard it, faintly.

And so she followed the sound, all the way to the end of the corridor, and what was clearly a "superior" room. On the corner of the wing, it boasted two windows instead of one, carpets on the floors, cheerful landscapes on the walls, and all the amenities of a fine hotel room. While the furnishings were not ornate as in the current fashion, they were of high quality, and made with an eye to comfort. Upholstery was not harsh horsehair, but pleasing velvets in the fashionable color of mauve, harmonizing with wallpaper of mauve cabbage roses. The bed—well, at first sight, the bed made Nan a bit envious: not one, but *three* featherbeds, a luxurious pile of pillows, and a coverlet of velvet to match the rest of the furnishings.

And in the bed, huddled up in one corner, was a girl in the throes of inconsolable grief, or so it appeared, at least. She had been dressed in a cambric nightgown with deep lace ruffles, the sort of gown that Nan had never actually seen before, only surmised from the elegant fashions worn by women in Lord Alderscroft's lofty circles.

Her dark hair was damp, and had been braided into a single tail down the back of her neck. She looked thin to Nan, and her face was a blotched mess, eyes swollen, cheeks raw. A pile of crumpled handkerchiefs beside her testified that she'd been at this for quite some time.

Her sobbing certainly sounded overwrought to Nan, and she could see where it would easily have been taken by a bachelor, unfamiliar with the ways of young girls, as madness.

But there was one thing above all else that literally *hammered* at Nan as she ghosted into the room. A single thought, so drenched in despair it brought tears to *her* eyes for a moment.

He doesn't love me! He never loved me!

Never, not once, in all her life, not even when she was living on the street with her gin-soaked mother and often went so hungry she'd suck on a stone to try to stave the pangs off, had Nan ever felt that depth of inconsolable agony.

And yet . . . the emotion seemed just as contrived and cultivated as it did crushing.

Oh no. You don't drag me down into your morass, my girl.

Ruthlessly, she walled herself off from the emotions accompanying that thought, and took Neville up on her hand. *I'm sending Neville to guide you all,* she thought to her teammates, and felt their assent. "Go get the others," she instructed the raven. "I think this must be the girl."

With a bob of his head, Neville flew off through the wall, leaving her alone with the sobbing mess in the corner of the bed. She considered her next move. First order of business, she decided, was to find out who "he" was—though from the information she had, a good guess would be that "he" was her cousin.

Now that she had insulated herself from the girl's hysterics, she felt vaguely sorry for her, but only because it seemed to her that the child had built up a romantic air-castle for herself that had ultimately proved to be founded on foam and had crumbled beneath the weight of reality. It was the same sort of thing she felt about Shakespeare's *Romeo and Juliet.* The tragedy was not in their love and suicide. The tragedy was that they had thrown their lives away before they ever had the chance to understand what real love was—and that it was not the mad passion they'd shared.

As Friar Lawrence had tried to point out . . . and of course, neither of them had paid attention to him.

At least this little idiot hadn't killed herself.

So let's just see what you're thinking. Just in case the girl was a sensitive, she eased herself back into the girl's thoughts, ghosting in softly, silently, and with luck, undetectably.

And found herself rocked back on her heels.

Because instead of the image she had expected . . . the one attached to "he" was that of a roguishly handsome fellow in the scarlet uniform of an army officer!

"Bloody hell!" she muttered to herself, withdrawing for a moment. She was fairly certain that if the "cousin" had been an officer in the Army, Alderscroft would have mentioned that fact!

Therefore. . . .

"Well, aren't you the darkest of horses," she said aloud, just as Sarah and Grey turned up. "And you have been up to some very impressive mischief, I fear."

At Sarah's inquisitive look, she held up her hand. "This is the girl, and the situation really is so different from what we expected that . . . I'm more than a bit taken aback. I need more information, and I want to wait until everyone is here before I say anything."

Sarah nodded, and Nan plunged back into the chaotic stream of the girl's thoughts, which were all of a muddle, to say the least.

But at the forefront of everything was the scene she kept obsessively reviewing in her mind.

She slipped out of the walled garden into the orchard, using the door she'd found hidden under the ivy. She saw him immediately in his scarlet uniform, pacing back and forth between two apple trees. He must have heard that her father was dead—

Well, now she was free. Now they could flee to Scotland and get married, just as he'd promised. He must have come to tell her to pack a bag, that they would leave tonight once the house was asleep—

"Robert!" she cried, and flung herself at him.

And found herself roughly shoved away, so that she stumbled and fell to the ground. "Robert!" she cried, shocked. "What—"

"You stupid bint," he snarled at her. "You swore to me that everything was going to be fine, *that all we had to do was run off and get married! You swore the will left everything to you!*

Couldn't you have managed one sick old man better? *Couldn't you at least have taken the time to look at the will before you had me wasting my time on a silly little slut like you?"*

She gaped at him from the ground. Her expression only enraged him more. "I bribed a clerk in the law office, and a damn good thing I did, too. Idiot! Even if your stepmother approves of a marriage, and you damn well know she won't approve of me, you don't get anything until you turn twenty-one. Years! And if she doesn't?" *He made the sign of an explosion with his left hand.* "PFFT! It's gone. It all goes to her, you stupid cow!"

"B-b-b-but money doesn't matter! I don't mind being poor with—"

"But I mind being poor, you fool! Why do you think I've been dancing to your tune all this time? Because of your looks? Because I was in love with you?" *He laughed, harshly.*

"But I'm going to have your—" *she choked.*

"And I don't care. Don't try to put that on me, as free with your favors as you were with me, you probably have been distributing them randomly with the stablehands, the gardener's boy, and the lad that delivers the groceries. I don't love you. I never loved you. The only reason I sent for you was to warn you not to tell anyone about me. If you do, it'll be the worse for you."

He laughed, nastily. The shock of his declaration left her speechless.

"I'm going now. My regiment's being sent to India. I'll never have to look at your pudding face or pander to your fragile sensibilities again. Thank God." *And with that, he strode away, leaving her half lying in the grass, which was where her maid found her, hysterically weeping.*

That memory led to another: a meeting at a party, a waltz in the arms of this handsome, fascinating officer. She shouldn't properly have been there. She wasn't exactly old enough . . . but her family also was not of the social class where she'd ever have a Coming Out, and her father got a great many invitations and didn't like to see her "sitting at home like a spinster." So there she was, and there he was, and it was just like a glorious romance when he began to court her in secret. . . .

And then do quite a bit more than "court" her. Somehow he had access to a cottage near her home. It was secluded, it was easily reached on foot, and all she had to do was say she was taking a walk. Not even her stepmother, a distant relative of her mother, seemed to think anything about it. But then, the stepmother was occupied with nursing her father, and it was trivially easy to get away whenever she liked. No one even questioned when she "went for a walk" on days that threatened bad weather, and when she returned dry after a downpour, no one seemed to think it odd.

Nan resolutely blocked herself from the memory of what had gone on in that cottage, but there was absolutely no doubt that the girl had been a complete idiot. Not only had she tried to tell "Robert" that she was pregnant, there was yet another searing memory.

The sly little maid who had been her confidant, carrying messages to and fro, and who knew about all of this, giving her a bottle of something that tasted like bitter mint, and the resulting, frightening rush of blood and the feeling her insides were tearing themselves loose. And *that* had led to the first fit of absolute hysterics that had brought her here.

It took the better part of a quarter of an hour to sort through all the memories, by which time all four of them were in the room—and the girl was well into sobbing herself into another round of vomiting. Which was, pretty much, what she'd been doing since she arrived here.

"Well," Nan said, as the last piece fell into place, "I don't know whether to laugh or throw up my hands in disgust. Here we were prepared to run to the rescue of a persecuted innocent, and instead I find a domestic disaster worthy of Jane Austen."

She paused for a moment to put her own thoughts in order, and after the silence had gone on too long, Sarah shook her finger at her. "Go on!" Sarah urged. "You can't just leave us hanging after a statement like that!"

"It appears that the fair innocent is neither innocent nor fair," Nan said bluntly. "While her papa was slowly fading, unbeknownst to him or the stepmother that was spending every waking moment at papa's bedside, she was canoodling in the shrubbery with a soldier-lad!"

Peter gaped at her. Sarah's mouth fell open. Suki just laughed. "Nor better nor she should be, aye?" the little girl crowed and tugged at Nan's ethereal skirt. "Well, go on then!"

"They met at a party. I am pretty certain the meeting was intentional on his part, and that the fellow had his eyes on her fortune and intended to elope to Scotland with her as soon as papa was conveniently out of the way. He discovered there are more entanglements as laid out in the will than would make that possible. By bribing a law clerk when the poor man was dead, if you please. He found out if she marries without her stepmother's permission, she's cut off."

"That makes sense," Peter agreed, shaking his head.

"The long and the short of it is that papa went to his reward, and our little fountain of tears here met up with her lover and informed him she was pregnant. In the meantime, he had found out the terms of the will, because instead of the response she expected, he told her bluntly he'd never loved her, he doubted the child was his, and in any event he was being sent to India, goodbye."

Sarah winced. "Cold," she said.

"As the glaciers of Norway," Peter agreed. "She's a silly goose, but *he's* a cad."

"She threw herself at him, he shook her off and beat a hasty retreat, and left her in hysterics in the garden, which is where her stepmother found her," Nan concluded.

"I think I can fill in the rest," Sarah said. "She's going to have a baby without benefit of father or clergy, so the first thing she thinks of is to declare her love to her unattached cousin in hopes of getting *him* properly shackled before it's too late."

"And when that hope fails, more hysterics followed by a miscarriage arranged by the maid she'd involved in her affair." Nan shook her head. "At that point, having no idea what was going on, her stepmother sent her here, where she has nothing but time to brood on her lost love, weep, and vomit."

"I . . . really don't know what to say," said Peter. "Or, more importantly, what to tell his Lordship."

"Arsk th' Watsons," Suki said wisely. "Or tell 'em, rather, an' leave it up t'them."

"Probably the best solution," Sarah agreed. "Should we do anything about—" she waved her hands at the room, and the sobbing girl.

"What *can* we do?" Peter asked. "We don't have any proof of any of this. So we certainly can't tell the doctor what's going on with his patient. The only thing we can do is just wish him well and leave him to it."

Nan shook her head. "The girl got herself into this mess, and I wish I *could* tell the doctors here what is really going on. But the best we can hope for is that he prescribes a course of dark rooms and a bland diet. She'll get tired of agonizing over the wretched man eventually." She clenched her jaw a little. "And that maid knows exactly what she's doing. She's going to be blackmailing her mistress with this until one or the other of them is dead. In fact. . . ." She paused. "You know, this might have been a scheme cooked up between her and this 'Robert.'"

"Do women really do that sort of thing?" Peter asked in fascination. "Betray each other like that?"

"Same as men do," Sarah replied. "And for the same reasons."

Grey made a rude noise. "Money," the parrot said, wisely.

"Grey's right." Nan cast a glance at the huddled figure on the bed that was anything but sympathetic. "Well, with the girl locked up here, the maid won't have a chance to extort anything from her for a while."

"I find it impossible to care," Sarah said in disgust. "Let's go back to the Watsons."

The return to their bodies was as instant as their departure, though they had to take a few moments to orient themselves before Nan unburdened herself of the sordid little tale.

The Watsons listened in stunned silence; Nan suspected that they had been coming up with all manner of suppositions, all of which included anything but the actual truth, and had been preparing a variety of plans to extricate the wretched girl from the facility. Without a doubt, the real story struck them with the same sense as a physical shock.

"Let's have dessert," Nan suggested, as the silence that followed her revelations stretched on and on. "I know that *I* could use something sweet to negate the sourness of what we found."

Mary Watson said nothing, but began to unpack the treats she had earlier put back in the hamper, and Nan took refuge in iced cake and fresh strawberries.

She still couldn't feel anything but irritation for the girl they had left sobbing in her bed. *Would I have been in more sympathy with her if we'd been of the same class?* she wondered. *Or if in addition to being an idiot, she'd had magic or psychical powers?* She didn't *think* so—but it was perfectly possible her irritation was a product of her own kind of prejudice.

No, damnitall. And I would feel just as much irritation if she'd been psychical or magical, because she exhibited no common sense and no willingness to do anything but grasp the immediate pleasure without regard for consequences.

John Watson was the first to speak when the last crumb had been eaten, and the plates and cutlery put away. He sighed heavily and fanned himself with his hat. "Well . . . I'll put the whole wretched tale in front of Alderscroft. I don't see any reason to try and find out who the blackguard is that abandoned that wretched wench. It won't do any good, he'll deny everything, and if any of it gets out, it will destroy not only the girl's reputation, but that of her stepmother. Because people *will* blame that poor woman. Since he's going to India, let us hope that Karma will see to his downfall."

Nan didn't have any hope of that; in her experience men like that got away with whatever they cared to, because they were so good at escaping before their bills came due. But Watson was right about the rest of it.

"I'll leave it to Alderscroft to decide what to tell the cousin," he continued, "And I thank God that's not something I need to decide."

"It could have been much worse for him," Nan felt impelled to point out. "If the poor man had actually *believed* what that stupid girl told him, and had gone so far as to marry her, she'd be leading him a merry dance indeed! He's well escaped from that particular trap! And can you imagine an Elemental Master saddled with that sort of wife?"

"It would have ruined him," Mary said flatly. "John, I think that's the tactic you need to take. We've uncovered some very sordid information that leads us to believe his Huntsman had a narrow escape from a budding adventuress. Then tell him the girl is neither psychical nor an Elemental Magician, and she's reaping some unsavory wild oats indeed."

John nodded. "Well, that was certainly a sordid little mystery. Quite unlike the ones we've been accustomed to solving."

"Just a reminder, I suppose, of how privileged we are," observed Peter. "Most of the mysteries ordinary people like Lestrade have to solve are sordid and unpleasant *and terribly boring*. At least ours are interesting."

5

Rain drove Ellie and Simon in from the garden, where they'd been pretending to weed while their mother milked the she-goat in the shed. Ellie didn't really want to go in, but she didn't want to be in the garden either. What she *wanted* was to be on the moor, with the goat, and not doing any kind of chore, so she lingered in the doorway, and Simon paused to loiter with her. Then lightning struck very nearby, and they shrieked, more in excitement than fear, as immediate thunder shook the stone walls, and dove in through the open door. The smell of rain followed them inside.

Truth to tell, they'd been doing a great deal of playing and not much weeding. Ellie was ravenously hungry, but neither she nor Simon had dared to touch so much as a cabbage leaf inside the garden wall. Mother knew, down to the exact number of pea-pods, just what was in the garden, and if anything was missing when the weeding was done, she'd whip both of them. Ellie had actually thought to sample the weeds, but the roots were tasteless and woody, and the leaves bitter, and nothing had tasted satisfying.

I druther be on moor, she thought, as Mother hurried in with her apron held over the bowl of milk. *Least there be things we can eat out there.* Nice things, too, sometimes, depending on their luck. Bilberries and gooseberries for instance. Her mouth fair watered at the thought of an apron full of gooseberries. Sowthistle in a pinch. Yarrow and deadnettle and saxifrage. Hogweed and chickweed and lambs'-lettuce. Most edible things were green leaves, and it took a lot to fill you up, but you could get your belly full enough that you could get to sleep before the thin provender wore off and you were hungry again. Mother's mouth pursed up when they brought home armloads of greens to cook, because cooked down there was generally barely enough to fill four bowls, but it *was* food, and Ellie didn't see any reason to turn your nose up at it. It wasn't like they had much of a choice.

But Mother was funny that way. Pa said she'd been brought up better than a stone cottage on the moor, and all the make-dos and shifts grieved her, but what were they to do? They were *lucky* that they'd gotten this cottage by way of Pa's Ma, and it had a bit of land they could put a garden on, after Pa'd lost a hand to the machines in the mill. They wouldn't even have the cottage in the first place, if Pa's Pa hadn't got all the laborers to help him on a day when all the farmers were away at the Fair, and they'd cheated a bit of freehold out of Squire by raising the cottage in a single day. Because that was the law, if you could raise a cottage, floor to roof, and have a fire burning in the hearth in a single day, it was yours, freehold, and any land it was on and you could enclose in a wall. Seemed impossible, but done it they had, and more than once, hereabouts.

And Pa had inherited the cottage from his Ma after his accident. So when they got turned out of lodgings because there bain't no more money, they had a place to go and a garden to eat out of. They were *lucky*, Pa would say, and there's an end to it. And Mother would thin up her mouth and nod abruptly.

Thunder rattled the shutters, and in the snug little shed attached to the cottage, the goat, Daisy, kicked her objections to it. They were lucky to have Daisy, too; Ellie and Simon had found her wandering on the moor as a kid, and no one had claimed her, and now they had her and a billy-kid, who was probably going to get traded for the services of another billy-goat when spring came around, rather than ending up in their pot. Ellie was just as glad; she didn't want to eat him, not when she'd seen him all wobble-kneed and vulnerable right after he'd been born. But there were only two fates for a billy-kid, and this one was probably not going to end up guarding a flock of sheep.

Mother put the bowl of milk in the very center of the table for safety. "That milk and the loaf-end's all we've got for dinner," she said, in that tight voice that meant she was upset about the lack of food. "So don't be larking about and spilling it."

Mother didn't talk like the folks hereabouts.

"Nay, Mother," she and Simon said together.

"Your father should be home soon." Unspoken was *"Pray he found work,"* because there wasn't much left in the flour crock, and the rest of the stores were likewise depleted. Not many people wanted to hire a one-handed man, and especially not a man who'd gone off the moor and only returned to take over his Ma's cottage, with a "foreign" (which meant "not from Dartmoor") woman to wife and her with hair as black as a raven's wing and tall and pale—and nothing like the people he'd grown up with. She didn't talk right, to their way of thinking—they'd look at her side-eyed, and make little sounds that meant *Who does she think she is?* And *Gives herself airs, she does.*

That wasn't true, but it didn't stop folk from thinking it.

As for her looks, most people here were round-faced and blond or sandy-brown-haired. Black hair meant "Travelers" and people were slow to understand that was what she wasn't. But things moved slowly on the moor, and that was that, and no point in asking a pig to dance, as Pa would say.

"Sweep the floor," Mother ordered. "And sweep the ashes from the hearth. No wasting them! Put them in the crock where they belong."

Ashes went into a crock with a crack across the bottom that Mother had found in the shed. It didn't hold liquid, which was why she hadn't used it for the milk, but the mouth was big enough you could scoop ashes in there, and Mother used the ashes to make soap. The crack across the bottom was useful for that; she put water in the top and a dish under it, and the lye-water that came out the bottom helped make soap and clean, and for some reason, she used it in cooking dried peas and beans and to make bread. Mother was clever like that, she could read and write and figure and all, and she had books that told her how to do things, like make soap. Last summer Ellie and Simon had found a wild bees' nest and come to tell her and the book had told her how to smoke the bees out, and collect the honey and wax. Ellie had joyfully expected a feast of sweets, but no, every bit, honey and wax and all, had gone to the market, and the only taste she and Simon had gotten had been the splintery licks scraped out of the inside of the tree, and they'd had to fight with ants for those.

Ellie went to carefully collect the ashes with a birch-bark scoop and a little whisk made of gorse twigs, when she realized Simon wasn't sweeping as he'd been told, he was galloping around the room with the broom between his legs like a hobby-horse.

"Oi!" she shouted indignantly. "And what'd Mother be sayin'?"

"'Es be 'ighwayman!" Simon shouted. "'Es be Dick Turpin! Stand and deliver!"

"'Ee bain't Dick Turpin, ye gurt loon!" she shouted indignantly. "'Ee be a dunderheaded dawcock!" Truth to tell she was angrier about the fact that *she* was doing chores and *he* wasn't than that he was pretending to be a highwayman, which was a very naughty thing to do. "Gi' un broom!" She seized the handle as he galloped past, and tugged at it. He hung onto it and tugged back.

Soon they were fighting all over the cottage, tugging and hitting each other and calling each other names. And of all the bad luck, Mother came in in the middle of it, and shouted.

"Helen! Simon! Stop this instant!"

And worst luck, startled, Simon let go of the broom just as she tugged, and the brushy end swept across the table-top, hitting the wooden milk bowl and sending it flying. It hit the floor and spun like a top, spilling every drop across the flagstones, where it soaked into the porous stone. And there went half of supper.

Mother went white as snow, then red as a sunset. In the absolute silence that followed the clatter of the wooden bowl on the floor, Ellie held her breath and waited for the explosion.

And oh, it came.

"Outside," Mother said, between clenched teeth. She flung open the door, and shouted. *"Out! Both of you! NOW!"*

"But, Mother, it be rain—" Simon began, his voice taking on that wheedling tone that usually got him his way.

Not this time.

"OUT!" Mother roared, and crossed the room in two strides to pick up the knife-strop. *"OUT! Onto the moor with the both*

of you, you worthless, feckless, miserable brats! OUT! And don't come home unless you bring a feast for four back with you, or I'll beat you both black and blue from the soles of your feet to the tops of your heads, and then I'll hold you while your Father beats you a second time!!"

She brandished the strap and made it snap, and even Simon realized that this time they had gone too far and ran for the door before she could use the strap on him. Ellie was right behind.

And no sooner were they out the door than Mother had slammed it shut behind them.

"Es th-th-think she do be meanin' it," Simon stuttered. Ellie boxed his ear. This was all *his* fault.

As they stood blinking in shock on the stoop, Ellie slowly realized the storm had been one of those short, violent ones: blown up in moments; gone again, flying down the moor, in another few moments. Blue sky and sunshine reigned once again, and a warm breeze lofted over the hills. Fat white clouds clustered like flocks of sheep, and the smell of the heather drying under the sun changed her mood from frightened to joyful, all in a moment. They were out of the cottage, freed from tedious chores, and free!

And Mother had just ordered them to do exactly what she had wanted to in the first place. The moor beckoned and she was only too happy to answer.

But of course, she wasn't going to let Simon know that.

She punched his arm. "This be *'ee's* fault," she snarled at him.

"Ow! That's a lie! 'Ee started it!"

"Nawt! 'Oo was th' gurt fool daggling about room like asneger, a shoutin' 'Es be Dick Turpin'?" she countered in triumph. "Mother had owten been cotten 'ee."

"Aye but—" Simon realized his arguments weren't going to hold up, and seemed to fold in on himself. "Ellie, she's desperd angry. What are usn's gawn to do?"

"What she told us." Ellie went to the storage shed—the one on the other side of the cottage, the one that didn't hold the goat— and came back with two willow-withy baskets. "Brung back a feast." She thrust one at him, and when he took it, marched out the gate and straight up the moor, glancing back to see that he followed. She nearly skipped, she was so happy to be out and about. The warm breeze made her feel like galloping like a moor pony. She was certain they'd have two baskets full of foraged food in no time, and come back to the cottage in triumph. Who needed stale bread and half a cup of goat milk and a few peas from the garden, anyway?

About a hour later, she realized the major flaw in this plan.

Every place they usually foraged was pretty picked over. All they had to show for their work so far was a couple of handfuls of cress in the bottom of each basket—quite a pitiful showing, and certainly not the "feast" Mother had demanded.

"We bain't got much," Simon said, looking doubtfully down into his basket.

"We go futher then," she replied, her chin set stubbornly, and waved her hand around. "Nobbut a soul out here food huntin'. It's just us an' sheep an' ponies."

"What if there's a storm?" he asked desperately.

"We outrun 't," she stated confidently. After all, they could see for miles. Little storms like the one that had just passed were easy to spot, and since there was no particular place that was any better for foraging than any other, they could just go where the storm wasn't.

"But what if we cain't?" he persisted.

"We find an 'ollow and lew." She squared her shoulders and started marching toward the sun. It was easy to get lost on the moor, but she reckoned that as long as she kept the sun in front of her as they foraged, and behind her when they returned, they'd hit some place they recognized on the way back to give them a more accurate guide home.

How hard could this be? It was the moor, and she was moor-wise. They'd come home with heaping baskets and Mother would admit it was better to let them "play" on the moor from now on.

"Cham afeerd, Ellie," Simon whined. She wasn't afraid, and she suspected that neither was he, but it was actually getting dark, their baskets were barely half full, and all of it was greens. Not very satisfying. Certainly not a feast.

And she was sure that they were lost, because she'd gotten turned round about when they'd scrambled down into a rocky valley with a stream in it, hoping to find some fish to tickle, and realized they couldn't get back up the way they'd come down. It had been a long, weary trudge that had taken them a good long time and twisted and turned them right round about before they'd found a place to climb out again. And now she didn't know where she stood.

She stopped where she was and closed her eyes, and thought hard. "I think we best lew," she said. "We can ate what's in our baskets now, and come morning, forage back. There's bracken t'make bed with, an' that 'ollow under blackthorn roots be nowt so bad."

She turned to peer at Simon in the fading light. He looked as if he was going to cry, but he nodded. Together they made their way back to the hollow, picking bracken as they went, until by the time they reached the place as the moon rose, they labored like a pair of donkeys under a pair of enormous piles of fresh-smelling greenery.

And she was right. The hollow, once lined with bracken, was cozy enough. No worse than their beds in the loft in midwinter; better in a way, because there wasn't any straw poking up into them. They curled up together, and began stuffing handfuls of greenery into their mouths from their respective baskets. The mingled tastes, sour, bitter, faintly sweet, and all very *green* were— not entirely nice and not very satisfying. They'd have been better stewed and more satisfying fried in a bit of pig fat. But food was food, and she knew everything they'd picked was edible, so she munched on, even though right now that cup of goat's milk and piece of bread to dunk in it was a lot more appealing than she'd ever thought it would be.

Meanwhile, red sky, which made her sigh with relief. *Shepherd's delight*, that. No storms tonight. Then darkness flooded over the moor, the sounds around them changed, and the wind changed from warm and sweet to cool and damp. Stars came out, twinkling between the leaves of the blackthorn overhead, and out into the distance over the hills. She thought she heard sheep in the far, far distance, but otherwise, nothing. And she kept putting her hand in her basket, and bringing it to her face, full of greenstuff, reminding herself that any food was better than no food.

Before she was done she felt a bit like a sheep, but her stomach was more than full enough to let her fall asleep, which was the important part. Simon finished wearily munching his last fistful, and whimpered a little. She put her arms around him to comfort him, pulled bracken over both of them, and finally began to drowse as their bodies warmed the bracken-lined cavity under the blackthorn roots.

As she was halfway down into sleep, she told over her nightly prayers in her head. She wasn't sure that saying them would help—could Jesus even hear you out on the moor like this? But she didn't want to take the chance that He couldn't. Besides, priest said that stars were the eyes of angels, and if angels could see them, surely Jesus could.

Please make Mother not angry at us. Please help us find something really good to eat tomorrow. Please make Mother realize we should be foraging all the time, because when Simon's inside four walls, he goes spare. Please don't let us be lost. Please— And then Simon's warm little body helped hers warm up completely and she drifted off, her prayers unfinished.

She woke up with thin sunlight streaming from the east, as Simon sneezed loudly and threw off most of the bracken covering both of them with a wordless grunt of impatience. Cold damp air struck her face, smelling of bracken and mud. "I be 'ungry!" he announced, as if it were a royal proclamation, or a fact of supreme importance, and looked at her as if he expected her to provide him with food.

"Drink some water," she snapped. "Find some cress. Feed t'y own self. I bain't a witch, t'conjurate up eggs an' toast a-cause *'ee* got usn's sent out on moor yestere'en!"

Whether it was the mention of the eggs and toast that they were *not* going to get, or the reminder that they were both out here with empty bellies because of him, Simon looked at her and burst into tears.

And ordinarily, she'd comfort him. But she was cross, her hair was full of bits of bracken and she hadn't a comb to make it right, she was hungry too, and the sound of him crying satisfied the part of her that wanted him to feel as badly as possible. Because it was all his fault. Every bit of it. If he hadn't been larking about, they wouldn't be here. If he hadn't fought her over the broom, they wouldn't be here. They'd be in their beds, and mayhap Pa would have brought home food last night, and Mother would be making hot porridge to eat for breakfast.

And right now, hot porridge with a bit of salt sounded wonderful. Not as good as eggs and toast, but wonderful.

She threw off the rest of the bracken, and clambered out of the hollow, and went off in the direction of where she thought that stream was without seeing if Simon was following. It wasn't as if she needed to see . . . she could hear him easy enough, stumbling after her and sniffing and blubbering, because he thought blubbering would make her feel sorry for him. Well, it wouldn't. Not this time.

Sure enough, the stream was where she'd thought it was, and she went to her knees to drink out of it. And as luck would have it, there was watercress right there. With a grimace—because she was still thinking about porridge and toast and eggs—she picked a handful and stuffed it in her mouth. "Cress, gurt loon," she said around the mouthful, and Simon knelt down next to her to join her until they'd pulled up and eaten every bit of it.

He rubbed the back of his hand across his tear-streaked face, leaving a smear of mud across his cheekbones. "Now what d'we do?" he asked her, looking up at her woefully.

"We gets our baskets, and we bring back feast," she told him. "We went west, now we go east, an' forage on the way."

She washed her hands and face in the cold water—Simon didn't, the little pig—and went back for her basket. After a good night's sleep and at least a sketchy meal of cress, she felt confident again.

They moved slower, this morning, peering carefully at the ground at their feet, and plucking everything that they knew was edible. The baskets weren't filling up fast that way, but when you combined baskets with bellies, they were making much better progress than yesterday. They had all day to forage, after all, and just because they were supposed to be filling their baskets, that didn't mean they couldn't eat some of what they'd found. In fact, even though she still felt like a grazing sheep, she reasoned that they'd be able to hunt better if their stomachs were full.

Since they were moving slowly and carefully, they found a lot more food than they had last night, when they'd been larking a bit, and careless. Simon started up a rabbit, and she *almost* managed to hit it with a rock. That was a disappointment; one rabbit or a fish would have been more than enough to purchase Mother's good graces again.

What she really wanted was something besides greens. Big baskets of greens did not a "feast" make. What she really wanted was to find either berries or something more substantial. She took a thought longingly for 'taties. Did 'taties grow wild?

And it was too late for bird eggs; all the nests they found were empty. She wouldn't have turned up her nose at baby birds, either; after all, they would net wrens and doves when they could, and cook up the entire birds into pies when they had the flour. But when they got down into wooded valleys, the nests were empty, and none of the tree hollows they explored yielded any stored nuts.

The going was easier to the north, and the foraging better, too, so they drifted in that direction for a while. She still wasn't worried about getting lost. After all, home was west. And she knew where west was!

And that was when they came upon a heavily wooded combe, which looked like the best place to forage yet. But on the other hand . . . the trees were bigger and darker than anything she'd *ever* seen on the moor. If there was ever a place where a witch would live, this was surely it.

They looked at each other. Simon licked his lips. "Bet there be mushrooms in there," he ventured. Mushrooms weren't a rabbit, but they were better than greens. She knew there was still a bit of fat left, meant to scrape over that stale bread. Fried mushrooms were *almost* as good as meat.

She nodded. Many of the trees were oaks, and everyone knew that the best mushrooms grew under oaks. "And 'ee see slip shell?" she observed. "Mebbe last year's nuts."

Nuts *were* as good as meat, and hard come by on the moor.

She led the way into the combe.

There *were* mushrooms, and they were the kind they'd been taught were safe. And in little tree hollows, the last few nuts from squirrel hoards. It seemed with every step they took, they found another bit of something to eat—not much, but every bit in the basket was a step closer to going home in triumph, the more especially since now it wasn't such thin stuff as greens. So they moved slowly and methodically, both their gazes on the ground, and ears cocked nervously for the voices of piskies. Because piskies there surely were here, and they were more likely to do her and Simon a mischief than bake them a cake.

"Ellie," Simon whispered. "I think we be t'end of combe."

She looked up; Simon was right. There was more light ahead. Was that the end of the combe, or something else?

They hunched over and crept forward, until they crouched behind a screening of slip shell bushes. Under the trees, it was dark—but before them was a clearing with the sun shining brightly down onto it. And in that clearing was a cot.

A bit smaller than the cottage they lived in, but it was still stone. The thick slate roof had green moss and even grass growing on it—the sure sign no one had tended that roof in a very long time. There were two small windows with no glass in them, one on either side of a half-open, crooked door. No smoke came from the chimney.

From here, it looked abandoned. There was a half-ruined wall around it; shutters gaped open over the two windows, which were dark, like a pair of hollow eyes.

Instinctively, they crouched down further. The first thing that Ellie thought of was that this surely must be a witch's cot. Who else would live out here, all alone and lonely, but a witch? And she waited for the hag to emerge and demand what they were doing there. But there was nothing. No movement. No sounds.

"Do 'ee think there's anybody there?" Simon whispered.

She shook her head. "Maybe a garden, though. . . ."

If there was a garden, there might still be edible stuff in it. Stuff Mother wasn't guarding like a watchdog! Even gone to weeds and seed, some garden stuff survived for a very long time on its own. This might be the best place to find Mother's feast.

Especially if the cot hadn't been abandoned for long. Weeds grew up powerful fast; what she could see from here might just be the growth of a single year, untended.

Ellie stood up first, and moved cautiously toward a gap in the wall. She winced a little as she moved out into the sunlight, and paused, waiting again for a challenge from inside the cot.

But no challenge came, and she peered around the wall into the weed-filled yard. And anything Ellie had in her mind until that point was completely driven out of it by the flash of bright red beneath trefoil leaves.

"Strawberries!" she shrieked, overcome with greed, surprise, and delight, and fell on her knees in the weeds inside the wall.

Yes, they were strawberries, and they were real, and fat and plump and there were a *lot* of them, more than enough to stuff her and Simon full and still have plenty to carry home!

She dropped her basket without any regard for how much she spilled, and gathered up as many berries as she could fit in both her hands. Beside her, Simon did the same. She opened her mouth as big as it could get and crammed them inside—

Ellie woke up with a hideous headache, the taste of strawberries in her mouth, and shivering with cold—and knew there was something terribly wrong. She wasn't in the sunlit garden by that old cot; it was dark and damp, smelled of mildew and wet dust, and all she could make out from the straw mattress she lay on was a dark, huddled lump on another straw mattress between her and the wall. She knew she was on a straw mattress—or rather, a burlap sack stuffed with straw that served as a mattress— because it crackled and prickled her when she moved, and the unmistakable smell of mildewed straw was all around her.

Her left ankle hurt. She sat up slowly and tried to move it, and was rewarded with a *clank*, and the bite of metal into her skin above her bare foot.

Frantically, she felt down her leg, and her questing fingers encountered a metal band locked around her ankle, a chain attached to it. When she tugged on the chain, she was able to drag a few more feet of it toward her, with a hideous rattling and clanking noise.

She'd been chained up like a dog! Why? Who had done such a thing? A thousand questions whirled in her aching head, and she had answers to none of them.

"Ellie? Ellie! 'Ee be awake!" The lump next to her shot up

straight and scrabbled over to her on hands and knees, his own chain rattling behind him. Simon threw himself into her arms, sobbing and shaking with fear. Well, she was quaking with fear herself. Where were they? How had they gotten here?

Had they been taken by a witch? But how?

Had the berries been bewitched?

"Where—" she began.

"Dunno!" he wailed. "Es et the strawbs, an' Es woket up 'ere!"

She took him by the shoulders and shook him, trying to get more sense out of him. "Where's 'ere?" she demanded, choking on the words, eyes burning with tears. One thing she did know, it couldn't be a piskie-barrow. Piskies couldn't abide iron and steel, and that was an iron shackle on her ankle. Was it a witch as she'd first feared? But witches weren't supposed to like iron much, either.

But if it was a man, why do *this*? Why not just beat them for trespass? All they'd touched were two double-handfuls of berries!

"We dunno," came a thin voice out of the dark, and she nearly dislocated her neck, swiveling her head around to find the source. "We dunno where's 'ere. Most on 'uns was like 'ee; come on garden, et somethin', woket up 'ere. Some on uns et somethin' else, e'en in town, ended up 'ere. But uns dunno where *'ere* is. 'Tisn't in town, 'cause there ain't no town-sounds. And 'tis bigger nor cot, we thinket."

She put her arms around Simon, who was crying in utter despair. She felt like wailing herself. "'Ow many of 'ee?" she asked, unable to really make out dark lumps against the dark floor.

"Ten, mebbe?" the speaker sounded doubtful. "Dark One comes twicet day, feeds 'un. There's water an' dipper by me, slop bucket for to piss an' shit in by you. Dark One feeds us good, but . . . anon the Black Sleep comes, an' 'ee'll wake up weak an' doattie an' addle-pated an' all a-biver. 'Ee don't really get strong again. An' it comes agin, an' ee'll wake up weaker. Then 'ee don' wake up, an' Dark One takes 'ee away an' 'ee don' come back."

"The Black Sleep?" she whispered, making it a question.

"Like real sleep, but 'ee don't dream, an it makes 'ee weary, nay rested," said the other child.

There was a weak chorus of "ayes" at that.

She strained her eyes to make anything at all out, but the

room's sole window was shuttered tight, and all she could see were four dim walls, vague shapes lying or sitting on the floor. Under the prevailing smell of mildew, there *was* the faint stink of shit and piss, but no worse than came from the chamberpots at night at home.

"If 'ee needs shit, there be bucket uv earth aside the shit bucket," said a female voice. "Cover the shit wi' earth or the Dark One'll beat 'un all."

She blinked back tears in the long silence that followed that helpful statement. Finally she spoke again. "Us be Ellie an' Simon," she said, finally.

One by one, the children—or at least the ones strong enough to speak—told her their names. Rose and Lily. Colin. Mark and Stephen and Bill. Sam and Ben. Deborah and Jess. And lastly, the speaker, Robbie.

"Who's be the Dark One, Robbie?" she asked, when the introductions were all made.

"Dunno," Robbie began, when the sound of footsteps approaching the closed door broke the heavy silence. "'Ee'll find out," the boy finished bleakly.

And the door creaked open.

Standing in the doorway, a pillar of black against the dim light of the next room, was a sexless creature with a hood hiding its face.

And it turned the hood toward *her*.

6

"Penny for your thoughts," Nan told John Watson.

The entire *ménage* had decided to visit that constant favorite, Hampton Court Palace. The venue was—somewhat more neglected than most of the Royal Palaces. The Queen didn't care for it much; it was, after all, a patched-together hotchpotch of several styles, and these days most of the people living in it were those to whom the Crown owed some sort of debt, and who were given living quarters here for life. The grounds and some of the parts of the Palace, like the Tudor section, were actually open to the public to stroll through. Large sections of the extensive gardens were utterly neglected.

But as far as Nan was concerned, that made the place all the more fascinating. The Royal School of Needlework was here, and she often thought about taking a class or two—until she reminded herself she barely had time to darn her stockings, much less learn complicated fancy-work. Suki adored the maze; it was much cooler than London—and it certainly *smelled* better than London in this heat. Both the girls' flat and the Watsons' were far enough from the Thames that at least the river-stench didn't get that far, but there were plenty of horses (and dogs, and cats, and the occasional human) making the streets less than fragrant. And she preferred the untidy, overgrown gardens with their illusion of wilderness to any other parts except the great maze.

And of course, there was always the chance that Robin

Goodfellow would put in an appearance, though Nan suspected he'd be more likely to do so for Suki than for the adults. He tended only to come to *them* when they called, but would often surprise Suki any place where you could find something like a green oasis. Sometimes she wondered if this was because they were no longer childlike enough to interest him—but then her knowledge of Robin suggested another reason entirely. This was possibly sheer politeness on his part. Adults tended to dislike surprises, and didn't much enjoy it when someone popped up unexpectedly, where children delighted in that sort of thing.

Since by this point, Suki knew the layout of the place as well as she knew the grounds of their nearest park, and since she could be counted on *not* to run riot or call attention to herself, or do anything that might be considered impolite, the adults let her roam on her own, admonishing her only to meet them at teatime at the front gate.

"My thoughts are mixed," Watson replied. "On the one hand, I am enjoying the peace and quiet. On the other, I begin to sympathize with Holmes' restlessness when he does not have a case. Half my patients are out of the city, the other half seem infernally healthy. But then I remind myself that there is always the chance of a cholera outbreak . . . which I would not wish on anyone, and which strikes the people who cannot afford a doctor. So I am pleased with peace and quiet."

"Not that a doctor is much help with cholera," Mary reminded him.

"Only one who is also an Earth-magician, and most of them cannot abide London even for duty, love, or filthy lucre." They had chosen the more overgrown portions of the Royal Gardens to stroll in; they were such frequent visitors here that the Palace Guards and guides merely smiled, waved, and allowed them to go where they willed. And the gardeners ignored them as if they were some species of wandering plant. It was much cooler here, and if you knew where to look, it was easy to find the old seats, since most of them were marble. Those marble benches were marvelously cool, too.

"Well, you've cursed us now, John Watson," Sarah laughed as Grey and Neville played tag with each other among the branches.

Grey was as safe as houses here—at the least hint that any other bird was going to trouble her, Neville would swoop in to administer a trouncing.

"Look, Mama!" cried a young child from somewhere past the overgrown arbors. "A Grey Parrot!"

"Don't be silly, dear," replied a woman, sounding hot and impatient. "This is not a menagerie. Come, let's go back to the Palace."

Grey snickered, and Neville outright laughed, and then the two went back to their game. But now it had a variation; Grey must have lost one of her red tail feathers, because she had it in her mouth—and Neville was trying to snatch it from her.

"What do you mean, I've cursed us?" Watson asked, as they finally found the seats within the arbor and sat themselves down in them. Nan sighed as the coolness immediately penetrated the thin cottons of her skirts and underthings. She much envied Mary Watson's linen trousers right now.

"Every time you complain about inactivity, a case finds us," Sarah replied.

Nan nodded. "I will bet you the cost of our tea that there is a letter from Alderscroft waiting for us when we return to Baker Street."

"There may well be a letter, but the only thing in it will be a reminder of the Hunting Lodge meeting tomorrow night," Watson retorted.

"Well, now you've *certainly* cursed us!" Mary exclaimed with a laugh. "John Watson, I believe you did it on purpose!"

Watson twisted the ends of his moustache and looked impish. "Well," he countered, "wouldn't you like the excuse to leave London in this beastly weather? And do so at the Lion's expense?"

"He certainly *spares* no expense when it comes to us when we need to leave," she replied wistfully. "Even if such expeditions are not precisely holidays, they are certainly comfortable."

That was an understatement if ever Nan heard one.

"And once outside of London," she added, "I could revert to being Mary again. These trousers may be comfortable, but the rest is certainly *not*."

Oh, of course not, Nan thought ruefully. *Good gad, the corset she has to wear to flatten everything must be ghastly in this heat.*

"I wouldn't mind," Sarah admitted. "And Suki would love it."

"As long as it's not Blackpool, or some other holiday city," Nan put in. "I do like my fun vulgar, but I don't like throngs where you're stepping on someone's skirt every time you try to move." She sighed. "I wouldn't mind going back to Wales, not at all. But our Selkie friends there seem to have matters well in hand. Not a word from them except letters about how the twins are growing in ever so long."

"Oh, now don't go cursing them as well!" Mary said with alarm. "Trouble involving the Selkies would be dire indeed!"

"I imagine the reason they haven't written much is because the twins are leading them a merry chase every single day," Sarah quickly said. "Twins can get into *quite* enough trouble when they are merely human. Just imagine what they can do when they elect to take a short stroll across the seabed because they can hold their breaths like seals!"

"I would not wish that fate on anyone," Nan agreed. "Honestly it might be easier for everyone if the entire family just stayed seals until the twins are old enough to reason with."

Grey and Neville had tired of their game and returned to the girls. Both birds hopped into laps instead of on shoulders, and settled in for a long, blissful scratch, for all the world like a pair of feathered cats. Nan was just glad that the birds would hop *off* and go somewhere else if they needed to relieve themselves.

A little blond-haired girl darted around the overgrown lilac bushes that half-hid them with a peal of laughter, and stopped dead in her tracks at the sight of the birds in the girls' laps. "*Mama!*" she called out in triumph. "Come see! I *told* you there was a Grey Parrot!"

Sarah's brows rose—Nan knew that look. It wasn't disapproval, it was surprise. A harried woman as golden-haired as the child, holding onto her hat with one hand and her skirts with the other, ran as fast as the tangled undergrowth and her skirts would allow her, and stopped beside her daughter, blushing with shame and chagrin. "Sylvia! I told you not to bother anyone! I beg your pardon, I'll take her away now."

"I didn't!" the child protested. Nan smothered a grin; this little girl was utterly irrepressible, and Nan was reminded strongly of Suki. But she still didn't see what made Sarah so surprised.

"Please don't go," Sarah said, with a welcoming smile. "And you didn't interrupt anything at all."

Then Mary Watson—whose expression mirrored Sarah's—did an astonishing thing. She pursed up her lips and gave a soft whistle.

Three of the little sylphs that were her primary Air Elementals whisked around branches and through the foliage and came to hover expectantly in front of her, waiting for any requests she might have.

They were lovely little things, although utterly shameless. The gauzy bits of "fabric" they wore did nothing to conceal any part of their bodies, which were not at all "doll-like" or sexless as the fairies that were based on half-remembered legends of them were. One had the wings of a dragonfly, one the barred wings of a hawk, and one the wings of a butterfly. Nan and Sarah were used to their nudity, but Nan wondered why Mary had called them just now.

Now it was the newcomer's turn to look astonished, although the child noticed nothing so far as Nan could tell. She clearly saw the sylphs, looking from them to Mary Watson and back again. "You—you're an Air Master!" she blurted.

"And you're an Air Magician," acknowledged Mary with a little nod.

So that's what Sarah saw! Masters could often recognize other Elemental Magicians on sight. Magicians generally could not.

"And *this* little one," Sarah added, "Is about to be some sort of Earth Mage, when she grows into it." The mother looked startled, but not exactly as if this were something unexpected. Perhaps she was startled because the child was allied with Earth rather than Air.

Sylvia, entirely oblivious to all of this, had crept closer to Sarah, eyes fixed on Grey. Nan thought it was rather endearing, how she kept her hands carefully to herself, though her eyes spoke of the longing to touch the parrot. "She's *beautiful*," the child said. "I've never seen a bird so close. May I pet her?"

"You can," said Grey herself, offering the back of her neck to touch. With her mouth pursed up in a little "o" of delight, the little girl gently petted the back of Grey's head and neck with a single, careful finger.

"Oi!" Neville objected. "Me too!" He hopped onto Nan's knee to shove his head aggressively under the girl's hand. With a laugh of pure joy, the child petted one bird with each hand. Her blue eyes danced and sparkled with happiness. Nan got the impression from her surface thoughts that this was a very kind and gentle child.

"My name is Doctor John Watson," Watson had been saying, while the girl made her enraptured acquaintance of the birds.

"But I know of you, of course!" the woman replied, blushing again. "My husband is in Lord Alderscroft's auxiliary—we're only Magicians, not Masters, so we are not full Lodge members. Once again, I apologize, I'm so sorry Sylvia disturbed you, we'll just be—"

"Staying, of course," Mary said firmly. "It's ever so much cooler here. As long as Sylvia is playing with the birds she won't be running you around Robin Hood's barn, so to speak, and you look as if you could use a rest."

"There's a twin to this bench just behind you," John added, and the woman searched hastily behind her and found it, dropping down onto the marble with a sigh. "Where are my manners!" she exclaimed. "I'm Sapphire Morrison. My husband is Gerrold Morrison."

The rest of them introduced themselves, and they all made some small talk—"small talk" for magicians, that is, which was scarcely like the gossip ordinary folks might exchange—while Nan carefully examined the woman, the child, and the surface thoughts of both.

Both Sylvia and her mother were dressed in outfits that did not match Sapphire's careful and cultured speech. Sylvia's dress, if Nan was any judge, had been cut down and pieced together from larger garments, while Sapphire's was of good quality . . . but either remade from an older garment in a more modern style, or secondhand. *Teacher,* she guessed. *Or governess.* The former seemed more likely than the latter, since most families of the means to employ a governess did not care for said governess to be married.

After all, in their minds, they were paying for the governess's attention to be on *their* children, every day, and every hour of the day.

Both Sapphire and her daughter were wearing light muslin summer dresses, but not *white.* Sapphire's was a pattern of blue-gray leaves on gray, with very narrow, conservative flounces, trimmed in white braid and a little white lace. Sylvia wore a dark gray pinafore over a solid blue dress with no frills at all. Neither color would be likely to show stains readily, at least, not as readily as white.

The woman's surface thoughts were mostly those of

embarrassment that her child had been so forward and mannerless, gratitude that John and Mary and the girls were so kind, and a kind of shyness in the presence of three Masters. Nan got the impression that she was in awe of Elemental Masters in general, but John Watson in particular.

By this point, Sylvia had Grey on her shoulder and Neville begging shamelessly for chin scratches, and Sapphire had just remembered something Sarah had said.

"Did—Miss Sarah, did you say that Sylvia was going to be some sort of *Earth* Elementalist?" she asked in a break in the conversation. By this time the sylphs had gotten bored, and since Sylvia could not see them, had fluttered off.

Sarah nodded. "Yes, I did. I cannot tell yet if she will be a Master or a Magician, but she is definitely allied with Earth."

Now Sapphire went from blushing to pale. "But—that's—" She seemed overwhelmed by anxiety suddenly. Nan was puzzled, until her next words explained it. "—we cannot afford to leave London!" she blurted.

Ah, of course! The Earth Magicians cannot tolerate living in London, with all the poisons in the soil, air, and water. The more Sylvia came into her power, the less she'd be able to stand living under such conditions.

"Which is why I will speak to Lord Alderscroft about a scholarship to the Harton School for Sylvia, now that we know her Element is Earth," John Watson said smoothly, as if he had been thinking of this all along. "There are several of them available, I believe. The Hunting Lodge has established a fund for such things. The school is outside of London, on one of his Lordship's estates. One can easily run down there in a few hours."

Sapphire's face reflected her mixed emotions. "That—that is uncommonly kind of you, Doctor," she managed. "I am incredibly grateful, and I know that Gerrold will be as well. . . ."

"But it's difficult knowing you will have to part with her during the school terms," Mary said with sympathy.

"Our ward Suki is enrolled there," Sarah added, with a kindly look. "It was hard at first to part with her, but she so enjoys being able to be among those like her, so that she does not need to hide her powers."

Sapphire nodded. "If she had been any other Element, I could have had her enrolled in the school where I teach."

"Well, perhaps Memsa'b will be in need of a teacher herself by that time," Nan put in. "I'll speak to her about that on your behalf if you like. But I should think she would be overjoyed to find an experienced teacher with powers to match the students. What do you teach?"

Overjoyed is understating it.

"English, Grammar, English Literature, and some Latin and Greek," Sapphire said with a blush. "I know the last are unusual, but Papa was a parish priest and thought all his children should learn the classical languages."

Memsa'b will turn cartwheels. "I'll do more than speak to her, then," Nan promised. "I'll write to her immediately. The summer term is nearly over, and if you can get away, you could start in the fall." She smiled reassuringly. "The position comes with housing, and your husband could go into London on the earliest train, and come back the same way in the evening."

A few years ago, that would not have been possible, but it was astonishing to Nan how many people were choosing to live in the "suburbs," as they were called, and take the now-frequent trains into London.

Then again . . . certainly in the summer I would not at all mind doing the same. In fact, if Suki had not been adamant about keeping her position among the Baker Street Irregulars, Nan would have been greatly tempted to close up the flat and move to the school for the summer.

"Here's my card," Watson said. Sapphire took it, fumbled in her reticule for a moment, and produced two of her own, as Nan handed over the card she and Sarah shared. "We'll be in touch, I promise you. Would you care to join us for tea?"

The look on her face told Nan without needing to read surface thoughts that she did, badly, want to join them. But instead, she sighed a little with regret and said, "Sylvia and I need to start back if we're to have supper ready for Gerrold. But thank you so much for your kindness! Sylvia?"

"Yes, Mama," the child said, giving Neville a final scratch, as Grey flew back to Nan's shoulder. "Thank you, Miss," she said to

Sarah. "And thank you, Grey and Neville. You are the *beautifullest*!"

Neville struck a pose on Sarah's knee. "Yes, we are," said Grey, and laughed, as the child giggled. After a few more polite exchanges, the woman tied her hat back on and led the child back out of the tangled garden and out of sight.

"Well, and that's the finest show of kindness I've seen in a while," said a very familiar voice from the opposite end of what passed for a "clearing" in this tangle.

Nan swiveled her head and stared at Robin Goodfellow in shocked amazement—because in all the time she had known him, except for great emergencies, the *only* time he had appeared to anyone besides herself and Sarah had been to Memsa'b.

The Great Elemental—or fairy—or Godling, you could take your pick of what he was—stood there, leaning on a spade, in his guise as one of Her Majesty's gardeners. To the uninitiated, he appeared to be a young, sandy-haired man in his mid-twenties, wearing tough moleskin trousers and a canvas gardener's smock, with a straw hat jammed down on his head far enough to conceal the points of his ears. But since Nan could see Elemental Magic . . . she actually didn't look at him in that way, because he was so very powerful it was not unlike staring into the sun.

"Puck!" Sarah exclaimed, and jumped up to run over and hug him, with no regard for conventional manners. But then, Robin didn't have any regard for conventional manners either, and hugged her right back, laughing.

"I trust I don't need to kneel in your presence, Highness," John said politely. "I do not think my knee will cooperate."

Robin gave Sarah a saucy kiss on the cheek, and grinned at him, going back to leaning on his spade. "I may be the Oldest Old One in all England, but I'm no Majesty, nor nothing like one. No crowns for me!"

Sarah had gone back to her seat beside Nan, and cocked her head to one side. "What brings you here today, Robin?" she asked.

"Oh, I just came to play with Suki, told her where you were when I tired her out, and went on ahead of her to pay my greetings," Puck replied. "And I could not help but listen to the goings-on when I got here. Well done, that. The more especially as we both know there's no 'scholarships' for young'un's, though there ought to be, and you tell the Lion I said so." He drew his eyebrows together in an almost-frown. "There's few enough of you not to tend to the needs of those that haven't two pence to rub together in their pockets."

John looked a bit taken aback, but Nan chuckled. "Next I expect to hear you've turned socialist, Robin."

Puck just shrugged. "You want magicians gone to the bad? Neglecting 'em young's one way."

"Well said," Mary put in, decisively. "And we'll either find scholarship money for that little girl or some other way to get her into the school, I promise you."

"You're uncommonly interested in the matters of mortals today, Robin," Nan observed.

Puck rubbed the side of his nose reflectively. "There's change in the wind," was all he said.

Nan wondered what sort of change was coming. Puck was very chary of helping adults—probably because he expected adult mortals to be able to help themselves. Except when matters spilled over into hurting the land itself, as they had when that creature from some other world had attempted to invade this one. If he was warning them . . . it must be because he sensed danger to the land itself.

"Soon?" she asked anxiously.

To her relief, he shook his head. "Not even by your mayfly counting," he admitted, then turned cheerful again. "I've run Suki up and down and round about and into a good appetite."

"It's a good thing that we'd planned a hearty tea, then," Mary laughed. "But thank you for the warning."

Robin exchanged a few more pleasantries with them, seeming to focus on John and Mary. Nan had a notion that he was examining them in his own way, and evidently was pleased with what he found. Mostly his careful questions centered around what they expected of *him*, which they both wisely answered in equally hedged terms, *nothing*.

Which makes sense, she reflected. *He's helped us a great deal in the past, but he's also made it very clear that he doesn't meddle in the affairs of mortals. I think he's making sure they aren't taking that help as a given.* In the end, he tugged on his hat, grinned at them, and casually took his leave just before Suki arrived.

Suki burst into the clearing like the force of nature she was, her hands carefully cupped around an extraordinary butterfly she wanted to show them all before she let it go.

"I'm fair famished!" she declared once it had been duly admired all around, and Suki nudged it with a finger to get it to leave her hand.

"Then it's a good thing we're visiting the tea shop next," Nan told her. "Just what we promised."

By the time they took the train home, birds riding on their shoulders to the bemusement of fellow passengers, Suki looked as if she was ready to burst, not from all the scones she'd eaten, but rather from all the things she wanted to tell them, and couldn't because they were in public. Nan was exceptionally pleased with her. Her manners at the tea shop had been so exemplary that even strangers had remarked upon them, and her ability to keep from chattering in public spoke volumes about how trustworthy she was these days.

"We met a lovely teacher and her daughter while you were playing," Sarah finally told her to distract her. "I think they might be good at the school. What do you think?"

Suki pondered that for a while. "Is they like the Watsons or like Memsa'b?" she asked—meaning, of course, *Are they magicians or psychical?*

"Like the Watsons," Sarah said promptly. "Only the little girl is Earth and her mother is Air."

Suki tugged at her earlobe while she thought, which was a much better habit than the one previous to it, which had been to stick her little finger into her ear. Sarah was now trying to get her to select a strand of hair on that side and twirl it around her finger. "Well," she said, finally. "Suzie Higgins, what went to a hoity-toity school afore this, an' Jess Masterson, what had a governess, says we need more teachers what can teach stuff universities want, on account of universities are likely to start lettin' girls hev degrees soon."

"Suzie and Jess are very intelligent girls indeed, and observant as well." Nan was pleasantly surprised by Suki's very mature answer. It seemed as if it was only yesterday that Suki's answer would have been something like, "On'y if she'll he'p me kick them boys in th' arse when they needs it."

"Do *you* think you'd like to go to uni, Suki?" Sarah asked curiously. "I'm certain it can be managed if you think you do."

Suki thought about that some more. "Dunno if I'm smart 'nuff," she said at last. "Leastwise, not book-smart."

"You can make yourself that smart, if you decide that's what you want," Nan said firmly.

"You can ask Peter about it if you like," Sarah added. "He can tell you how much work it will be, and also what benefits there are. I know he is enjoying himself."

Suki nodded.

"If you chose, you could even go to Oxford or Cambridge, and live away from home with other girls." Nan could tell Sarah had made that observation to see if Suki might be more receptive to the idea than she would have been before she started attending the Harton School.

Suki continued to tug on her earlobe. "Thet might be fun," she admitted. "But whut if I make a slip-up in talkin'? They might make a guy outa me."

Nan laughed at that. "When women can get degrees, girls will come from all over England. The first time a girl from Yorkshire says *Eeh I'll go t'foot of stairs!* when she's surprised, they'll forget all about you."

Nan was rather proud of her Yorkie dialect; she'd been studying it at the feet of their dustman, who was only too pleased to earn a couple bob a week for the privilege of teaching her.

Suki laughed at that. "Mebbe I'm better off findin' people t'teach me that!" she pointed out. "'Specially if I keeps on doin' fer You Know."

"You have a point," Sarah acknowledged. "But at least keep the idea in mind. You might discover something you want to study more than you want to do for our friend."

Suki laughed, but promised she would.

They arrived home about sunset, and Mrs. Horace had left a cold dinner for them—some lovely fresh veg for Grey and raw meat for Neville. After the long walk through the gardens and the equally long walk from the 'bus stop to their door, everyone was pleasantly tired. One of the great benefits of having this flat

THE CASE OF THE SPELLBOUND CHILD

was an en-suite bathroom—this had been a new house when Mrs. Horace's husband had bought it, with all the modern conveniences.

In fact, now that Nan came to think about it, the mere existence of not one but two entire bathrooms in what should have been a middle-class home was yet another hint that Mrs. Horace and the late Mr. Horace had been more than they seemed, and another possible suggestion that Lord Alderscroft knew them.

Most houses on this block still had outdoor privies. And the ones that had indoor, flushing toilets didn't have bathtubs with a water supply and a linkage to the drains, nor a gas-fired copper to heat the water (though, to be fair, you had to be incredibly careful with that, and watch it every minute just in case, as they were known to explode if left untended). There were so many things about this place that only someone rich could afford—so either Mr. Horace had had some source of wealth that dried up on his death, or Lord Alderscroft was somehow involved.

And I'm betting on Lord Alderscroft.

Well, all this meant that she and Sarah and Suki enjoyed an unprecedented level of comfort, especially when it came to bathing. So one by one, they took their turns at having a nice cold bath before bed, both to sponge off all the sweat and dirt of their trip, and to cool off to get to sleep easier.

Nan was the last, and she didn't consider it that much of a chore to pump up the water from the basement cistern to give herself a few inches of cool water in the bottom of the tub to sponge herself with. But once again, she found herself thinking longingly of Criccieth, where they all could not only have had refreshing sea-baths, but there was a cool running stream near the cottage they had rented for a refreshing dip.

Well, refreshing if you don't mind being fully clothed having a dip in it. One can't run about the hills of Wales starkers, even if you think you're alone. This might be much better, after all.

Bathed and dried and feeling much more comfortable, she put on her nightdress. Sarah had made her nightdress out of nearly transparent cotton muslin. Nan had gone a different route, getting her hands on an old, worn silk sari that one of the ayahs at the school had been willing to sell her, and stitching up a scandalously bare-armed shift out of the least worn part of it, and a patchwork dressing gown out of the rest. She rather thought her solution was superior.

She strongly suspected that Suki was continuing the practice of her childhood and stripping naked to sleep when it was hot. But Suki never appeared in the morning without one of the shifts she and Sarah had sewn for her, so at least she no longer graced the breakfast table wearing nothing but air.

She left the bathroom feeling deliciously cool, and settled into her bed with a book. But she kept looking out the window at the slumbering neighborhood, which looked so very peaceful, and wondered about Puck's warning.

What can he have been talking about?

The papers were full of war, but it was all distant. Uprisings in India and China, war with the Boers in Africa. The closest was so far away—Egypt and the Sudan—conflicts she and Sarah had carefully managed to skirt around when they had visited Sarah's parents in Africa. *Thank goodness they're not in the Congo anymore. The South Sea Islands seem much safer, and a great deal more pleasant.* She felt frustrated with her own lack of information. *I don't know nearly enough about things outside our borders,* she thought, ruefully. *And yet, isn't there trouble enough here already?*

But Puck's ominous words had seemed to speak of something coming that was much, much larger, something that would erupt to engulf even peaceful England. It seemed impossible. And yet. . . .

Puck was not given to exaggeration. Nor causeless warnings.

But he also said it was nothing that would come any time soon. I'll just have to remember this and watch for signs. And maybe get Lord Alderscroft to find someone who does *understand all those complicated international politics to keep me informed.*

It was about as peaceful out there tonight as it ever got in London. Only the occasional passerby or cab; a few carts out making late deliveries now that the streets were clearer. Music from the pub on the corner, but distant enough that it was muted and softened into something that gave her a bit of a chuckle rather than something annoying. Puck's warning seemed like a faded nightmare, something to be dismissed as nonsense on awakening.

But I know better. And I'll be on the watch. And I'll make sure anyone else likely to listen to me is, too.

7

Ellie still didn't know their captor's name. She didn't even know if it was male, female, or a monster. It never removed its long robe and hood, and spoke only in a harsh whisper. She was utterly terrified every time it put in an appearance, and so were all the other children, even though so far nothing worse had happened than it snarling at them to be quiet. When the Dark One opened the door, they all shrank back to the wall and tried not to be noticed.

Once, and only once, Simon had tried to flee to her for protection. The Dark One had come all the way into their room, snatched him up by his collar and flung him back onto his own mattress. Simon never tried that again.

She and Simon had been here for four days now, and every day had been the same. It started at dawn, when the thing brought a basket of bread and a fresh bucket of water, and directed one of the children to bring it the slop bucket, grumbling under its voice the entire time. At noon, the thing brought a basket of raw garden produce, one of bread, another bucket of water, and took the slop bucket away again. At dinner time, it was bread and a hard-boiled egg apiece. No one went hungry—at least not as far as she knew. Robbie saw to it that everything got shared out alike, and if someone had more than he or she could eat, it got passed on to someone else so nothing was wasted. Robbie confessed that he was afraid that if they left anything, they'd get less food the next time.

There was one window in their room, shuttered close, so

all they saw was thin lines of daylight between the boards and around the edges of the shutter. She thought that the walls were solid stone; the floor was definitely pounded earth. There was no doubt that the roof was slate; she heard mice over the top of it all the time, and occasionally something larger walking about on it.

It was hard to make out what the other children really looked like, and not because the light was so dim. They were all filthy and dirt-caked, their hair was all mud-colored, and they cried so often there were runnels down their cheeks in the dirt.

Their mattresses were nothing but grain or flour sacks stitched together and stuffed with straw, and whoever had been doing the stuffing hadn't made sure the straw was completely dried when he'd done it. That was why they smelled like mildew. They each had one "blanket," which could be anything from an actual scrap of a blanket to someone's old coat. Their chains were fastened to iron staples driven into the earthen floor; Ellie tried, and failed, to pull hers loose. She couldn't understand how that was possible; it was as if they'd been driven into stone, not earth.

It was hard to sleep. Not only was she plagued with nightmares of her own, but all night long the other children whimpered and cried in their sleep. During the day, they didn't have the heart to do much except huddle on their mattresses, talk very quietly, or cry softly to themselves. They tried to keep every sound at the level of a whisper; anything more brought the Dark One in, and if the monster was able to tell who the offending party was, there would be a beating.

But Ellie woke up with the feeling that today was going to be different. And a few moments after she woke, the Dark One entered the room. As always, it hurled the door open so that it banged against the wall. As always, it set down the basket of bread and the bucket of water. But this time it looked at her. Straight at *her*. Even though she had no idea how it could see her in the darkness.

"Ellie," it rasped, as the hair stood up on her head and she was struck with such fear that her teeth chattered. "Come 'ere." And it pointed at its feet. Or where it would have had feet, if it hadn't had a robe on so you couldn't see feet.

She couldn't move. Every limb was frozen. She started to cry, to sob helplessly, as her entire body seemed to turn to stone.

Impatiently, it strode over to her, as every other child in the room tried to press itself into the wall or somehow become invisible. It grabbed her by the forearm, hauled her to her feet, and shook her like a dog would shake a rat. It smelled, oddly, of sweat and beer, and its breath stank. "When Es say, then tha'll *do*, an' tha'll do *now*!" it snarled in that whisper. Then it threw her onto her bed, bent, and unlocked the shackle around her ankle with a huge iron key.

Suddenly, at the feeling of that shackle falling open, she could move again. She had just enough wit left to try to make a bolt for the open door, but it caught her before she got off the straw mattress, hauled her up off her feet, and dragged her out the door, by one arm. Behind her, she heard Simon wailing; no words, just a terrified, anguished wail.

She only got a glimpse of the next room before the Dark One threw her down on the hearth. There was a good fire going in the fireplace, and a pot full of pease porridge over it, rich with bacon by the aroma. Her first thought when the Dark One let go of her was to try to run again, but before she could scramble away, it knelt beside her, seized her left hand by the wrist, brought out a giant knife from under its robe, and splayed her fingers out on the hearthstone. He raised it high, and she froze again, eyes fixed on the shining blade. In an instant, the knife had come down, and she stared in horror at the end of her little finger lying on the hearthstone, detached from the rest. And then came a fountain of blood and pain.

Screams of agony and terror erupted from her as she writhed, still held fast by the wrist. The Dark One seized a poker that was in the fire and applied it to the wound, searing it off, and blinding her with redoubled pain. The Dark One let go of her and she fell on her side, vaguely aware that it was chanting something over the little piece of flesh. Then it lifted the hearthstone and dropped the finger-end into the hole, and put the hearthstone back.

She fainted.

When she came to herself again, she was lying on her mattress, and Sam had dragged himself and his chain over to her and taken her wounded hand in his. It was the pain of that that had awakened her. She whimpered, wanting to beg him to kill her, but she couldn't articulate anything but moans.

"'Eh, lass," he crooned. "Tha'll be areet. 'Ush 'n less 'un work."

She couldn't help it, she wailed softly in agony, tears streaming down her face, her nose running, and her hand throbbing so badly she prayed for darkness to come again and take her, this time for good. Beside her Simon whimpered and called her name.

And then . . . a miracle.

A sensation of cool came from Sam's hands, centered around her wounded finger. Then her whole hand began to tingle and numb. And the pain began to drain away.

She sucked in her breath, unable to believe what was happening. But it was true; the pain ebbed with every passing moment and with every heartbeat. Each throbbing stab was less than the one before it. In the dim light all she could see was that he was bent over her hand as if he was praying over it, but the hands holding hers had started to shake.

Finally, as the pain dimmed to a dull and distant ache, like a bad bruise, he dropped her hand with a gasp. "Sorry, lass," he said. "That be all us can do fer 'ee."

"It doesn't hurt anymore!" she exclaimed, still not able to believe it. She was afraid to move her hand lest the pain start again.

"'Twill if tha's bump it," Sam warned. "Best get rag an' wrap tha' oop."

There was a sound of ripping, and a moment later, as Sam crawled back to his mattress and his bread, Rose brought Ellie bread and a strip torn from her petticoat, and Simon brought her the cup filled with water. After thanking both of them, Ellie carefully wrapped the abused finger—and Sam was right, it did hurt if she bumped it, but by the feel, the burn *and* the wound had somehow half healed and scabbed over.

"'Twas witchery, that, wut 'un done to 'ee," Ben said, darkly. "The Dark One's th' Divil's own witch, certain-sure."

Ellie certainly didn't see any reason to argue with him, although what purpose cutting off her finger and burying it under the hearthstone could have, she had no idea.

It was only when she had finished her loaf, picking off bits and eating them slowly, along with sips from the tin cup of water, that she realized there was something missing from her leg.

The shackle.

The Dark One had taken it off, and had never put it back on.

Carefully she felt for it, with her good hand, and found it lying beside the bed, still open.

For a long moment, she sat there; her mind, numbed by pain, took a while to take in what that meant. Then elation replaced fear. She could escape!

Or at least, she could, if the Dark One ever left the cottage. But surely the creature did at some point. It would *have* to leave to gather the stuff it brought from the garden. There were no sounds out there like there would have been in a village, so this must be some place far out on the moor. Maybe even the very cottage she and Simon had found in that lonely combe.

She looked up after a moment. The door to their prison was closed, and she couldn't make out any sounds on the other side.

Her hand throbbed; she cradled it in the right as she stared at the door. Not really thinking, just gathering her courage. She didn't dare think past escaping. This might be her only chance.

She slowly got to her feet, a moment of light-headedness stopped her briefly, then she made her way to the door and put her ear to the crack between the door and the frame, trying to hear.

"Ellie, *don't*!" Robbie hissed, urgently. "When t' Dark One catches 'ee, 'e'll 'urt 'ee *bad*!"

Someone else whimpered. "'E'll 'urt usn's too," spat Colin.

She turned her head. "'Ee wanter go 'ome?" she demanded.

There was no answer to that. Of course they all wanted to go home. Of course they wanted to get away. And of course they all knew that the only way that was going to happen was if someone escaped and brought help back. Right now, the person who had the best chance at that was her.

There was no sound of anything on the other side of the door. Now she moved to the other side of the room, where the slop bucket and the window were. Moving with great care for her hand, she tried to open the shutters, only to find them nailed shut, with great, huge iron nails rusted into place. Not even a miracle would give her the strength—much less the tools—to pry those out.

No help for it, then. It would have to be through the next room and out the front door.

She moved back to the door, and tested it. It opened the smallest of cracks.

She put her eye to the crack, peering into the next room.

The fire in the fireplace burned merrily on. There was no sign of the Dark One anywhere near the hearth. She tried to get a look at the rest of the room, but her range of vision was limited by what she could see through the cracked door.

Finally, she eased the door open enough to get a good look around to the sound of the rest of the children collectively gasping.

There was no one in the room beyond.

There would never be a better chance.

She slipped through the door and closed it behind her, then dashed across the room and to the door on the other side. The savory aroma of the pease porridge was almost too much to bear after four days of bread and raw vegetables, but she ignored it, and eased open the outer door.

Sunlight blinded her, and she squinted against it, eyes watering. After a while her eyes adjusted, and what had been a multicolored blur resolved into a neatly tended garden on either side of a straight, short path of beaten earth that ended in a stone wall with an open gate in it.

She swallowed hard, puzzled by what she saw. Because that was almost certainly the wall and the wooded combe beyond it that she remembered. In fact, she particularly remembered the lightning-struck oak with the deep burn scar down it that stood to the right of the gate.

But the garden wasn't the weed-grown place she remembered. . . .

And yet, there was the strawberry patch, to the left of the gate.

The Dark One certainly hadn't cleaned up all those weeds in four days!

Yet, except for the unkempt state, this definitely *was* the garden that had lured her and her brother into captivity. This made her head hurt. Was her memory at fault? Had she imagined all those weeds?

Her mind reeled, trying to reconcile what she knew with what she saw, until she felt dizzy. And for one moment, she was tempted to go back inside, snap the shackle on her own leg, and lie down on her mildewed mattress.

But if I don' go—'oo will?

She clenched her jaw, took a firm grip on the door, and wrenched it open, flinging herself in a headlong dash toward the beckoning gate. There were no shouts. No dark-clad form dashed out of the garden to stop her. With triumph surging in her, she reached the gate and—

Stopped cold. Stopped so abruptly, in fact, that she tumbled to the ground, right in front of the gate itself.

Frantic, she scrambled to her feet and flung herself through the gate.

Or—tried. Because once again, her feet stuck to the ground right at the gate, and then her knees failed and she fell.

She tumbled backward, and landed on her arse. It was as if her feet had stuck on something invisible, right where the gate closed. And then as if her legs suddenly gave out.

Sobbing with frustration and confusion now, she got to her feet, and made to leap over the low wall—

And her legs gave out again, failing her, and she landed in the middle of the patch of beets that was next to it.

She ran between the rows of beets and made another attempt at the wall, this time from the beans. This time it was only by dint of flailing that she managed to not land on her wounded hand. Once again, her legs went to rubber the moment she attempted the jump.

Again and again she tried, her panic and confusion growing with every attempt—and discovered during the process that the entire cot was surrounded by the garden, and the wall at the back joined up to a scarp that not even a goat would attempt to climb. Time and time again, she flung herself at the boundary only to find herself sprawled in the dirt. And it wasn't as if she met some kind of barrier, either. When she ran out of panicked breath and energy, and tried climb instead of jumping, she discovered that right at the base of the wall her feet stuck fast in the earth and she could not move them, not even to lift them an inch. It was as if her whole body rebelled against what she wanted it to do.

How was this even possible?

Finally she found herself at the front gate again, and stared at the open gate, tears running down her face in frustration and anger and growing fear. This *was* witchcraft! The Dark One was some kind of witch! That was the only possible explanation for why her own feet betrayed her just when she was about to reach freedom.

She put her face down in her hands and sobbed helplessly. All around her, the birds that had been frightened away by her struggles returned, and began to sing. And it seemed to her as if they were mocking her.

And just when it seemed as if things could not get worse . . . her sobs were interrupted by the sound of slow applause.

With a gasp of fear, she dropped her hands and looked up.

Standing in the forest beyond the open gate was the Dark One, face still hidden in the shadows of its hood. Clapping.

She froze in absolute terror as the Dark One dropped its hands to its sides.

"Learnt yer lesson, then?" rasped the Dark One. "No runnin' off fer 'ee. 'Ee be *mine*. No gettin' awa'. An when Es say, tha'll *do*. Do 'ee ken?"

Numbly, she nodded, too terrified to do anything else but agree with what the thing wanted.

The Dark One stalked to the gate and through it, stood beside her for a moment, and beckoned for her to follow. With a last despairing glance over her shoulder at the false freedom the forest promised, she followed the creature back into the cottage.

What the Dark One wanted of her that was different from what it wanted of the other children, she soon learned.

The first thing it did when they had crossed the threshold was to thrust a broom into her hands and order her to sweep out both rooms, watching her carefully to see that she got up every speck of dirt. It might be thought by some that a pounded-earth floor would just create never-ending dirt, but that was not the case as long as the floor got regular coatings of linseed oil and wax, and the roof remained intact. The conditions in the prison room might not be the best, but the conditions in the main room were as good as Ellie's mother could have wished. It was clean, well furnished with a kitchen table, a larder, a big cupboard, two stools, a real chair, and a bed. The fireplace drew well and did not smoke, and there were a flitch of bacon, a couple of hams, and several strings of sausages hanging from the rafters above it to demonstrate the Dark One's prosperity. Ellie could not remember the last time her family had seen more than a single sausage, much less a string of them *and* hams.

The fireplace had ovens on either side of it, so that explained where the bread was coming from. In fact, as she swept, the Dark One began to remove hot loaves with a bread peel, and drop them into the food basket. Then it took eggs from the larder, one for each child, and dropped them carefully into a pot with water in it that it put on the hearth to boil.

Having swept out the house to the Dark One's satisfaction, Ellie was then instructed to carry out the slop pail, empty it into the privy, rinse out the pail with water from the rain barrel, and return the pail and a fresh bucket of earth to their proper places.

"Tha'll do thet mornin', noon, an' night," the Dark One rasped.

Next, she was told to check the chicken house for eggs. She had been so focused on trying to escape that she hadn't even noticed a chicken house, much less chickens, but sure enough, following the directions, there was the shed with four shelves of nests, a total of twenty-eight in all, and there were a dozen eggs in the nests. Two of the chickens were sitting on their eggs and pecked at her, drawing blood, when she tried to reach under them. But she was more afraid of the Dark One than the chickens, and managed to get the eggs without too much damage to herself.

When she returned to the cottage with the eggs, she found the Dark One prosaically tucking into a bowl of that delicious-smelling pease porridge and one of the loaves of bread with bacon grease smeared over it. Her mouth watered and her stomach growled audibly.

"Tha'lt do chickens mornin' an' night. Naow. Feed t'others," the Dark One ordered. "Bring 'em water from pump. Then feed tha'sel'. Tha' may hev grease on tha' bread," it added magnanimously, waving at the dish of carefully saved bacon grease on the table it was sitting at.

She picked up one basket of bread and the waiting bowl of eggs, and brought them into the other room, reserving an egg and two small loaves for herself. The others looked up at her with varying expressions—mostly of relief that so far the Dark One hadn't killed her for her escape attempt (or so she supposed), but also some despair that she hadn't gotten away. Only Simon was unreservedly happy to see her, and hugged her when he came to get his share of the food.

She closed the door behind her, and stood a distance away from the Dark One, torn between want and fear. She *wanted* that scrape of bacon grease. It had been a long, exhausting day, she was starving, and the promise of a taste of baconey fat made her mouth water with anticipation.

On the other hand, she didn't want to get any nearer to her captor and tormentor than she was now.

"Well?" it rasped, when she had stood there indecisively for long enough it had finished its own meal, with a long drink of beer to finish it off. "Do 'ee want it or no?"

It didn't wait for her to answer. "Put 'un away, then," he ordered. "Put parritch off t'side t'stay warm. Clean dish an' table. Bank fire. Put tha'sel' t'bed. I' mornin', there be other chores."

And with that, the thing got up and stalked out of the door, closing it.

She took her two loaves to the table, broke them in half and smeared the halves with fat, and put the bowl of fat away in the cupboard. Only when she had done everything the creature had ordered her to did she sit down and eat her own meal. And she did wonder for a moment if the thing would notice if she helped herself to the porridge . . . but then decided that a hellspawn thing that could keep her own feet from obeying her could certainly tell if she ate its food, and confined herself to her bread, egg, and water.

And then, with an aching heart, burning eyes, throbbing hand, but a full belly, she opened the door to the prison room, and took her place among her fellow captives.

"What happed?" asked Robbie.

She explained as best she could, as the light on the other side of the shutter faded, and they gathered around her.

"Witchcraft," spat Colin. "Black witchcraft."

"Aye, not like Sam's. Or mine," Robbie said wisely. "Tha's why t'crathur keeps un. T'crathur eats our witchery. But 'ee, Ellie, 'ee got na witchery, so 'ee'll be th' Dark One's slavey."

"Did th' Dark One hev a slavey afore?" she asked.

"Aye. An' be keerful an' do all t'crathur says," Rose said fearfully. "'Er name wuz Liz, an' she didn' do like Dark One said, an' t'crathur do makeit 'er lie a bier. Snappit 'er neck, like a coney."

They all shuddered, Ellie not the least. "Do wut Dark One says, Ellie!" Simon cried frantically, on the edge of tears. "Do wut Dark One says, even if 'tis t' 'urt me!"

"Gi' un yer 'and," Sam said, cutting curtly through Simon's hysteria. She did, willingly, hoping he could work that miracle of healing he had earlier.

Once again, as he cupped her wounded hand in his, a cooling sensation spread from his touch, and the pain of her much-abused finger abated until at last it was down to little more than an ache that she could certainly ignore enough to sleep.

All the exertion of trying to run away, followed by more work than even Mother had ever put her through, made her feel as if the straw-stuffed sack was like a cloud as she lay back down on it. She was aware of the other children talking softly, but within moments, she was asleep, to wander restlessly in nightmares.

In the morning she woke to the sound of the door crashing open. "Op," came the rasping voice from the door, and Ellie scrambled to her feet and fetched the bucket of earth and the slop bucket before the Dark One could order her to do so.

"Good," it said as it stood aside for her to go out into the gray dawn light and take care of the buckets. She was pretty sure what order she was to do things in, so after bringing the others their food and water, she left her two loaves at the hearth on one of the stools and went to open up the chicken house to let the chickens out.

Only then did she return to eat her breakfast.

It was almost more than she could bear to watch and smell the Dark One eating fried eggs, fried bread, and bacon, while she ate day-old bread with nothing more than water. But all it took was to have the thing raise its head and look at her—or rather, have that dark *nothingness* under the hood be pointed at her—for her to decide that bread was not so bad after all.

"Sweep oop," the thing ordered, when she had finished. "Then tha'll mek bread."

"I dunno—" she squeaked in panic.

The Dark One interrupted her. "Chell tell 'ee 'ow," it whispered, impatiently. "Naow sweep oop."

She swept out both rooms, the eyes of the other children on her the entire time that she worked, and returned to the main room to find that the Dark One had laid out a cloth, a wooden bowl, a sack of flour, a bowl of lard, a bowl of salt, and the crock of bubbling, fermenting stuff Mother always used to make the bread rise on the table by the window.

"Coom 'ere," it said, and instructed her, step by step, in the first stage of bread-making. "Nah," it said, "Tha'llt learnet t'make bread. An' that'll be wut tha'llt et, 'ee an' th' rest, raw or burnet, dry or doan, so best learn quick." Trying not to panic, she made several batches of dough, enough to fill the largish table and the window ledge with wooden bowls for the first rise, before it was satisfied.

"Garden," it ordered, and she went out with it and the familiar basket to pick ripe produce. It supervised her for a while, then apparently satisfied that she knew what she was doing, left her to fill the basket with whatever was ripe. Except for the cabbages, or, of course, the berries. It told her to leave them alone, then the Dark One picked a cabbage itself and went back into the cot with it.

She noted the cleverly set rabbit snares among the veg, and wondered how often the Dark One caught conies. And then why it needed to set snares when it had magic—because surely it could catch them easier with the magic.

When she lugged the filled basket back inside, it was frying chopped cabbage in bacon grease for its luncheon, and the smell nearly drove her crazy. "Feed 'em," it rasped at her as she entered. "An' yersel'."

She took the last of the baskets of bread into the room after she brought in the basket of raw vegetables. Robbie saw to it that everyone got a fair share of the food, and she took hers to eat sitting next to Simon on her bed. "'As 'e 'urt 'ee, Ellie?" Simon whispered fearfully, when she sat down beside him with her loaves and skirt full of three carrots, some radishes, an onion, and some beans. She was so hungry she ate even the leaves of the root veg, putting them between the two halves of one of her loaves for palatability, and to add a bit of much-needed moisture to the otherwise dry day-old loaf.

The "loaves" were not actually loaf-size, not a proper pound loaf, but more like a large bun shaped like a round loaf. *I could eat a whole pound loaf, I could,* she thought wistfully. But then again . . . so far she and Simon had been eating better than they did at home, except for when they were allowed to forage on the moor. Well, and better than they often did even when they were foraging, since there were only a few days every summer when they could eat to gorging and still bring home enough to share.

When she came out of the prison room, the Dark One had just finished a dish of berries, and she stared with all her eyes at the bit of juice in the bottom of the dish when it shoved its luncheon dishes at her to clean. She didn't dare even stick her fingers in it and lick them, though, not with the creature watching her every moment. No telling what it would do.

Then as the thing instructed her, she punched down the dough, divided it into little loaves, and laid them out on every flat surface for the second rise, cleaned out the prison room and the buckets for the second time that day, fed the chickens—and that was when she noticed something that set the hair up on her head again.

As she filled her big wooden bowl with grain for the chickens . . . the amount of grain in the bin didn't become any less.

In fact, she could take out a wooden scoop full—and watch the level actually rise again.

She dropped the heavy lid on the mouse-proof bin and couldn't get away from it fast enough. Where was the new grain coming from? There was the magic again! Black witchery, for surely he was stealing the grain from someone else, somewhere by magic! Grain didn't come from nowhere!

She noticed something else. All of the chickens had the end of one toe missing. And none of them left the garden. Had the Dark One worked the same magic on them as it had on her? Poor chickens! They were prisoners as much as she and the other children were!

With the chickens fed, it was time to put the first of the loaves into the ovens to bake. The Dark One showed her how, after taking out a pie that was clearly for its own dinner. It was hot work, and she was terrified of the oven. Mother never let them near the oven at home, on the rare occasions when there was fuel to bake things or things to bake. It took down a sand-glass that was on a shelf near the bed and set it on the table with the rest of the waiting loaves. "When last grain runs oot, loaves come oot. Remember, tha'llt be ate it, raw or burnet, dry or doan. Raw kin go back. Burnet is burnet. So make sure 'tisn't burnet." And it laughed. "An' git on wi' tha' work a whiles."

The work didn't take long, just bringing in an armful or two of wood from outside.

And then it was time to take the stops out of the oven, and with her face and hands feeling as if they were aflame, get the bread out and put the new loaves in, dropping the fresh bread into the first basket. *Please let them be all right,* she thought frantically, as she opened the first oven and shoved the peel into the depths where the loaves sat like inscrutable stones. She actually did sob a little with relief when her bread came out all right.

"Long as fire's burnin', loaves tak a turnit th' glass," the thing told her. "So mind th' glass."

When all the bread had baked and was piled up in the baskets, the cot was filled with the glorious smell of fresh bread and her stomach growled. She wanted so badly to break into one of those fresh loaves and bite into it!

But there was more work, of course; the water barrel next to the big bowl that served as a sink to refill from the pump outside, one laborious, sloshing bucketful at a time. Then taking a cloth and rubbing a coat of linseed oil on the earthen floor, where she'd been walking and spilling water and going to and fro while making the bread.

All the time the thing just lounged and watched her, never pulling its hood off, that empty darkness more terrifying than a monstrous face could have been. Her resentment of its laziness grew to match her fear of it.

And finally, when she actually felt faint with exhaustion and hunger, the thing decreed she could feed the others and eat. Robbie took pity on her when he saw how weary she looked and heard her stomach complaining, and apportioned three loaves to her. Then it was the cleaning and the slops, and cleaning up after the Dark One's supper. There were scraps of ham and the ham grease on its plate, and an end of a loaf, and her hands trembled as she took the plate from it.

"Tha' canst hev scraps," it said, magnanimously, and laughed as she gobbled them down. "Tha' canst hev pot scrapin's as well."

At long last the rest of the chores were over, and the thing let her go to bed. The last she saw of it was with its feet up, a pipe incongruously sticking out of the darkness under its hood, smoking away.

She closed the door behind her as she entered the prison room. By this point, she had gotten the feeling that the other children thought of that door more as the thing that kept the Dark One temporarily out, not as something that was locking them in. After all, they couldn't go any further than the chains on their legs.

No more can I, she thought, as she wearily dropped down onto her mattress, ignoring Simon's insistent attempts to talk to her. *My chain's just one ye cain't see.*

8

"Let's stop by the Watsons on our way home," Sarah suggested, as they left the cool marble environs of the British Museum with Suki in tow. Suki looked up hopefully.

They had been visiting the Elgin Marbles, now that Suki was old enough to understand the controversy about how they'd come to the Museum in the first place. Nan had thought it would be a good lesson in both history and politics—for both of them. She only wished she had been able to consult someone more involved in the Greek side of things before they visited. The British argument seemed to consist mostly of, "Well, they weren't taking care of these priceless treasures, and we got permission to take them—"

The "permission" claim was dubious. The Greeks had not had self-government at the time. The Turks that had been in control had not cared to take care of such things, since human images were blasphemous to their religion, which was hardly the fault of the Greeks. So—well, Nan could *almost* make a case for Elgin, but surely the Museum could simply have made plaster casts as they had of so many monumental pieces and restored the marbles to their proper owners.

That subject had never actually come up, however, since on entering the cavernous gallery where the marble frieze was displayed, they immediately encountered a group of artists whom Beatrice Leek numbered among her friends. Nan and Sarah were instantly recognized from their meetings with Beatrice at her favorite tea shop. The artists were there to sketch the marbles, but were . . . easily distracted by the sight of new people whom they *knew* Beatrice numbered among her other, occult friends— people who might be persuaded to talk about such things more than Beatrice was.

Beatrice styled herself as "just an old witch," and never talked about the sorts of things their romantic and over-imaginative minds wanted to hear about. Elaborate occult ceremonies, mystic visions, dramatic visitations by supernatural beings.

So they found themselves besieged by questions. Were they Magickal? (Nan could practically hear the capitalization and extra "k"). Oh, they were Psychical? (Nan sensed their disappointment with some amusement. They could see "Psychical" people any time they wanted for a shilling, and they all knew how to hold a seance.) Was the adorable little girl as well?

At least they had the good manners not to ask for a demonstration, but then the questions veered off into another path, triggered by Suki, who had gotten bored with the questions, trying to imitate the poses of the statues. Would they be willing to pose for sketches or paintings? And would their little ward pose as well? It was hard to find child models. They (the artists) could pay—

"I can't promise anything," Nan had replied. "We're actually employed irregularly, and might be called away at any moment. Just now we're between commissions and enjoying a bit of a holiday."

"If you would be satisfied with sketches only, for single days at a time, we could manage that," Sarah had offered, seeing their disappointment. She had looked down at their ward. "Suki, could you be very still for half an hour at a time?"

Suki had looked utterly scornful, and had taken great care with her pronunciation in her reply so as to leave no doubt that she was a very superior person indeed. "I can sit so still and for so long a wild bird will come to eat from my hand," she had retorted. She hadn't been lying or exaggerating either; Nan had seen her do just that, and in fact, the local starlings and sparrows would eat from her hand as she sat at the window of her room. Puck had probably taught her that level of patience, as he had taught her and Sarah at that age.

They had exchanged addresses, Nan with some doubt, Sarah

with amusement, and Suki with impatience. And by the time they had finished with all of that, there was just time to explain the figures to Suki—a task one of the grateful artists gladly undertook—before they needed to leave if they were to catch their 'bus back home.

"I think dropping by Baker Street is a capital idea," Nan agreed, as Suki pranced in glee at the prospect of going to see the Watsons. Nan whistled and held out her arm, and Neville flew down from the top of one of the famous lions guarding the entrance to land on it, as Grey came down from where she was hidden between the ears of the other. "What do you think?" she asked Neville.

"Supper sooner," Neville said with a nod.

Nan wasn't worried about putting out Mrs. Hudson with unexpected supper company. Fortunately, like Mrs. Horace, the Baker street landlady, Mrs. Hudson, was very understanding about unexpected company. On the other hand . . . Nan was well aware that Holmes and the Watsons were not behindhand in making that understanding worth her while.

Nan took out her notebook again, and wrote a quick note to Mrs. Horace and gave it to Neville. "Go let Mrs. Horace know we won't be home for supper, oh pirate," she told him. He took it in his beak, nodded, and flew off. Nan readied herself for the thankless task of trying to hail a cab in front of the British Museum, which was not an easy thing for a woman to do. Men—either outright rude, or simply thoughtless scholars with their minds on getting home to their work—tended to nick them right out from under Nan's nose, and cabbies, who thought women didn't tip well, let them.

Just at that very moment, a hansom stopped practically in front of them, dropping off three young men who looked rather like university students, who had somehow managed to squeeze themselves into a space meant for two. Nan moved quickly to claim it before a rather officious-looking and somewhat overweight man came puffing up to grab it for himself. Nan took that as a good omen.

When they got down at 221, Neville was waiting for them on the rooftop, and flew down to Nan's arm with a note in his beak. Nan took it and read it right there on the street. "Mrs. Horace thanks us, and says she'll leave 'a little something' for us when we get home."

Sarah shook her head. "That woman spoils us," she declared as Nan rang the bell. "Well, that means if we catch the Watsons as they finish dinner, we can just ask Mrs. Hudson for tea and bread and butter and not put her out."

Mrs. Hudson answered the door, and actually looked pleased to see them as she let them in. "My word, you young ladies must have magical powers!" she exclaimed. "You're wanted just this very moment! The doctor just got a letter, and was writing out a message for one of the lads to take to you! That'll save a shilling," she added, frugally.

"Shall we go on up, then?" Nan asked politely.

"Certainly. I'll bring up dinner for all of you." Nan winked surreptitiously at Sarah, and they gathered up their skirts and climbed the stairs up to 221C as Mrs. Hudson retreated to her own little flat.

Nan tapped at the door, and Watson opened it immediately, already saying, "I hope you found Tom—" and his eyes lit up when he saw it was them. "By Jove, I was just about to send for you! Come in!"

"So Mrs. Hudson told us," Sarah replied, and they all followed him into the Watsons' airy and cool sitting room.

"Oh!" Mary Watson exclaimed. "Let me get the stands for the birds." And from the broom cupboard she brought out two smoking stands that had been converted to perches, and spread the morning's newspaper beneath them.

The table was already laid for dinner for two, but Mrs. Hudson bustled in before they could settle themselves, with more place settings, and dishes of water and fresh peas for the birds.

"I've gotten a letter—well, actually, Sherlock got a letter, but I've been reading his mail in case there was anything in it for us," Watson continued, as Mrs. Hudson brought up supper (which was centered around cold sliced beef and ham) and left them to their own devices. "And it's a good thing I did. The moment I opened the letter, I sensed the hint of Earth Magic on it!"

"Why would an Earth Magician write to Holmes?" Nan asked in astonishment, serving fork pausing in midair.

"Her children are missing!" Watson exclaimed. "Well, wait, let me just read it to you—take care of my plate, would you, my dear?"

he added to Mary, who chuckled a little, but did as he asked.

"Dear Master Sherlock Holmes," he read. *"My husband and I are writing to you in some desperation. I sent my two children out to forage on the moor, and they have not returned. We have searched as far as Sheepstor, without success. I beg of you to help us! Yours truly, Roger and Maryanne Byerly."*

"Well, I don't know what she thought Holmes could do for her," Nan replied, "And that letter is uncommonly short on details. We don't know when the children went missing, nor how long they've been gone. We don't know how old they are. Or if this is the first time their mother sent them out on the moor alone, or the first time they haven't come home. Isn't it supposed to be dangerous?"

"It can be," Watson replied. "As for why—well, Holmes gets letters like this all the time, and usually he just answers that the person in question must go to the local constabulary—" He rubbed the back of his head. "—and that he gets them is mostly my fault, what with all the stories I write about him. But the point is, this is one of *our* people, and I feel obliged to at least—" Now he stopped, clearly feeling helpless to further explain himself.

"Can I see that?" Sarah asked, reaching for the letter.

Watson handed it to her.

She didn't read it. Instead, she held it in her hand, her forehead furrowed in a little frown of concentration. "I think the woman wrote this, but the man is the one with Earth powers, and I honestly don't think he's aware of them," she said, finally. "John, I know you're bored with your practice and looking for a case, and I understand that you miss the excitement of running off with Sherlock into the unknown at frequent intervals, but—this probably isn't a 'case' at all. For all we know, the 'children' are fourteen or fifteen and ran off on their own, or they've come home or been found already."

Mary Watson had that look on her face that told Nan she'd already said as much to her husband. John Watson just sighed.

"I know it seems thin—" he began.

"It's thin enough to read the newspaper through," Sarah corrected him.

"But I just have a feeling. And yes, I *am* bored. I'm beginning to understand why Sherlock indulged in cocaine when he hadn't had a case in too long. Not—" he added hastily, "—that I'm in any danger of doing likewise. But I can sympathize, now that I myself am experiencing the discomfort of a buzzing brain with nothing to work on. Even *Suki* has had more exercise than Mary and I have had."

"An' yew has them Elementals t'play with, all the time," Suki piped up. "An' I don't. So I reckon it's fair."

"She's got you there, John," Mary said, smothering a laugh with her hand.

John Watson changed the subject, but Nan could tell he was still thinking about it. And after they set the dishes out on the landing for Mrs. Hudson to clear away, he brought it up again.

"I have to tell you, I have the strongest feeling that it's important that we follow up on this letter," he said. "I can't tell you why, because I don't know myself. I know for a fact that Holmes gets at least one 'please help me find my child' letter a week and almost never does anything about them. And even though he's supposed to be dead, he still gets them, from people who seldom see newspapers, I suppose. And you're right about it having so little detail as to make it fundamentally useless. But this one . . . just *feels* different to me. And I don't know why."

Nan exchanged a look with Sarah, then with the birds. The birds didn't show any interest in joining the conversation, instead sitting on one leg on their perches, stuffed full of new peas, and content to drowse. Nan shrugged, and nodded to Sarah.

"Well," Sarah said slowly. "It can't hurt to forward it to Lord Alderscroft and tell him about your strong feelings. For all we know he'll be able to pick out more from the letter than I can. Or there might be something moving out in Dartmoor that none of us have been privy to. Besides, he has his entire network of Elemental Masters *and* the Hunting Lodge, and he's in a position to undertake a quick investigation without even leaving London."

As John sighed again, the girls and Mary exchanged another of those looks that said this was precisely what Mary had advised. But he also nodded. "I'll do just that in the morning," he said. "And thank you for talking sense into me before I ran out and booked tickets for some remote village none of us has ever heard of."

"Sheepstor does not have a name that inspires visions of

comfortable inns with ample accommodations," Nan agreed. "But I will tell you this. We've just started Suki's Summer Holiday, and if he sends you out and wants us to come with you, we'll make a family party of it. Peter ought to be able to come as well, since it's the Long Vac at University."

Watson perked up at that. "That would be splendid!" he replied.

"It would be cooler and healthier than London," Sarah pointed out with a laugh. "And we've never visited Dartmoor."

The look on Mary's face told Sarah that in Mary's opinion they hadn't missed anything, but she didn't comment aloud.

It was still light enough when they left to let the birds fly home while they took a hansom. They would have taken the 'bus, but John Watson insisted, and went out and fetched one himself.

"Oi'd loike a bird loike Neville or Gray," Suki said sleepily, as the hansom took its time navigating the streets back to their flat. It was an indication of how tired she was after their long day that she let her speech slip so far back to the streets.

"Well," Sarah said slowly. "Gray was given to me by a wise man in Africa, and her mother gave the shaman permission to take her to me when she was very young. I don't think you'd want a parrot that comes to England by the usual way, which is to be kidnapped out of its home by cruel men and taken away from its flock and friends."

Suki sighed. "No," she agreed. "But . . . I'd loike one if it could come to me. Loike Neville came to Nan."

"Nobody can make that happen, Suki," Nan reminded her. "But the next time you see Robin, you might ask if he can do anything about that. He's in charge of all the wild things of England, and if anyone knows how, he does. If we go to Dartmoor, we'll be on Robin's ground, and you'll probably see him if you call him."

"And if we don't go to Dartmoor, we'll go to Hampton Court Palace again, and he'll likely come to you there," Sarah added, and looked out the front of the cab as it pulled to a stop. "And here we are, and meanwhile, Neville and Grey are very much your friends."

Suki went to bed immediately. She didn't even stay up to share in the lemonade and digestive biscuits that Mrs. Horace had left for them.

"So, do you think we'll be going to Dartmoor?" Nan asked.

Sarah shrugged. "I have no feelings about it. But what I *do* know is that if we do, I want Lord Alderscroft to be paying for the trip, not *us*."

Nan burst into laughter at that, and Sarah smiled. "Do you blame me?" she asked.

"Not a bit," Nan replied. "And I completely agree with you!"

The next morning, Nan and Sarah moved around the flat, aided by Suki, making a thorough cleaning of it. Nan found herself whistling "The British Grenadiers," and Suki responded happily by marching in time as she beat a cushion held up by Nan, or brought Sara a whisk or a dustrag.

"You're in an uncommonly good mood this morning," Sarah said.

"I'm sensing either that we're going on a paid holiday, or that we're *not* going on a holiday we have to pay for ourselves," Nan laughed. "In the case of the latter, I think we can find ways to keep ourselves cool and entertained until the end of August."

"Peter alone can do that, although he's as full of mischief these days as a monkey house," Sarah replied, replacing the last cushion. "Well, that's that. If we go, we come back to a clean flat. If we don't go, we *have* a clean flat."

Mrs. Horace tapped on the door with her foot with their luncheon, and surveyed the morning's handiwork with approval. "You young ladies have earned your meal this morning, and that's certain," she said with a decisive nod of her head. "I couldn't have made a better job of it myself."

"High praise!" Nan laughed, and the three of them fell to with a good appetite.

When the dishes were cleared onto the landing, Nan turned back to the others. "Well, we haven't—" she began, when her words were interrupted by the bell. Suki stuck her head out the window.

"It's Tommy!" she cried, and waved. Presumably Tommy waved back, but Nan was already on her way down the stairs to see what had brought the lad.

Mrs. Horace was just closing the door with a note in her hand. Nan took it from her as Sarah and Suki stuck their heads out of the door to the flat.

"Get your hats and pack up the birds," Nan said. "And make up overnight kits. We're going to the Lion's bungalow."

Within the hour they were on the train, bird carriers in one hand, small suitcases in the other. In the summer Lord Alderscroft followed the example of every other person of means who didn't *have* to be in the city, and left for a summer residence. This one happened to be on the grounds of his former manor, which he had deeded over to Memsa'b Harton and her husband for their school. Nan was not sure how he had divided the property, but he still apparently held a goodly portion of it, more than enough to surround his Indian-style bungalow with beautiful gardens and plenty of cool, green woods to ride through when he cared to.

A carriage was waiting for them at the station, with ginger-haired Paul Sterling, his Lordship's second coachman and permanent driver for the bungalow up on the box. Paul knew them all very well, as they knew him. "Let them pore birds out uv captivity, miladies," he said as he handed them up into the coach. "They mun be fair weary uv bein' in there."

"*Lemme out!*" shouted Neville, and laughed wickedly.

"As if I wouldn't, you pirate," Nan scolded fondly, and opened the door to his leather carrier. He and Grey popped out like rabbits out of burrows as the coach rolled away; Neville took up a perch in the open coach window while Grey sank her claws into the horsehair upholstery of the seat next to Sarah for a more secure grip.

The bungalow was closer to the station than the school was, and it wasn't too long before the coach was rolling down the beautifully smooth drive to Lord Alderscroft's summer residence.

Much, much newer than the manor that now housed the school, the bungalow was built in the style of those that wealthy officers and businessmen in India would construct in the hills in order to escape the summer heat. It had been built over a stone-walled cellar and had two stories above that; it sprawled over quite a lot of square footage, and had seven guest bedrooms on the first floor to allow his Lordship to do the requisite entertaining, as well as ample servants' quarters. And since it had been built so recently, and since his Lordship was always further modernizing it, it had all the latest conveniences: real bathrooms such as the girls enjoyed, shared between pairs of bedrooms with hot and cold water on demand, gas lighting, and a telegraph in the butler's pantry. Many of the original servants from the manor had moved to work here as soon as Alderscroft finished it, and his chief cook swore the kitchen was so good she would die in it rather than leave. The rooms all had *punkah*-fans, to be brought into play if the breeze died and the heat became oppressive. In India these would be powered by a small boy; here it was by an ingenious clockwork mechanism on the wall which kept the great blade gently wafting to and fro. But the chief jewel of the house was the enormous veranda that wrapped around four sides of the house and served as a sort of outdoor sitting room, where one could lounge and enjoy the cool breeze in the worst of the summer heat.

They were met by John Watson—and two of the footmen, of course. From here they could see his Lordship and Mary Watson (who was wearing something cool-looking and white) sitting at their ease on comfortable rattan "peacock" chairs, up on the veranda. Mary waved to them, and the birds immediately took off to join her—doubtlessly in anticipation of treats.

"Traitors," Nan chuckled, and turned to John. "I see you beat us here."

The footmen took possession of their luggage and the bird carriers, and whisked it all off into the house as John replied. "By several hours. The Lion has some details he'd like to discuss with you. Come on up."

They followed him up the stairs and around the veranda to where Alderscroft and Mary were sitting. Sure enough, the birds were being treated to digestive biscuits—Grey had considerately broken Neville's up into smaller pieces he could gulp down as he stood on the veranda floor, while she sat on the back of an empty chair and held an entire biscuit in one claw and was nibbling it around and around the edge, taking neat little divots out of it.

All three of them took empty chairs, and an attentive servant appeared as if by magic to ask if they would like something to drink. When they were all settled, Alderscroft turned to Sarah.

Lord Alderscroft resembled his nickname remarkably well, with a great mane of tawny hair kept unfashionably long and unfashionably full, and strong, leonine features. He wore a cream-colored linen suit in concession to the heat, and in further concession, had hung the jacket on the back of his chair (probably to the dismay of his valet) and sat back in his shirtsleeves and crisp waistcoat. Watson had taken similar liberties with his wardrobe. Mary was wearing a white muslin teagown that looked. . . . suspiciously brand-new. And Nan realized at that moment with both amusement and a touch of dismay that his Lordship had probably had all their bedrooms stocked with brand-new clothing he'd had run up just in case they might be persuaded to visit this summer.

We needn't have packed at all. . . .

We won't allow him to shower us with presents, so he is getting around that by presenting them in this way.

On the other hand, this was good planning, if instead of a visit, they ever had to come here as an escape from danger in London.

"Now, are you fatigued, or can you undertake an experiment for me?" Alderscroft asked without preamble.

Since he was looking at Sarah at the time, Nan kept her mouth shut.

"A short train journey and an even shorter trip by comfortable coach is hardly going to fatigue *us*," Sarah replied with amusement. "We're here to be at your disposal."

"In that case—" Alderscroft picked up a folded square of silk from the rattan table that lay between them and extracted a by now familiar piece of paper from it. "When you were examining this letter, I know you were concentrating on the sense of Earth Magic, which came from the husband. But did you do any attempt to learn anything about the letter writer herself, his wife?"

"I—no, I didn't, actually," Sarah admitted, with deep chagrin. "I suspect that may have been a mistake?"

"Let's just say, an understandable omission, given the circumstances." He handed the letter to her. "Rather than exercising your new abilities as a Spirit Master, I would like you to exercise your psychical gift as a reader of the history of objects. Indulge me, please."

Sarah took the letter from him, held it carefully between her palms, and closed her eyes. Fleeting emotions passed over her face for the next several minutes as she probed where the letter had been and tried to glean facts about the writer.

Finally she opened her eyes, and . . . from her expression, Nan was pretty certain she was annoyed with herself. She confirmed that with her opening words.

"Sherlock would certainly have given me a good scolding," she said, biting her lip. "At the time the letter is postmarked, the children had been gone for three days. They never stayed out even overnight before; the writer actually spoke about just that to her husband as she was writing the letter. The woman was frantic with worry, but doesn't know how to express her fears without coming off as hysterical, so she restrained herself. She was also laden with guilt because she sent the children out of the house to forage after they ruined the little there was for dinner in the course of romping about their cottage. There are no near neighbors to ask for help, but even if there had been, she knew she was regarded with suspicion by the people living around them because she is from a town and is *much* better educated than they are. And—" Sarah held up a finger, "—after the letter was sealed and the stamp put on it, she learned that her husband's enquiries at the village of Sheepstor suggested that at least three or four *more* children have gone missing this summer. I say at least, because itinerant worker families and Gypsies and Irish Travelers have been passing through, and some of them were missing children as well, though how many, neither the woman nor the man know."

"I've sent salamanders to my Earth Masters in the vicinity, as they are the most likely to pick up on signs of dark powers at work," Alderscroft said. "So far today I have gotten two replies in the negative. But even if they all reply in the negative—"

"The absence of a sign does not mean there is not something nefarious going on," John said, frowning.

"In the absence of Sherlock Holmes, I would like you four— five if you take Suki, and six if Peter can get free—to investigate, once we have gotten all the information we can remotely gather. You have resources the local constabulary won't; you can nudge them in the right direction if you learn anything." He frowned fiercely. "If something *is* going on beyond a lot of extraordinarily careless parents and a combination of children running away and terrible accidents, we cannot let it persist. Since Sherlock is no longer with us, we must carry on his work."

Nan had never loved Lord Alderscroft more than at that moment. The missing children were all lower class, even despised classes, and yet, here he was, fiercely declaring that something must be done if there was someone preying on them. There was not one man in a thousand of his rank or wealth who would have given a burnt matchstick about the lives of those children.

"It will take at least a day, and probably more, before I am ready to send you, if I send you at all, rather than merely putting the force of my rank behind a local inquiry with the police," he cautioned them. "John, I'll give you and Mary the tokens to contact the Air and Water Masters of the area arcanely, I'll send salamanders to the Fire Masters, and we can all begin doing that tonight. Nan and Sarah, is there anything *you* can do from this distance?"

"Possibly," Sarah answered for both of them. "We'll try. And you're right, while we have all the possible tools, arcane, mundane, and psychical, all here in this one spot, it's best to learn what we can before we venture into the unknown."

"My Lord, I am beginning to suspect you are turning into a socialist," John said, with a smile.

Alderscroft shrugged. "You could as easily say I am following in my aristocratic ancestors' footsteps and taking *noblesse oblige* seriously. We have great powers, John. It is incumbent on us to use them when and where they are needed. In a situation where mundane authorities are clueless or helpless, honor requires that we step in."

"Well said!" Nan enthused.

"Meanwhile, you, Nan, and Sarah and Suki are sharing the lavender room. John and Mary are across the hall in the cornflower room. Would you like to go up and unpack and freshen up, then return to discuss all of this in more detail?"

"I think that's a capital idea," Sarah agreed before Nan could answer. Nan had the feeling that this was more because Sarah had already guessed there was an entire new wardrobe waiting for them up there, and wanted to see it.

Alderscroft summoned a servant to take them there, since they hadn't ever been past the sitting room of the bungalow before.

The lavender room was exactly that; the wallpaper was patterned with pale sprigs of lavender, the oriental carpets were lavender, the furnishings were upholstered in lavender brocade, the twin beds and the truckle under one of them were decked in lavender counterpanes, and even the china was lavender and white rather than blue and white. And the bouquet of flowers on the dresser was mostly lavender.

As Nan had expected, Sarah went straight to one of the three wardrobes in the room, opened the doors, and began laughing. It was obvious why. The wardrobe was packed full, and the clothing they had brought with them was absolutely unnecessary.

Nan opened one of the bureau drawers and was unsurprised to see brand-new underthings. Silk, and the particularly delicate cotton that was nearly as expensive as silk.

"Well, at least we know we won't have to go back to the flat if we are sent out from here," Nan said with a sigh as Suki ran to the child-size wardrobe to crow over cool linen sailor suits and lace-trimmed little-girl versions of tea gowns. "We might as well change, so we don't embarrass the Lion with our normally shabby selves."

But once she, Sarah, and Suki had changed, she realized that Alderscroft's generosity had not been merely to indulge his own whims. She felt energized, exceedingly comfortable, and ready to face this potential problem head-on, not overheated and muddle-headed.

And it's just as well, she thought, as they rejoined the others on the veranda. *Now we can keep our minds completely on our job. Every bit of advantage may be crucial.* Because it certainly looked as if John Watson's instincts had been right and hers had been wrong. And the game, as Sherlock would say, was almost certainly afoot.

9

A foot in her side jarred Ellie out of sleep so deep she woke not knowing where she was for a moment. "Op," commanded that too-familiar, harsh voice. "Start chores. Tine door behin' 'ee."

Without even stopping to scrub the sleep from her eyes, Ellie obeyed, stumbling into the other room and closing the door behind her—and only once the door was closed did she realize that she had closed the Dark One in *with* the other children.

Simon! she thought, fear clutching at her throat, and tried to open the door again.

But it was stuck fast. Not *locked*, because there was no way to lock it from the other side. But stuck fast in the doorframe, as if it was all one solid piece and not a door at all.

For a moment, she dithered, not sure what to do, as silence reigned on the other side of the door. But what *could* she do, really? She couldn't get in from here—

The window! There was the window into the room from the back of the cottage! Maybe she could see what was happening! She groped her way hurriedly across the main room and opened the door, creeping out into the gray light and around the cottage wall until she came to the back, where she cautiously tried to peer in through the crack between the shutters.

But all she could see was the tall, black figure of the Dark One standing in the middle of the room. Just standing, doing nothing else.

But the silence in that room sent chills down her spine. She had never heard a silence quite like that before—it was a silence that had weight, and cold; it filled the room and spilled out to where she was standing, and she started shaking. The other children were always making some sort of sound; whimpering, whispering, coughing—but now she couldn't even hear them *breathing*.

It won't kill 'un, she told herself, trying to quell her rising panic. *It wants 'un . . . what'd Robbie say?* She thought she remembered the others saying something about a kind of sleep, a sleep that they dreaded, that frightened them. . . .

Robbie had said the Dark One ate their magic when it put them to sleep, that was it.

So they're just sleepin', like, she reassured herself. *They'll wake up, an' be all right.*

She had to believe that. Because . . . she just had to.

But her feet dragged a little in the dirt as she made her way back and got started on the chores, and she had a hard time concentrating on the work. That heavy silence on the other side of the prison door weighed on her heart like cold stones.

By the time the Dark One unstuck the door into the prison room and emerged, she had already swept the outer room, made up its bed, laid out everything for its breakfast, and turned the chickens loose. And—the chickens hadn't liked what was going on in the prison room either. They'd gone to the front of the garden and huddled against the wall together, only pecking at things as an afterthought, and mostly staring at the cot with suspicious, beady eyes. The sun was halfway to noon, and she'd been in a mire of worry the entire time the creature had been in there.

When it came out, there was something different about it, something that Ellie couldn't quite put into words. It seemed stronger somehow, or more alive. "Change buckets," it whispered. "Sweep oop. 'Ee'll nae need t' feed 'un till they waket."

She stumbled over her own feet in her haste to do as it ordered, and when she entered the room, the thick, cold, and above all, uncanny silence made her heart stop.

She ran to the back of the room where her brother's bed was. "Simon?" she whispered, putting a hand to his shoulder and halfway expecting him to be cold and dead.

But he wasn't. He was cold and clammy when she put the back of her hand to his forehead, but he was alive and breathing.

But she also couldn't shake him awake. No matter how hard she tried, he remained locked in a sleep so deep nothing got him out of it.

She peered around, and tried the next child—Rose. The girl was in exactly the same state as Ellie's brother.

They're just asleep, she reminded herself. *It said they'll wake up.* She had to believe the Dark One. What else could she do?

She swept up, changed the buckets, and since the others were still sleeping, took the dipper to the sink to wash it, because the last time she'd had a drink herself, it was getting slimy. The Dark One was having pease porridge, the last in the pot. It called her over to the table and thrust the pot at her. "Clean thet," it ordered. "'Ee kin hev scrapin's. Et it all. No wastin'!"

She had absolutely no appetite, and she was pretty sure the Dark One was well aware of that. But to refuse would only get her in trouble. So she sat on the floor with a spoon and carefully scraped the sides and bottom and shoved each overcooked, half-burned spoonful into her mouth, swallowing it. The porridge she had so longed for only yesterday was dry and scorched, and it nearly choked her to swallow it. But even if it hadn't been rendered almost inedible, it still would have choked her.

The Dark One lounged in its chair and watched her every moment, now and then encouraging her to scrape the pot harder. "Nae wastin' a morsel, or 'ee may be sorry," it said ominously, and laughed.

Finally she showed it the pot scraped down to bare metal, her mouth tasting like ashes. "There now, that's a-reet," it said. "Less work cleanin' pot. Get sand an' scrub it."

Fortunately she knew what it meant, since Mother had taught her to scrub pots the same way. There was a cracked and otherwise useless pot of silver sand on the floor by the table with the sink. She got a handful, and a little water, and scoured the pot with sand, a rag, and nothing else. When the bottom was perfectly smooth—and her fingers felt sanded—she rinsed it and was about to put it aside when the Dark One snatched it out of her hands and felt inside. "Tha'll do," it said grudgingly, and filled it with dried peas from a sack in the pantry, then water, and put it on the hearth.

But Ellie wasn't watching the Dark One. She was watching the fustian sack of peas. He'd taken out almost a quarter . . . and as she watched, she shuddered with fear, for *she could see the sack moving as it refilled!*

The Dark One didn't seem to pay any attention to what she was looking at, nor her reaction. Instead, it got a loaf, cut it in half, and smeared both halves thickly with mustard before reaching up to the rafters and cutting two slices of ham from the ham hanging there and laying them on the bread. Ellie watched the ham sharply—but the ham did not miraculously become whole again.

The Dark One sat down and cocked its head in the direction of the prison room. "Feed 'em. 'Em be stirrin'."

She seized the basket of morning bread and ran in. The Dark One was right. The others were moving, some more than others. She knew now that each of them was to get two loaves, and if there were extras, who Robbie would give them to. "One t' Sam, first," he always said. "Sam keps un from sickenin'." *How* Sam did that, she had no idea, but Sam had magically made her chopped-off finger heal like a miracle, so she was willing to believe Sam could keep any sickness away, too.

The others were just about able to sit up and accept their food; she brought the water around to them and made sure they each had a dipper-full, and had just finished when the Dark One called her back into the room.

"Leave 'em be," it ordered. "Get ovens warm."

This cot had ovens like she had never seen before. In the oven in the fireplace at home, you started a fire in the oven itself, let it get hot, raked out the ashes, then put the bread and the stop in. When the bread was done, you put in a cake or a pie, which would need less heat and more time to bake. When that was done, you'd put in beans or taties or meat if you had it, which would cook slowly using the last of the heat.

Both these ovens, one on either side of the fireplace, had additional fires under them, so you could keep the ovens as hot as you liked for as long as you liked. That meant she could get three bread bakings done—or, really, as many as she wanted. But it meant that she had to lug a lot of firewood, enough to keep the fires going all that time.

And . . . now that she was noticing these things, she saw that the pile of firewood never seemed to get any smaller.

There certainly was a pattern here. It looked to Ellie as if the Dark One was using magic to replenish things that wouldn't trigger someone into looking for a thief—firewood, grain, flour, peas. Wasn't that how witches were said to steal things, whisking them away, little by little, so folks would just think they were mis-measuring, or that mice or insects were eating them, or there were other natural explanations? But something that would be missed—a whole ham or a side of bacon—those must come some other way.

Did it trade with someone to get these things, or buy them? She couldn't imagine the Dark One strolling into a village and popping into the butcher for a ham!

But there were folk who were said to deal with witches. Travelers, for one; most people said Travelers were witches themselves, or half witches, and everyone knew that Travelers would steal anything that wasn't watched, and trade it back to you to boot.

Maybe that was it. The creature was trading with Travelers for the things it couldn't steal. Or maybe it had killed a pig in the fall, and the hams and bacon were all that was left. She could imagine it creeping up to a cottage by night, and letting the pigs out, luring one back here, and killing it. The cottager would never know what had happened, and would just lament his bad luck in not checking over the sty before he went to bed.

As she built up the two fires under the two ovens and thought these things over, a curious thing happened. Her mind stopped scurrying around like a terrified mouse, and she found herself able to think. And she realized that, as frightening as this witchery was, and as terrifying as the Dark One could be . . . it had limits.

It had to eat. It had to sleep. It was clearly using magic that it stole from its captives to make its life more comfortable, but "more comfortable" wasn't a palace, it meant using magic to steal food so it didn't have to work to buy it, using magic to steal firewood so it wouldn't have to cut it, and to hold someone—her—in thrall so it didn't have to do the work around the cottage. That *didn't* mean that it could steal everything it needed. That *didn't* mean it could do all the chores magically, or have some sort of magic servant to do them.

So . . . it wasn't all-powerful. Maybe it could be beaten.

Without being prompted, she made the first batch of bread dough and set it aside for its first rise, then went out to the garden to collect vegetables for the other children.

That was when she found the two dead hares, strangled in the nooses the thing had set out in the garden. She felt a pang as she touched the soft fur. They were both still warm.

She stopped what she was doing, and went back in empty-handed. "There's conies," she said timidly from the door, before it could hiss at her.

"Good," it said, and went to the kitchen and selected a knife. "Tha'll learnet t'butcher."

She was given no chance to object. The thing seized her by her left wrist and dragged her out into the garden again. "Show 'un!" it ordered, and so she showed the thing where they were among the beanpoles. It showed her how to get the noose off and reset the noose in the natural path the rabbit or hare would take, so that it would put its head through without thinking, then feel the noose close around its neck, panic, try to run, and pull the noose tight. It made her set the second noose after it had demonstrated with the first.

Then it showed her how to strip the skin from the hare in one pull, how to slit the skin up the belly, and where to stretch it out to dry it. How to clean the hare, and save the good bits of offal and discard the guts. That wasn't as bad as it could have been, though she didn't like it at all. It sent her to wash up at the pump while it took the carcasses and liver and lights and kidneys and all the good things inside.

But when she had come back in with the basket of veg, the hares were stewing in the biggest pot with onions and carrots and peas and beans, and he sent her back out again, this time with a smaller basket, and a curt order to fill it full of gooseberries, blackberries, and currants.

"Naow feed 'em," it said when she returned. "Wi' fruit, too." So she brought it all in at once, bread, veg, and berries, and Simon showed her how they'd all eat the center out of one of the loaves, fill the hollow place with berries, and bruise them a little, so the juices mingled and soaked into the bread. Gooseberries could be mouth-puckering tart, but mixed with the currants and blackberries, they were fine.

"Dark One allus gi's un sweetie arter Dark Sleep," Robbie explained slowly, sounding as if he'd been chopping wood until he was exhausted. They were all that drained, even Simon, who barely spoke to Ellie and ate his food slowly and mechanically. Sam was in the best shape—Ellie wasn't sure why.

Rose was in the worst. She could scarcely keep her eyes open, and Robbie moved over to her mattress to keep prodding her to eat. When she'd finished, long after the rest were done, she drank water and laid back down to sleep again, under Robbie's worried gaze.

But he wouldn't tell Ellie what had him so concerned when she asked, just told her she needed to get back to her work before the Dark One got angry.

Today was different, though, she sensed it. The Dark One seemed restless, and kept looking out the window impatiently. It started the eggs boiling early, and set the stewing rabbit to cook as slowly as possible. The moment she took out the last of the three batches of bread, it got to its feet.

"'Ee knows what t'do," it said. "Do't an' don' shirk." And without waiting for her response, it pulled a couple of leather bags connected by a strap down off the wall, and stalked out the door, closing the door tightly behind it.

She couldn't have stopped herself if she'd wanted to—she rushed to the window in time to see it standing outside the gate, its hands raised to shoulder height—and it was glowing.

She rubbed her eyes to make sure she wasn't seeing something that wasn't there, but sure enough, when she looked again, the Dark One was surrounded by a sullen, gray-gold glow. It was enough to freeze her where she stood. This was magic, real, and in front of her! And it was every bit as terrifying as she could imagine.

It stood there for some time—long enough to have baked a round of bread at least—until at last, a chestnut moor pony with a black mane and tail came toward it, picking its way out of the trees of the combe.

The poor thing's shaggy coat was dark with sweat, its eyes

rolled nervously, and every step it took seemed against its will.

Oh . . . the Dark One's caught it with magic! This was a confirmation of how she'd thought it might have lured a pig to the cot. Her heart surged with sympathy for the poor beast, and she thought she knew exactly how it felt.

When it finally reached the Dark One, the creature flung the bags over the pony's shoulders, put a rough sort of bitless bridle on it, and threw itself onto the pony's back. They poor pony didn't even try to buck. With stiff legs moving in a trot, it headed down the path she and Simon had taken to get here. Before long they were both gone into the trees.

Somehow she managed to do the rest of the chores, but when she came to feed the others and told Robbie what had just happened, his eyes went wide.

"So *tha's* whut it do!" the boy exclaimed. "It made nary soun' arter a Dark Sleep, an' we ne'er knowed why!"

"Liz didn' tell 'un?" she asked.

He shook his head. She bit her lip, trying to think of something she could offer that might give him—and the others—a little comfort. "It bain't 'ere naow, un c'n do as we like. Do 'ee wanter wash-ep?" she asked, finally.

His eyes lit up.

There was plenty of heat in the fire, and no fear of going short of wood. So she heated up a pail of water, dragged in the tin tub, and brought in some rags and soap, and everyone that wanted to got a turn at washing themselves. After so long in captivity, they had no more shame than a bunch of apes, stripping themselves naked. Then each of them took turns scrubbing down. The floor in here was not waterproof, but at least it didn't turn to mud as she brought in more pails of warm water. When they were all clean, the ones that felt up to it lent her a hand, giving their clothing a quick wash. Then they spread the clothing and clean "blankets" out on the mattresses as she emptied the tub out as best she could with the pail, then dragged it out and dumped the rest of it. Then they relaxed, sitting there naked until their clothing was dry enough to put back on. Not everyone did this—Rose was back asleep again—but most of them seemed happier for being clean. It was the first time Ellie had seen Robbie's features under all the tear-streaked dirt. It wasn't a revelation. He actually didn't look much different from the boys at Sheepstor, the nearest village to their cottage. Brown, untidy longish hair, round face, round eyes, pug nose. He didn't look anything like her or Simon, who took after their mother, with her raven-black hair and angular face. And the rest of the children were a lot like him, true Dartmoor children.

All this had made extra work for her, but she didn't care, because it made the rest of them so happy to be clean again.

Well, it made *her* happy to feel clean again too.

"'Ow long'll tha crature be gone?" she asked.

Robbie shook his head. "Dunno," he replied. "Door was allus tine."

"Best figger any time, then," she said wisely, and although she was ready to drop, she made sure to put everything to rights before going to bed. She'd have *liked* to have stayed up to see exactly when it returned, but . . . that was not even remotely possible, as tired as she was.

And so the first she knew of the Dark One's return was when it toed her awake the next morning.

The savory smell of stewed rabbit permeated even back here, wafting in through the open door. She scrambled to her feet as ever, and staggered into the outer room to seize the basket of bread.

But the thing stopped her. "Bide," it ordered, and took out one of the loaves, cutting it in half and hollowing it out a bit and putting one half in each of her hands. Then it dipped out some broth and a bit of rabbit meat and stewed veg and ladled the stuff into each half. "Git," it said curtly, nodding at the prison room.

By this time the others were awake, and when she handed Robbie his bread and meat, his eyes widened with excitement, and he went at it regardless of burned fingers. So did they all, and even Rose roused up enough to eat without prodding. Ellie brought them all a second helping, then the rest of the loaves, then at last she got to sit down and enjoy her first taste of meat in a very long time. The Dark One got the lion's share, of course. Mostly what they got was broth soaked into the bread, small bones stewed until they were soft, a bit of veg, and what meat came off the bones, and chopped up bits of liver, kidney, lungs, or heart. But it tasted so good she almost cried, and she crunched up her tiny rib bones with a rare spark of pleasure.

Then it was the usual sort of day, except she had to scrub the stew-pot, which scarcely needed scrubbing since the Dark One had mopped up every bit of broth left with his own bread.

The usual sort of day—except the Dark One went out again.

He left at the same time as he had yesterday, and by the same means. She stood at the window and watched him go, this time on a mottled brown and white pony that acted the same as the chestnut had.

The palpable atmosphere of relief that came over the room when she reported the creature was gone seemed to make them all relax as much as a lot of prisoners ever *could* relax. Robbie in particular seemed as if he was ready to have questions asked of him.

In fact, when Ellie sat down at the foot of his bed with her bread and egg, he cautioned her. "Don' reck on meat agin," he told her solemnly. "Us'n on'y gets un arter Dark Sleep an' *if* Dark One catches conies. It don' gi' us'n no pig nor mutton."

"Why?" she asked simply.

"Brung un' strenth up. An' coney don' keep."

She nodded wisely, because of course it didn't. The meat went to tasteless nothing if it was stewed too long, and while you *could* smoke rabbit to make it keep longer, unless you had a lot of them to smoke at once, it was a great deal of work for little reward.

Not like smoking a pig, for instance.

And there was potted rabbit, but you had to know how to make it. The Dark One didn't strike her as the kind of creature that knew anything about preserving outside of smoking and brining, if that. Not that Ellie knew how, but she did know how much work Mother had gone through to make potted rabbit the one year Papa had been invited to the warren clear-out.

"Wut's Dark Sleep like?" she asked.

Robbie shuddered. "Ain't like sleep. Tis like—'ee be lyin' a bier, but 'ee knows 'ee be lyin' a bier. Cain't move, cain't see, cain't 'ear, but 'ee *feel*. An' 'ee feels, like blood drainin' oot, 'cept t'ain't blood, 'tis somethin' else 'ee needs like blood. 'Ee gets tireder an' tireder an' then 'ee wakes oop, still a-weary."

"Tha's t' crathure stealin' our witchery," Ben said wearily, as some of the others who had been listening shivered at Robbie's explanation and nodded in agreement. "'S part uv us'n. If't take too much or too fast, 'ee don' wake oop."

She gulped. "Tha' 'appen?" she whispered.

The others nodded.

"An what'd t' Dark One do?" She really didn't want to know the answer, but felt she needed to hear it. She had to know what she was protecting her brother against.

"Dunno," Ben admitted, after a very long pause. "Dark One picks 'em oop, takes 'em oot, us'n niver see 'em no more."

Well, that gave rise to all kinds of horrible thoughts. Had there been spots that could have been graves out in the yard? Or did the thing just take the comatose child out onto the moor and leave it for the wild animals? Or dump it in a fen to drown? They were all horrible to contemplate.

I have to keep Simon's strength up, she thought desperately. *Or somehow get help.*

No, she had to do more than that. *I have to keep all of their strength up. That way he won't take too much from any one of them.*

As a couple of the others gathered around, she related what she'd seen so far—how the flour had been replaced, and the grain and the peas, but the ham and bacon had not. How there were chickens, how the chickens were kept in the yard, and all of them were missing a toe.

"Witchery," Ben said firmly. "I know how 'tis done. Dark One witched a bean, or a stone, or more like a bit uv lead. Droppet i' some'un's flour or peas or feed. Sinks to bottom, an' 'tis a hole whut goes from *there* to *'ere*." He illustrated what he meant with a sort of pulling motion, but they all instinctively knew what he intended. Ellie felt her jaw go slack. "Do same wi' bit uv bark, leave in someun's woodpile."

"'Ow 'ee know thet?" she demanded.

Ben shrugged. "Grammar wuz witchy. *Good* witchy, but tol' me tales, afore she lay a bier."

"Then 'ow'd 'ee get 'ere?" she demanded, because she couldn't see how a child who had been warned about these things could have ended up in the Dark One's hands. "Grammar warnit 'ee, no?"

"Grammar lay a bier," he repeated. "Ma an' Pa gone year afore. No sooner was they in ground, then m'lor' come fer cottage, an' turnet me out. Parish said, 'work'ouse or get 'ee gone.' Twas summer, so I were livin' rough on moor, found the combe, same as 'ee." He sighed. "Thought, 'ere's a cot left t'rot, mine t' take an' make snug an' bide. Saw garden gone t'weed, et a gooseberry. Next Es knaowed, Es be 'ere, a-chained."

One by one the other children told her their stories, but they were all depressingly similar. Robbie, too, had lost his parents. Rose came from Travelers, as did Ben and Deborah. Lily, Colin, and Mark's single parents were all itinerant workers with a gaggle of children to keep track of. Stephen, Bill, Sam, and Jess had all been left with a grandparent who had died, leaving them to be turned out by whoever owned the land their cottage was on. Like Ben, Sam's grandmother had been "witchy," but in her case, she had been noted for her healing powers, things she had taught to Sam, whereas Ben had not been taught anything but tales by his. For one reason or another, either getting lost from the family group, or going out foraging, or taking off on their own because the choice was the workhouse or the moor and everyone was terrified of the workhouse, they had all found their way here and been caught the same way. They'd see the combe, take it as a good place to forage and shelter, find the cot, see that it looked abandoned, and eat something from the garden.

"Why don't no growed-ups find cot?" she wondered aloud.

Ben, Robbie, and Sam looked at each other. Robbie shrugged. "Reckon 'tis 'id from growed-ups. Dark One don' want 'em. The crathure on'y wants childer."

She nodded. That made sense. Children couldn't fight back, weren't big enough to be a threat, and obeyed.

And that might be another reason why the Dark One did some things the ordinary way, and some with magic. Any magic it used, say, to draw water, would be magic it couldn't use to hide the cot from adult eyes. In fairy tales, magic always seemed to be an inexhaustible resource, but the fact that the Dark One had to harvest it from the children here told her that it was anything *but* inexhaustible.

Not that this helped any of them. Except that she desperately needed to figure out how to make them all stronger so none of them *(Simon!)* was in danger of being exhausted to the point of collapse.

"'Oo bin 'ere longest?" she asked.

Ben nodded. "'Twa yearn," he said. "'Twas three more 'ere then. They be gone. Rest came arter."

They talked for a long time, while the room grew dark, and finally Robbie sighed. "W'as matter?" she asked.

"A-hungert agin," he confessed.

Her own stomach growled a bit. And that was when she decided that "keeping up their strength" was going to start right that minute.

Without saying anything to them, she went back out and built up the fire, and mixed up a big bowl of flour, salt, some of the bubbling yeast, eggs, honey, and water, making up pancake batter as best she remembered it. Pancakes were the one thing Mother had taught her to make that she was pretty sure she could do without mucking them up too badly. She used as very little of the lard as she could manage to grease the big frying pan, put it on the hearth, and made pancake after pancake until every drop of the batter was gone. Then she cleaned up the bowl, spoon, and pan and took the pancakes to the others.

They weren't the best; they were thick, a bit doughy in the center, rather tough, and a bit burned around the edges, but nobody complained and everyone ate every crumb. "'Ee thin' 'ee'l get inter trouble?" Sam had asked with some alarm when she brought the cakes in.

"On'y thin's Dark One don' witch up's eggs an' honey," she replied. "If it sez, Es say eggs was cracked an' rotten, an' Es dun use much honey i' the makin'. If it don' cotch on, when it gae oot, Chell make pancakes."

Sam rubbed his stomach thoughtfully. "Right swant, goin' t' sleep all full," he said, but looked worried. "Don' go makin' Dark One think 'ee's twily, Ellie!"

"Nae be so unket," she told him. "I got ideers."

"Ideers wut's got Es ageest," Sam countered, but went back to his bed and lay down anyway. Ellie made a last check of the Dark One's room to make sure everything was neat and tidy and there were no signs of her illicit meal-making.

As always, she woke with the Dark One toeing her awake, and without a word, she stumbled straight into the other room and went to work. Right now, she reckoned her best chance at getting away with doing things for the other children was to make herself so useful that the Dark One stopped paying attention to what she did and she could sneak comforts in.

Although this morning when she took a sidelong look at the creature, it didn't seem to be paying attention to much at all. It moved about as if it were still half asleep, it made its breakfast out of the pease-porridge instead of eggs, bacon, and fried bread, and once it was satisfied that she was doing her job, it actually went to bed again!

Greatly emboldened by that, she started the baking early, and increased the number of loaves she was making by half again. She didn't dare do quite as much in the way of cleaning as usual for fear of waking it up, but she had an idea, and she decided to try it.

She dragged her mattress out while the others watched, and hauled it to the compost heap, where she carefully unpicked the stitches at the one end and saved the string, then dumped out all the mildewed and rotting straw. Then she cleaned the bag as best she could and left it over the gooseberry bushes to dry while she gathered the day's veg. It was dry by the time she brought the basket of veg in, and the Dark One was *still* asleep, so she punched down the dough, portioned it into "loaves," and left it for second rise. And while it was rising, she got the now-dry bag and took it to the straw-heap, where she stuffed it half full again.

Then she watched. And to her glee, saw the straw replacing itself.

She made a crude sort of needle—or at least something she could use to thread the string back through the holes in the sack—and stitched it back up again.

Then she dragged it back to her sleeping-place, got the blanket, took it out, and washed it too, spreading it out over the bush. By that time the Dark One was stirring, and she had begun feeding the others their veg and bread. Unsurprisingly, everyone that could fit joined her on her less-filthy bed.

But now would be the moment of truth. Would the Dark One notice how many *more* loaves there were, waiting to rise and bake?

Well, it didn't say anything. It just silently went about its business as she shoved as many of the loaves in the oven as would fit, then went on to the second batch of dough. For its part, it went out and got a cabbage and made fried bacon and cabbage for its nummet, ate it, and then watched her work.

It finally spoke up when she pulled out the second batch of loaves. "Tha's more then I shewed 'ee—"

She turned around, shaking so hard she could barely stand. "Uns 'ungry. Sleepin' makes uns cruel 'ungry. . . ."

"Do it, naow. . . ." It contemplated her. "But not 'ee. 'Ee didn' Sleep."

"Bu' Es works," she pointed out, trembling at her own temerity.

She waited for a long time, while that dark cowl just stared at her. Finally—"'Ee's lucky 'ee's useful," it hissed. "'Ee kin make more bread."

She thought she was going to faint with relief.

But she didn't. And as soon as she could manage to make her trembling legs work again, she went back into the prison room, dragged out Simon's bed, and hauled it past the unspeaking Dark One, hauling it back in again, cleaned, without it saying a single word.

She got one more of the beds and blankets done—Sam's—before it was time for supper, and the now-increased bread ration. The children fell on the extra loaves like wolves—all except Rose, who still seemed foggy-minded and had to be coaxed to eat her share. Robbie watched her worriedly. "Un's daver," he whispered to Ellie, who he seemed to have decided was now his right-hand person.

"Can Sam—?" she asked.

He shook his head. "This ain't what Sam kin mend," he replied. "Un's givin' oop."

"Cain't blame un," Ben put in, sadly. "Usn's bein' et, alive. Us'ns ain't niver gettin' oot."

"'Ee best remember that." The Dark One had slipped up to the open door when they weren't paying attention, and had evidently heard that last. They all jumped—except for Rose, who just slowly looked up at the creature, dull-eyed. "Yer *mine,* niver ferget. 'Tweren't fer me, ee'd be layin' a bier on moor. Be grateful."

It walked away. Ellie sat frozen on Robbie's bed for a very long moment. Finally she got the courage to creep out into the Dark One's room—

Just in time to see it going out the door again. She ran to the window and watched it summon a pony, mount, and leave.

"It's gone!" she called out, and ran back to them.

"It said Es kin make more food," she told him, in case he hadn't heard the Dark One giving her permission. "It didn' say Es couldn' make pancakes, so Es will!"

Some of the children let out feeble cheers. Some burst into tears. She well understood both reactions. Robbie fell on her neck and hugged her fiercely. "'Ee's a angel, Ellie. 'Ee's a angel for certain-sure."

She shook her head. "Bain't nomye angel," she said. "But *thet's* a divil."

And us'ns got to fight it, she thought, but dared not say. *Or . . . us'ns all lay a bier.*

10

Breakfast at Alderscroft's bungalow, so Sarah discovered before going to bed by asking a housemaid, was a buffet at which everyone was to help himself, and the laying-out of it was signaled by the sound of a gong. Since this was at approximately the same time that breakfast was taken at the school, the three of them were already up and dressed and about to make a foray into the rest of the house to discover what the arrangement was for themselves.

That had been at roughly seven in the morning, which was, by fashionable standards, horrifyingly early. But when he was not hosting guests who kept fashionable hours, his Lordship himself followed a schedule closer to that of common, working people.

Alderscroft already knew they'd refuse any offer of servants to help them dress, so none had appeared, but a housemaid was lurking just outside the door to the lavender room and whisked inside to start cleaning and tidying up as soon as they had vacated.

"You know she would have materialized like a djinn if we'd rung the bell," Sarah said in an aside to Nan. Suki giggled. They'd all helped themselves to the coolest possible outfits in the wardrobes, without regard for whether or not the outfits would have been considered "appropriate" for breakfast. Which meant Sarah had chosen a tennis dress, and so had Nan.

Evidently the Watsons were used to this arrangement; they were in the dining room ahead of the girls, and Alderscroft and his secretary came in shortly after Sarah and Nan and Suki. The buffet spread was impressive, but Sarah confined herself to toast and fruit. The day was already warm and she really didn't want to even think about the heavy meats that were on display. She just hoped the staff had heartier appetites than she did.

"I regret to say," Sarah announced once everyone was seated, "that our results last night were disappointing. There don't seem to be many ghosts in the part of Dartmoor we were able to explore, and there is quite a lot of Dartmoor."

"The ghosts we found were also not terribly communicative," Nan added.

"They was all a-tatters," Suki confirmed, and tapped the side of her head with her finger. "Addled, mostly."

"I spoke with several Earth Masters and several Earth Magicians," Alderscroft told them. "None were aware of anything untoward, but I still have another evening of communications ahead of me—most Earth Mages are either physicians or healers of some sort, or landsmen, and it's simply not feasible to pull them away from their work by day."

Mary Watson nodded to confirm this. "While we could send an Air, Water, or Fire Elemental to alert a magician that Alderscroft wishes to speak with him, we have no way of knowing if we're interrupting something important. So we send an Elemental to speak with *his* Elementals, who will know best when to get his attention."

"It sounds terribly complicated," Sarah observed, brows furrowed. "Like court etiquette, or something."

Mary Watson laughed. "You're not far off. A great many Elemental Magicians are quite touchy about how they are approached. The Earth Magicians very often are quite particular and set in their ways. They tend to be the most old-fashioned of all of us."

"I've also sent a telegraph to the constabulary at Yelverton, which seems to be the nearest town to Sheepstor—which is not saying much," Alderscroft continued. "Sheepstor is in the middle of nowhere, and we already can guess from the letter that the letter writer lives a further distance still from Sheepstor, perhaps in one of those 'villages' with only two or three families in it, too small to have a name. Sheepstor does not have a telegraph office, but hopefully Yelverton can spare a constable to ride over to get us more details, or possibly even interview the writer herself and find out just how long it has been since the children went missing—or if in fact they have returned."

"I'd very much like it if it turned out to be a false alarm," Sarah admitted, and found herself flushing a little. "Although I wouldn't mind if we could impose on your hospitality here for a little."

"My dear child, you are always welcome!" Alderscroft laughed. "By all means, stay until we have an answer that will let us know what we need to do next, and beyond. Besides, it makes it all the easier to dispatch you, if you are here rather than in London. You needn't even send to your flat for anything; I can supply whatever you'd need for the journey."

"I'd noticed," Nan said, just a touch dryly. But Alderscroft knew her too well to take offense.

"What I would like you to do today while we Elemental Masters work," he said, as they finished the last bites of breakfast, "is to see if the Oldest Old One will be willing to tell you if there is anything afoot out there."

"He probably *won't*," Sarah warned. "He's told us before that mortal affairs are mortal affairs and he doesn't meddle in them." *Not that long ago, in fact,* she remembered, and wondered if, by deliberately coming to tell them that, he was already warning them that there was something going on that needed their intervention.

"In that case, *just* in case, you should ask him if he can teach you the dialect of those that live near Sheepstor," Alderscroft continued. "I know he has done that for you with the Welsh tongue, so he should be willing to do that much. Otherwise, when you get out there, neither you nor the moorfolk will be able to understand one another."

"Now, that I think is certainly possible for him to arrange, if he'll answer us," Sarah confirmed. "And it's a cracking good idea."

With that in mind, she, Nan, and Suki took their leave and went out the garden entrance. They decided to consult with Alderscroft's head gardener as to the best place to summon Robin, and it certainly wasn't hard to find him, directing a couple of underlings who were replanting some herbs. It was quite a relief to be able to talk to the servants openly about magic and psychical matters—all of Alderscroft's people were entirely cognizant of what their master was, and many of them had a touch or more of magic themselves.

The gardener rubbed his bearded chin, and his eyes had a faraway look as he considered every inch of his Lordship's property. "Well, miss," he said, after a very long time—the girls made sure to show no signs of impatience, although the same could not be said of Suki, who was hopping from foot to foot. "I've naught but the barest touch of Earth Magic, meself, but if I was to pick a spot where it's thick on the ground on this property, I'd pick a special little clearing surrounded by firs just off the east bridle path."

He gave them very explicit instructions, and sent them on their way, returning to his task of replacing herbs that the cook had decimated.

The bridle path in question began just past the stable and stableyard, and curious horses gazed at them with wide eyes as they made their way past the paddock and took the turfed path that led eastward, rather than the other two that began there. The path very soon led them beneath the thick branches of a mixed forest of oak, beech, hornbeam, and birch, a beautiful green tunnel through forested land that held trees that were at least several hundred years old. Sarah remembered what she and Nan had learned about Alderscroft's land, when he'd given over the family manor to the school. It went back in the family almost all the way to the Norman Conquest, and the woods that stood here now were at the least the direct descendents of the woods that had stood here in those times. That was not uncommon, among the families of Elemental Magicians who were among the landowners, whether mere farmers with property or the landed gentry. They tended to hold onto their properties much better than any other group of landholders.

Probably because their loyalty is not primarily to the Crown or any political group, but to the land itself. So they don't get embroiled in anything that could cause them to lose the things they have pledged themselves to protect. There were probably those who would consider that treason. Sarah just thought of it as a "higher calling."

"Well, that's one of the three," Sarah observed, as they passed by a very old oak. She stooped and picked up a twig off the ground; there were five leaves, still green, and a half-grown acorn attached. She tucked it into her waistband, and they moved on, with Suki scampering away ahead of them or lagging behind, just within sight. One thing that they knew would always help summon Robin was the combination of Oak, Ash, and Thorn— three trees that had a very long tradition in magic.

The canopy was so thick that the atmosphere was a kind of deep, green twilight, scented with old leaves, and lightened by birdsong and the occasional calls of rook, wood pigeon, and crow. Neville and Grey kept themselves busy by keeping up with Suki— not that she *should* need watching here, but it was good practice as well as good exercise for them. The deep shade was welcome, given the warmth of the morning. Nan had already rolled the sleeves of her dress up above her elbows, and Sarah did the same.

The path was bare dirt now, and the woods on either side of it thick with trees slim and stout, heavy bushes, and clumps of fern. Not something Sarah would have considered forcing herself into, but apparently Suki didn't feel the same; thrashing in the undergrowth signaled her presence off the path up ahead.

A few dozen yards more, and Suki came running back to them out of the woods, holding up a hand-sized and verdantly green twig from an ash tree. She handed it to Sarah, who tucked it in her waistband with the oak twig.

And finally, just before they were to take the turning that would lead them to the clearing the gardener had promised, a sudden gust of wind tore through the branches overhead, and a third twig came spinning down to land right at their feet. Although there were no thorn trees about, it was a thorn twig that Nan carefully plucked from the ground and handed, wordlessly, to Sarah.

Sarah smiled to herself, and handed all three to Suki. "Run on ahead of us, dear," she said to the child, who was only too willing to do exactly that, the birds following her in the air.

"Do you think—?" Nan asked.

Sarah laughed. "That thorn twig was no accident. I'll bet a new pair of stockings he's waiting for us when we get there."

And sure enough, when they pushed their way through the

fragrant ring of balsam firs that edged the little clearing, Robin and Suki were busy playing leapfrog in the center of it, while Neville and Grey watched from a nearby tree and laughed at them. They both tumbled in a heap, laughing, into the long grass, as the two young women shoved their way into the clearing. Sarah was just pleased they'd put Suki into a green dress today, in anticipation of grass stains.

"How now, Old One!" laughed Nan at the two of them, scrambling to their feet.

"How now, mortal!" Robin retorted, making a mock bow. "A little bird told me you and the Masters are interested in my moors."

Robin was at his most *other* today. He made no attempt to hide the pointed tips of his ears, which poked their way through a tumble of brown curls festooned with a strand of ivy and a few leaves tangled here and there. Sarah wasn't quite sure *what* to call the outfit he was wearing. Jerkin? Tunic? it was sleeveless, green, looked something like leather, and was laced up the front. He wore baggy green trousers of something soft she couldn't identify, and bare feet. So—he wasn't Prince Robin Goodfellow today, he was just Robin, or Puck. She wasn't sure if that was a good thing for what they were about to ask of him, or a bad one.

"Well, we are," Nan replied, sobering immediately as Neville flew to her shoulder, and Grey to Sarah's. "Obviously we needed to talk to you, so thank you very much for obliging us. It's a bit of a story, and we're not sure how much more might be going on—or even if it's something magic is involved with."

"But given how unlikely it is that something has come *our* way that doesn't involve magic, we thought we'd better ask your advice," Sarah finished.

"Then sit, and tell!" Puck urged, patting the ground beside him.

He watched with amusement as Nan selected a rock, and Sarah, a log, to spare their white dresses. Then he grew serious as Sarah began telling him everything they knew, starting with the letter to Holmes.

"Well," he said, when she had finished—it hadn't taken long, because of how little they actually knew—"This is mortal business, and I don't meddle in the affairs of mortals."

"Much," Nan amended, fearlessly.

He flashed a grin at her. "Much," he admitted. "I do have a weakness for protecting mortal children, as you two know."

That's what I was hoping you'd say, Sarah thought. "But we just wondered if there is anything at all you can tell us about the comings and goings on the moor, since there *are* mortal children involved, two at least," coaxed Sarah. "Is there a magician on the moor, do you know?"

"Pfft. There's a mort of 'em," he replied, surprising both of them. "Not powerful, not like some of the ones you've taken on in the past, but the witchery blood runs strong in that part of the world, and there are plenty who can see through a millstone better than most. Good *and* bad; the moors can be dark and dangerous, and attractive for them as has good reasons to hide from other mortals. But there's not one that stands out, and not one that hunts children *that I know of.* But that can be hidden."

"Even from you?" Nan asked, surprise written all over her face.

"Especially from me." He nodded, and the pointed tips of his ears showed just for a moment among the tousled locks of his chestnut hair. "Horseshoe nails and Cold Iron's not proof against me, but there are spots out there that have been held by generations of them that are no better than they should be. Those places have been witched for long generations against my interference and my sight. And the pity of it is, I can't even tell where they are by finding the blank spots; it all just blurs away into the waters and the wild." He scratched his head. "So my answer is, aye, this is possible. Lots of things go astray on the moor, and plenty of those things are human children. But if there's magic involved, I can't find 'em, nor can I find who took 'em, nor where. If anybody did at all. Remember, all you know for the moment is that you just have one lone woman who chased her kiddies out of the house herself."

"Well . . . fiddlesticks," Nan said, slumping. "I guess we'll have to rely on the mages and the constables to know whether and *maybe* where we should go. But can you at least help us by giving us moor-speech in case we do go on the hunt?"

"Moor-*speeches*, there's more'n one, though the differences are small," Robin corrected. "Aye, I can do that. Open your mouths and stick out your tongues."

They obeyed, even Suki. Robin put three petals on each of

their tongues. Nan couldn't tell what they were from, but had the suspicion they were flowers that only bloomed on Dartmoor. "Now swallow without chewing," he ordered, and they did. The taste was floral, not bitter, but also not sweet. For a moment, Sarah was disappointed, because nothing happened.

But then—suddenly, it felt as if her head had swollen until it was about to burst, and her ears rang with what seemed like a cacophony of a dozen voices babbling at her, all at once.

Her head swam, she put both hands down beside her to steady herself—

And then everything was back to normal, and the voices were no longer in her ears, if they had been in the first place.

"Crikey!" Suki said, sounding a little dazed. "What were *that*?"

"That was the voices of the moor settling into your heads," Robin said cheerfully. "You won't get the full mastery of them until you've slept on it, but they're there, just as if you'd learned another language, and if you'll take my advice, *don't* pick the voice that sounds exactly like the person you're talking to. Pick one for yourself that sounds more east or north, or west or south. You're still all *Dartmoor,* but you won't cause suspicion if you sound a bit foreign to whoever you're speaking to. Otherwise they'll be bound to wonder why you sound like you come from their very village, but they've never seen you in their lives."

"That's good advice, thank you," Sarah said gratefully. "What about John and Mary?"

"Oh, they're Masters, they can get their education from their Elementals, once they arrive on the Moor," Robin said blithely.

Sarah sighed a little. "I can see where being a Spirit Master just isn't as useful as one of the other Elements. Most of the ghosts I encounter aren't particularly helpful."

"Hey now, ho now, if you weren't a Spirit Master in the making, you'd never have met *me*!" exclaimed Puck. "For us Old Ones are more Spirit than Elemental, you see. And I'd be sad to never have had our acquaintance, 'deed I would."

Then he cocked his head to the side, as if listening to something. "Methinks your friends have got *some* news, if not all the news you need, and they'll be hoping you can give them something. So . . . I'll tell ye something more, and that will be all that's in my budget.

Just as I can't see the bad 'uns who've hidden themselves while they are working small evils rather than great, no more can John and Mary. And if you were to ask my advice, I'd say to you, take speech of Holmes. The bad 'uns that are doing small, small things are gen'rally doing the same small, bad things they'd be doing if they weren't using magic to do them. And your Mister Holmes is *good* at tracking down that sort."

He winked, and a moment later a whirlwind whipped around in the clearing, making them all shield their eyes from the dust and bits of debris. And when the wind died just as quickly as it had come up—Puck was gone.

As soon as they were within sight of the bungalow, they saw Alderscroft at the edge of the bridle paths, peering anxiously in their direction. As soon as he spotted them, he waved vigorously to them; the birds took off for the veranda and Sarah and Nan picked up their skirts in both hands and sprinted for him. "I've had a telegram from Yelverton," he said. "The district constabulary there says there have definitely been more children than normal going missing without explanation over the last four years. He couldn't go into detail over a telegraph, of course, but I hope one of my Earth Mages will have more information tonight."

"And if not, that's enough to send us out to investigate," Sarah said firmly. "Will you send a message about this to Mycroft? Robin told us that if we can get him, we need Sherlock involved."

"Did he now?" Alderscroft looked astonished. "I wouldn't have thought that would be something he'd suggest—but let's not talk here. Come up to the veranda and Mary and John and I can tell you the little we learned while you were talking to the Old One."

The telegram, it transpired, was just as terse as one might expect from someone who was paying by the letter to send one. *4 yrs chldrn mssng stop cld use hlp stop,* it read. "Clear and concise, but not exactly informative," John remarked. "But I suspect a chief constable who was *not* obsessing over a problem he can't explain would not have sent that last, even to Lord Alderscroft, agent of the Crown."

"Good observation," Alderscroft agreed. "It tallies with my

experience of rural constabularies. They don't much like to ask for help."

"Well, you can't blame them," Watson pointed out. "Londoners come swooping in and solve their cases and they get written up in the newspapers as a lot of provincial dunderheads. Which is unfair, very unfair. They're shrewd on their own ground, it's only when things outside their experience impact them that they flounder, as would anyone."

"Well, this one has *asked* for help, so I suggest we work *with* him rather than around him," Mary put in.

Sarah nodded, as did Nan, and reiterated what Robin had told them about not always being able to see where magic was being worked even though it was on *his* own ground, as it were.

". . . and he thinks, given that these places on the moor have been used as bolt-holes for centuries, that you won't be able to find them by magic either," she concluded. "Which is why he suggested contacting Holmes."

"If the Oldest Old One suggests it . . . he's probably given us as much as he's able to. I'll telegraph Mycroft," said Alderscroft. "He'll be predictably annoyed at being made into Sherlock's letter-box, but we've done him yeoman's service lately and haven't asked for much."

All this time, Lord Alderscroft's secretary had been sitting close by, taking notes. Finally he spoke. "Shall I see about train schedules to Yelverton, and possible accommodations with your peers, my Lord?" he asked, with polite practicality. Then he allowed the faintest of expressions to cross his face. "One supposes one *might* be able to telegraph for reservations to an inn. . . ." His tone suggested that he doubted it.

"By all means, please make the inquiries, but I might have an alternative for accommodations," Alderscroft said. "It will depend on what one of my Earth Magicians says."

Sarah waited for him to elaborate, but the conversation passed on to other things. It seemed that learning anything more was going to have to wait until after dinner.

* * *

"Would you like to see how I communicate with other Masters and Magicians?"

The Watsons were using the magical workroom Alderscroft had set up for guests—the Fire Master really *had* thought of everything when he'd had this bungalow built. Suki had gone to bed lulled into a state of near-torpor by generous helpings of Eton mess—that meringue, whipped cream, and sliced strawberry delight that was her very favorite of desserts, rated even above the most decadent of chocolate cakes and mousses. The birds had gone off to their perches in the bedroom to sleep. Nan and Sarah had been sitting on the veranda, listening to the sounds of the night, when Alderscroft addressed them from the doorway.

"Definitely," Nan replied, getting to her feet. "And we'd like an explanation of that so we can figure out how we can do the same."

Sarah was a mere pace behind her as she joined Alderscroft at the door, which he held open for her. "I confess, I am not sure of that myself," Alderscroft replied. "Most of us use some form of physical object to communicate with. Air Mages generally use a crystal ball, Water a shallow bowl of consecrated water, Earth a polished slab of obsidian. Fire Magicians—use a fire. I have no idea what a Spirit Magician could use."

They continued down the hallway from the sitting room that led to Alderscroft's study.

Nan sighed. "Like so many things involving us, a mystery. How do you communicate with a magician that's not of the same Element as you?"

"With the help of our Elementals, we use the objects we normally use; the Elementals are the bridge between us, rather than the power itself," Alderscroft said, unlocking the door to a room along the hallway just after the door to his study. He gestured for them to go in.

It was not a large room, and it was not as ornate as she would have expected, although it was papered in red damask. There was a closed, floor-to-ceiling cabinet along one wall, something not unlike an altar on the south side of the room, and—somewhat incongruously—a set of three comfortable red-plush chairs facing a small fireplace. "I like to come here to read, or discuss things in a very private setting," Alderscroft said, with a slight smile. "There is no reason why a workroom can't serve more than one purpose. But this arrangement will be quite convenient for our purposes as well. Please, take a seat."

They did, one on either side of Alderscroft. There was a small, very bright fire already going in the fireplace. He gestured toward it. "This is what a Fire Master uses for scrying or communication; the Element itself, rather than a representation of it." He took his seat, and pulled a notebook out of his waistcoat pocket. "And the first on my list is Harold Linwood, the proprietor and owner of the Rock Hotel in Yelverton. He is due for attempt to speak with me at any moment."

He gestured—Nan sensed, rather than saw, a rush of Fire energies toward the flames, but Sarah nodded as if she had seen something that made sense to her. *Well, good, at least one of us is getting something useful from this.*

For a very long time all three of them just sat there, staring at the fire. The two small windows on either side of the fireplace were open, letting in the cool air—a good thing, or even though the fire was small it would have gotten very warm and stuffy. And just when Nan was about to ask if the innkeeper might have gotten delayed, the flames moved in the fireplace in a very . . . peculiar fashion, and a voice came from it.

"Are you there, my Lord?"

It was a strong voice, though it sounded as if it was coming from a great distance, and the tone was diffident. When Nan leaned over and peered more closely at the flames, she thought she saw a tiny figure of a man in the midst of them. Or half a man, to be precise; he was only visible from the waist up.

"I'm here, Linwood," Alderscroft replied. "I need to be brief. I have reason to believe someone is abducting children around Dartmoor, and it may be a magician. Have you gotten wind of anything?"

"Well . . . perhaps? Over the past several years I have heard of children going missing, but it has mostly been Travelers, itinerant workers, and orphans about to be sent to the workhouse." Nan bit her lip to keep from blurting something rude as the figure of the man in the flames shrugged his shoulders dismissively, as if to say, *and those people don't matter. "Dartmoor is a dangerous place, children run away from their parents, and really, what can one do?"*

Nan saw the corner of Alderscroft's eye twitch a little, but he didn't rebuke the other man. "In that case, I am very likely to send five people down to you to investigate for me. Two are a married couple, three are sisters. The couple will be there to paint the moor. The sisters are from the Harton School; the two eldest are teachers, the third is a pupil, and they are all getting away from London during the Long Vac. This is what you will tell people who ask, and we both know they will ask."

The man shrugged again. *"It's a village, my Lord. Anything and anyone new is talked about."*

"Our mother died in Sarah's infancy. Our father married an Italian woman, who died giving birth to our sister," Nan said, speaking clearly into the fire.

The figure started a little. *"I didn't know you weren't alone, my Lord,"* he said.

"Well, now you have some gossip to use to prepare your regulars," Alderscroft told him. "Suitably tragic, which should give them plenty of fodder for speculation without alarming anyone if there *is* something afoot. Oh . . . and on that head, please do not start making inquiries about missing children yourself. I don't want to make any potential quarry go to ground. Remember, the potential to be gained from blood magic is the same regardless of who the child's parents are. If there *is* something of the sort going on, the perpetrator is crafty, has been operating freely for several years, and is likely someone people know and think harmless."

"In Yelverton, my lord?" the innkeeper asked nervously.

"Possibly, possibly not. So guard the secret, Linwood."

"Yes, my Lord. Absolutely, my Lord. When can I expect the visitors?"

"Just hold your two best rooms. I'll pay for them regardless," Alderscroft replied dismissively. "It will be some time within the week. Not sooner than tomorrow, not later than four or five days from now."

"Certainly, my Lord," the innkeeper said. *"Is there anything else I can assist you with?"*

"Just take care of my agents, keep your ear to the ground, your eyes sharp, and your counsel to yourself, and thank you, Linwood. I'll send you a sign by Elemental when my agents leave from here."

"*Thank you, my Lord,*" the innkeeper returned, and the flames died back down.

Four more times he spoke to Earth Masters or Earth Magicians through the flames. All had heard rumors of missing children, none had thought anything of it. They all said the same—children were known to run off rather than allow themselves to be sent to the workhouse, Travelers and itinerant workers couldn't keep track of their hordes of offspring, the moors were dangerous. Nan could tell Alderscroft was losing his patience with these attitudes when he sat back in his chair and allowed the fire to die down to coals, staring at it without speaking.

"Well," he said, finally. "There is not a great deal I can do to rectify these deplorable attitudes, if their own preachers and padres have not been able to instill the basics of decent Christian thinking in them."

"It's lazy thinking, or so my parents would tell you," Sarah replied. "If something doesn't affect them directly, they are too self-centered to care about it. The more foreign someone is from the circles they move in, the less they care. By the time you get to Travelers, well, to their way of thinking, Travelers are scarcely human at all."

Alderscroft's thunderous brow told wordlessly just what he thought of that sort of attitude, *especially* among the Magicians and Masters of whom he was the loose head.

But then he sighed, and passed his hand over his face. "Hopefully now that I have raised the specter of a Blood Magician working out there, the fates of Traveler children will seem a bit more important. And you two should go to bed. You might be packing tomorrow."

"Yes, sir," Nan replied, offering her hand to help Sarah up.

They left him alone in his workroom, still brooding over the dying fire.

11

Ellie had gotten all of the beds cleaned and restuffed with clean straw; she'd washed what passed for blankets, and everyone's clothing, at least once. Odd, she had never done so much hard work in her life, yet somehow she was getting it all done, and feeling all right when she went to bed, not utterly exhausted. Maybe it was that she was doing it to make all the others feel better. Or maybe it was because Simon was chained up in his corner and not making twice as much work by undoing half of what she did and wasting the other half of her time by skylarking around.

Once, and only once, the Dark One had stopped her. "Tha's doin' a mort of work for *them*," with the emphasis on *them* as if her fellow prisoners were beneath her, and an unspoken implication that they weren't worth her time. But she didn't take its bait. It was clearly trying to get her on *its* side, pitting her—and possibly about to dangle the bribe of getting better treatment and better food before her—against them.

As if she'd believe it. As if chopping off her finger and making her as much a prisoner here as they were was worth its table scraps! So she'd just looked down at the ground, her legs shaking, and replied, "Ev'un needs ter sleep an' eat good so they's strong. Tha' needs 'em strong." And when she got no answer, she looked up, and saw that it was just . . . staring down at her, apparently as astonished as if it had heard a toad talk.

So she'd left it standing there staring, and went back to the washing.

One huge advantage of doing all that washing was that *she* was cleaner than any of them. She'd always hated being dirty, and before she started doing this, she'd wanted to claw her skin off.

Her hard work paid off; the others were all looking better, stronger as she had hoped, and not quite so much in despair. They had energy and the inclination to talk, and even to help her with the chores in the prison room, which gave her more time for the other things she was doing. And on the one hand, that was more than good, it was excellent.

On the other hand . . . it meant the Dark One was sending them into the Dark Sleep a lot more often, and now it didn't even bother to shut her out of the room when it did so.

But on the third hand . . . that meant that it was leaving after supper a lot more often. And it was coming back with things, as she would discover in the morning. Mostly those things were only for its own comfort, but it seemed to have decided that treating the prisoners better meant it was getting more of what it wanted from them. So when it came back from wherever it went, sometimes things appeared piled in front of the prison door in the morning. More blankets—adult shirts and smocks they could wear if they rolled up the arms, so that they could strip to their skins and get their clothing washed regularly and have something clean to wear instead of huddling in a blanket like a naked heathen, as Mother would have said.

And the Dark One was bringing back more food. Most of it, like a couple more fletches of bacon and two strings of sausages and a half-wheel of cheese, didn't self-replenish, so none of that went to the prisoners, but some did, and that meant Ellie had more things she could make for them when the Dark One wasn't there. For instance, it brought back a huge sugarloaf that must have weighed more than five pounds—something Ellie had only ever seen in a grocer's window. And the sugar had been enchanted just like the flour; no matter how much she scraped off, the loaf never got any smaller.

That meant she could make sugared pancakes with bits of candied carrot in them for everyone every night the Dark One was gone. The treat seemed to make everyone feel better, even when they were recovering from the Dark Sleep.

The Dark One still allowed her to make extra bread, too, and if the Dark One left early enough, while the eggs were still boiling, she would go for a second foray into the garden and make a sort of vegetable stew to go with it. The extra food seemed to be helping everyone—except Rose.

But what the Dark One *didn't* know was that she was also baking hard biscuits a few at a time, the kind that kept forever, and they were all hiding them in their beds. The others were hiding them against the day the Dark One might decide to punish them by withholding food. *She* was hiding them against the day that she could figure out how to run away.

She'd put the others to limited work, besides having them take over the daily sweeping, now that they were all in better shape. When they swept, they swept the place clean from wall to wall. She'd had them move the beds to one side of the room, sweep the entire room thoroughly, oil and rub down the floor, then do the same with the other side. Then she'd laid sprigs of rosemary, lavender, and mint along the base of the wall. So now they had clean, dry beds, a floor that wasn't oozing damp and cold all the time, and most of the vermin had been chased out by the herbs she laid along the wall. In fact, if it weren't for the chains on their ankles and the Dark One . . . they'd probably have enjoyed living here. At least the ones that didn't have homes and families to go back to.

The only one that wasn't doing better was Rose. She *had* changed to a clean smock that she was practically lost in, and she *had* washed, but she still spent most of her time curled on her bed in a kind of half-doze, and still had to be roused to eat. Even Ellie could tell she'd given up, and nothing anyone said to her made any difference at all.

Something had broken inside her the last time the Dark One had sent them all into the Dark Sleep. Sam and Robbie were both worried about her, but what could they do? They'd tried coaxing her, tried putting some heart back in her, tried begging her with tears in their eyes for her to not give up. . . . She was indifferent to it all.

Ellie regarded the girl with pity, but in her own mind, Ellie had already consigned her to a grave. It was like that kid the goat had had. There was no use getting attached to it, Mother had told her. It was only going to end up sold or stew. And Ellie had hardened her heart and *not* gotten attached, and stupid Simon had and would have blubbered buckets when it was gone. Ellie had seen the hand of Death in the form of the Dark One on Rose a long time ago. While Rose lived, Ellie would make sure the girl got everything Ellie could provide—but she wasn't investing any emotions in the girl. Not the way she had already with Sam and Robbie and yes, even her pestiferous little brother, who was the one responsible for them being here in the first place.

One of these times, Rose wasn't going to wake up from the Dark Sleep. Sam and Robbie would probably go billid when she died. And then—God and his Saints only knew what the two of them would do after that. Ellie had already resolved to make sure to protect them from the Dark One if they did anything the creature didn't like—

That devil'd likely do a lot worse than just smack them crost phizog.

So she had already thought of all the ways she could intercept one or both of them, and keep them locked up until their reason returned. It wasn't as if it would be hard. They *were* chained, and she could get Simon to sit on their chains if need be. The others would probably even help her, to avoid getting the Dark One all riled up.

So when the inevitable happened to Rose, she was ready. Meanwhile . . . Ellie tried to puzzle out how she could escape.

The Dark One was restless, a sure sign that it was going to drain the others and vanish for the night, and probably repeat the nightly visits to wherever it went for the next couple of nights after that. Instead of just lounging, it was playing with something—jewelry, Ellie thought. Threading rings onto a chain with a locket, and unthreading them again. By this time, Ellie was pretty sure the destination had to be a village or even a town, because of what it'd been bringing back to the cot when the creature returned. But this village couldn't be anywhere nearby, because it was catching moor ponies to ride there and back, and she was pretty sure it was forcing them to gallop all the way there. So the goal was probably thirty miles away, maybe more. This cot was hidden well, and distance from any other human beings undoubtedly factored into that. Good for *them*, because that meant the Dark One was gone for the better part of the evening and night and slept heavily and late when it got back. Bad for *her*, because when she finally ran, there would be no path to follow, and a long, long way to travel afoot.

But this time . . . this time Ellie caught the creature staring at Rose through the open door every time it was about to turn and pace in the opposite direction, staring in a way she could only think of as "predatory." Like a stoat sizing up a wounded bird. And she got a cold feeling in her chest when she thought she understood just what that meant.

Tonight the Dark One was going to drain Rose completely. It must have been going easy on her, the way it did on Sam, but something had changed.

Why had it suddenly decided to do this tonight? Ellie had no idea. Maybe it had noticed that Rose was not producing very much of the mysterious "magic" that Robbie said it ate, anymore. Maybe it had decided that Rose was consuming more than she was worth to keep alive.

Maybe it already had a replacement in mind.

Her insides went cold and her stomach flip-flopped.

That might have been the most horrible thought in this horrible place that Ellie had yet had. To know that the Dark One was about to be rid of Rose, *and* that it was going to kidnap some other child, *and* that there was nothing she could do to stop it—

It was awful.

And all she could do was wait helplessly in the other room, up to her elbows in bread dough, while the Dark One strode in, raised its arms, and gathered that dark-light around itself.

And this time, when the procedure was done, it did something it had never done except with her. It bent over Rose, took a key from somewhere inside its robes, and unlocked the shackle. That moment of the shackle dropping open dropped Ellie's heart, too. This was the end for Rose. And despite her determination not to feel anything, her eyes stung and she swallowed down a sob.

Robbie and Simon protested weakly from where they lay, dazed and barely awake—Robbie because he likely knew what was coming, and Simon because Robbie was doing so. Simon had taken to copying the older boy slavishly, which mostly was a good thing, but Ellie held her breath and hoped that Simon wasn't going to earn a beating this time.

Evidently, the Dark One was in a good mood. It slung the limp and lifeless-looking body of Rose over its back, and all Ellie could think was, *is she dead?*

There was no way to tell. The Dark One strode past her without a second thought—except to look down at her and hiss, "Es be gone. Feed t'others. Finish tha' work."

And then it was through the door. She ran to the window, and watched as it paused only long enough to summon a moor pony. It slung the usual bags over the pony's shoulders, dumped Rose on top of the bags, and off the creature went, with Rose's body slung in front of it over the pony's withers.

And in the other room, Robbie, Sam, and Simon began to cry, quietly. She hardened her heart again. This was probably the best chance she was going to get, and she needed to have a clear mind.

Save th' tears for thasel's, she thought. Rose was gone, either dead already, or unconscious and the Dark One was going to take her off to die elsewhere. She had to shut down her feelings and concentrate on the living, and they should, too.

She finished baking the bread and sweeping up. Finished boiling the eggs, and cleaned everything she used to make the bread. Last of all, she made candied carrots to give them with their bread and eggs. All the while, Robbie sobbed softly in the other room.

When she had done everything she could, she brought in their food; half-loaves hollowed out and filled with carrots, and the other half with the egg in it. Robbie was red-eyed, but seemed resigned to what had happened when she brought him his half-loaves. He seemed about to say something to her, then just shook his head. She went back out and brought in the basket with the remaining bread and made sure everyone got his fair share. There was, of course, one extra boiled egg. She considered it a moment, then sat down next to Robbie, between him and Sam.

"Es gonna scarper," she said matter-of-factly.

That startled him out of tears. "'Ow?" he gasped.

"Been thinkin'. Dark One chopped off m'finger an' put it under 'earthstone, an' now Es cain't get past wall. Chickens all got one toe off, an' *they* cain't go past wall. So mebbe if Es get m'finger an' throw it or take it through gate, Es c'n leave." She let out the breath she'd been holding. It had taken her a long time to try to reason her way through how the Dark One must have been holding her here, and that was the only thing that made sense.

"Wut c'n us'ns do?" he asked immediately.

"Tha'll tell th' Dark One thet tha 'eard door close an' thunk Es was come t'bed, late," she ordered him. "Tha'll tell thet *all* uns were too weary t' do more'n eat an' sleep an' thet's all tha 'member."

"But—" he protested.

"No nort," she told him firmly. "Do wut Es sez."

"Ellie, do tha' get finger from under th' stone, an' try. Then come back here an' tell us'ns," Sam said just as firmly as she had. "We'll spare tha' half our'n biscuits, do tha' take Rose's clather an' blanket an' tha'n. Then run, run till tha' canst run no more."

She nodded, and went out to look for the fire iron to pry the hearthstone up with. She fought hard to maintain her determination, because it was oh, so very tempting to give this up right now and just let things go on as they were.

The stone came up surprisingly easily, and she levered it over to the side as she remembered it lying when the Dark One had dragged her here.

And then she was confronted with a problem. There was not one finger end. There were two.

Both were in the same withered, mummified condition. She hesitated a very long time between them—then firmed up her lips and took both. The other one must have belonged to that girl who had been the Dark One's slavey before Ellie. Well, she was dead, and taking her finger would neither help nor hurt her.

She marched straight out the door, down the path, and to the gate, and holding her breath with trepidation, her stomach a tight little ball, she thrust the fist holding the fingers in front of her, closed her eyes, and walked forward.

She more than half expected to bounce off that invisible fence and land on her bum again. Ten slow, cautious steps later, when she hadn't done so, she stopped, and slowly opened her eyes.

She was not only well past the gate, she was well past the lightning-blasted tree.

She clapped her free hand over her mouth, and indulged herself in a much-muffled whoop of joy.

Then she ran back into the cot.

"Did it—" Sam began and saw her face. "It did! Ellie! Tha' can get help!"

"Chell! Chell!" she pledged fiercely, and then saw that the others had made the smock Rose had been given into a pack that presumably contained her biscuits and theirs, her own spare shirt, with shoulder straps rigged from the arms of the smock, and the two blankets rolled up tight and secured on top with the strings from the smock collar.

"Naow run, Ellie!" Robbie said, his eyes overflowing. "Run! The futher tha' gets, the less like Dark One'll keep chasin'!"

"Chell bring back help!" she swore, and then did one of the hardest things she had ever done in her life.

She closed the door on them.

She stopped long enough at the baskets of bread for tomorrow to take the loaves she and Rose would have eaten and stuff them into her pack, along with the two boiled eggs, hers and Rose's, that she had not eaten.

And then she stopped in the garden just long enough to pick enough strawberries to fill a pocket she made out of the corner of her own smock, to eat as she went. It was a pity she couldn't take more, but they were only going to end up a sticky, smashed mess if she did.

She didn't run, despite Robbie's orders. Running would lead to tripping and falling. But she did set out with the longest stride she could manage, eating strawberries as she went.

She had no idea where "home" was from here. But she did remember one thing that Pa had told her. How, if she ever got lost on the moors, she was to walk until she found running water, and follow it downstream. "Water be where folk be," he'd said. "So follow water."

So that was her goal. Find water. Follow the water. Follow it until she found people, and tell them everything she knew. And fortunately, she had proof, of a sort—

—two chopped-off fingertips.

* * *

It was long, long past moonrise when she finally could not go another step. She still hadn't found running water, but she had found a little rain-pool where she'd gotten a drink and eaten one of her loaves.

The moon was full, and her eyes were used to the dark. It was a clear night, so she knew she was in no danger of getting rained on, but she felt vulnerable out in the open, so she looked around for some cover.

It wasn't much, just some bushes, but she crawled under them and made a nest out of her two blankets. At first, she started awake at every little sound, thinking it was the Dark One that had found her at last, but eventually her exhaustion overcame her, and she fell asleep.

And she didn't wake until the sun was high in the sky—and a wild pony was nuzzling her cheek curiously.

She sat up with a yelp, frightening the pony into flight and immediately tangling her inexpertly braided hair in the branches of the bush she had gone to sleep beneath.

When she got herself out of that cawtch, she took a long and deep breath, and peered around from within the shelter of the bush. Because the Dark One could be sitting *right there,* waiting with cruel patience for her to wake up so it could have the pleasure of her terror.

Nothing.

Slowly, she crawled out from under the bush, stood up, and looked around.

For as far as she could see in any direction, there was nothing but the low, rolling hills of the moor, covered in grass and flowers, dotted with bushes, with dark patches that might be groves of trees in the distance. No sign of the Dark One. No sign of any sort of pursuit. The only living thing within sight that wasn't a plant was the moor pony, standing off in the distance at the edge of a little herd of six more, staring warily at her.

Her stomach growled. And that decided her actions for the next little while.

She ate an egg and two loaves, packed up, and considered her options. Last night she'd had the mother-wit to lie down with her feet where she'd been and her head where she'd been going. East, was where she'd been going, and that seemed good enough to her for lack of any other signs.

She did pause for a long moment to scan the horizon with extreme care, looking for the thin threads of smoke that signaled a hearthfire going. But either the hearthfires out there were not putting out any smoke, or (more likely) there just wasn't anyone out there.

Find running water, her Pa reminded her in her head. With a last hitch of the improvised shoulder-straps, she started walking east.

When Mother had chased them out to forage, Simon had been wild with joy. Who wanted a half a cup of milk and a single piece of dry bread when there were berries and nuts and all sorts of good things to eat out there for the taking? And who wanted to waste time doing boring chores when there were hills to run over and fun things out there to get into?

He'd begun having second thoughts when all he and Ellie could find was green stuff, and not even cole, but thin, unsatisfying cress and the like. He'd been on the verge of tears when they gave up for the night and lew under a hedge and such disappointing sheep-fodder had been all they had to eat.

Then he completely recovered his spirits the next day when their hunting went so much better, and he'd practically shouted for joy when they'd found that deserted garden. Everything was good again! They'd come home laden with food, Mother would be proud of them, and they'd have a feast and Mother would stop making them do chores and turn them loose on the moor every day!

Except, of course, it wasn't deserted, and that had been the last happy moment he'd had.

At least through all of the ordeal, Ellie had been there, making sure he got fed and was warm enough, keeping between him and the Dark One. And doing all that work! Baking and sweeping and cleaning and all that other work like a regular slavey! He huddled on his bed, consumed with guilt when he wasn't crying to go home, because it really was all *his* fault that they were here.

But even though the fact that Ellie had said that she was going to try and get help was known to every one of the prisoners, he hadn't *really* believed she was going to do that. Not without him, anyway. So as the others packed her clather and the biscuits into Rose's clean smock, he waited for her to appear with the key to unlock his shackle. Because of course, she was so fitty, she could manage anything, including stealing the key.

And he watched with open-mouthed disbelief as she shouldered her burden, marched out the door and shut it behind her, and left without him.

It wasn't possible! She surely would be right back!

But she wasn't. And as the others laid back down, as dizzy and drained from the Dark Sleep as he was, he remained staring at the now-closed prison door, still in complete disbelief that she had left without him. Wasn't she supposed to protect him? Now what was he going to do?

Eventually he found himself starting to slump over, and he gave up: laid himself down on his bed, covered himself, head and all, with his blanket, and began to weep, softly.

He must have cried himself to sleep, because the next thing he knew, he was jolted awake by a scream of pure rage right beside him.

Instinctively, he pulled the blanket tighter around himself, trying to hide. *Not me! Not me! Not me! I didn' do anything!*

To no avail, of course. He felt the blanket being ripped off his body and out of his grip. He squeezed his eyes tight shut, trembling in every limb. Felt a pair of cruelly strong hands seize him by the shoulders and lift him into the air, shaking him. *"Where is she?"* screamed the Dark One, as he tried to avert his eyes from the empty hood where its face should be. *"Where is she?"*

"Dunno!" he bleated, the exact truth, since he had no more idea where his sister was than a hen would. *"Dunno!"*

The creature shook him until his teeth and the chain on his ankle rattled a fine counterpoint against one another, then threw him back down on his bed.

It knocked all of the wind out of him, that did, and he lay there struggling to get a breath as it berated Robbie.

Robbie just repeated what Ellie had told him to say, as the Dark One got angrier and angrier. And just at the moment when

Simon was certain the creature was about to strike him, Jess spoke up timidly.

"Chave made'a mort'a bread," she whispered. "Really."

Deborah spoke up as well. "Cham good at cleanin'."

The Dark One whirled and stared at them both. For a moment, Simon held his breath, afraid that it was going to beat *them*.

But instead, the Dark One bent down and seized Jess by the wrist, unlocked her manacle, and dragged her out to the hearth. There was a scream of absolute terror and pain, and the Dark One dragged her back in, her fingertip severed as Ellie's had been. He flung Jess onto Sam's bed, and went for Deborah.

Deborah did not scream, but that was because she fainted as soon as the Dark One touched her. In mere moments it had flung her limp body on Sam's bed too. "Fix them," the thing snarled, and stalked off to bring back the basket of bread and the broom, which it flung at Colin.

Then it slammed the door.

Sam was already working on Deborah's finger, having dealt with Jess's. The rest of them stared at each other in stunned silence.

Robbie recovered first. "Ben, get broom. Bill, take buckets an' put 'em at t'door. Rest bar Sam, haul back beds fer sweepin'." And he suited his words to his actions by getting up and pulling the beds belonging to Jess, Deborah, Rose, and Ellie out into the center of the room.

When all the debris was swept out the door, Jess and Deborah were both awake and Sam had finished bandaging their fingers with some clean rags. That was when the Dark One appeared at the door.

It looked around the room—as best it could in the gloom—and then down at the buckets. "Tha," it hissed, pointing at Deborah. "Take buckets an' foller. Tha—" and it pointed at Jess, "Get t' makin' bread."

Both scuttled to obey the creature, sniffling into their sleeves. The thing cast another glance around the room, and shut the prison door behind it.

Simon pushed his bed back where it belonged and went to sit on it, still too terrified to do anything but sniffle as the occasional slow tear born of fear crept down his cheeks. Sam laid himself down flat, looking exhausted. The rest put the room back in order and took to their beds as well.

As the fear wore off, Simon realized he was dizzy and lightheaded, and that *might* be because none of them had eaten, even though the basket of bread was sitting right there. So since no one else was apparently thinking of that, he got up and headed for the basket.

His original intention had been to snatch two or three loaves and take them back to his bed and devour them. But he paused with his hands full of bread and looked around himself, peering through the dimness.

They'd all been heavily drained by the Dark Sleep. And it hadn't been easy, cleaning up while dragging those cursed iron chains behind them. With a sigh, he took his loaves to Ben, poking at the boy with his toe until Ben rolled over, and holding out the bread to him to take.

Only when everyone else was fed did he claim the last of the loaves for himself. He'd curled up on his bed with his treasure in hand when the door opened again and he practically jumped out of his skin.

But it was Deborah with the two buckets. "Dark One be gone," she said in a low voice, as if she was afraid it would hear her regardless. "Left door all abroad."

"It's arter Ellie," Mark said flatly.

"Nay sar unket," Robbie retorted. "Dark One don't know where she go. She moorwise, Simon?"

"Aye," he replied, cautiously.

"So usn's pray." Robbie seemed perfectly sincere in this, and Simon, schooled by Mother in daily prayers, abandoned his bread and got on his knees, following Robbie's example. Deborah just took her share of the bread off her bed and sat down to eat, but Steven and Bill and Lily knelt and bent their heads as well.

Simon couldn't think of anything but a wordless plea to a nebulous God that the Dark One not catch his Ellie, and that she find help, but from the way Robbie's lips were moving silently, he had a very great deal to say to that same nebulous God.

Jess came in during the middle of this, and with a curious glance at the children praying, dropped down on her bed to pick at the bread waiting for her there.

"Chell weed garden," she said quietly. "Dark One got our fingers hid, so no hope of follerin' Ellie." She sighed. "Grammar knowed me plants. Us'ns c'an eat a lotta them weeds, an' Es can fix 'em tasty."

That perked Simon up no end.

"Deb'ra'll do bread. Chell do other vittles. Dark One don' stop un, us'll et good." There was a quiet defiance in that statement that made Simon wonder what had put courage into *all* of them? Had it been Ellie? Or had it just been the improvement in their food that Ellie had managed that had given them all twice the strength and heart they'd had when he and Ellie were first captured?

The Dark One returned for nummet; the door had been left ajar and Simon could see that Jess and Deborah leapt to wait on the creature, bringing it a fresh loaf and a vegetable stew. It reached up to the flitch of bacon hanging from the rafters and cut a rasher, throwing it at Deborah. She caught it without flinching and fried it up. It was impossible to read the damned creature, and it said nothing the entire time it was in the cot, but at least it didn't hiss any orders at either of them, and when it stalked out again, it also hadn't struck or otherwise punished anyone.

So, *their* nummet was the same as the Dark One's, without the bacon. Bread and vegetable stew, which was ever so much more satisfying than the raw veg they'd gotten before.

Everything was quiet and tidy when the Dark One returned again, still empty-handed. Deborah presented the creature with more vegetable stew and bread, and a mess of gooseberries cooked in sugar. It grumbled and hissed under its breath, but once again, meted out no punishment, not even over the extravagant number of loaves Deborah had turned out.

It went out a third time; Jess ran to the window to watch, and called back over her shoulder after a silent interval.

"Dark One's gone. Called up moor pony, like Ellie said, and 'tis gone." She left the window and joined Deborah at the table, where they were making something. "Reckon it's give up cotchin' Ellie."

Simon bit his lip in mingled anxiety and hope. Could they be right? Had the thing given up? Ellie must be halfway across the moor by now! Surely it could not be long before she found people and could bring back help and rescue!

"'Sa big moor," Ben said glumly. "Don't need Dark One huntin' 'ee t'get inter trouble. They's fens, mires, wild dogs, storms, breakin' leg—"

With every reminder of how dangerous the moor was, the more tears welled up in Simon's eyes. And when Ben said "breakin' leg," he couldn't bear it anymore; he burst out crying.

"'Ere!" Robbie barked sharply, catching him by surprise. "Will tha' blatherin' an' blubberin' 'elp tha' sister?"

He sniffed loudly, but it didn't look as if he was getting any sympathy from anyone. "N-no," he admitted.

"Then stop tha' crewnting," Robbie ordered. "Tha' blubbers like a chrisemore."

The two girls brought in supper; the usual bread and boiled egg, but also a wonderful surprise. Not the candied carrots that Ellie made, but a half-loaf loaded with candied rhubarb. Simon tucked into it first, greedily, and sucking his fingers free of every sweet little drop. He gathered from what Deborah told the others that the stuff was overtaking the garden in the rear of the cot; evidently the Dark One had no idea it was edible. It was Deborah's idea to leave a big dish of it waiting for the creature. "Might sweeten its temper," she said, and went to Sam for another dose of his healing powers.

The Dark One was still not back by the time the cot was all but completely dark except for the fire left banked for the morning. And so Simon went to sleep in a state of decidedly mixed emotions. Afraid for Ellie. Angry she hadn't freed him to come with her— he ignored the fact that she didn't have the key for his chains. She was smart, she should have thought of something! Hope she would bring back rescue. Fear that she would be lost out on the moor and never seen again.

But riding above everything else . . . the terror of the Dark One.

12

Nan was going to be very glad to be off this train. While they *were* in a First-Class compartment—Alderscroft would never pay for anything less—it was not a Parlor compartment. So the main advantages were some extra padding on the bench seats, no need to actually share the compartment with anyone, and enough room that Suki could move about a bit. The disadvantage was that it was a very hot day, and since this was a First-Class compartment, there were only windows to open on *one* side, the other side being taken up by the windowless wall on the corridor.

Suki alternated her time between having her head out the window and playing with the birds. She had conceived of the idea of "teaching" them some of the same tricks that dogs performed, and fortunately the birds thought this idea was highly amusing as well. The birds could and would do anything on the first command; the real question was how to adapt dog commands to them. "Beg" was easy enough; both birds could say "Pleeeeeease," in the most plaintive of tones. "Shake hands" was not difficult, and neither was "wave." "Sit" provided some challenges, until Neville solved the problem by squatting down as if he were in a nest. "Lie down" was obviously lie on the back. "Play dead" was to lie on the back with the head and neck stretched out and the feet tucked up against the body. Both birds thought "Roll over" was hilarious good fun. Nan finally got involved by teaching them both something Suki couldn't do because her hands were too small: balancing first Grey, then the much larger Neville, in a kind of headstand on the palm of her hand, where their heads were in her palm and her fingers supported their bodies in the headstand.

Not that the countryside was boring—it was extremely pretty. But it was also extremely *sunny*, and right now, Nan wanted off the train and into a room where she could get a sponge bath or give herself a cologne rub to cool off. Travel by train might be fast, but it was also dirty, and the sturdy dark brown linen suit she wore was definitely not best suited to the weather.

So it was with a great deal of relief that she felt the train slowing for Yelverton. She knew it was for Yelverton, because she had been obsessively keeping track of the stops.

"It's bigger than I thought," Sarah said with surprise, as she craned her neck out the window with one hand firmly on her hat to keep it from flying off.

"Yelverton is not that far from Plymouth," John replied. "Many people feel that it is worth a lengthy commute to live in the country. Suki, can you put the carriers on the floor for the birds?"

"Yessir," Suki said obediently.

By the time the train finally stopped at the platform, the entire party had gathered up belongings and were more than ready to exit. Nan was the first out, and immediately began looking up and down the platform for their promised transportation to the Rock Hotel. She noticed that there was a turntable at the far end of the station, and her curiosity was piqued. She'd never seen one in action, and it appeared that in order to go on to Princeton the locomotive had to be detached and re-hooked to the carriages . . . and for a moment she was distracted from her search.

But their transportation spotted them before she saw him. "Pardon me, miss," said someone behind her—

Well, her *ears* translated it to "pardon me, miss," but she had the feeling that if it had not been for Puck's "language lesson" she would not have been able to understand him at all.

"—be tha th' party Lord Alderscroft sent?"

"We are," Nan replied, as the rest of them gathered around her and the gentleman who had addressed her—who was dressed respectably, though not in recognizable livery, in a brown coat, trousers of a slightly lighter color, and a brilliant scarlet waistcoat.

He was holding his Derby in both hands and gazed toward John Watson deferentially.

"We are," John repeated, at which the man beamed.

"Well, then if tha'll coom this way." He took one hand off the hat brim and gestured, then moved off briskly.

"You all follow him, I'll organize the luggage and meet you," John told them. Suki didn't need to be told twice; she scampered after the man and caught up with him. Mary, Nan, and Sarah got a firm grip on their bird carriers and carpetbags and hurried their steps.

They caught up with him just as he rounded the corner of the station, and there, waiting at the street, was a coach with a signboard proclaiming *The Rock Inn* on the side. To Nan's relief, there was nothing else on the signboard but the name of the hotel in elegant Gothic letters, red outlined in gold on white. In her experience, when hotel coaches advertised the quality of their rooms or other amenities on their coaches, the accommodations rarely matched the descriptions.

The coach itself was of much older vintage than the sign, but it didn't look in disrepair, merely "well-used." And Nan didn't care; it was big enough for the five of them and all their luggage, and that was all that mattered. And to Suki's delirious delight, it was pulled by two enormous "Shire" horses, with thickly feathered feet, platter-sized hooves, and gentle eyes. Suki had wanted to be near and pet such horses since a previous trip to the country outside of London. She completely won over the coachman by standing near their noses with her hands firmly clasped behind her back and asking, "Please, may I pet them?" Which is, of course, the proper and respectful way to treat both a coachman and his horses. So while John directed the porters in loading their luggage, Suki was introduced to "Daisy" and "Dandy."

Eventually, they were all rolling down the uneven streets of Yelverton. It was a lot prettier than Nan had expected; most of the buildings were either made of gray stone or had had the stone plastered over and whitewashed. Many of them still had thatched roofs, although modern shingles were replacing those roofs rapidly. And as John had mentioned, there seemed to be a great many new houses—what he called, ironically, "suburban villas," the homes of prosperous businessmen who worked in Plymouth and spent an hour each way commuting on the train.

The main street was cobbled, but most of the side streets were not. It was, however, not at all long before they were pulling up to a two-storied structure that to Nan's eyes looked as if it must have once been someone's country house. But that must have been a good long while ago, since the bold brass letters proclaiming it to be *The Rock Inn* had been over the door for quite some time.

They all alighted as a porter appeared from the doorway to take care of the luggage.

Inside it was evident that this was a very old building. The ceilings were low, whitewashed plaster with exposed beams. The walls were whitewashed plaster, and the floor polished flagstones.

John was already in deep conversation with their host as the rest of them entered the first room, which appeared to be the public bar.

A lot quicker than Nan would have thought, she, Sarah, Suki, and the birds were established in their "room," which was rather larger than she would have anticipated. There were two beds plus a trundle for Suki, a lounge, three padded armchairs and a little table, a desk and desk chair, a dressing table and stool, a wardrobe and a blanket chest, and a washstand. They had their own (currently cold) fireplace. Nan was resigned to using a non-flushing toilet, but at least it was indoors, down the hall and at the bottom of the stairs. In the last country inn they had stayed at, the facilities were in a small, divided outbuilding in the stableyard. *And I am so spoilt. As a child I squatted with a bare bum in the corner of wherever. I didn't even have knickers to pull down.*

Suki immediately pulled out her trundle and flopped down on it.

The walls were whitewashed plaster; the floor was varnished wood, with scattered, hand-braided rugs; the curtains were a faded floral with lace trim that matched the coverlets on all three beds. And someone had followed Nan's directions for the birds to the letter. At the foot of each bed was a rectangular wooden umbrella stand. Newspapers had been spread beneath them, and two pairs of old, handle-less teacups had been bound into each end with some extremely clever rope-work. She let the birds out of their carriers and got the pitcher of water from the washstand, pouring them both drinks.

At that moment, the porters came up with their trunks. Alderscroft had supplied trunks for all of them, pointing out that *they* were not going to have to be moving the things around, porters would. Nan had given in, knowing she'd never win the argument with him.

When the trunks had been placed, Nan shut and locked the door. "I am having a quick wash and a change," she said firmly, already stripping off her jacket. "I am hot, and sticky, and I am not remaining that way a minute longer."

"Me too!" said Suki, jumping up off the bed.

It was not the first time that the three of them had shared a washbowl. There was *just* enough water in the two pitchers to get them all reasonably clean, and once all three of them had changed into much more comfortable cotton lingerie dresses, Nan unlocked the door, to find one of the hotel servants waiting patiently outside it with two cups of food for the birds. Chopped vegetables for Grey, and chopped offal for Neville.

"Thank you!" Sarah said, taking them. "We'll need more water and fresh towels, please."

The servant nodded, as if she had expected exactly that. "Chell fetch 'em for 'ee, Miss," she said. "Public room be open."

"Thankee." Nan actually *felt* things shifting around in her head to make what she was saying come out in the local dialect. "We'll just be lookin' in on our friends." She gestured to Sarah and Suki to come with her, and then moved down the corridor to the Watsons' room.

Mary answered the door in a lingerie dress of her own, and when she let them in, even Watson had changed to a much lighter suit and had his jacket off. "Hungry?" Nan asked. "I've been informed that the public room is open."

Her own stomach growled, and Mary Watson laughed. "That sounds to me as if there is no question as to what we should do next. Are the birds tended to?"

"As well as at home," Sarah confirmed. "And I'm perishing. Let's see what's on offer."

* * *

The Rock evidently was very popular with people making holiday excursions to "see Dartmoor," though the vast majority of them would never go further into the moors than a few hundred yards off the road. The public room was full, mostly with fit, young men (though there seemed to be a heavy contingent of locals in the adjacent taproom), and there were a few equally hearty-looking young women in sturdy linen walking suits, and even a couple brave souls in the hiking version of a bloomer suit!

Just as they were finishing the last of their drinks, one of the barmaids paused by their table. "Master Linwood would like to invite you to his private parlor," she said. "If you'll follow me?"

Nan glanced at Suki, and sure enough, Suki was starting to nod. The sticky toffee pudding she'd tucked into at the end of the meal probably had something to do with that. "Suki, do you need me to show you where our rooms are?" she asked.

Suki shook her head. *I can just follow Neville's thinks,* Nan heard in her own head.

Excellent, Nan replied the same way, and eased off the bench so Suki could get past her. Suki bade them all a polite goodnight, while the barmaid waited with just a tiny bit of impatience until the girl trotted off.

They followed their escort down narrow passages all the way to the back of the place, then up a set of stairs next to the kitchen. This proved to be the way to the landlord's private apartments, and they were ushered into a shabby-comfortable back parlor not unlike Sherlock's sitting room—except with fewer chemical smells, bullet holes, and laboratory equipment.

The room, with its worn brown leather furniture, plain whitewashed walls, and bare wooden floor, was uncompromisingly masculine—not that there wasn't just as much clutter as in a room decorated by a woman. But this was actual *clutter*, not attempts to decorate with all the latest frou-frous. Fishing flies in a case on a side table, a stack of poles in a corner, newspapers piled up under the table, scatterings of coins, a pocket knife and a half-formed carving. . . . Now that Nan was paying attention, she noticed one other thing missing: any sign of tobacco or tobacco products. Which made sense. This man was an Elemental Magician, and tobacco was basically a poison. It affected Earth and Air particularly; Fire Mages *could* smoke and get away with it; Water could but generally didn't because smoking didn't suit their natures. But Earth and Air were both affected badly by the stuff.

Harold Linwood himself did not appear until a few minutes later, although the barmaid made sure that they didn't need anything before she left them. When he finally came clumping up the stairs, he appeared much less harried than Nan would have expected.

He was older than Nan had thought, given she'd only seen a miniature version of him in the fireplace flames. Taller than John Watson, wearing a smock and moleskin trousers, with a full apron on which he was wiping his hands. "Harold Linwood, Earth Magician, at your service," he said, holding out his hand to John.

John rose and shook it. "I'm Doctor John Watson, Water Master; this is my wife, Mary, Air Master, and my friends Nan Killian, Spirit Magician and Psychic, and Sarah Lyon-White, medium and Spirit Master."

Linwood shook hands all around, though his eyes had widened when John introduced Nan and Sarah. "Well! Well, well, well! Spirit Mages! Well, well!" he said, sounding very much as if he couldn't think of anything else to say.

"Our little sister is also a Psychic, and we don't know if she has any bent toward magic," Nan continued. "She's very tired, so she went to bed. The two birds we brought are . . . intelligent."

"I'll reckon ye mean more'n that they can say 'Polly wants a cracker,' then," Linwood said.

Nan laughed. "Very much more. And thank you for the accommodations for them; what you supplied was perfect. I promise you that your linens and floors have nothing to fear from them. They are better behaved than many humans I could name."

Linwood laughed, and took a seat. "Naow, I dunno if there's anythin' to this business His Lordship sent you on—"

"Actually, we already know there is something odd going on," John Watson interrupted him. "The chief constable here in Yelverton believes that an unusual number of children have gone missing on the moors over the past four or five years. We just don't know why. Our only clue at the moment is a pair of children from near Sheepstor that vanished." He frowned. "Actually, we don't know at the moment if they are still missing. But we have to start somewhere."

"Well!" Linwood said, taken aback. "Well, well, well. Big doin's for wee little Yelverton. I'm fair ageest. Wust I would'a thought is them thievin' Travelers." His brow wrinkled. "But if thet's so, why hev' none on us—" He paused, obviously not wanting to insult them, but also skeptical that these *Londoners* would know about evil doings before the resident mages did.

"We talked to the Oldest Old One," Sarah said bluntly, eliciting a gasp from their host. "He said that magicians have been up to no good out on the moors for generations, and that plenty of them made themselves dens that are so well-guarded and hidden, that not even *he* can find them. He reckons that this is a new magician, but using one of these ancient dens to hide his work."

"Or her," Linwood put in. "No reason cain't be a witch." He pulled on his lower lip. "Every reason why't might be. Young 'un coulda took over her Grammar's cot. Old 'un could be workin' mischief outa spite, or t'keep 'ersel' young an' bowerly."

"No reason it can't be a woman," Nan agreed, although she was more than a bit skeptical about the notion that someone could use magic to keep herself young and attractive. . . .

But then again, she didn't really know all that much about magic, did she? And even then, it was only magic as practiced by ethical magicians. Maybe it *was* possible?

She just listened quietly as John Watson and Harold Linwood discussed all the local Elemental Mages that Linwood knew, consigning all that information to memory. Sarah, however, was taking notes.

"And where'll ye go from 'ere?" Linwood asked, when he had delivered all the information he had.

"Talk to the chief constable, and probably make a trip out to Sheepstor to talk to the parents of the missing boy and girl," John replied.

"Can any of you ride?" Linwood asked, in tones that suggested he thought it was unlikely that a bunch of London city-dwellers knew one end of a horse from another.

"All of us, including Suki," said Nan, dryly, before John could reply. "Quite well, in fact." She thought about mentioning the fact that Suki had taken to going out on one of the school ponies every Hunt day, intercepting the fox and carrying it over her saddlebow to safety, through terrain even the seasoned hunters would think twice about. She decided against the idea. These country people took their fox hunting seriously. She was just glad it wasn't Hunt season right now. "I'd venture to say that as far as Sarah, Suki, and I go, you'd be hard put to find a horse we couldn't handle."

"I wouldn't go that far for myself, but I can ride," John said.

"Father and I rode with the local Hunt," said Mary, with an amused glance at her husband.

"Well then, I'll loan tha' nags out of m' own stable," Linwood offered. And when John started to protest, the mage cut him off. "Reckon it's least I c'n do, given what His Lordship's payin' for." His eyes twinkled as he added, "Don' stin' thasselves in my housen. His Lordship's got a open purse."

Linwood promised to arrange for equipment needed to safely tramp over the moor as well; not just Ordinance Survey maps—which John providentially knew how to read—but compasses and sextants and other things that eventually blurred together in Nan's mind. No matter, both John and Mary knew what the landlord was talking about, so she dismissed these things for the moment. When the time came she'd learn how to use them.

Meanwhile, shadows lengthened outside the parlor windows; the sky moved from blue to red, to deep purple, and finally to black spangled with stars.

Finally Linwood looked up at the night sky outside the windows, coughed, and said, "'Scuse, but—"

"But you need to get back to keeping an eye on your establishment," John finished for him. "Please, lead back to the front of the hotel. We can find our way from there."

Linwood was only too happy to do that, but Nan wasn't quite ready to go to bed yet. At the stairs she paused. "Goodnight," she said to the Watsons. "Police station tomorrow, I assume?"

"That was my plan," John replied. He hesitated. "I was planning on going alone. . . ."

Sarah laughed and Nan waved a dismissive hand at him. "Unless you discover this chief constable is more amenable to taking mere females more seriously than most of his kind, that's probably best. You are John Watson, medical doctor, sent by Lord Alderscroft, and colleague of Sherlock Holmes. We, however, are delicate little flowers best shielded from unpleasantness."

Watson rubbed the back of his neck ruefully. "You are, sadly, correct."

"Well, we don't want the poor chief constable being distracted by the issue, so the best thing to do is for you to go alone, at least for now," Nan admitted. "On the bright side, that means we can sleep late and take a leisurely breakfast while you share bad tea and a stale biscuit with the police." She grinned wickedly as John winced and Mary giggled. "I'm going for a little walk around the grounds. I'll be up shortly, Sarah."

Sarah nodded, and as Nan headed for the front door, the three made their way up the stairs.

In both the taproom and the public room there were still good crowds, and checking the watch at her waist, Nan saw that there was still plenty of time before closing. The buzz of conversation and the faint aroma of ale followed her out the front door, where she paused, and took stock of the evening.

Scent told her there were roses growing somewhere nearby, but then, this was an English village in Devon in high summer, and it would have been more notable if there had *not* been roses. After all that sitting in trains, she definitely wanted to stretch her legs a bit, but as dark as it was and with no lights except the candle lanterns at the doors of the buildings on this street, she didn't want to go far. Living in London had certainly spoiled her. She was accustomed to gas laid on at the least, and the "best" rooms in this hotel were not equal to the comforts of their flat.

Exploring the neighborhood more completely could wait until morning, but it seemed to her that it would be a good idea to get some notion of the general layout of what appeared to be a building that had been much added upon over the years, and in a very haphazard fashion.

She set off on her walk in a leisurely fashion, taking great care with her footing. The last thing she wanted to do was to trip and tear this brand-new and rather delicate lingerie dress. As she walked, she took mental stock of the trunk she had packed. She was reasonably sure she had covered all possible contingencies—although it remained to be seen what Yelverton in particular and Dartmoor in general would make of the divided skirts and bloomer suits she and Sarah had brought.

She had not gotten past the first corner when she heard someone walking behind her.

This is a public house. It could be a customer on his way home.

Still, she put her hand carefully through the slit in her pocket and petticoat and got a firm grasp on the baton she had strapped to her thigh. In London—in some neighborhoods at least—she'd have had her Gurkha fighting knife there instead of the baton, but she didn't think she'd need anything that lethal in Yelverton. Still, she didn't like being anywhere unprepared, so when she and Sarah had dressed for the train trip this morning, she had strapped on her baton, and Sarah had taken her umbrella with the sharpened ferrule and the solid steel shaft. They'd allowed Suki to have her little knife as well; Nan's philosophy was that in a case like this, it was better to allow Suki to go armed and stress that she was not to use her knife unless Sarah and Nan had taken their own weapons out of hiding. She reasoned that if they forbade Suki to wear it, she'd disobey and wear it anyway, and then everyone would be shocked if she overreacted and pulled it out. But if they made her a part of "defending the family" she'd be more inclined to take her cues from Nan and Sarah, and *they* would know she was armed.

The footsteps following her were quite deliberate, and slowly catching up. She turned another corner, and the person behind her kept following. She didn't make the typical female mistake of trying to hurry; instead, she slipped the baton out of its sheath, maneuvered it out of her petticoat and skirt, and kept it ready at her side, all without breaking stride.

The follower—a man by the sound of the footsteps; heavy, solid, and without the distinct clicking sound that a woman's heels made on cobblestones—slowly closed the gap between them.

She turned the next corner. The man was nearly within touching distance. . . .

"Excellently done, Miss Nan," chuckled the familiar voice of Holmes. "If I had not been watching you closely, I would never have seen you slip out your weapon."

Nan breathed out the breath she had been holding and maneuvered the baton back where it belonged. "Thank you for the compliment, Sherlock," she replied, and turned to face him, if you could call peering through the starry darkness at a tall shadow "facing" someone. "You must have eyes like an owl."

"I've merely been away from artificial light since sundown," Holmes replied. "Now, before you ask, I am here in Yelverton because I too have a case here . . . and given that both your case and mine have unnatural elements to them, it seems rather more likely than not that our two cases coincide somehow."

"I thought you preferred to leave the esoteric cases to John," Nan said mildly.

Sherlock nodded slightly. "I assume that I can call on all of you, at need, since you are here."

"A fair assumption," she agreed.

"But even if our cases do not overlap, I can pursue the mundane aspects of yours without losing any time on mine. I would discuss it further with you, but . . . it's a very delicate matter that involves the reputations of several young women who took me into their confidence." She heard the hesitancy in Holmes' voice. There was, of course, the simple fact that Holmes very much enjoyed keeping information to himself and bringing it out like a conjuror at the perfect moment, but she got the impression that he really was concerned for those reputations.

"Tell us if you need to. If not, we have our own case we should be concentrating on," Nan replied. "We are investigating what appears to be a rash of missing children out on the moors."

"And this is why I am fond of you young ladies. You know how and when to keep secrets." Holmes' shadow nodded. "So I will be using my own methods to discover what is amiss here in Yelverton, and if I learn anything that pertains to your case, I know where to find you."

"Well, I'm very glad you're here and are willing to help us, even if we aren't on the same cases," Nan said gratefully. "Is there some place we can leave messages for you?"

Sherlock chuckled again. "Of course there is. Leave letters at the post office for 'Benjamin Hubert.' I'll be checking there every two or three days."

"John's going to be pleased and relieved, and thank you for letting me know you were here, Sherlock." Not that Nan thought John Watson had any need whatsoever of Sherlock, but just knowing that his friend and colleague was in the same town would give Watson an extra bit of confidence that would certainly not come amiss.

"My pleasure." Sherlock touched his hat . . . and somehow melted into the shadows.

I really need to learn how to do that.

She walked the rest of the way around the hotel without incident, though coming into the front door she had to step aside to let two men who were at the "hail fellow, well met" stage of intoxication step past her into the road and stagger homeward, singing. She didn't recognize the song. Their words were very slurred, and their voices—well, she'd heard donkeys that were more melodious.

She found Suki already dead asleep on her trundle, splayed out like a starfish. Sarah was still awake, but in bed, reading by the light of an oil lamp on her bedside table. She had thoughtfully lit the other one for Nan. She had taken down her blond hair but left it braided in two tails that fell over her shoulders.

"A maid unpacked our trunks," she whispered. "She put everything away in the wardrobe and chest."

"Not everything," Nan corrected, with a low laugh. "We'd have found her in a faint on the floor if she'd gotten under the false bottom." But that meant one less chore to handle, which was a good thing. She slipped out of her dress and hung it up, and pulled her nightdress out of the chest of drawers, wondering what the maid had thought on seeing such a gypsy-like garment in the belongings of a respectable young woman. *Well, it's a hotel. I'm sure the maids have seen things far more scandalous.*

The maid had scrupulously put her things on one side of the chest and wardrobe, Sarah's on the other, and divided them from each other with Suki's. A very clever arrangement.

Evidently the "best rooms" got extra special treatment even if the amenities were not outstanding.

As she doffed underthings and got into her nightdress, she did note a new addition, a covered pail under the washstand which a quick sniff told her held bleach-water. Well, if they were here long enough, that would definitely prove useful. And at least she and Sarah would not have to figure out how they were going to wash their monthlies. It appeared the hotel had provided for that.

Well, if they do that, then they'll do our laundry as well. That was a cheering thought. Back at their flat, Nan knew they were very much spoiled by Mrs. Horace, who sent all their laundry out to the laundry at the end of the block. She had assumed they'd have to figure out something here. "Is there a hamper for laundry?" she asked, holding up her bloomers in one hand and her chemise in the other.

"Yes, silly. This is a first-class hotel and we have 'best rooms.' It's over there," Sarah replied, pointing. "The maid very helpfully told me that anything we leave in it will be washed, dried, starched and bleached if needed, and put away for us within the day."

"The fewer things we have to worry about, the better we'll be able to concentrate on our job." She dropped her underthings into the hamper and sat cross-legged on the bed. Suki slept on, oblivious. "Sherlock is here."

"Oh! Did he get the Lion's message?" Sarah put down her book immediately.

"I don't know. He did say he has a case here—and he didn't say that it was related to Moriarty's gang, which probably means the trail has gone cold there, so he's keeping busy with this new project. He also said it involves the reputations of more than one young lady, and that there are 'unnatural' aspects to it." She waited a moment for all that to sink in. "He thinks our case and his *might* be linked, so while he works his, he's going to keep ours in mind."

"Well, it's good to know he's here. I know the Watsons will be relieved." Sarah set the book aside, now much more interested in whatever Nan had to say than in what was between the covers of her book. "Although I don't know why John thinks he's any less of a detective than Holmes is."

"Because he's naturally modest. Which is a very good thing for an Elemental Master to be," Nan pointed out. "Now, since you and I are still awake, I think it would be a good idea for us to take advantage of the fact that we are relatively rested to have a quick look around in the spirit realm."

"I agree," Sarah replied.

Approximately an hour later, they both emerged from the spirit realm together, without much to show for their effort, except an acquaintance with the few local spirits. There were fewer now; many of them were mere shadows of their former selves, and Sarah had coaxed as many of them as she could across the threshold of her Portal. Three of those had been in this very hotel. It was impossible to tell just what they had been in life, as they were mere sketches of their former selves, and what could be made out of their clothing had not offered much in the way of clues.

No matter, Sarah and Nan had spoken soothingly to them, and they seemed more lost than anything else. It had not taken much to get them to cross over.

"Well, that was a good night's work, even if we didn't accomplish anything on the case," Sarah sighed.

"I wish we knew more about Sherlock's case." Nan sat up and took her own hair down—which she had forgotten to do—laying the pins carefully on her bedside table. "We might at least have learned something pertaining to his rather than ours."

"Well, that's unlikely until and unless we have more information." Sarah yawned. "We can range further afield tomorrow. Right now, the best thing we can do is sleep."

13

Simon woke up from a nightmare in which the Dark One pursued him across the moors. He leapt out of sleep with a yelp of terror, only to discover the Dark One leaning over him, staring down intently at him, while all the rest of the prisoners huddled as far away from them both as their chains would permit. A scream died in his throat as fear choked him.

"Simon," the Dark One hissed, looming over him ominously. "Where be tha' sister?"

Simon could only stare at the darkness inside the Dark One's cowl, the ash of pure panic choking him and making it impossible to speak. He tried to say "Es dunno" twice and couldn't even manage so much as a squeak. All he could do was shake his head frantically.

"Where be tha' fambly?" the Dark One persisted. It reached out its hand and seized Simon's shoulder in an iron grip, closing its fingers so tightly that the bone grated in its socket and Simon gasped in pain. And it was the pain that startled an answer out of him.

"Sh-sh-sheepstor!" he finally managed to stutter.

The Dark One let him go, and he fell back on the mattress. "If tha' has lied—" it said threateningly.

Simon shook his head again. The Dark One straightened up, turned, and left the room.

"Simon, tha' gormless asneger!" Robbie whispered angrily from across the room. "Tha' cawbaby dawcock! Tha's set Dark One on tha' fambly!"

Tears spilled out of Simon's eyes and his mouth worked without him being able to utter a single word. He hadn't meant to! He was *scared*! The Dark One had frightened the words out of him! But he couldn't manage to say a single word. Instead, he broke out into hysterical sobs, and buried his face in his blanket. Dimly, he heard the others palavering over what he'd just done. Clearly they saw him as a traitor to his own family.

And he was! Now all he could do was imagine what would happen—how the Dark One would come to the cottage, confront Mother there alone, and—

Well, he wasn't sure what the Dark One would do to Mother or Pa, but it would probably be horrible. And what if Ellie was there? What if she *wasn't* there? Would the Dark One hurt Mother and Pa to make them talk? Would the Dark One just kill them and wait for Ellie?

All the horrible things that could happen, and vague hints of things he couldn't quite imagine, swarmed around him, and he cried until his cheeks were sore and his nose was running so much snot he couldn't breathe except out of his mouth.

Finally, he felt someone grab his shoulder, and froze again. The Dark One was back! What would it do?

But it wasn't the Dark One. It was Robbie.

"Tine tha' unket mouth, tha' gurt noodle," Robbie said wearily. "None on us'ns kens tha' fambly name. Dark One don't ken, neither. Dark One ain't goin' door t'door, arsking 'bout thee an' Ellie, naow, is it? Think! What'd 'appen if it went clompin' 'round Sheepstor, a-lookin' like it do?"

Slowly, Simon shook his head.

"Even if it c'n make itself look like 'armless ol' Gatfer, it ain't goin' about arskin' arter uns. 'Cause if it did, people's want ter know how it knowed tha' was gone, it bein' a stranger an' all an' *not* a constable. An' *why* it wanted ter know. So tine tha' mouth, an' stop blubberin'. Get tha' lazy lump outen bed an' help wi' sweepin.'"

Simon wiped his eyes and nose off with his sleeve, and dragged himself out of bed. The other children had already pulled their mattresses into the middle of the room. The new schedule, as determined by the two girls, was for the room to be cleaned *before* anyone ate, rather than afterward. Resentfully, he was pretty sure that was because of him, because he spent so much time huddled up on his blanket. They'd already threatened to withhold his breakfast if he didn't start helping.

It wasn't fair.

Nothing was fair. Ellie should have taken him with her. It wasn't *his* fault she'd decided to run! And she clearly hadn't gone to get help, otherwise help would be here already! Wouldn't it? *Wouldn't it?*

But as he helped shake out the blankets and move the mattresses back as Sam finished sweeping where they'd been, his resentment turned again on himself. Maybe the reason Ellie hadn't brought help was because she was dead. Maybe she fell into an old mine and broke her neck. Maybe she blundered into a mire and drowned. Maybe she got lost and was wandering with no idea where she was. Maybe a wildcat or a wild dog killed and ate her!

All these dismal thoughts set him to crying again, but he did it as quietly as he could, because he didn't want Robbie to yell at him for being a cawbaby again.

His spirits sank so low that at that moment, he just wished he was dead. He was never leaving this awful place—except as a barely breathing body the Dark One would haul out to leave for wild beasts on the moor. Everything was horrid. And the only thing he had to look forward to was the food.

When the room was put to rights, the food came. There was always plenty of it now. The Dark One didn't seem to care anymore how many loaves were baked, or how much vegetable stew was made. It didn't even seem to care that in the morning and at night one of the loaves each of them got now had sugar-syrup drizzled over it. Simon always saved his sugared loaf for last, though today it was sprinkled with the salt from his tears as well.

But today, as soon as they'd finished eating and drinking, the Dark One came abruptly back into the room, and Simon knew what that meant.

The Dark Sleep.

He whimpered with terror as the Dark One stood there, waiting for all of them to take their places on their beds. Even Jess and Deborah, because, like Sam, the Dark One left them with enough strength when the Dark Sleep was over to do their work—at least after a brief rest—but whatever it was the Dark One was taking from them, he wasn't going to exclude the girls.

When they were all in place, the Dark One raised its arms.

And Simon dropped into blackness.

It was awful. Like he'd been bound hand and foot and blindfolded, while something drained everything out of him. Energy. Life. Even thoughts. Everything was held in a suffocating paralysis, and all he could do was endure in a complete and utter panic, alone in the dark, with the sense that *this time* he would never come out of it. *This time* the blackness and the paralysis and the terror would go on forever and ever.

But then, just as abruptly as it began, the Dark Sleep ended. He could move again. He could open his eyes. But as always, the Dark Sleep left him too drained to move much, head muzzy, impossible to hold on to a single thought for long. The Dark One stood there for a long moment, while a distant part of him wondered what it was thinking. Then it turned and left the room, pausing only long enough to pull Jess and Deborah out of their beds and drag them into the main room of the cot to start their work again.

It knows where Mother and Pa are. . . .

But then, he realized, that wasn't true.

He'd told the thing they lived in Sheepstor. But they didn't. They lived well outside of Sheepstor on the moor.

And with that realization, relief and real sleep came.

Suki was up at the break of dawn, as she always was. Reasoning that if Suki could take care of herself on the streets of London, she could certainly take care of herself on the streets of a Devon village, Nan sleepily gave her permission to get dressed, get breakfast downstairs, and go exploring, but asked her to leave an order with the kitchen for food for the birds later. Hardboiled eggs in the shell for Neville and chopped veg for Grey would do very well for now, and Neville could always hunt mice and bugs for himself later if he craved meat. Suki was so quiet about getting dressed that Nan was asleep again before she left.

She and Sarah both woke a couple of hours later, well in time to pick something as cool but not as delicate as a lingerie dress to wear for the day. Their white shirtwaists with the sleeves rolled up as a man's would be for the sake of coolness showed probably a great deal more bare arm than Yelverton was used to, but they *were* visitors, and from London to boot, so Yelverton would probably gossip behind hands and show a polite face in public. It was the divided gray linen skirts that would cause a stir, if anyone noticed. Nan was always amused by that—the polite fiction that women were some sort of solid object from the waist down never ceased to give her the giggles.

Neville and Grey were still on their perches, so they hadn't felt the need to supervise Suki either. Nan and Sarah were dressed and ready to go down to breakfast when a polite tap on their door signaled the arrival of Mary Watson.

Mary had quite sensibly donned a similar outfit to theirs, although hers had more modest sleeves, buttoning at the wrist. "John already got up and snatched a rusk and some tea and was off to the police station," she said with amusement. "Where's Suki?"

"She went off to explore." Nan paused a moment, and carefully sought for Suki's mind. *Hungry again?* she asked, and got back a wordless affirmation. "She'll join us for a second breakfast."

"Well, with luck, so will John," Mary replied, and they all went down.

Breakfast was served to order in the public room, and Suki and John both joined them at about the same time.

They were all less interested in the food than they were in what John had to say, which was quite a lot, and very detailed, when it came to the case files the chief constable had been keeping.

"So, that's almost a full dozen missing children *that he knows of*," Mary mused. "How did this happen?"

"Why is no one up in arms, you mean?" John countered. "Oh, he reported his findings to his superiors, and they told him not to bother. Because all these children are children of the poor. One of them was only reported missing because the old devil that employed him as a shepherd was incensed that he'd 'run off' and left the sheep unwatched. The blackguard assumed that the lad had eloped— rather than assuming that something had happened to him!"

Mary Watson's brows knitted with disapproval. "Well, what about the couple that sent us the letter?"

"So far as the chief constable knows, the children are still missing. So that's a place to start. I'm afraid we won't have much luck with any of the others; their parents are mostly gone from the area now, if they still had any. Several of them were orphans, and about to be sent to the workhouse, so there is no one that cares about them. And if they had any possessions at all that we could have used to try to trace them magically, those possessions were all on their persons when they went missing."

Sarah had been taking all this down in her neat hand, having pushed her plate aside.

"Well, my news will cheer you. Holmes is in the village on a case of his own he thinks might overlap with ours. His involves young women, and I surmise from the little he told me that they are not missing, but have been . . ." she paused for delicacy, ". . . I'm going to guess, *interfered with*, given that he was concerned about their reputations. But it seems there are some outré elements to his case as well as ours. He finds it unlikely that there are two cases involving magic in the same area are that are not somehow related, and he wants us to keep him apprised, as he will us."

John perked up quite a bit. "By Jove, there's luck! Did you encounter him when you took your walk last night?"

"I did indeed," Nan smiled. "Sarah will leave our notes for him to collect at the Post Office, and then—where do we go from here?"

"Sheepstor, to interview the parents and let them know we are on the case. We'll take advantage of our host's offer of mounts," John replied.

John went off to make the arrangements, while Nan made sure the birds were fed and ready to travel, Sarah went to leave her notes at the Post Office for Sherlock to collect, and Mary Watson arranged for an abbreviated picnic lunch that could be packed by the horses. No packed, fancy hampers or leisurely lunch while they pretended to paint today—but after all, they were not here on a holiday. Nan was just glad she, Sarah, and Suki had all worn their divided skirts. She very much doubted that the horses that would be supplied by the inn would have sidesaddles.

And she was right. The four horses and sturdy moor pony that were led out for them had ordinary astride saddles. The stableman looked more than a little shocked to see the three women and the little girl mount astride as easily as a man (and without using a mounting block) but Nan reckoned that was his problem, not hers.

She was no judge of horseflesh, but the horse she'd been given didn't seem inclined to shenanigans, and that was all she asked of a mount. Although she and Sarah seldom rode these days, both of them, like Suki, had grown up with the ponies provided by Alderscroft to the school, and by the time they were out of the village and following the track that led to Sheepstor, it all was second nature again—though her leg muscles were protesting, and she knew she would be paying for this by tonight.

Once they were out of the village and on the moors proper, she suddenly understood how easy it would be to get lost out here. The moors stretched out on either side of the track, rolling hills covered with grasses, native moor plants and low bushes, occasional clumps of trees, and no roads, not even a path in sight. One hill or clump of rocks looked very much like the next to her eyes. She had thought that the land around Criccieth in Wales was wild, but there, at least, if you looked hard enough, there was always some sign of human life in the distance. Here, there was nothing. And they were on what passed for a road!

Grey and Neville flew in front of them for a bit, but soon got bored, and came back to ride on Nan and Sarah's shoulders. Suki amused herself by seeing what she could make her pony do, without getting out of sight of them.

But there was so much . . . space . . . out here. It was a little frightening, and at the same time, invigorating. And peaceful; she could see why people came here for walking tours, although for the life of her she could not imagine what they found to paint if they were artists.

There was no wind; there were, however, larks overhead, singing their hearts out as they flew, as there had been in Wales. There was a lot of other wildlife as well—plenty of birds, though she mostly heard rather than saw them. Rabbits and hares crossed the track before and behind them. She was fairly certain she heard sheep in the far distance, and once a herd of moor ponies came briefly into sight before moving over the crest of a hill and out of view again. The air smelled faintly of flowers, strongly of grass warming in the sunlight, slightly of dust. The horses were content enough with the pace that John set, a brisk walk. *He must have learned to ride in Afghanistan,* she thought. *If he hadn't already known by then.* It was curious, she tended to think of him as a creature of London, more at home on his own two feet or in a cab, and the sight of him on horseback was a bit disconcerting at first.

She didn't wonder if Sherlock could ride; she had yet to discover very much that man couldn't do.

Sheepstor wasn't so much a "village" as two clusters of houses, one around the parish church, and a second cluster several hundred yards away, almost on the edge of a great reservoir. And there was a manor off to the opposite side of the church from the second cluster, also several hundred yards away. Perhaps two dozen families in all lived here, aside from whoever owned the manor. She couldn't tell from the road if there actually *was* anyone at the manor, but there was activity all around the houses. Women were hanging clothing out, people were working in their gardens, or walking on the paths. As they rode in, the birds having alighted on the girls' shoulders some miles back, John made the intelligent decision to head for the church and the rectory, since the parish priest would probably be the fount of all information here.

They found him in his garden, assiduously picking caterpillars off his cabbages. He was an older man, with a head full of gray, curly hair, in dark trousers and a shirt and waistcoat—clerical collar and all—with his sleeves rolled up. Neville immediately flew down from Nan's shoulder, and stalked down the row to give him a little "help" with his task. The priest looked up at the sound of hoofbeats to find himself staring directly into Neville's black eyes, which were fastened on the caterpillar in his hand.

"My word!" was all he could manage, when Neville hopped three times to reach him and snatched the insect out of his hand.

"Good morning, padre," John said, tipping his hat. "I'm Doctor John Watson; this is my wife Mary; and my good friends and helpers are the Lyon-White sisters, Sarah, Nan, and Suki, and—"

"Doctor John Watson!" the elderly man exclaimed, climbing to his feet. "*The* Doctor John Watson? Intrepid companion of the late Sherlock Holmes? My word!"

"Well—yes—" Watson began.

"Are you here about the missing children? Helen and Simon

Byerly?" the priest asked eagerly. "Maryanne Byerly told me she had written to Sherlock Holmes before I could tell her that he was, sadly, with us no more, and I didn't have the heart to tell her Holmes had met his fate—"

"That's precisely why we're here," Watson replied with great relief. "This is making things much easier, padre. Can you tell us anything?"

"Where are my manners?" The poor fellow really was flustered—probably as much by the unexpected visitors as by the fact that one of them was famous. "Please, come into the rectory. I'll have my housekeeper make us some tea—I don't suppose you'd care for anything else—"

One look at the man's somewhat worn trousers told Nan that the poor priest's offer of hospitality would probably leave him with a gaping hole in his budget if they took him up on his offer, and John, student of Holmes as he was, had undoubtedly noted the same thing. "Actually, water would be preferable to tea on such a hot day," he replied, and the priest's relief at that made Nan feel great sympathy with him.

"We have a lovely well, spring-fed," he replied, and gestured toward his home. "Will your horses be all right tied up?"

"They should be fine if you can spare some buckets to water them; we'll tie them in the shade of that shed over there, well away from your garden for the sake of your cabbages," John replied, and smiled. "And our pet raven is taking your place in ridding the garden of pests."

"My word, so he is! And he's your pet? Remarkable!" Only then did he notice Grey. "And you have a parrot as well! Can she talk?"

"I can talk, can you fly?" Grey replied, and laughed. The priest actually clapped his hands with glee.

"Remarkable!" he said. "Remarkable! Please, let's go in and be comfortable."

The housekeeper met them at the door, very much in a ruffle about the unexpected visitors, and fussing worriedly that she had nothing to serve them. John soothed her with his most professional manner—Nan could easily see why he was popular with his patients—and assured her that glasses of water would be just ideal.

The reverend led the way into a parlor that was as scrupulously clean as it was austere: white-painted walls, with a few small pictures on them, plain woodwork, two braided rugs on the floor, an ancient brown sofa, a matching chair at the hearth, and a dozen rush-seated ladderback chairs around a large table, showing that the room was probably used quite often for meetings of various parish groups. The only luxury in it was an upright piano whose yellowed ivory keys were a testament to its age. The real ornaments were bouquets of common garden flowers in mismatched vases of varying age. The priest nodded at it as they chose seats—John and Mary side by side on the hard horsehair sofa, Nan and Sarah on rush-seated ladderback chairs, and Suki on a stool. He gestured apologetically at the piano. "This is a very poor parish, as you might assume. I took degrees in both music and divinity, so I play the organ as well as tend to all the other duties here. Oh, what I am I thinking! I never introduced myself. Father Donald Shaw, at your service."

The housekeeper brought in a tray of glasses and filled them from an ancient pitcher. They all shook hands, and the priest took a seat on a third ladderback chair. "Well now, I don't know the Byerlys very well. Nobody in Sheepstor does, although that was not always the case. I knew Roger's mother, Sally Byerly; she was still alive and in the cottage when I first came here. Everyone in Sheepstor used to come to her for remedies for their ailments and those of their animals. The old woman—Sally Byerly that was—had one of those freehold cottages built for her by all of her friends here in the village, on some fundamentally waste land that belonged to the manor—"

"Excuse me—freehold cottages?" Nan said politely. "What's that?"

"It's an old custom out here. If you can erect an entire cottage between sunrise and sundown without the owner of the land it's on stopping you, it and everything you can enclose in a wall around it is yours," he explained. "Obviously Sally and her husband were very popular, and when the squire turned them out of their old cottage here in the village to give it to his children's old nurse, there was some hard feeling. So when he and his bailiff and all the people at the manor who *would* have put a stop to the doings were away, the villagers banded together and built a freehold for them. Obviously, they took land that wasn't being used for anything, but the squire was *that* put out about it, though if you ask me, I must speak and say he only got what he had coming to him. Unchristian as that sounds—"

"My aunt and uncle are missionaries, and they would agree with you," Sarah replied, and the old man brightened and ran his hand over his crop of white curls. "It was wrong of him to evict someone else from their cottage. If he'd wanted to give a cottage to the nurse, he should have had one built specifically for the woman."

"Well, picking waste land *and* land they could build on without anyone noticing it until it was too late meant that they were quite far from the village, though, you see," he continued. "So their son really was never *part* of the village; there was no one to apprentice him. As for farm work, the squire would *never* hire him out of sheer spite, and no one else dared to for fear of the squire, so once he was full grown, he went off to foreign parts to find a job in a factory."

"Foreign parts," obviously, meant *anywhere not here*.

"Then he had a terrible accident and lost a hand, and came back to live with his mother. Now that would not have set the village against him—well, not *against* him, exactly, but . . . well . . . when he brought back a wife who had a cultured way of speaking, and wasn't from *here*, well, people thought he thought he was a cut above them, and kept their distance." The priest ruffled his own hair again. "I heard she was a teacher somewhere, but they would never come out and *tell* me anything about her other than her name, Maryanne. Very close-mouthed, she is. Polite, oh my yes, but close-mouthed. They only had two children, the ones that are lost. Simon is eight, or thereabouts, and Helen is eleven. I understand she teaches them herself, and the few times I have seen them, I have asked them the usual catechism questions that they should be able to answer at their age, and they gave me the correct answers. They were quite bright and seemed as well-educated as the children here in the village. The entire family comes to services every Sunday like everyone else. Helen takes after her mother; dark, and very responsible. Simon is a little devil, I can tell he's bursting to make mischief during services, but his mother keeps him under control."

"Do you know why their mother was schooling them herself?" Sarah asked.

The reverend shrugged. "We only have a day school in one of

the cottages for the handful of village children, and between the two of us, the teacher isn't very good. In fact, she's only three years older than the oldest of the children in the school. I assume Maryanne thought she could make a better job of it *and* have the children right there to be useful at the same time. I cannot find it in my heart to blame her. We're poor, and she wouldn't be the first person in the village to keep her children out of school in order to get some useful work out of them."

This was painting a very familiar picture to Nan—things weren't that different here in Sheepstor than in the poorer neighborhoods of London. Plenty of children got no further than 1-2-3 A-B-C before their parents found them work or employed them in their own labors, or kept them home to mind the younger ones while the mother worked.

"One offers what help one can, but . . . Maryanne did not precisely *rebuff* me, but she did make it very clear that help was not wanted, and charity forced on someone is no charity at all." Reverend Shaw sighed. "So that was all I really knew until, three weeks ago, Roger came tearing into the village just at dawn with a story of how the children had gone out on the moors and hadn't come home at sunset."

"And the village went looking for them?" John asked.

"Well, of course! Everyone who could be spared, and a few who couldn't, but left their duties anyway. But it's Dartmoor. There are mires, I've heard of feral dogs, there are rumors of wildcats, and there are certainly old mines to fall into, and if you get lost, it's not easy to find your way again, you see, because there isn't much in the way of landmarks. We all went out and searched. Even the old squire forgot his feud and brought out his hounds, but . . . nothing. There had been storms sweeping through all afternoon and evening, and the rain just washed out any scent there was." The priest sighed. "We kept it up for three days, but after that . . . there really was no point. Maryanne evidently decided she was going to write to Holmes, apparently, but the first I knew of it, she had traded a little glass bead necklace to my housekeeper for a penny stamp, she'd sent Roger all the way into Yelverton to talk to the chief constable there and mail it, and it was too late to stop her."

Nan sipped her water, then spoke. "If that's truly all you can tell us, then we should interview the Byerlys ourselves."

"That would probably be best, although to be honest I really don't know that there is anything you can do that we haven't already done. . . ." Once again, Father Shaw seemed undecided about something. "I should probably show you the way, but I haven't a horse or a pony myself—"

"No need, padre," John replied, pulling an Ordinance Survey map out of the inside pocket of his jacket. "This and a compass is all an old hand like me needs."

"Oh, of course, you were an old campaigner, I recall from your stories. Afghanistan, wasn't it?" Father Shaw said with relief. "Let me get my own map. I promise you it's accurate to the foot, and I can mark yours to match."

He hurried away and returned quickly with an Ordinance Survey map of his own. "This parish has few people. Some of them are very scattered abroad, not just the Byerlys—my predecessor thought it prudent to mark every cottage on a proper map in case he had to direct someone else or guide a visitor. Here, let's take them both to the table. I've brought a pencil for you as well."

Maps compared, all the houses of Sheepstor parish laid out (including the Byerly cottage), there was nothing left but to get on their way. As they filed out the door, Neville flew up from the garden and landed on Nan's shoulder. "All clear, guv'nor!" he announced, looking straight at Reverend Shaw, radiating satisfaction.

"My word! He talks as well!" the priest said, eyes wide with astonishment.

"Yes, and he was telling you he's cleared out your cabbage caterpillars," Nan replied, and took Neville's beak in two fingers to turn his head to face hers. "Did you steal any strawberries while you were there?"

"Maaaaaaaaybe," Neville replied cagily.

Reverend Shaw smiled.

"If he has cleared out those pesky caterpillars and saved my old knees, he is welcome to strawberries as well as my thanks," the good father said with gratitude. Neville laughed, sounding very like Nan.

Map in hand, horses collected, they were soon on their way, leaving the plain track at the second—barely visible—trace, a deviation marked only by a small cairn of stones at the side of the track.

"Do us a favor, and scout ahead for a cottage, will you?" Nan asked of Neville once they were off the track.

"Arm," Neville demanded, and obligingly she held out her arm for him to walk down. With a heave, she threw him into the air, and he labored upward and forward, becoming a small black silhouette in the sky. There he hung, keeping just ahead of them, for about three quarters of an hour. And about the time Nan would have hoped they would spot the cottage, he came winging back and landed again on her shoulder.

"House," he said.

"I'm happy to hear that," John called from the front of the group. "That tallies with my navigation."

They crested a hill, and spotted a small, thatched, gray stone cottage, with a lean-to shed against one wall, and a matching stone wall around it. There was a garden within the wall, and a woman working in it. There was a goat tethered to a post by a long rope, well out of reach of the garden. Their movement caught her attention; she stood up, shading her eyes with her hand, and waited for their approach.

"Mrs. Byerly?" John called out as soon as they were within hailing distance.

She made her way to the gate in the wall, but did not open it. "I'm Maryanne Byerly," she called back. "How may I assist you, sir?"

The very first thing that Nan noticed was that Maryanne Byerly did not speak with the "countrified" drawl that everyone else around here but Father Shaw had used. In fact, she would have taken Mrs. Byerly for a graduate of the Harton School, so well-spoken was she. The second thing that she noticed was that the woman's skirt, apron, and blouse, though threadbare and visibly patched, were painfully clean. And the last thing was that Maryanne Byerly was a beauty.

Beneath the cloth kerchief she wore, her hair was the same blue-black as Neville's neck-feathers. Her finely sculpted face would have prompted the artists Nan knew to beg her to let them draw her. And her cornflower-blue eyes, though they were puffy with weeping, were like a pair of blue stars.

No wonder the little brown hens of Sheepstor hate her, she thought, and looked back at Sarah, who nodded. Clearly they had had the same thought.

"I'm Doctor John Watson—" Watson began, in answer to her question.

Maryanne Byerly gasped, and clasped her hands together under her chin. "Sherlock Holmes' great friend! Did he get my letter? Is he coming?"

John dismounted and handed the reins to Mary, before walking to Mrs. Byerly and reaching for her hand. She gave it to him without hesitation, and he held it carefully. "Mrs. Byerly, I am here, because he cannot be. I lost my great friend in Germany at the hands of that evil fiend, Professor Moriarty. But when I read your letter to him, I knew he would have wanted to help you, and so I and my friends came in his stead."

Maryanne's eyes began to gleam wetly and a moment later two tears trickled down her cheeks.

She even cries beautifully.

"I'm so—" she stammered.

"My dear lady, do not be concerned for me. Your children are gone, and yours is the greater grief. May we come in, and see what we may do about this dire situation?"

As ever, Watson's "bedside manner" won the day.

When the horses were seen to (bits slipped, reins tied to posts alongside the wall, but outside it, so they could graze without getting into the garden), they all crowded into the main room of the little cottage. This room, with its stone walls, flagstoned floor, wooden shutters over glassless windows, held a wooden table, two benches, three stools, a cupboard and a kitchen counter under one of the windows, and not much more. There was a loft above, and a boxed-in area beneath it just big enough to hold a bed and perhaps a clothes chest. Nan, Sarah, and Suki mostly just got as far out of the way as possible to allow John and Mary Watson to take the lead. And shortly after they had all found something to sit on, as if by magic, Roger Byerly appeared at the door.

"Es bain't found nawt, m'love," he said wearily, as he appeared on the threshold. He looked *terrible*, as if he had not slept in weeks, which probably accounted for why he hadn't noticed four horses and a pony tied up along his wall. "Es—" And then he stopped, and stared at all of them.

Roger was just as handsome, in the moor manner, as his wife was beautiful. He had brown hair, cut roughly, and wore the usual canvas smock and canvas trousers. In him, the usual features of the locals were refined, and his dark brown eyes were particularly fine. Not even the fact that his right arm ended in a stub detracted from his looks. Once again, Nan completely understood some of the attitude of the locals—particularly the women—some of whom had probably had hopes of catching this fine fellow for themselves.

"'Oo's this, then?" he asked, bewildered.

"This is John Watson and his helpers," Maryanne replied. "You remember, I read you his stories about Sherlock Holmes. Master Holmes has met with a terrible accident, but the doctor is here to help us in his stead."

"Thank God!" the man replied, and sat down heavily, just staring at them all. He was either too worn to speak, or too dumbfounded by the company he found himself in, or both, but after that, Maryanne spoke for both of them.

And the first thing she said, tears pouring down her face, was, "Oh, Doctor—I am afraid I have murdered my babies!"

14

"...And I was so *furious* I drove them out of the house and onto the moor, and told them not to come back until they had foraged enough for all of us to have a feast," Maryanne said between clenched teeth, with tears streaming down her cheeks. She was too self-controlled to wail, but Nan sensed that if she had been alone, she would have. There was complete silence in the little room as she spoke; it was quiet enough that the steady munching as the horses cropped grass was clearly audible. "I drove them out, because I knew if they stood there with that gormless expression on their faces, I would completely lose my sanity and beat them until they were black and blue. I should have known better. I should have *been* better. I taught school for four years before I met Roger. I should have been able to handle my own children better."

John Watson reached out and took her hand and patted it, as her husband put his arm awkwardly around her shoulders and held her. "You were weary, and very hungry, and Reverend Shaw told me he considered your Simon to be a little monkey of a mischief-maker. You only taught girls, am I correct?"

She did not withdraw her hand, though she used her free hand to wipe the tears away as she nodded.

"Then you were ill-prepared to handle a boy, particularly a lively one with a penchant for deviltry," John soothed. "You let your hunger and your own temper get the best of you for a single moment, but you did *not* beat them black and blue, and you sent them out where, unless I am wrong, you thought them safe and where they really wanted to be in the first place." He paused, perhaps waiting to see if she would stop weeping, then went on. "As it happens, I have just come from a discussion with the chief constable at Yelverton about this very situation of yours."

"Naowt 'elp that pinswell's been," mumbled Roger, flushing with anger.

"Actually, more help than you think," John corrected. "He has been seriously alarmed at the number of children who have gone missing on the moor this past four years, and has been begging his superiors to give him the men to attempt to do something about it. It is those superiors in Tavistock who have been no help at all."

"*What?*" sputtered Roger, and "There are *more*?" gasped his wife.

"Many more. Mostly the children of Travelers and casual laborers," John told them. "A few were employed by farmers, and it was presumed they ran away to avoid hard work. Most of the rest were orphans left on the parish, about to be sent to the workhouse, who left their villages on their own—but never arrived elsewhere. No one bothered to look for any of them to discover they, too, were missing, except the chief constable." John nodded at their shocked faces; Maryanne's tears had dried right up, and Roger had gone white as bleached linen. "There is a very dark pattern there. And Roger, I am going to ask you something that is very pertinent to these disappearances. How long have you known that you can—err—" he glanced at Nan.

"Eh lad, 'ow long has 'ee knowed 'ee can see futher into a millstone than most?" Nan asked.

Roger turned startled eyes on her, as if he had forgotten she was even there, and was shocked to see her sitting next to his hearth with a raven perched on her shoulder. With that question, she could tell without reading his mind that she had gone from "inconsequential girl with the Important Man" to "Oh dear Heavens, she's witchy!"

"Me Grammar an' me Ma—" he choked out, and shook his head. "Cham not much better nor a bee-boy. Grammar, she had the Sight and Ma, she were herb-wise—"

"And there it is," said John, and nodded. "We all know certain things run in Travelers' blood. At least one, possibly more, of the orphans came from families with known wise women in the past. We think now the missing children all have this in common. They have the Sight and the Blood and they were lured away because of it."

"But 'ow—"

Mary Watson whistled, and a trio of Air Elementals, as pretty as butterflies and naked as babies whisked in the open window to dance expectantly before her at eye level. A certain shimmer about them told Nan that Mary Watson had ordered her Elementals to reveal themselves to any magician.

Roger gasped and crossed himself. His wife looked at his shocked face, then to the Watsons, bewildered. Clearly Roger could see them, but she could not.

"We have the Blood and the Sight too," John Watson explained to Roger. "We sensed that you had it before we came here thanks to the letter you carried to the Post Office. That is why we are here."

Roger fainted.

It took some convincing of Maryanne Byerly, once Roger had been revived, that magic really *did* exist, and the five of them *were* magicians, but it turned out the easiest way was for Nan to read Maryanne's mind—with her permission, of course. Once Nan recited a list of things that only Maryanne—not even her husband—knew, she was convinced.

"But this doesn't help anything!" the poor woman finally cried, helplessly. "You know *why*, but not how, or who, or where they are, or if they are even still alive!"

"Actually . . . I should be able to tell you right now if they are still alive," Sarah spoke up for the first time. "My special gift is to communicate with the spirits of the dead. Do you have some plaything or possession that Simon, Helen, or both were attached to?"

The parents looked at each other. "We bain't got much, an' none t' spare fer trupperies," Roger said, a flush of shame spreading over his face, as if the fact that he could not afford a single toy for his children gave him great guilt. "Playthin's they made from sticks an' grass an' suchlike. On'y clathers wuz on they backs. But—'ould a piller do?"

Something they laid their heads on *every single night*? Nan had no doubt that would do, and neither did Sarah. They both nodded. Roger got up and made his way awkwardly up the ladder to the loft, coming down with two little grass-stuffed squares of flour sack.

Sarah took them on her lap. "Need me?" Nan asked. Sarah shook her head.

"With this, I can even tell if they've passed the Portal to the Other Side," she said quietly. "Just give me a moment."

Grey huddled into Sarah's neck, and Sarah placed one hand on each pillow on her lap, closed her eyes, and slightly bowed her head.

Nan didn't think she'd need to join her friend in the spirit realm, but she held herself ready, just in case. If the children *were* dead . . . well, she thought it unlikely they'd be haunting anything but this house. While some spirits clung to the place of their deaths, most clung to the places where they had lived, and here inside this cottage they would be safe from the ravages of sunlight. So if they were on this side of the Portal, chances were they would be *here*. Which would be why she and Sarah would never have found them, since they had not known where to look, and had been asking other spirits about wandering child-ghosts on the moor itself.

Once again silence reigned in the little cottage, and a lark singing outside made an ironic counterpoint to the solemn quiet.

It took longer than Nan had hoped, but less than she'd feared, for Sarah to open her eyes again. "They're not dead," she said with absolute conviction, leading Maryanne to let out a cry of pained relief, and fall weeping onto her husband's neck.

"Cans't tha' cast a findin' spell, like me Grammar?" Roger asked, both his arms around his crying wife.

All of them shook their heads. It wasn't entirely true—they all *could,* in one way or another, but if the children were being held in one of those places Robin had told the girls about, a spot that had been enchanted so that it literally could not be seen magically, then there was no way for any of them to find the youngsters.

No point in confusing the Byerlys with that information. John was right to keep things simple. They were just lucky that Roger

Byerly already was aware that magic existed and believed in it—that, with Nan's demonstration, had been enough to convince his wife. That made things ever so much easier when it came to speaking openly about all of this.

"That doesn't mean we're going to give up, Byerly," John Watson said firmly. "It just means that now that we are sure the children are alive and being held somewhere, we'll use other methods to find them. Some of which will involve what Sherlock Holmes taught me. Don't despair; I know they've been gone a long time, but the mere fact that they are still alive means that they are in shelter and being fed, which is more than you knew this morning. We're staying at The Rock Hotel in Yelverton. If we discover *anything*—" John paused for a moment, obviously unsure what to say next.

"If we learnet aught, chell send Black Bird 'ere with letter," Nan said, reaching up to ruffle Neville's feathers, showing *which* Black Bird she meant, ending John's uncertainty. Neville bobbed his head enthusiastically, but did not speak—probably because in the bird's judgment, the Byerlys had had more than their share of the "uncanny" today and did not need to be confronted with a talking raven. "'E can be 'ere an' back t'me faster nor moor pony at gallop. I' fact, chell send 'ee letter ever' second day, so's 'ee knowed usn's bain't forgot 'ee."

"You'd do that?" Maryanne said, lifting her tear-stained (still beautiful!) face from her husband's shoulder.

"Black Bird bain't cost a penny-stamp," Nan said shrewdly, which startled a weak laugh out of both the Byerlys.

And at that moment, poor Roger's stomach gave an audible growl.

Both of them flushed. *I think they're both really, really hungry,* Suki said, speaking up in Nan's mind. *I bet they haven't eaten much because they were so worried.*

Or because they haven't much to eat in the first place, Nan reminded her.

Can we share our lunch? Suki begged. *They can have all my cakes.*

"It do be 'round 'bout nummet," Nan said, as if she had not heard Roger's stomach proclaiming its emptiness. "Usn's brought enough an' more. Usn's admire if tha'd share an' bile oop water for tea."

"Capital plan!" John exclaimed heartily, and forestalled any objections by getting up and going out to the horses. He returned with the packed (and bulging) burlap bags that had been slung behind his and Mary's saddles, went straight to the table, and began to unpack them, leaving Maryanne no choice but to bring out wooden and pottery plates and cups, and put an ancient, much-patched kettle full of water over the hearth.

Fortunately, the hotel kitchen had either grossly overestimated their appetites, or had anticipated that they might be feeding guests. Out came sausages, cheese, hard-boiled eggs, ripe plums, radishes, a packet of tea, another of sugar, four big loaves of bread, and two tins of digestive biscuits. Maryanne ran out with a cup and came back with just enough milk (presumably from the goat) for everyone to have milk in their tea. Roger brought a pot of homemade coarse mustard out of the cupboard. Watson and Mary took turns in urging the Byerlys to "try this," and "do have some more sausage," and Suki pushed an entire tin of biscuits to their side of the table and refused to take any for herself. Nan ate just enough to keep from feeling hungry on the way back, and she was fairly certain she was not the only one refraining from eating too heavily. Neville took himself out to the garden, where they heard him chortling. Evidently he was wreaking havoc among the insects. Grey very politely ate digestive biscuits.

There was even a generous amount of leftovers, which Watson insisted the Byerlys keep. "Those eggs will surely go bad on the trip back," he said mendaciously. "I know the bread will go stale, and I've no wish to be smelling of sausages when we dismount at the hotel. Smelling of horse will be quite bad enough." Flushing a little with gratitude and a little with embarrassment, Maryanne put the food away in their cupboard. Nan couldn't help but wonder how long she'd make it last.

After that, there was nothing more to be done. It was just a matter of saying goodbyes, collecting their mounts, and heading back to Yelverton.

* * *

When the trace joined the larger track, and once they had passed through Sheepstor without stopping, John waved all of them to come up and cluster around him. A breeze had sprung up, enough to make all the ladies tie their hats firmly down. "This is as good a time for a palaver as I can think of," he said. "We're out in the middle of nowhere, no one can eavesdrop on us, and I very much doubt that whoever is behind this, they have any notion that we are even here, much less that we are on their track and out on the moor at this spot. So, what should our next move be?"

"Mary should send her Air Elementals out searching for Helen and Simon," said Nan. "Being in a place invisible to magic will not prevent the Elementals from spotting them visually if they are out of doors. I know exactly what they look like; I got that from Maryanne's mind and I am fairly certain I can impart that to the Elementals. I should send Neville out looking for cottages past Sheepstor, in case they are being held at a cottage, and we can note those on your map for further investigation."

"We should find out where the abandoned mines are, too, and if there are any caves," said Sarah. "The children might be hidden in a mine. That's what I would do. Nobody wants to go near those things for fear of falling in, and that's an excellent place to keep people you don't want escaping. You just lower them down, pull up the ladder, and there you go. They could call and cry with all their might, and the only thing anyone would hear they would probably take for a hawk or a kite calling."

"I think we all know why a magician would kidnap children with magic," Mary said grimly. "To feed off them."

"Yes, but the good news is that this magician, either by accident or design, is not draining them to death," John countered. "But there is quite another reason why a magician might take children with magic. Such children are *much* more susceptible to coercive magic than children without, and could easily have been lured into a trap that way. In fact, now that I am thinking about it, I would guess that the magician *hasn't* taken them to drain them. He—or she—has taken them as a labor source."

"What now?" Nan asked, then looked over to Neville, who was bobbing his head furiously. "A labor source?"

"Suppose one of the mines still had tin veins?" John replied.

"What better labor force to use than children, who won't fight back, won't demand wages, and are small enough to crawl down small tunnels? That would account for *everything*. Why they haven't been seen. Why none of them have escaped. Even where spirits are, if any of them have died! The ghosts wouldn't know where they were, so if they didn't pass to the other side, they'd haunt the mine, not anywhere else!"

"John, that's diabolical—" Sarah said, aghast.

He shrugged. "No more diabolical than employing poor souls afflicted with dwarfism for a similar reason, as we found on one of Sherlock's cases." Then he paused. "Well . . . actually, you're correct. It is more diabolical. It's using unpaid, stolen children to do the dirty, dangerous work. But if that's the case, then using coercive magic to catch them is all the magician would need to do. Once he got them into the mine, *work or you don't eat* and *work or you get beaten* would certainly suffice. Why, out here on the moor, there is even a ready supply of moor ponies to carry off the ore to a smelter!"

Sarah shivered. "We should definitely check all the mines for signs of activity, then."

"Neville can do that without arousing any suspicions," Nan replied. "All right. We have some things we *and* Sherlock can do immediately. When we leave our notes for him, I'll ask him to find out of there are any smelters with a new source of ore in the last four years. He can do that faster than we can. And that gives me something I can send the Byerlys in their letter in two days. I intend to dole out the information we have carefully, so they get some sense of progress, rather than letter after letter of 'no news yet.'"

"That's an excellent strategy," John agreed. He appeared lost in thought for a moment. "There is a technique Mary and I might try that involves pendulum dousing to see if we can find 'magically null' spots on a map. I've never done it, and neither has she, so I have no idea whether we'll have any luck at it, but it's certainly worth trying."

They had to stop at that moment, to let a young shepherd drive his flock across the track. The sea of wooly backs with the myriad of legs beneath it did not look *anything* like any cloud that Nan had ever seen, which made her wonder briefly why it was that poets were always comparing clouds to flocks of sheep. They brought with them the smell of dust, lanolin, and trampled grass. The young shepherd was in a bit of a hurry, although Nan could not tell what made the other side of the track better than the one he was on, and the sound of what must have been a hundred or more sets of hooves on the ground was punctuated by protesting *baas* and the clank of the bells on the bellwethers' necks.

The horses were clearly used to this, and waited patiently, even when the flock inexplicably decided to divide in the middle and flow around them. When the path was clear again, the horses picked up their pace, probably understanding now that the humans on their backs were definitely heading to the home stable, where hay and grain awaited them. They were definitely moving more briskly than they had been this morning.

"So," Sarah said. "I can't think of anything more we can do right now. Does there seem to be any great urgency about this? Shall we proceed methodically and carefully, or—"

"If the children are still among the living at this point, I think it's fair to assume their captor has no wish to kill them," Watson replied. "Methodical is our best approach. When we arrive back at the inn, I will apprise the chief constable of the more ordinary aspects of our investigation, while you and Nan, Sarah, write notes to be left for Sherlock. Mary, you send out your sylphs while there is still daylight for them to see by. Although they will be of limited utility, I'll have my undines see what they can discover, if anything."

"What can I do?" Suki demanded.

John moved his horse over beside her pony. "You, my dear, should go make friends with the village children. The ordinary ones, best of all, the ones who are working rather than playing. You know what to do."

Suki grinned up at him. "Investigate!" she said gleefully. "Nan can show me what Helen and Simon look like. I can arst—*ask*— about them. See if any of the other children know about 'em. An' see if there's any stories goin' about—if there's supposed t'be witchery goin' on!"

"Exactly. The adults are probably not going to talk to us about that sort of thing. The upper-class ones will pretend such things don't exist, and the working-class ones will avoid anything that makes them look—" John sought for the most diplomatic way to phrase things.

"—makes them look like a lot of superstitious country bumpkins," Mary supplied, not at all diplomatically. "The children will have no such concerns, which makes them our best source of information local to Yelverton." She smiled as Suki looked back at her. "You're going to be absolutely vital to us, Suki. Use all the training you've had with the Irregulars."

"Not *all* of it," Suki said thoughtfully. "I don' think I'll need t' threaten t' stick anyone."

They divided up as soon as they reached the stable, John setting off afoot immediately, Mary, Nan, and Sarah going up to their respective rooms, and Suki sauntering off down the street in search of the children of the village, after a brief pause for Nan to set the images of Simon and Helen into her mind.

Grey and Neville flew to their perches. Sarah took the desk; Nan sat down on her bed with paper and a book to use as a temporary desk, and they both wrote out everything they could remember as concisely as possible. They didn't bother to consult with each other beforehand or afterward. Sherlock had taught them both that it didn't matter if they repeated information, as independent observations of the same event were of great importance to an investigation. They finished at about the same time. "Do you think the Post Office will still be open?" Sarah asked, as Nan folded her sheets and passed them to Sarah to be put in the same envelope.

Nan consulted her watch. "Just, I think. I have longer legs. Let me run out, and while I am out, I'll get another map like John's."

She ran down both the hallway and the stairs and while she did not run in the street when she reached it, she managed to walk so fast it was almost a run. She reached the Post Office just in time before it closed.

The Post Office was in a newish building, probably built to accommodate all the new villagers who worked in Plymouth; two-storied, with the Post Office on the bottom floor and living quarters for the Postmaster and his family on the upper floor. Spacious and modern-feeling, the public area was the size of an average store, with a counter across the middle. She bought a stamp for the letter, and an Ordinance Survey map, and left the letter for Holmes to pick up. Fortunately the cheerful young lady at the counter was not annoyed at having to wait a few minutes past the technical closing time. That certainly would *not* have been the case at a London Post Office! In fact, she remarked in quite a friendly manner that Nan was obviously a visitor, and asked a little bit about her.

Bearing in mind the story they had concocted, Nan supplied her with the gossip fodder she obviously desired. "My sisters and I are here on a painting holiday with our married friends, a doctor and his wife," Nan replied. "We're at the Rock. We have a friend who's here on a walking tour of Dartmoor; that's who the letter is for. He asked us to keep him apprised of our own sightseeing so that he won't miss anything interesting."

"Oooh, a sweetheart?" the girl asked, giggling coyly. Nan smiled and uttered a completely genuine and hearty laugh, since the notion of Sherlock Holmes as her sweetheart was absolutely absurd.

"Goodness gracious no," she laughed. "He's *far* too old. Perhaps I should have said 'a friend of my late parents.'" She wondered if she should elaborate on the letter she was leaving for Holmes, but decided against it. There was such a thing as inventing *too* much information. "But I'm keeping you from closing up—thank you very much, and I'm sure I'll see you again soon!"

Back at the hotel, Nan popped into the kitchen to ask for raw meat trimmings, which the cook (having been warned to expect her) very readily gave her, and some cooked barley, raw chopped carrots, and shelled peas. Just as she got the two cups, she heard a very plaintive *Supper?* in her head from Neville. *Coming,* she replied, and hurried up to the room.

Both birds greeted her with wingflaps of joy and anticipation. She emptied the two teacups of food into the respective tin cups fastened to the perches, emptied and refilled their water cups, and gave herself a quick wash at the basin and tidied her hair. Suki came in a moment later and did the same.

Sarah, of course, had made her own preparations for dinner and was sitting quietly, reading a book. "Shall we go down and start without the Watsons?" she asked, looking up.

"I'm not so starved I'm ready to eat my own leg off," Nan

replied, with a glance at Neville, who was greedily wolfing down bloody scraps of meat, and Grey, who was beak-deep into the warm barley and succulent peas.

"*I* am!" declared Suki. "There's treacle tart! I smelt it!"

Nan laughed and gave in. So they were already into the bread-and-butter course by the time John and Mary joined them. The bread was warm and fresh, and good enough Nan would have been quite ready to make an entire meal out of just that.

They were surrounded by other diners, so John kept up the pretense that the girls were here to paint by waxing eloquent on the quaintness of Sheepstor, the picturesque old church, the distant moor ponies, and the young shepherd and his flock. They returned the favor by remarking on the colors and "light" on the moors. Both of them had been hanging about Beatrice Leek's artist friends enough to be able to babble about such things quite as if they actually were painters. *It's a good thing there don't seem to be any actual artists here at this hotel, however,* Nan thought ruefully. *I really don't know what I would do if I was asked to produce my sketchbook.*

Suki got her treacle tart, in no small part as a reward for her forbearance at lunch, and when the last plates had been taken away, Nan realized that all of them were blinking with that sort of numb-witted glazed gaze that hinted at satiation combined with a very tiring day.

"I don't know why *riding* should tire one out so," Mary said, suppressing a yawn. "The horses did all the work."

"Not so much, my love. Your own muscles do quite a bit of unaccustomed work just staying in balance with the horse," John replied. "I suggest an adjournment until morning. I don't think I'm quite up to a discussion of the day over a pint in the parlor."

"A pint would put me to sleep immediately," Nan retorted. "John, may I borrow your map briefly? I just got one of my own and I want to copy your notes onto mine."

"Certainly. Let's go up, shall we?" John looked across the table at Suki, who was blinking like a sleepy little owl. "Before we have to carry Suki up there."

"'M awake!" Suki protested, but did not object to heading upstairs. Sarah and Suki went straight to their room. Nan went on to the Watsons' room and got John's map.

She returned it a half hour later; the long day was really catching up with her, and she'd asked Sarah to make sure she'd made all the notations correctly. She was really yawning by the time she returned to their room, and a bed had never looked so good.

Sarah was already in her nightdress, and Suki was face-down in her pillow when she entered their room, but Sarah's raised eyebrow at her yawn reminded her that they were going to have to make a visit to the spirit world before she could actually sleep. There were things they could see in the spirit-world version of the Byerlys' cottage that they had not had time to look for during their brief visit.

"No rest for the wicked," she sighed, and got ready for bed.

"Need us?" asked Grey, and yawned herself. Neville gave all his feathers a huge shake, and clacked his beak.

"I don't think so—" Sarah began, but Nan shook her head.

"Let's not be overconfident," she cautioned. "We know now that there definitely is a magician somewhere out there on the moors. I'd rather have all our defenses and not need them, than need them and not have them."

Slipping into the spirit world out here in the country was a lot different than doing so in London. For one thing, it was easier; there were almost no distractions. For another, the spirit world itself was somehow quieter. Definitely more peaceful. Because they were going to be on a close watch for ghosts, they didn't plan on going straight to the cottage. Granted, they had done a cursory inspection before, but now they could make a better job of it. Passing through the walls of the hotel, they and the birds took to the air, orienting themselves on the shadow-street beneath them, gaining height until they were able to make out the track they had taken to Sheepstor, then cutting across country directly rather than following the meandering track.

The spirit world, a shadowy replica of the real world, stretched out beneath them, illuminated not by the weak shadow-moon, but by its own luminescence. The track to Sheepstor was a sort of black snake winding among the glowing moorlands, and the distant walls of Sheepstor rose dark gray among the faintly shining trees and bushes. Beatrice had explained that what they were seeing was literally the "light" that life gave off here in this half-world. This was nowhere near as apparent in London as it was here in the country.

They'd only recently learned to "fly" when in the spirit realm, and it saved an immense amount of time. Grey and Neville kept pace with them easily, and if the situation hadn't been so serious—and she hadn't been so tired—Nan would have very much enjoyed this journey. It was almost exactly like the dreams of flying she'd had as a child, and now she wondered if those had actually been dreams, after all, or if she had slipped into the spirit world when she slept back then. It was certainly possible; such things were easier for children. Look how easily Suki had taken to it!

They came down out of the sky and walked carefully the last few feet to the Byerlys' house. There was always the possibility that Roger had unconsciously imbued the cottage walls with defenses, and they didn't want to trigger them.

But she needn't have worried. There was nothing about the place that suggested he had done anything of the sort, and having been invited inside in the flesh earlier today, they were able to pass through the door in spirit as if it weren't there at all.

There were, however, faint and fading signs of benevolent magic everywhere. There was very little doubt that someone—probably Roger's grandmother—had been an Earth Magician, and a good one, though not a Master. The hearth in particular glowed as brightly with power as if there were a roaring fire there.

"Well, that answers that question," Sarah said. "With this heritage behind them, one or both of the children is almost certainly a magician. Potentially, with the power of a Master."

But Nan shook her head. "Not a Master, or the child would be seeing Elementals already, and even if Maryanne had no idea magic existed, her husband would certainly take notice if one of his children started babbling to things invisible to him. And that's a good thing; think of what our criminal could do with the power of a Master if it came into their hands."

"Well, we've seen all that we can see here, and until Neville scouts for us tomorrow, there's not a great deal more we can do," Sarah replied after a pause. "We need actual targets to investigate."

"I don't disagree," Nan replied. "Just one more thing. Let's go back outside and see if we can sense anything trying to lure us away."

Sarah nodded, and they passed through the door and out into the glowing yard. Nan did notice something, once they were out, something she had not paid much attention to when they first arrived.

"Look at the garden," she said.

Because the plants out in the garden were definitely glowing more brightly than the plants outside the wall. It was a healthy glow, and when Nan moved among them, she felt a little bit stronger and more energized.

"Roger only has one hand," she reminded Sarah. "There is no way that he affected the plants this way."

"Do you think it could be left over from the mother or the grandmother?" Sarah replied, then shook her head before Nan could answer. "No, I don't think so. This feels too recent. Could Maryanne have some trace of magic herself?"

"It wouldn't surprise me, though not enough to see my sylphs. I *very* much doubt this was either of the children. This has the feel of someone who loves this garden." Nan pulled a face. "From the way Maryanne spoke, neither of the children thought of the garden as anything but a place they longed to raid for food, and didn't want to spend any time working in."

"It also has an undertone of desperation," Sarah said, after a long moment of simply standing there and allowing the feeling of the place to seep into her. "I think it has to be Maryanne. This place feels not only like something she loved, but something she saw as the last bastion standing between her family and starvation."

Well, that's a depressing note to end the evening on, Nan thought.

"Well, I don't sense anything trying to lure us away from here. So whatever got the children, did so out on the open moor. Tomorrow we'll begin the real work," she said aloud. "In the meantime—let's get back and get some sleep. This is going to take painstaking and exacting precision. And I am determined to find those children before anything happens to them that is worse than what already has."

"Let's hope, whatever *has* happened to them already, it's not irrevocable," Sarah said somberly. "Returning them to their parents as empty, walking shells, like those poor girls in Battersea, would be worse than not returning them at all."

15

Simon was not sure whether to be happier or not. Whatever was taking the Dark One away from the cottage in the evening was leaving the creature in an extremely good mood, and he wasn't sure if this should make him more or less nervous.

The last time it had gone, it had taken a second pony with it, and come back with both animals laden with luxuries. Sausages, bacon, and ham, a small keg of beer, bags of sweets, a huge bag of 'taties, another of barley, a jug of gin, cheeses, even butter!

Now it was clear to Simon that if the Dark One was a normal human being, it would have been poor. Not as poor as his family, because it certainly had enough to eat with its garden and the snares and all, but still, poor. So where had the creature gotten the money for such things? And where was it getting the jewelry it took out and played with? Simon could not even make any kind of a guess. He just hoped the thing hadn't murdered some poor soul for the money and jewels.

It was worrying. Very worrying. He feared for the people of Sheepstor—though only the squire had anything worth taking, and Simon didn't give a fig for the squire, who would come riding over about once a month to glare at them and their little cottage, as if the cottage was robbing him of actual sovereigns. But the Dark One was so gleeful when it returned that Simon just hoped it had forgotten that Ellie had escaped its clutches.

Although so much time had passed since Ellie's escape. Days!

And with every day no rescue came, the more Simon feared that something awful had happened to her out on the moors. Weren't there supposed to be wolves? He thought he'd heard about wolves. He already knew about the mires you could step into and get sucked down to your death, and the mines you could fall into and break your neck. And there were Travelers out there! Everyone knew Travelers were dangerous. If they didn't murder you outright with their long knives, they'd rob you of everything you owned and beat you and leave you for dead. And there were criminals too, horrible men who'd escaped from the prison somewhere vaguely "out there on the moor" and lived wild like beasts. And there might be more witches like the Dark One! Where there was one witch, there was bound to be more! What if Ellie escaped the Dark One only to be recaptured by someone even worse?

It all made his stomach knot up and his throat close, and made him cry into his pillow several times a day, much to the disgust of some of the others. He just couldn't seem to do anything right when it came to Robbie. Robbie was always looking at him and muttering to himself. He knew why, too. Robbie thought he was useless, and wished they had Ellie instead of him.

And there was more to worry about. Unfortunately, whatever the Dark One had been doing that brought it such treasures seemed to require even more of whatever it was the creature took from its prisoners. It had only rested for a single day and a night after putting all the new treasures away and Simon had only just recovered from the last Dark Sleep when the thing stalked into their prison in that way that told them all the terrible spell was going to be placed on them all *again*.

Simon went cold all over. *Not again*, he thought. *Please, not again*. But no matter that Father Shaw said that sincere prayers were always heard, God evidently had no interest in his. *Maybe the Dark One has us locked away where God can't see*, he thought as his throat closed up again.

It stood in the middle of the room as they all huddled as far away from it as they could, and some of them—Simon included—whimpered in fear and despair.

"Cease tha' crewntin'," it chuckled. "It all be good, fer tha' an' fer me. Whenst tha' wakes, tha'll get a sweetie. And tonight—tha' gets bacon with tha' bread! A swant supper! There be nothin' to blubber like a chrisemore for."

That only made Simon more terrified. He didn't want anything that creature could give him! What if it was going to tie them even tighter to itself with the food? Or maybe there was a worse reason for the promise. The thing wouldn't promise them treats unless it intended to make the Dark Sleep longer and more fearful than it ever had been before—

But he was not given any time to dwell on that, because the Dark One raised its arms and he fell into the black and the terror, and as ever, it felt as if it would go on forever. He feared he would die. Or worse, he feared that the Dark One had learned how to keep them in this place for years and years without end, and just keep draining and draining them without ever letting them back to the world and the light again. . . .

But then it did end, and the terror let go of him and he sensed that for now, at least, the Dark One couldn't keep them there forever. When he fell out of the spell again, he felt so weak he could barely move his head.

And the Dark One was standing over him, gazing down on him from that empty hood.

He wanted to scrabble away. A scream started in his head, but all that came out of him was a pathetic whimper. All he could do was wait for the Dark One to seize him again and—

His imagination failed him as to what the Dark One would do to him. All that he was sure of was that it would be terrible.

But the Dark One just . . . stood there. Gloating, he thought. As if he was some sort of special dish that the Dark One was about to enjoy.

"Ah, Simon, Simon," the thing crooned, which somehow was more horrid than if it had hissed at him as it had before. "Sech a treasure tha' be. Worth twice tha' sister, an' I dain't even mind she run. She were doan compared t' 'ee. Tha'rt a right guit. Es could et tha' right oop."

Oh God! Was the thing going to actually kill and *eat* him now? He fell to shaking, and his eyes starting right out of his head with terror. He wished he could faint, if only to get away from that terrible stare.

The thing laughed, and stood erect again, then stalked off, slamming the prison door behind it.

Simon shook so hard his teeth rattled, trying to parse out what the thing had meant. Was it going to eat him later? Was something worse in store for him? What did it mean? What did it want?

"S'aright, Simon," Sam said wearily from his own bed. "Don' be afeerd more'n tha' already be. It meant tha' gives it more witchery-power than usn's. Shoulda said it were gonna guddle 'ee, but it don' think that way."

Despite Sam's words, meant to comfort—or maybe because of them, because being drunk up like a pint was no more comforting than being eaten—it took him until the girls brought round a bag of sweeties—bull's-eyes—and gave each of them one to suck now and a second one for later—that he finally managed to stop shaking.

The sweetie helped. It was something good to concentrate on, in the middle of all the horror. He'd only ever had a bull's-eye at Christmas, before Pa had lost his hand and they'd moved to Grammar's cottage. He and Ellie had got three each in the toes of their Christmas stockings, and a gingerbread man, and new stockings, and warm jumpers, all thanks to the parish. Mother had made sure that they told the priest thenkee and not to prate no nonsense about Father Christmas. He wasn't sure if that was because Father Christmas didn't exist, or because Father Christmas only came for rich children, or because Father Christmas left the distribution of gifts to poor children to the parish. He rather thought it was the last, but he didn't dare say anything with Mother being so firm about thanking the priest. He'd done what she told, and the priest had seemed very confused, but said he was welcome and patted him on the head.

The sweet, so good, and so full of peppermint that it made his nose feel cool and soothed a throat sore with crying, made him feel a little better. He did his best to think about nothing else. He nursed the treat as long as he could, sucking on it slowly, until at last it was nothing more than a tiny speck on his tongue. He *thought* about keeping the other for later, he truly did, but the knowledge that he had it was like a fire, and the fear that the Dark One would come in here and take it back like ice, so he popped it in his mouth and lay back, trying to think only of the bliss of sweetness and the cool of mint and imagine himself somewhere, anywhere else. Back in the little room where they'd lived when Pa still had a hand.

"Robbie," Sam whispered across the room. "Do tha' think Dark One's a man or 'ooman?"

Well . . . that got his attention.

Robbie snorted. "Don't think. *Know.* 'Ooman, a'course."

"But—it be sa *mean*," Sam objected.

Simon agreed. He didn't think anything could be as horrible except a man. Even Mother, when she was at her angriest, never was anything like so cruel.

"Thinkee 'ooman cain't be mean? Tha' shoulda met me Ma," said Ben, with a snort of derision. "Faster w' stick on me bones than Pa, an beat me like a drum, she did, any time she felt it. An' put a pint'a gin in 'er?" He whistled. "Felled a prize-fighter oncet, she did."

"'Sides," Robbie continued. "Wears a *dress*."

"Robes," Sam objected again. "Like priest."

Well, Simon had to admit the thing *did* wear something that looked like the fancy robes a priest wore for Sunday. A lot like them, in fact. Only with a hood. Well, that just cemented his certainty that it was a man.

"Dress," Robbie sneered, sounding very sure of himself. "Tis a 'ooman. Mean, hard 'ooman, cold an' narsty as winter."

"Don't matter," Mark said harshly. "Man, 'ooman, don' matter. Jest th' mean part. An' that it got us, an' it ain't gonna let us go, an' we'll be 'ere forever an' ever unless usn's fall inter Dark Sleep an' don' come out again."

Simon was inclined to agree with Mark. Unless, of course, the Dark One was neither man *nor* woman. . . .

Inside he wanted to scream, because that, of course, was the answer. And everything Mother had told him about being a bad boy was true. A devil *had* got him, only it hadn't waited for him to die to take him.

"'S a *devil*," he blurted around the last of his sweetie, the sugar tasting now like ash.

"Cawbaby got it aright," Robbie agreed, though the fact that Robbie called him a cawbaby took a lot of the pleasure out of being called right. "'S a devil, outa Hell. An' it got us t'do what it wants."

"Wut's that make usn's then?" asked Mark.

"Whatever it wants." Simon opened his eyes to see Robbie turning over on his bed, putting his back to them all, and ending the conversation.

But he couldn't help thinking about that . . . because surely not everyone here was as bad as he was, that a devil would come up out of Hell to torment them all?

And besides that, what would a devil want with draining them of witchery power? Wouldn't a devil have power of its own? Weren't devils supposed to be able to offer you anything you desired to tempt you?

And the Dark One certainly ate, and ate well. And why would a devil need to eat at all?

Worrying over all of those things, like a dog with a rag, exhausted him further, until he fell asleep with the taste of sugar and peppermint still in his mouth . . . to find Jess shaking him awake again, with his three loaves of bread, one drizzled with sugar-water, one full of vegetable stew, and the third, as the Dark One had promised, smeared with bacon fat, with two slices of crisp bacon in the middle.

Thinking was too hard. He was already worn out. There would be no Dark Sleep for at least another day, and right now the best meal he had ever seen was right in front of him. And that was all he cared to think about.

Today, lovely as the day was, Nan was going to spend it in the privacy of their room. It was time to send Neville to deliver her letter to Maryanne Byerly and out to cross-quarter the moor, one carefully marked out a bit at a time, so that they could add all the outlying cottages and deserted mines to her map. At the end of the day, she and Sarah would enter the spirit realm again, and carefully check through all places he had found.

She opened the windows wide, got into her most comfortable, lightest gown, and prepared the desk for the task at hand. Neville watched with interest.

While she and Neville worked, Mary's sylphs and John's undines would be doing the same for them. Nan wasn't sure if they were going to use the same technique that she was, which required that she "ride" as a kind of passenger in Neville's head, or if they were just going to send the Elementals out and have them trace what they found on John's map. She rather thought it would be the latter, though. There was nothing she knew about other Elemental Masters that suggested they could do what she and Neville could. "Here's your letter," she said, handing it to Neville, who took it carefully in his beak.

Neville hopped to the windowsill, then flew out into the morning. Suki got into her *oldest* clothing, so as not to stand out too much. She would continue her interrogation of the local children, looking for anything of interest.

And Sarah was going to go out and try a bit of interrogation of her own. She had a knack for getting people to talk to her, and she was going to start with that fount of all local gossip, the wife of the priest of Yelverton Parish. If there was ever anyone who would know practically everything about anyone in a village, it was the preacher's wife. It was too bad Father Shaw had been a bachelor; Sarah could have gotten a *lot* out of the wife.

Besides, Sarah had a secret weapon when it came to preachers and their wives. Her parents were missionary doctors, and she knew all the right things to say when she was talking to a priest, a minister, or a vicar. That very fact opened many, many doors to her. She was just going to have to remember to say that her *aunt and uncle* were missionary doctors, and not her parents. Her parents, after all, were supposed to also be Nan's parents. Their mother was supposed to be dead, Suki's mother—who would have been their stepmother—was also supposed to be dead, and—

"Oh lord," she groaned, as Sarah set her hand to the doorknob to go out on her own mission. "How many wives is our father supposed to have had?"

"Three," Sarah said promptly. "Two died; the first died having me, the second died having Suki. The third is an heiress who spoils us rotten, which is why we get painting holidays with Suki. That explains *everything*."

Nan sighed with relief. "It does, nicely. Well done. Off with you. Find out as much as you can. And you know, if you have time after you get done with your parish gossip, try seeing if there are other hotels here and who frequents them. That might come in useful."

"I shall. Have fun flying!" Sarah and Suki whisked out the door, leaving Nan to settle into the chair at the desk, compose herself, and "join" Neville.

Neville was already back from taking the letter to the Byerlys, waiting on the roof of the inn, with a fresh-killed mouse from the stableyard. Sensing her in his head, he gulped it down quickly and launched himself into the air.

Ravens were laborious flyers, rowing through the air like muscled watermen. The view from Neville's head was truly remarkable when Nan thought about it. The position of his eyes gave her a much wider field of vision than she got as a human. His eyes were much sharper, too. There wasn't much he missed; he could spot a mouse from a truly remarkable height, for instance. He would have no trouble spotting hidden cottages or overgrown mine shafts.

When he found a column of rising air, he switched from rowing to soaring, using it to gain even more height with a lot less effort.

Not that Nan was merely *sitting* there passively. She had to keep part of her concentration with him, and part of it on her map, with her pencil in her hand, adding details to the map that the surveyors had deemed irrelevant. Copses of trees, combes, cottages, ruins, all the variable things that the surveyors had not noted because they were changeable. Trees and brush could be cleared, after all. Only actual topographic elements were static and reliable. They might have noted walls, but there were almost no walls on the moor except for those that were around gardens to keep wandering ponies and sheep out.

It was very hard work, but it was vastly interesting too; Neville's point of view was fascinating, and it was even better than flying in the spirit world. Everything was so bright, and there were colors she did not even have a name for, only that they were more than purple. If anything moved, anything at all, things as small as a beetle or a cricket, Neville spotted it. This was by no means the first time they'd flown together like this, so she wasn't distracted by the novelty, but if they hadn't been searching for lost children, this way of seeing the moors could have had her entranced for days.

And then Neville spotted a dead lamb. *Pleeeeeeeease!* she

heard him begging her. *Hungry!*

Fortunately, it was at just that moment that she felt a beak gently close on her left hand index finger.

It was Grey, who, having gotten her attention, looked up at her and said, "Hungry now." And she realized that she herself was both hungry and very thirsty. And stiff. And a little sore from sitting so long.

All right, she told Neville. *Lunchtime for everyone. Just watch out for angry shepherds. They'll assume* you *killed that lamb.*

She sensed Neville's amusement at the idea that any shepherd could harm him, and reminded him of the existence of shotguns. When she was sure she had impressed on him the need for caution, she detached herself from his mind and looked down at Grey.

"What would you like?" she asked.

Grey cocked her head to the side, and thought. "Beans," she said. "Brown bread."

"Those should be easy enough," she replied, stretching. She really felt very stiff; she'd been sitting a long time—four hours, by her watch.

"How hungry are you?" she asked Grey—and then remembered the tin of digestive biscuits they had in their room to stave off a growing child's neverending hunger. She fetched it and gave Grey one, refilled her water bowl, and went down to the public room to get herself—and Grey—proper lunch.

When she came back and gave Grey the beans and brown bread she'd asked for, Neville had gorged himself and was ready to fly again. She settled back into her chair.

At some point she was aware that Suki had returned and was reading quietly on her trundle with Grey on her knee, but the child knew better than to disturb either of her guardians when they were working, so she kept right on with her task.

Finally Neville made it wordlessly clear that he'd had enough, he was hungry again, and he wanted something besides some beakfulls of dubious sheep. She told *him* wordlessly that he'd done a capital job and to come back for his reward, and separated herself from his mind.

Suki was playing with jackstones and a ball on the floor, and Sarah was back sitting on her bed and giving Grey a good cuddle. When Nan stretched, both of them looked up.

"Done for the day?" Sarah asked. "John says he has more information from the chief constable, and he's gotten *another* map he wants us to fill in with everything we know to pass on to Sherlock."

"Well, that sounds like an evening's work," Nan told her, with a wry smile. "I must admit, when we began this business of helping Alderscroft, the one thing I never envisaged was that it would involve filling out tedious detail on maps. But Neville has done a circle with Yelverton in the middle, and he's got well past Sheepstor, so we'll call this a good day."

"Apparently John's information will give us a better direction to aim our searches," Sarah told her. "He has a list of all of the last known locations of all the missing children that he knows about."

Quiet night sounds came in through the window. Nan sipped a cooling cup of tea. "It's a good thing we already know that at least two of the children are not dead, or we'd be asking the police to drag the reservoir," Watson said a bit glumly. "Because the general center of our missing children *is* the reservoir."

They were all in the Watsons' room, since it had more space than the girls' did. Or rather, it had the same amount of space, but only had the one bed, not three. Instead of a second bed and room for the trundle, there was a table with four chairs they could use while Suki sat cross-legged on the floor, listening attentively. They'd left the birds back in their own room on their perches; Neville was already asleep. He'd had quite the strenuous day and Nan didn't want to tire him further.

"It isn't the exact center," Sarah pointed out. "It isn't even close to the exact center." She contemplated the map, tracing an irregular line with her finger from red dot to red dot. "You know, if this were a penny-dreadful, the villain would turn out to be that nice Father Shaw. Though what he would be using the power stolen from children *for* I cannot imagine. He's harmless as a dove and poor as a churchmouse."

"He wants to live forever?" Mary Watson suggested, though Nan could tell she was making the suggestion purely in a spirit of mischief.

"Good Gad, like *that*?" Sarah giggled. "Presiding over the endless wranglings of this and that Ladies Circle full of people who made poor Maryanne Byerly unwelcome because she was pretty and had a posher accent than they do? Teaching Sunday school to a handful of squirming children who would much rather have been larking about on the shore of the reservoir? Running back and forth between an out-of-tune piano or wheezy old organ and the pulpit? The man is either a saint, or this is his Purgatory!"

"He didn't have so much as a hint of magic about him, either," Nan reminded them.

"Maybe it's his housekeeper," John suggested, entering into the spirit, as Suki grinned. "And secretly she has a hidden room in her house full of forbidden pleasures like—"

"Chocolates and hampers from Fortnum and Mason?" Nan countered. "She looked more likely to succumb to bonbons and pheasant than anything else. Or perhaps she has an opium habit? Or do you propose that she is a classic witch from the Dark Ages and is gathering the power for her master, Satan?"

"Maybe she's turning the children into sheep to supplement her flock," John put in. "There's a nice, practical application of traditional witchery for you."

"She *also* had not a hint of magic about her," Nan reminded him. "In fact, so far, the only magic we've found was the weak magic displayed by the Byerlys, and they are genuinely stricken with grief and loss."

This reminder of the seriousness of the situation put a damper on the levity.

"But this is very useful," Nan continued, tapping the map that sat in the middle of the table—John's copy, since Nan had folded up and stored hers, and tucked Sherlock's away into an envelope to be left for him at the Post Office tomorrow. *It's a good thing we are supposed to be on a painting holiday. Those colored pencils Alderscroft supplied are exceedingly useful on the maps.* Blue dots for "haunted places," red dots for "the last known locations," and there was still a nice variety of pencil colors for other purposes. "Knowing they were last seen in a limited area means I won't have to send Neville haring off too far in a direction that seems impractical."

"It could be much worse," Sarah observed as she sipped her own now-cold tea without seeming to notice it had gone cold. "At least we won't have to search the *whole* of Dartmoor. We'd be here months."

Suki had already given them her budget of information—the locations of every place the children could reach that was said to be haunted, a veritable Grimm's compendium of local legends, and the name of every woman, old or young, said to be a witch. The last, they had agreed to eliminate for now, on the grounds that whoever was doing this was almost certainly doing her (or his) best to keep from being noticed at his (or her) work. And having every child in Yelverton and the surrounding countryside calling one a witch was certainly *not* going unnoticed. . . .

Except that Nan suddenly got an idea that made her groan.

"What is it?" the other four all asked at the same time.

"Well . . . the missing children are being ignored by both the authorities in Tavistock *and* all the locals because they're nonentities or worse—the poor about to go on the parish, Travelers, itinerant workers, the children of outsiders. Well, what if our villain actually *is* one of these local witches, who's using power extracted from captives *to help all her local people*? She'd think she was doing right! These children don't matter to anyone, according to her lights. Plus, even if she is keeping them prisoner— even if she's *killing* them eventually—while she has them she'd have to feed them, house them, probably in better conditions than they had on their own or with their parents. You saw how close to the bone the Byerlys lived for yourself, Sarah. It would be easy to justify using up a few children no one wanted, whose own parents couldn't feed them, in the interest of healing people she knows, and bringing them prosperity."

She looked around the table and saw that even Suki was struck by the logic of her argument.

"And there goes the argument against Father Shaw—" Sarah said, then corrected herself. "No, it doesn't. He's not magical and neither is his housekeeper."

"And the only person we know of who was, in or near Sheepstor, was the Byerly mother and grandmother." Mary Watson tapped a finger on the map. "But we need to find out where all of the purported witches that Suki found out about live and eliminate them."

"Parish records, somehow get access to the Postal records, or once more see if the chief constable can help me, then, tomorrow," said John. "It's a good thing that I'm quite the hand at tedious tasks. On the other hand, I'm quite sure our Elementals can help there, particularly the sylphs. They'll sniff out any hint of magic in a moment, and can move on to the next potential target."

"I can do better than that," Mary told him. "I can tell you that today my sylphs found neither a trace of any form of counter-magic within Yelverton, nor any place where they could not go, which would be one of those protected spots where a magician could hide. So unless your witches are living out on the moor somewhere, we've eliminated that much."

"Some of 'em are," Suki said. "Or in little places like Sheepstor."

"Searching the empty moor would be faster," John Watson grumbled.

"I could play bait," Suki offered. "I done it in Lunnon."

"And in London you had all of the Irregulars and Sherlock or Lestrade waiting to swoop in and save you when the bait was taken, Suki," Sarah reminded the child. "It's a very brave thing of you to suggest, but until we have some idea *where* to look, we can't have you wandering about, shields down, playing the honeypot."

Suki sighed, looking crestfallen, and looked down at the hands clasped in her lap. Nan sympathized. Suki lived for the adventures she'd become involved in.

"Suki, I am absolutely keeping your offer in mind," John promised. "And if we *do* have a situation where we have a potential villain we have to draw out, and all four of us—five, if we can bring in Sherlock—waiting to pounce, then we may well make that sort of use of you."

By this time, Suki was a seasoned enough member of the team that she took that as it was meant—that the adults considered her a valuable asset, and she would be given the opportunity for very material help, if the situation warranted. She looked up at John gratefully.

"Well, the sylphs will expand their search tonight and report to me in the morning, and—oh! John, I just realized something!" Mary exclaimed. "You can easily simply *talk* to an undine or a nixie tonight to find out if there are bodies in that reservoir! Then at least we'll know one way or another if someone has been using it as a dumping ground."

John made an exasperated sound. "Well done, my dear. I should have thought of that myself. I was so focused on the *land* that it never occurred to me. Although, my love, you have come a very long way since I first met you. The young lady I courted would never have casually used the words *dumping ground for bodies*. She likely wouldn't even have considered such a thing."

Mary patted his hand. "Do I make your blood run cold, my love?" she asked.

"You make me grateful that I have a true partner," he countered. "And you make me feel very sorry for Sherlock that he hasn't anyone like you."

"But he has," she contradicted him. "He has his Watson. And you have yours. I simply don't chronicle your adventures—not because you don't deserve it, but because it would be a very bad idea."

There was not much more to discuss that night, and the girls all returned to their room shortly thereafter. When they had all prepared for bed, rather than fling herself down on hers, Suki sat up cross-legged and looked from Nan to Sarah expectantly. "Are you going to the spirit world?" she asked.

"I don't know," Nan said frankly. "I'm not sure what we can accomplish. I'm tired, but Sarah probably is not."

"We should check the whole of the reservoir, just in case," Sarah replied after a moment of thought. "We didn't get near it before, and if someone is drowning children, there should be at least one ghost. That shouldn't take too long, and it will be good 'flying' practice for you. Neville is tired, but Grey should be additional protection enough."

Nan nodded, and the three of them composed themselves in their beds.

It took a moment for Suki to "pop" in—probably because, although she had made no complaints, she, too, had had an active day. She had probably covered as much ground afoot today as she usually did on her most active days with the Irregulars.

It was very useful having Suki with them; Nan and Sarah could take the north and south banks of the reservoir, and Suki could cover the middle. If there *were* spirits haunting the place—well, they would all be very recent, since the reservoir itself was very recent. There could not have been many—if any—accidental drownings yet. Not like London, where every body of water from the Thames down was thronged with restless spirits. Even the Serpentine had its share, from murder victims to suicides to people who had merely fallen in drunk at night and drowned by accident.

But they found exactly nothing.

They met at the northernmost point of the reservoir, and from the look of the other two, neither were going to be good for much more tonight. Sarah capped that observation by saying, "I am knackered. We've done all we can for now."

"You're right," Nan agreed.

"Time for *real* bed," said Suki.

The one good thing about all this spirit-world travel was that they did not have to *fly* back to where they had left their bodies, they merely had to will themselves out of their respective trances, and they were snapped back into those bodies in an instant.

Which was a good thing, because Nan, at least, fell into a real sleep as soon as she had.

16

John's map was spread out on the table in the Watsons' room after they had finished breakfast, and they were all studying it. Red dots for the missing. Blue dots *had* been for hauntings, but last night Sarah, Nan, and Suki had eliminated all of them. There had been ghosts—fewer than were reported—but the three of them had persuaded or tricked all of them to the other side.

All those blue dots had been erased, and now blue stood for blanks—places the sylphs reported they could not see into nor enter. Green for purported witches . . . and that was where things got interesting, because three of those were also at the same location as blue dots.

Which was, of course, exactly what you would expect if the purported witches were real witches, perhaps ones who had magic running in their families for a very long time, and had carefully protected their working places for generations, until the protections layered on top of protections had become permanent.

The question was . . . were any of them up to no good? Or more to the point, were any of them kidnapping children?

"You know," Sarah said, something suddenly occurring to her. "What if whoever is taking these children is doing so to save them from neglect, starvation, and privation? What if we're entirely wrong about this, and the children aren't being used, they're—"

"And how likely is that?" Mary Watson asked dryly.

"And if so, why take the Byerly children? Their parents love

230

them. They're poor, but not starving. Maryanne had a *single* moment of losing her temper, and did the right thing by sending them out of the house," John added.

Sarah sighed. "You're right, of course. There are no Fair Elves or Good Witches who only kidnap neglected or abused children. That would make a lovely story, though."

There had been no word from Sherlock, although they really didn't expect any. He would work according to his own methods on his own mysterious case, and he would make contact with them only when he thought he had something that pertained to theirs as well. Sarah did wonder where on earth he was staying, though. One generally did not use "Post Office General Delivery" for an address unless one did not actually have an address, and he wasn't at any of the hotels or inns in or around Yelverton. Not even at the Drake, which did not have individual rooms, only the exceedingly old-fashioned custom of paying for one in a double line of beds lined up in the single upstairs room. Such accommodations were generally used by farmers who were too distant from Yelverton to make it home before sundown on market day. There were fewer and fewer of those nowadays; with the railroad coming to Yelverton, it was more profitable for even small farmers with a couple bushels of produce or a few dozen bundles of flowers to sell all their goods to a wholesaler who would take them to Plymouth, rather than taking them to a local market and risk going home with goods unsold.

"Do we divide up, or do we go as a group?" Sarah asked aloud. "There are hazards to both options."

John and Mary looked at each other. "We . . . could do both, in a way?" Mary replied for both of them. "We go as a group, but we approach the area with no more than two of us at a time."

"Or we let Suki do the initial approach," Nan suggested. "By saying she's lost, perhaps. . . ."

John opened his mouth to object, then closed it again. "I can't say I like that idea, but Suki volunteered, all four of us—six, counting the birds—will be there with her, and given that children are the targets of this unknown person, she does stand a better chance of flushing the villain out."

Suki looked as if John had just gifted her with a new silk

gown. "I'll go get ready," she said, and darted out the door.

Sarah's feelings on this were decidedly mixed. Suki was as prepared as she could be. She was as prepared as an adult would be. They could send Neville to go sit on the roof, or over the cottage door before she approached, and woe betide anyone who opened the door and tried to snatch Suki. Between Neville's beak and Suki's knife, any kidnapper would have a very bad few moments, and then the adults would have reached them.

But Suki was still just a child. Granted, she had volunteered, but did that give them the right to use her as bait?

Memsa'b and Sahib used us like that. Though I'm sure they had just as many qualms then as we're having now.

In the time it took her to think all this, Suki was back, dressed in an old, worn smock-dress with a patched apron over it, her hair tucked under a straw bonnet with a faded ribbon holding it on. When Suki was inclined to, she could get changed faster than anyone Sarah had ever seen.

"I think that's the best plan," Sarah said, finally. "We send Neville first, and put him on the roof. Then Nan and I can come set up with our easels and begin sketching. Then you and Mary, John, can stroll by and pause to gawk at us. *Then* Suki can make her approach."

"Wouldn't it seem odd to just set up and start sketching someone else's house without a by-your-leave?" Mary wondered.

Sarah gave a delicate snort. "Every one of the artists I know would not hesitate for a moment to set up and sketch anyone or anything he thought was interesting. I've seen them do it a hundred times. They seem to think they have the right to make a picture out of anything they please. It's not unlike the tours well-to-do people make of the slums; they simply don't think about it at all. I suppose in their eyes the poor are not entitled to the finer things, like feelings."

John winced. Mary shrugged.

"At any rate, I am fairly sure they get enough artists and would-be artists and painting dilettantes around here that this is something they have seen before," Sarah continued. "I would love to be able to eavesdrop on some of the over-the-fence gossip about such encounters, however."

"Well, in that case," John said, "That does seem to be the approach that will arouse the least suspicion."

"I'll get the sketching kits," Nan volunteered. "There are two locations that we can reach this morning, here and here." She pointed to one spot within Yelverton itself, though just barely, and another between Yelverton and Milton Combes. "Then this afternoon we can get the horses and try this one, here, south of Sheepstor."

"A-hunting we shall go," agreed John. Nan left for the kits, Suki snatched up her hat, and Sarah took Grey on her hand.

"Will you be all right coming with us, but hiding in the trees?" she asked the parrot. "We'll be making enough of a spectacle of ourselves as it is, but it will be an *expected* spectacle. With you on my shoulder, we might attract a crowd."

"Yisssss," Grey replied, and bobbed enthusiastically. Sarah got the wordless impression from her that the parrot was as impatient of results as any of the humans were.

She picked up Neville on her other hand and took them both to the window. "Stay out of sight, and Neville, watch for danger to Grey," she cautioned them, and tossed Neville out first, so he could guard Grey from crows or hawks, then let Grey take flight.

Then she retied her straw hat firmly just as Nan arrived back with the two sketching kits. These were clever wooden boxes about the size of a lawyer's briefcase, with easel legs built into them that could be slid out and clamped into place. No really serious artist would use them for anything; a real collapsible easel, bulky as it was, was the only thing that would stand up to vigorous painting or sketching, and most real artists would carry one along with their palettes and paints or charcoals, crayons, and pencils regardless of its bulk. But the kits were exactly the sort of thing that "ladies on a painting holiday" would use.

"Fellow painter?" Sarah said with a little bow, as she took one kit from Nan.

Nan made a face. "It's a good thing we're unlikely to run into any actual artists, that's all I can say," she replied, and gestured to Sarah to precede her out the door.

They made what Sarah thought was an admirable show as they walked down the street, of considering this Tudor building, or that one that clearly dated to the Civil War, absolutely oblivious to the feelings of the people who actually lived in the places they were "considering."

The only fear for their ruse that Sarah had was that their destination would prove to be much less "paintable" than anything in the area, thus casting a great deal of doubt as to why they were setting up there.

But her fears were completely cast aside when they turned the corner of the lane, and there it was. It was a small, single-storied stone cottage with a thatched roof. There was an actual rose bush spreading along the front wall, and two potted geraniums, one on either side of the door. The tiny window behind the rose bush had its shutters flung wide open, and a pair of muslin curtains fluttered half in, half out of it. It looked as if it had sprung straight out of a fairy tale.

"Oh *look*, Sarah!" Nan exclaimed needlessly. "That's perfect!"

They set up their kits, side by side, across the lane on the verge, chattering away about "light" and "chiaroscuro" (Sarah had no idea what that meant, but Nan threw the word out so they tossed it between them for a while) and "aspect," doing a great deal of talking and a lot of fussing over getting the position of their easels just right. Sarah had actually just started something like a color sketch of the place when John and Mary came strolling up, arm in arm, and exclaimed to find them there. At that point, Sarah thought she saw someone moving in the shadows behind the curtain, but no one came out.

They chattered aimlessly for a while, and then Suki appeared, coming from the opposite direction, carrying a basket of pears. Where she had gotten them Sarah had no idea, but it was a very clever ruse. She stopped at the house next to the cottage, while Neville positioned himself on the roof above the door of the target, and Grey fluttered into the branches of the tree above Sarah. Suki actually managed to sell the householder half a dozen pears before proceeding to the target, marching boldly up to the door and knocking.

It was answered by a very old, stooped woman in a fustian skirt and worn linen blouse, with a canvas apron over it all. She had a very old-fashioned cloth cap over her perfectly white hair. She was honestly just as "paintable" as her cottage, and Sarah found herself hoping that this *wasn't* the kidnapper.

John says she's definitely a magician of some kind. Fire, he thinks, she heard in her mind.

"How d'ye fadge, Ganmer?" Suki said politely. "Would 'ee try me pears? Penny each!"

The old lady laughed, and reached out—

—Sarah held her breath—

—and patted Suki on the head. "Bless'ee, child," she said indulgently. "Chave nobbut three teeth in me head! Try Gaffer Flint, two cots adown. Or ast t' fine leddies crost road, there." And she nodded at Nan and Sarah and laughed. "Reck they still got all their teeth!"

Suki looked up—she didn't have to look far—into the old woman's face, then did a quick rummage in her basket and came up with a very yellow pear with brown speckles on it. She held it up while Sarah and Nan sketched. "This un's soft, but nay aprill'd nor deef," she said. "She'll go bad afore Es can sell 'er, so please, have 'er! Tha' can et 'er with a spoon!"

The old woman smiled broadly, showing that she did, indeed, have but three teeth, two above and one below. She bent down further. "A trade then? Fancy a fresh scone?"

Sarah held her breath. Was the old woman about to try to lure Suki into the cottage?

"Iss, please," Suki said with enthusiasm.

"Bide 'ee," said the woman, and took the pear and vanished into the dark interior of the cottage, returning with a scone, which she handed to Suki, who took it. "Fair trade, little coney, and now tha's got somethin' fer nummet, aye?"

"Aye Ganmer, an' thank 'ee!" Suki exclaimed, and the old woman chuckled again and shut the door. Suki put the scone in her basket and crossed the road to where they were standing. "How d'ye fadge, leddies?" she asked. "Fancy a pear? Penny each!"

You little monkey, that was a clever ruse, Nan told her, then said aloud, "I do believe I do."

Suki grinned broadly at her, and sold each of them a nice, juicy pear, then sauntered on down the street, bold as Neville, who followed her. Mary and John strolled on, Nan and Sarah put their pears aside and "finished" their sketches, then with many exclamations of admiration for each other's work, packed up and followed after the Watsons.

As prearranged, they all met on the outskirts of town a few

hundred yards away, well out of sight of the cottage they had just been watching. Suki came last, swinging her now-empty basket and munching her scone. "Wherever did you get the notion to sell pears, you little monkey?" Sarah exclaimed as Neville and Grey landed on a branch overhead.

"Bought 'em off a boy that was doin' the same," Suki replied. "'E was right by the Rock, I saw 'en as I come out, an' bought the whole basket. 'E didn' want t' sell the basket at first, but then I ast as 'ow I was gonna carry 'em elsewise, an' made 'en a fair offer."

"Did you make a profit?" John asked, highly amused.

"By one scone, an' the pear I et meself, so reckon I'm ahead," she retorted. "I didn' think that 'Help me, I'm lost' was going to work in the middle of town, 'cause why would I knock on *that* door of all of 'em around?"

"That was shrewd thinking; Holmes would be proud of you," Mary Watson said warmly. Suki blushed with pleasure at the praise. "And how was the scone?"

"Worth a pear!" she replied, and licked her lips. "Was currants in it!"

"Well, what ploy are we going to use on the second target?" John asked.

"'Hev ye got any work? I'll take me pay in nummet,'" Suki said, promptly. "That's the sorta thing what'll tell some'un I wouldn' be missed."

"And what will you do if the person actually *does* have work for you?" John countered.

"Same as when I run that in the Irregulars. Do it," she replied.

John nodded. "All right, then. This time Mary and I will keep ourselves concealed. Nan and Sarah will set up again. Neville will come get you when they are ready."

Neville *quorked* agreement, and they were off.

The second target was just far enough outside of town up Dousland Road that Yelverton itself wasn't visible, only the top of the church above the treetops, off in the distance.

Like the first, this was another small stone cottage, this time with a wall around it, but with slates instead of a thatched roof. There was a big garden, much larger than the one the Byerlys had, and Sarah wondered if this, too, was a "freehold" cottage.

It looked as if it was small enough to have been built in a single day by a crew of determined workers, and the plot of land was certainly near enough to Yelverton that quite a few people could have been recruited to help construct it—certainly far more than the couple dozen houses at Sheepstor could hold!

This one was much, much older than the Byerlys' cottage, though. Ivy clambered over the walls and up onto the roof, and the gray stones were green with moss and white with patches of lichen; time and weather had eroded the stones until every mark of man's hand on them was gone.

"Earth Magician," John muttered. "If this is the one . . . well, the prospects are ugly. When Earth Magicians go bad, they go very, very bad, and even a minor mage can do major harm. Tell Suki to be very, very careful, Nan."

Suki, of course, was nowhere to be seen, which was the point. John and Mary stepped off the road into a screening of bushes. Nan and Sarah carried on.

They set up without all the fuss this time, playing the part of serious artists rather than silly dilettantes. They also set up a bit slantwise from the cottage, so that their compositions would have it as a part of the landscape rather than the focus of the sketch. With all of Yelverton to choose to draw, they'd needed to make excuses for *that* particular cottage. This prospect was a bit more natural, as if they had been looking for a "moorland with cottage" scene and this was about as far from the village as they cared to walk.

There was a lot less in the way of tree cover for the birds to choose from, so the other reason they had picked the spot they did was because there was a nice big tree to offer shade for themselves and a landing spot for Grey. Once they stopped moving, Grey and Neville came flying out of a tree where the Watsons were hiding, and divided, Grey coming to roost above the girls, and Neville looping around the cottage once to make sure it was the right one, then heading back to get Suki.

A moment later, and Neville came back, more or less following the road, passing them and landing on the roof of the cottage, disturbing a flock of sparrows. Sarah, whose eyes were very good, saw with astonishment that he managed to snap one as it took off and swallow it whole. She'd had no idea he could do that—she'd seen him take mice before, but never sparrows!

That little cannibal! Or . . . is it cannibalism, if it's not your species? He does eat chicken with us. And pigeon pie when we do. And eggs of every sort. . . .

Then, in the distance, came a forlorn little figure trudging along the verge of the road, head down, basket clutched to her side, looking discouraged and weary.

What a good little actress she's become!

Sarah continued to sketch with one eye on Suki, the other on her work, all the while thinking that this was *not* ideal. They were a great deal farther from the cottage than she would have liked, and John and Mary were farther still. She had to keep reminding herself that Suki ran with the Irregulars all the time, in some of the meaner parts of London. That she was armed, and she knew very well how to defend herself, both with her knife and with fists and feet. That she'd been trained by the same men—and their nephews—who had trained her and Nan. Suki could certainly hold her own for the few minutes it would take for the girls to get there.

None of this helped her nerves, of course.

Finally Suki reached the cottage, trudged up the path, through the gate, and knocked on the door.

This time a man answered. He spoke too low for Sarah to hear the words, but the short greeting didn't sound unfriendly. Suki said something else, and the two of them—

Oh heavens, she's gone inside!

The logical half of her reminded her that *this was the plan.* Suki was to go inside if need be. If the man actually had work, she was going to have to perform it. And if she needed help, she and Nan were both telepaths and could speak to each other as easily as with words.

But then Suki came out again, without her basket this time, with a pail instead. She went straight to something within the walls . . . *ah, a pump!* . . . and filled her pail with water.

Then she went back in. Neville hopped about on the roof, cocking his head and seeming to listen. Finally he flew down to the ground, then up to the windowsill.

Suki is scrubbing the kitchen floor, Nan said, amused. *The man is telling her she's doing a good job, and saying his old knees aren't up to that anymore. Now he's gone to sit by the hearth and smoke, while Suki works. Now they're both chattering away about what fruit makes the best pies.*

Sarah felt faint with relief.

Oh good Lord. He's spotted Neville.

Oh, no! The man was an Earth Magician, according to John! What if he—

He just gave Neville a cheese rind and called him an 'alkitotle.' I have no idea what that means, but the man is very amused. Neville's bowing his head. Neville's letting him scratch the nape of his neck, the cheeky little slut.

When the man finished giving him a scratch, Neville flew back up to the top of the roof with his cheese rind, pecking bits off and swallowing them. It was obvious their target did not have any captive children, was not a danger to anyone, and had the approval of Neville. So poor Suki was going to have to scrub away at the kitchen floor until it was clean, and they were going to have to stand here and pretend to paint until it was over.

On the other hand—that was two prospective magicians eliminated as their kidnapper.

And then Sarah had a brilliant idea. "Nan, tell John and Mary what's going on, and suggest that they just come up and introduce themselves to the fellow, why don't you?"

"Why? Oh! Of course! He's a magician, we know he's not the one we want, it would only be polite, *and* he's a potential ally! I don't know why I didn't think of that myself." Nan went very quiet, and then John and Mary emerged from the copse and came strolling down the road. Meanwhile they packed up their kits, joined them, and they all went up to the cottage and knocked on the door.

"I really *am* sorry to have deceived you in this way," John said apologetically.

John and Mary had been given the only two chairs in the cottage aside from the one the old man occupied. Nan and Sarah sat on the floor, the birds on their shoulders. They had all been invited inside immediately once John declared himself.

The cottage was very like the Byerlys' except for the dozens and dozens of bundles of drying plants hanging from the rafters. There was a small fire on the stone hearth, it did not have a loft, and the old man's neatly made bed was right out in the open in one corner, but otherwise it might have been the same building.

The man—calling himself "Gatfer Cole"—waved a dismissive hand at him. "'Ee has a black mage t'cotch," he said. "Es'd'a done likewise, 'ad Es th' mother-wit t' think of it."

Suki, who had insisted on finishing the floor "because the Gatfer's knees hurt," listened as she worked. Gatfer Cole glanced over at her and laughed. "A'sides," he added. "Es gets clean floor."

Suki laughed heartily. "It bain't fust time I done floor t' get inside a housen."

"So you've heard or seen nothing?" Mary asked. Gatfer Cole shook his head. "Nomye," he said with regret. "But Es don' leave house much, and Es bain't the dab Es were at magic. Ac'chully, the real dab were me wife." He waved his hand at the house. "She done all the wardin', clear an' sheer. Es did the potions an' all, an' her-ubs. Tha's why Es don' need t' leave house. Folk come t'me from Yelverton up an' Milton Combe down t'trade, so they brings what Es need. When yon lass come knockin' on me door, I thought 'twas for that."

Finished with the floor, Suki stood up, took the pail of dirty water outside, and dumped it. "They said Gatfer were a witch," she pointed out, when she came back in. "We just didn' ast what kind."

"Now, me little maid," Gatfer said, getting laboriously to his feet. "Es was gonna pay 'ee in potions an' nummet, but Es got somethin' better." He went to the mantelpiece, opened a small wooden box, and took out a leather cord on which something was strung. When he turned around with it dangling from his hand, Sarah saw that the pendant was a highly polished piece of cherry-amber in the form of an inverted "T"—the bar of the "T" was thick, and the stem of the "T" was short. "This 'ere been in th' fambly a cruel long time, an' I got no one t'leave it to. So Es'd take it kindly if 'ee'd have it, gift o' mine fer gift o' work o' tha's."

"Good Lord, sir, that's a real amber Viking charm, an amber Thor's Hammer!" John exclaimed, as the old man slipped the leather cord over Suki's head. "Suki, that's hundreds and hundreds of years old!"

"Aye, 'tis," Gatfer said with quiet pride. "But this lass's got th' Favor of the Oldest Old One; Es sees it on 'er, plain as plain. Ain't she a Raven friend then? Reckon 'tis in good hands."

"Chell be *very* careful of't Gatfer, Es promise," Suki said, fervently, cradling the charm in both hands and looking down at it.

"Aye, an' it'll take care'a tha'." Gatfer was clearly very pleased with his decision, and Sarah decided there was no point in trying to get him to take it back. "Noaw, wilt share nummet wi' me?"

Gatfer Cole evidently did a very brisk trade in "potions and her-ubs," since his larder was packed as full of good things as the Byerlys' larder was empty, and he had been happy to treat them all to a fine "ploughman's lunch," quite as good as they could have gotten at the Rock. The walk back to the Rock to collect horses had gone much faster than the walk out to Gatfer Cole's cottage, fortified as they were not only by the lunch but by mugs of Gatfer's very potent home-brewed scrumpy. Suki, to her vast disappointment, had *not* been permitted to indulge; Gatfer had provided her with a much less alcoholic cherry cordial instead.

Now they were riding north and east of Yelverton, out on the moor itself, to a point south of Sheepstor, where there was no road, no track, barely a trace to follow. But they really did not need a road, not when they had Neville, and Neville not only knew the way as shown to him by Mary's sylph, he had a literal bird's-eye view of the countryside beneath him.

Their destination was a cottage at the back of a combe—a sort of dead-end valley, with a steep cliff at the end of it. This was going to be tricky; the combe was heavily wooded, the cottage in a clearing up against the cliff, surrounded by both a garden and a stone wall. It was definitely inhabited; Neville had already made a scouting flight overhead, and not only was there smoke coming from the chimney, the garden was well-tended. And there were chickens scratching and pecking in between the rows of vegetables, providing pest removal, tilling, and fertilizing all at the same time. The fact that they weren't pecking about *outside* the walls, John said, was circumstantial proof that whoever lived there was, as suspected, another magician, who used his or her powers to keep the birds where they belonged.

There were good and bad things about this situation. The good thing was that unless the magician had some sort of warning system set up, there was no way they'd be seen as they approached. And because of the woods, they should be able to slip up quite close to the cottage without being seen.

The bad thing was that while John was dressed for skulking through woods and brush, the ladies were not. Suki—well, Suki was still small enough to be able to skulk no matter what she wore.

So this was going to take a very careful approach.

They tied the horses and the pony up at the very edge of the woods, well in the shade. Sarah kept Grey on her shoulder; granted, these woods were not that different from the jungles Grey was born in, but Grey was decidedly an urban bird these days, and they had both decided that Grey was rather too out of practice to be trying to get those skills back at such a crucial moment. Sarah also had the feeling that Grey still remembered with some trepidation the time that she had been pursued by a hawk and only Neville's intervention had saved her. Sarah didn't remember that time with trepidation—she remembered it with horror, and the memory still made her want to collapse in a heap and weep.

So Grey clung to her shoulder as she attempted, with the handicap of skirts, to follow noiselessly in John's wake.

Once again, Neville was ahead of them, perched on the roof of the cottage.

This time Suki would use, "Help me, I'm lost." And her story, if interrogated, was that she was from Meavy, her parents were dead, she was going to be sent to the workhouse, and she had decided to strike out and try to find a place as a kitchen maid rather than be sent to such a dire place. She had been heading (she thought) to Yelverton and had gotten all turned around. It was a good story, and a believable story. And if this particular lone magician was their child-thief, it would be an irresistible story, particularly with Gatfer Cole's Viking amulet around Suki's neck. Any magician worth his or her salt would give a great deal to get hold of something like that. John had not yet had a chance to examine it closely, but such things generally had power—some more, some less—but they all had *something*.

When the walls of the cottage were just barely visible through the trees, John crept forward until he found a spot with enough brush to hide all four of the adults, then motioned them to join him, one at a time. Sarah moved in a crouch, trying to move as silently as possible, sweating with fear that she'd be spotted.

Once they were in place, it was Suki's turn to come walking openly through the trees, past them and up to the wall. Sarah watched with her heart in her mouth as Suki opened the wooden gate set into the wall, went up the bare earth path to the door of the cottage, and knocked.

There was no response.

Damn! Did we somehow have the bad timing to turn up here when the magician is away? But surely that's not possible—the chickens are out in the garden. Surely, if the occupant was going to be away for any length of time, the chickens would be penned up!

Suki knocked again.

This time the door flew open.

A woman stood there, dressed in dark—well, it wasn't a dress. It was more like robes, like a monk's robe or something of the sort. She had an apron tied over the garment, but it was definitely a *robe*, and not a dress or a skirt. And her hair was chopped off at chin-length, very roughly, as if she had done it herself.

Without a word, she seized Suki's hand and yanked her inside.

Neville sounded an alarm and plunged into the open door. John leapt over the concealing bushes and the wall, and followed. Sarah, Nan, and Mary paused only long enough to haul their divided skirts up above their knees and vaulted the gate behind him, plunging into the darkness of the doorway in time to hear John thunder, *"Let that child go, you—"*

They all ended up in a knot just inside the door.

Suki did *not* have her knife out, and Neville was just *standing* there, not attacking. *Something's—not right!* And Nan shouted even as John raised the pistol he had brought with him.

"John! Don't shoot!"

Behind the woman were two pallets on the floor near the hearth. There were two children on them. One, terribly still and unmoving, was an adolescent girl that Sarah didn't recognize.

But the other—oh, the other she knew very well from the images Nan had plucked from Maryanne Byerly's mind.

It was little Helen Byerly.

The woman had dropped Suki's wrist.

"What are you doing with those children, you villain?" John shouted.

The woman faced him, a tigress to his tiger. *"I'm tryin' t' save their lives, tha' gurt noodle!"*

17

To Sarah's astonishment, the woman turned completely away from John—a big, angry, and clearly dangerous man—and grabbed a bucket from the floor. She shoved it at Suki. "Out! Pump! Right o' th' door. *Now!*"

Suki took it and ran.

Then she took two steps past Sarah to Nan and seized Nan's arm, hauling her toward the pallets. "Tha' looks least like aslat asneger o' any body here—hold lass oop, she cain't get breath."

Dumbfounded, Nan dropped to the floor beside little Helen, and did as she was told, and Helen did indeed stop laboring so much to breathe.

Suki came back with the pail full as the woman dropped to her knees on the other side of the pallet, and stripped the blankets and the oversized smock from the girl, leaving her only in her smalls. "Bring water!" she ordered Suki, and seized a rag, dipping it in the water and sponging Helen down. "If Es cain't get fever down—"

That decided John. He holstered his pistol inside his coat, dropped to *his* knees beside the pallet, and shoved the woman to one side. "I'm a doctor," he snarled. "Have you something like willowbark tea? And put her right on the stone floor, it will pull some of the heat out of her."

The woman pulled the pallet out from under Helen and looked at Mary. "Kettle's at 'earth. Willowbark's in square wood box on mantle." She continued sponging Helen. "This be a cruel cawtch.

245

Fever sparked oop nay long agone, an' me havin' nobbut twa hands. Fetch water, brew tea, cool th' lass down? Cool th' lass, fust, but with what?" She appeared to be talking to herself, but since she hadn't given Sarah a task, Sarah went looking through the larder for something she recognized by opening lids and sniffing, and found a pot of honey just as Mary finished boiling the willowbark and the child began a series of racking coughs. Sarah snatched up a cup, not caring if it was dirty or clean, poured in a generous portion of honey, and held it out for Mary to fill. She brought it to the woman, who blew vigorously on it to cool it, then held it to Helen's lips. "Drink, honey-sweet," she coaxed. "Drink, little lass."

Helen hardly seemed to notice the words, but she did start drinking, or rather sipping. Mary took over sponging the child's face, neck, and body while the strange woman continued to coax Helen to drink.

"Where did you get this child?" John demanded harshly, all the while counting Helen's pulse, and leaning down to listen to her chest.

The woman didn't get a chance to answer, as Suki pulled the leather cord over her head and held the amber amulet under the woman's nose. The woman started back, eyes wide. "Will this help?" Suki asked.

"Shan't 'urt," the woman said shortly, took the amulet, and held it to Helen's chest. She closed her eyes, and bowed her head, lips moving silently.

For a long moment, nothing happened except the wheezing of Helen's breathing.

And then Helen heaved a huge sigh, and her tortured features softened.

"Fever's going down," Nan said, and picked the child up, moving her back to the pallet. Mary covered her back up with blankets. The crisis had been averted.

The woman handed Suki back her amulet, and sat back on her heels, but looked at John defiantly. "So. Water Marster Es-A-Doctor, 'oo be tha' an whyfore tha' comes burstin' through my door?"

* * *

". . . an' then Es found that'un in fever, lyin' on moor like t'other," the woman—who in the course of things mentioned her name was Maude Rundle—said. "'Cept whate'er ails the fust un, 'tain't what ails this 'un. This's lung-fever, from sleepin' wet. T'other?" She shrugged. "Dunno."

Now that they were not dealing with a crisis, Sarah was able to examine the woman in detail. There was no doubt about it, what she was wearing, if it was not a brown linen monk's robe, was certainly virtually identical to one. It even had a hood. There was also no doubt that the poor woman was utterly exhausted. Her short brown hair hung in lank locks about her square-jawed face, there were dark circles under her deep-set brown eyes, and her tanned skin was dull. Sarah wondered when she had last slept. She didn't think it was recently.

John checked both girls; made certain that Helen's fever, if not broken, was at least not to a point that it would kill her outright; then knelt at the pallet of the second one and examined her. He glanced over at his wife and the girls. "I think we've seen this before," he said, reluctantly.

Sarah knew exactly what he meant—this second girl looked not unlike the soulless husks of the young ladies who had been the victims of that madman in Battersea, who had tried to open a Portal into a strange and terrifying other world to bring in the thing that ruled over it.

"Well, there's one way to be sure of that," she replied. She took her own place next to the pallet, placed her hand on the girl's pallid forehead, closed her eyes, and reached out with her own magic.

It was dark, very dark. And cold, and empty. But . . . there was something in the darkness, something hiding just out of reach. Out of reach, because every time Sarah tried to touch it, it skittered away again. As if it was afraid of her. Or . . . afraid of something, something that it thought she was and was going to flee and flee so she could never catch it.

She retreated back into her body, and opened her eyes. "Not like the Battersea girls," she said definitively. "The soul is there, but it's afraid and hiding and very, very weak."

"What the devil. . . ." muttered John, and cast a suspicious glance at the woman, who shrugged, as if to say, *don't look at me, I had nothing to do with it.*

John scowled. Clearly he suspected Maude had done this herself—and Sarah didn't entirely disagree.

But she didn't agree, either.

She glanced at Nan, who nodded, and at Neville, who was calmly sitting on the back of a chair, and at Grey, who was doing the same. Suki sat at the hearth, toying with her amulet and alertly watching the faces of all of the adults in turn.

"There's a very simple way to determine the truth, here," she said aloud, and turned to Maude. "You allow my friend Nan to read your mind."

Now Maude looked bewildered. "Wut, naow?" she asked.

"Nan can see inside your head and know what you are thinking, even see some of your memories, if you will let her," Sarah began, then rephrased it. "Nan can see i' tha' head," she repeated, tapping her own temple. "Canst see wut tha' knows. Canst see the truth. But tha' mus' say 'aye.'"

Maude looked at her as if she thought Sarah was crazy, but then shook her head. "Yon *doctor* brung 'is pistol," she pointed out wryly. "'Es'd soon as not be shot." She gestured at Nan. "Es gi' 'ee leave."

It grew very quiet in the cottage again, giving Sarah the chance for another covert look around. It was smaller than Gatfer Cole's, and the ceiling was lower, but otherwise it looked pretty much the same. She could not imagine the amount of work it must have taken to haul all the stone needed for the walls and floor and the wall around the place here. She wondered how the woman—or whoever had built the place in the first place—had ever managed to get a crew of thatchers out to this remote spot.

There was a tangible aura of peace around it, however, that had been missing from Gatfer Cole's cottage. Not that there was anything wrong with the Gatfer's place—but this one almost felt like a religious retreat.

There were six small windows in the stone walls, each of them fitted with shutters currently standing wide open to allow the breeze to flow through, and the sounds of birdsong and the gentle clucking of the chickens. The air held so many different faint scents that Sarah couldn't really sort them out; they all mingled into a sort of faintly sweet hay scent that had a slightly bitter, medicinal undertone. That was all the drying herbs, she supposed.

"Well," said Nan, bringing her attention back to her friend. "I'm afraid you're going to have to look elsewhere for your villain, John. Everything is just as Maude told you. She found first this girl, then Helen Byerly, lying on the moor. There were many days between finding the first and the second. She was led to both by the circling of kites and ravens."

Neville made an embarrassed *quork*, as if to apologize for the uncouth manners of his brethren.

"She brought both of them back here. The only thing she hasn't told you is that Helen has been here for about four days, very sick, and unable to tell her anything, even her own name."

Maude shrugged. "One day like th' next, out 'ere. Get back se fore sometimes. On'y ever see shepherds, come fer sheep doses, trades fer wut Es needs. Reck it were a week, no more'n nine day 'tween findin' fust an' findin' second."

A rapid succession of emotions crossed John Watson's face, but the final one was disappointment. "Damnit," she heard him mutter under his breath. "Another dead end."

"Nay, lad. . . ." Maude, who certainly was not *that* much older than John Watson, reached out and patted his hand as if she were his grandmother. "Tha' knows some things naow. Tha' knows twa wee lasses can't ha' gone *too* far fra' th' monster what kept 'uns."

John's face lit up again. "That's true," he admitted. "I very much doubt they crossed the reservoir, for instance."

"Sur-e-ly they'd ha' seen th' smoke of Sheepstor an' gone there, ha' they come from North an' went round reservoir," Maude agreed. "Well, yon Helen would. T'other lass were maze as a brush."

"And if she had done that, she'd have known her way home," Mary Watson pointed out. "So she *had* to have come from south of the reservoir. That eliminates a vast amount of Dartmoor!"

"So it does," John agreed. But before he could continue with his musings, Maude interrupted him.

"Mayhap this will 'elp?" she said, and got up from where she was still sitting on the floor, went to the mantelpiece, and brought back a dirty bit of rag with something in it. She handed it to Watson, who opened it—and his face went white.

"*Dear God in Heaven!*" he exclaimed in something close to a yelp. "Where did—"

"Yon Helen had 'un knotted up in corner of 'er smock," Maude said, just as calmly as if she came across severed finger-ends every day. "Reckon it's her'n. Reckon th' lass *needed* t' 'ave it. Powerful magic on't, I cain't parse. 'Ee be th' Marsters 'ere." She gave John a long and measuring look. "Mark 'ee, there be twa bits, an' th' lass on'y lost one."

"One is clearly older than the other," John said, his voice shaking just the slightest bit.

"Well, then. Tha' be doctor. I bain't slept i' twa, three days. So . . . if tha'll watch forbye, I'll be 'avin' a sleep. Bring tha' horses up t'cot, tie 'em oop outside garden, gi' em what tha' wilt an' water an' watch lasses. When I wake, tha' can take the bits, hie 'ee back t' Yelverton an come back i' mornin'." She gave John no chance to object; she marched straight over to her bed, flung herself down on it, and was asleep in moments.

"I suppose," John said into the silence, "we had better do as she says."

There was about an hour to sundown. That was not the problem. All four of the adults had the skills in their various forms of magic to conjure enough of a light so the horses wouldn't step in something and break a leg, throw them, or both. And Mary's sylphs could easily find their way from this cottage back to Yelverton, even if Neville couldn't guide them in the dark.

No, the problem was what Sarah had found.

". . . so I don't know who that older bit is from, but we can dismiss it. If it ever connected to someone, it doesn't anymore." Sarah gulped around the lump of anxiety, and yes, fear, in her throat. "We know it's not from the comatose girl, because she has all her finger-ends, and that's what matters right now. But the other thing that matters is that Helen's *bit* is connected to her so powerfully that she literally cannot move beyond a certain distance from it. I saw it manifesting in the spirit world, and so did Nan and Suki."

Just to be *sure* that the comatose girl was not . . . call it "semi-dead" . . . and her spirit was somehow lurking in the spirit world,

Sarah and Nan had taken the time to go there themselves. And that was where they had seen it—a kind of twisted lump in the spirit world that was connected to little Helen. And when they had used their powers to look from the spirit world into the real world, they'd seen that what they had taken for a "lump" was a sort of perverted version of the cord that bound a soul to a body until the dissolution of death. Except this ugly, festering, pustulent thing looked like nothing so much as a half-rotten umbilical cord that tied Helen to that bit of finger.

"Wait a moment," said Mary, running her hand through her hair as she tried to remember something. "I think I've heard of this. There's a folk charm to keep an animal from straying. You take a bit of it, do the spell, and bury it in the center of the place you want to keep it from straying out of. It's good for chickens, or a goat or two you want to keep near your house, or a cow or pig if you're better off. Nice people use something like a dropped feather, or a toenail clipping. Nastier people—"

"—use a toe. Or a finger," John finished, as Mary shuddered. "I would imagine the further from 'alive' the bit is when you take it, the weaker the spell would be."

Sarah snapped her fingers. "I've heard of that, too! It's African magic as well—or, I guess I should say it's Elemental magic, just the African version."

"Very, very primitive Elemental magic," John corrected. "I very much doubt you'd find it in anything but the oldest of village-witch grimoires. But that's probably how the kidnapper kept Helen for so long." He cast a glance at the child, still huddled in her blankets, still caught in fever, although doing a little better after John got an extremely nasty mush of comfrey, lobelia, and bread mold into her. The bread mold was something else Sarah had remembered from Africa. Her parents had learned the use of it from the African shamans and healers they worked with, and had told her it worked too often to merely be a "cure by suggestion." He'd been dubious, but willing to try, since in his expert opinion, Helen had clearly contracted pneumonia as a result of her ordeal.

It seemed to be working, with a powerful assist from both John and Mary. Water Magic was far from ideal as a healing power, but John had been doing the best that he could with his powers for as long as he'd been a doctor, and it was beginning to look hopeful that Helen would recover.

Certainly more hopeful than when they had arrived here.

"Well, the point is, we can't just carry that rather grisly relic away with us," Sarah continued. "It has to stay with Helen, at least for now. *I* don't know of any way to sever the connection."

"It's amazing that she had the mother-wit to figure out she needed to take it with her," Mary mused. She was taking her turn at Helen's side—the other nameless girl didn't really seem to need much tending. Like the Battersea girls, she was something like an automaton; she ate when you put food in her mouth, drank when you put a cup to her lips, and otherwise needed nappies like a giant baby. Sarah was amazed that Maude had the patience and fortitude to tend someone in the girl's condition. Sarah wasn't quite sure how to bring her soul out of hiding—it wasn't in the spirit world—but perhaps if they just waited long enough, she'd wake up on her own. . . .

Or perhaps, if they could get her to a Fire or Earth Master— Earth, more likely—one of them would know what to do with her.

Right now, that was the least of their worries. They needed Helen to recover. They needed to find out where Helen had been, and if her brother was still alive. They needed to find whoever had taken them and bring him or her to justice.

"Well, obviously we leave the bit we can't take with Helen, and carry off the other bit," Mary said. "Surely we can learn as much from it as we could have from Helen's finger!"

Sarah wasn't at all sure about that, but what could she say? John and Mary had both been trained in their powers since childhood, and since then had had the assistance of Alderscroft's extensive circle of Elemental Magicians to learn more. She had only just learned she was a Spirit Master, only to find that Spirit Masters were so rare that there was very little known about them.

She just got the sense that time was getting away from them. Not just for Simon Byerly, but potentially for most, if not all, of the missing children.

The worst-case scenario is this blackguard finds out someone is looking for him—or her—gets the wind up, kills all the children, and escapes to hide somewhere else to start all over again. If that happened, the odds of tracking the bastard down were very low. Dartmoor was not the only remote place in the world. It wasn't even the only remote place in the British Isles. In fact, truth be told, the best place for her—or him—to hide would be in a big city like London or Plymouth. You could buy children right out of a workhouse or an orphanage, or off the street from their own parents. And if the magician confined him- or herself to using very little magic, it would be a nightmare to try to find him. Or her.

Especially if it was a her. As every woman knew, men, the police included, tended to overlook and underestimate women. Women got away with a *lot* of criminal activity for that very reason. And women had the excuse to have any number of children with them.

"I don't know, but until we know how to safely part Helen from that bit of herself, trying to pry some information out of the other finger is the only choice we have," John admitted. "I can't see any other way of finding out more about her captor."

"Actually," Nan said, slowly, "*I* can. With your permission, I can read her memories."

"Nan!" Sarah exclaimed with alarm. "The child's in a state of delirium! That's *incredibly* risky!"

"For anyone else, maybe," Nan replied with a shrug. "I have Neville, you, and Suki to anchor me and pull me out if I get caught up in a fever dream."

"Even so—" John and Mary protested together.

"I'll repeat what you just said—what other choice do we have?" Nan countered. "Besides, I want definitive proof that will convince you that Maude doesn't have a bevy of children locked up somewhere else. Do I have your permission, since it's a bit impractical to get it from the Byerlys?"

"My reluctant permission," said John, frowning. "Mary and I still do not trust this woman." He glanced at his wife, who nodded.

Sarah tried not to show her exasperation. "I think this is perhaps not the best idea, but we are running out of options," she admitted. "Right, Neville?"

The raven nodded.

"All right. We'll anchor you. Go ahead."

* * *

Nan had been itching to do this, since she sensed John and Mary's disbelief—and she was fairly certain that disbelief was entirely rooted in how unconventional Maude Rundle's appearance and way of life was. Here she was, a middle-aged woman who by all rights *should* be living the life of a Dartmoor housewife, off in the middle of nowhere living and dressing like a hermit, and a male hermit at that. And, perhaps, the fact that Maude gave him absolutely none of the deference he was accustomed to getting by virtue of being a doctor and a man of authority figured prominently into his attitude.

Actually, that's probably the entire cause of his disbelief. He expected to be treated with awe and gratitude when he announced that he was a doctor, and all he got was "shut up and help me get the child's fever down." Poor John. That must have been a dreadful shock.

She'd have been a lot more amused if the situation hadn't been so serious. Not that she didn't like and admire John Watson immensely, and usually he was humble to a fault, but every so often . . . well, every so often, he was a *man* instead of her peer in magic and her inferior when it came to strictly Psychical matters, and there was a certain faint condescension in his voice that grated.

At least he never says, "Don't worry your little head about it."

She composed herself next to Helen, sitting cross-legged on the floor next to her *(thank goodness for split skirts and a lack of corseting . . . and come to think of it I have suspicions that Maude Rundle hasn't a stitch on underneath that peculiar robe)*, then placed one hand on Helen's burning forehead and let herself sink gently into the child's mind.

The surface was a roil of hallucinations—and at first, that was *all* Nan thought they were. But as she drifted deeper into memory, and caught glimpses unclouded by fever, she nearly snapped out of her trance entirely. Because those hallucinations were not just the result of fever! They were the things she'd endured and feared, amplified, and only a *little*, by the fever! Everything in those visions was mirrored in the girl's memories!

Central to all of it was something Helen thought of as "the Dark One," a menacing figure neither obviously male nor female, wearing a robe not unlike Maude's, probably to hide its shape.

Helen thought of it as a "witch," gender uncertain, and indeed, in her mind a "witch" could be either man or woman. Helen was utterly terrified of the creature, and Nan didn't blame her in the least. The most unnerving part was that there was nothing inside the cowl of the robe but shadows, and Nan was absolutely certain this was *not* a product of the fever, that this was, in fact, the creature's actual appearance, at least to the children.

And, oh yes, children. There were children, more than Simon. Nan sank deeper into Helen's mind, and picked through memories rather than hallucinations, willing herself to go as deep as she needed to in order to glean as much information as she could.

The first thing that formed up clearly was the prison that held them all, along with their captor. This was a two-room cottage, roughly twice the size of Maude's. The walls were stone, the floor of pounded and treated earth. Nan watched as the memories unscrolled, Helen going through the work of the day under the control and direction of the Dark One. She cleaned, cooked, baked a great deal of bread, fed the prisoners—eleven children including Simon, all of them chained up by one leg in the second, comfortless room. She tended a garden and some chickens, fetched water and wood. Meanwhile the Dark One lounged about, eating far better food than it fed its captives, and Helen's emotions boiled with terror mixed with rage.

Nan delved further. *Show me what happened to your hand*, she commanded gently, and after a moment of resistance, the memory opened up for her. She experienced the horrible moment when the Dark One chopped off Helen's finger. And the subsequent moments when one of the children (*Sam,* said the memories) actually healed the stump right before Nan's astonished eyes!

He must be an Earth Magician—potentially a Master!

And then she witnessed something she had expected from the beginning, a moment when the Dark One chased Helen from the room, raised its arms, and all of the children in that room dropped instantly into what looked like sleep.

This was not sleep, obviously, and the Dark One was not there to do those children any favors. This was, as she and the others had suspected from the beginning, some sort of way of draining those children of magic power. And why was Helen spared?

The answer is obvious. Because she hasn't a particle of magic in her. But her brother does. She was only useful to the Dark One as a servant.

Well, she had some of the answers, if not all of them. Not yet.

She had to wade through other memories first, including Helen's first attempts at escape, and the Dark One summoning moor ponies to ride off—somewhere. But the answer to *where* this prison-cottage was located was not in those.

She went deeper, to the moment they found this place. This, like Maude's cottage, was at the back of a wooded combe, and again, there was no real way of telling *where* it was. There were no landmarks. She was nowhere near familiar enough with Dartmoor to tell one valley from another. The siblings had been lost when they stumbled on it—

Or did they stumble? Helen had no idea where to go after that first night on the moor. What if Simon was lured there? That would make perfect sense; he's the one with magic, so he would be the most sensitive to a lure like that. In fact, the lure might just have been set to only bring in children with magic. All Simon had to do was drift in the right general direction for them to find the place. They were busy foraging; Helen wasn't paying attention to where they were going as long as they continued to gather food.

She moved forward to the moment in time when Helen escaped successfully, and ran out of the woods that were hiding the cottage and got up on the first hill and looked about herself, trying to orient herself—

—absolutely nothing looked familiar. Not to Helen, and not to Nan.

Damnit! These cursed moorlands all look alike!

There was nothing in any direction in the way of any sort of notable landmark, no distinctively shaped rocks or bodies of water, no tree taller than the rest, and no thin skeins of smoke rising on the horizon that would have indicated a cottage or even a village. Just the moor, a few ponies in the far distance. Poor Helen, there was not even a sign of a single sheep—if she'd found sheep, she could have found the shepherd eventually.

But Helen had known she had to put as much distance between herself and the cottage as she could, because the Dark One would be on her heels as soon as it returned and found her gone. So she just picked a direction and started walking. The only thing in her mind was her father's advice; if lost, find water and follow it.

But she never found water. And a storm found her.

Caught out in the open after dark when she thought she had settled into a good enough shelter, a storm came racing across the moors, the sky poured rain down on her, and she was soaked to the skin. By morning she was aching and nearly frozen and starting to sniffle. By noon, she sat down and never got up again, exhausted, too tired and sick even to eat, and by night she was semi-conscious and in a fever.

It's a wonder she survived that night.

Nan carefully pulled herself out of the memories, wishing they had that boy Sam with them now. When she opened her eyes, everyone was staring at her—except Maude, who was still asleep.

Outside, birds sang. Inside, Helen wheezed (though not as badly as she had when they first arrived). Otherwise it was completely silent in the cottage, with everyone, even Suki, watching her intently, as if they expected her to have the answer to everything.

If only she did!

"Well," she said, "I still don't know who had Helen, or where she was held. But I learned a lot, and I absolutely know Maude Rundle is completely innocent."

The one thing that Sarah regretted *not* having with them were those wretched sketching kits, which they had left behind when they'd gone back to the Rock for the horses. They were full of paper and colored pencils and would have proved immensely useful in making drawings of the Dark One and the Dark One's cottage and its surroundings. If only they'd had the kits, they might have been able to *show* them to Maude or Gatfer Cole, and they might have recognized something about the cottage.

But at least *now* Nan had the information to convince John and Mary that Maude was not the villain here.

"But wait!" John, of course, protested. "Maude is wearing the same sort of robe the Dark One was! She could have invoked the shadows within the hood—"

"Shadows, maybe," Nan countered. "But unless Maude can cast the illusion that she's nearly a foot taller than she is now, and hide her very ample breasts, that's unlikely. I can show you the memory again, if you'd like, but we know how tall Helen is, we know how tall Maude is, and we know that the Dark One did not have bosoms big enough to nurse quadruplets."

"But—" John began.

"You're the Master. You can rate lesser Elemental Mages, and they can't hide their power from you. You can tell how much power she has. So how much power *does* she have?" Nan interrupted.

John sighed. "Not enough," he admitted. "Not for that big an illusion, that close to the subject, and not for as long as Helen had the Dark One in sight."

So by the time Maude woke again, the Watsons were no longer assuming she was the kidnapper.

Maude listened very carefully to Nan's description of the cottage where the children were being held, but shook her head with regret. "Dunno 't. Moors be full'a combes an' ancient cots. If'n 'ee arst me 'bout a *person*, might could tell 'ee. But cot in combe on moor? Nomye. Could 'ide a circus an' a dizzen nelly-fants on moor. No more 'ould Es've laid eyen on't, sin 'ee reck there be spells on't t' hide 't."

"At least we know who this girl is now," Sarah observed, gesturing at the one that was still comatose. "Her name is Rose." She glanced back over at Maude. "Can you use that to bring her out of her sleep?"

Maude scratched her head speculatively. "Aye," she said slowly. "Reckon Es can. Need t'make th' lass feel safe, an' 'earin' a 'ooman callin' 'er name saft-like, that'd 'elp."

John glanced out the window, into the growing dusk. There was an owl calling out there. "We need to go. The horses need to be back to their stable, and we need to think of a way to find that cottage. Can you manage without us?" John asked. "Because if you can't, one of us will stay here with you to help you with both girls."

"Oh aye," Maude replied, "Naow Es got some sleep. Right fitty uv 'ee, Marster Doctor, t'gi th' wench th' mold. Niver recked on that. Knowed it were good fer wounds, niver thought it were good et."

John shrugged, but Sarah could tell that he was pleased.

"Go an' find that divil," she continued, her tone turning wrathful. "Stop at Gatfer Cole, tell t' awld woodquist, Maude needs 'im, an' all tha' lidden, an' 'e'll be 'ere aggoon. Can crost moor t' 'ere 'oodman-blind, 'e can."

John gaped at her. "You know Gatfer Cole?"

She snorted. "Don' Es? Pisht. *An'* Ganmer Dolly down t' Yelverton. An' Linwood at Rock, though 'e thinks 'e be too 'portant t'know usn's. Off wi' 'ee. Soonest begun is soonest done!"

18

If Simon had not been so mind-numbingly weary, he would have been crying again.

There was no doubt in his mind now that Something Bad had happened to Ellie, because otherwise she *would* have found people, and help, and someone would have come—for him, if not for the other children. He and the others had had a single moment of hope, a day or so ago—it was hard to keep track—when the Dark One came in with another rough-looking man, *wearing his own face and in normal clothing.* Because they hadn't known at that point that it *was* the Dark One, and seeing two strange men come in the door, they'd all thought it was rescue at last, and had started crying out for help.

Only to have their hopes utterly crushed, as the weedy little man turned toward their prison and grinned, showing a mouth full of crooked yellow teeth.

"Oh 'ee thin' usn's 'ere t' '*elp* 'ee, does 'ee?" And he had let out a guffaw as the other man just stood there, like a mommet.

Simon had understood what was going on immediately, and so had Robbie, though it took several long moments while the weedy man laughed and laughed and laughed. "Look 'ere, mate," the weedy man had said to the other. "See, Es gots own slaveys an' all. 'Elp me 'aul in t'goods."

The weedy man was the Dark One! Either this was the Dark One's proper form, or, more likely, the Dark One had been taking the shape of a proper man in order to visit whatever place he was going where he was getting all his booty. Either way, whoever the second man was, mate, ally, or another devil, there was no help coming from him, either.

Slowly the other children realized this too, and shrank back against the wall as they brought in bottles and bags of stuff and stowed them on the floor next to the hearth. It was enough to have required the services of four ponies, which explained why the Dark One had needed help.

When they brought in the last load, the other man finally spoke. "'Ow 'ee cotch 'em, Anglin?" he asked casually. "They ain't got kin?"

The Dark One picked his teeth with his thumbnail. "Witchery, mate. Th' cot's th' flower, they's th' bees, they vaught 'ere. Lost, run-off, lost kin, don' matter. They on moor alone, 'ear th' cot callin' an' they come. An' that's 'ow Es get lasses. They chillern got witchery-blood too, else they'd not've heerd th' call, an' I c'n take the witchery from 'em." He leaned back against the doorpost, arms crossed casually over his chest. "'Ee wanter see?"

The other man looked intrigued. "Aye! Ain't never seed no witchery!"

"Bide 'ee," the Dark One said, and walked into their prison room like he always did.

No! Simon thought in anguish, because the Dark One had *just* put them into the Dark Sleep yesterday!

But of course, no one cared what Simon wanted, least of all the Dark One.

When the terrors broke their hold on him, he couldn't open his eyes, but his ears worked just fine. "Eh, Anglin," said the stranger. "That were a wunner!"

"Aye mate," the Dark One said, laughing. "Too bad 'ee ain't gonna 'member none of 't!"

And exhaustion pulled Simon down into true sleep.

With one of Mary's sylphs guiding them and John conjuring a light for the horses to see by, they moved across the moor at a quick trot. The moor was both beautiful and eerie at night; owl calls traveled for miles, and all the shadows seemed to hold secrets.

The temperature was dropping quickly, and Sarah shivered in the damp breeze, and wished she had brought something heavier to throw over her shoulders. The Gatfer was still awake when they rode up to his cottage, and when he heard what they had to say, he quickly threw a few things into a sack. Then he did something odd. He took some small object down from his mantelpiece into his cupped hands, whispered to it, closed his eyes and waited for a moment, then put it back. Sarah could not be entirely sure what it was . . . but it had looked like a little bundle of twigs.

When they all went outside, there was a most peculiar-looking little black dog waiting patiently just outside the door. And when Sarah took a look at it with the Sight, it nearly blinded her with the amount of magic packed into its body.

"Eh, Grim," Gatfer said by way of a salute. "Well come, an' thanks t' tha Marster. Twa maids be desperd cruel sick over t' Auld Maude's. Wilt guide un's safe there?"

The dog let out a surprisingly deep and pleasant-sounding bark. Neville and Grey eyed it, and nodded their approval. Gatfer turned to John. "No fear, Water Marster. Th' Grim be a friend, nay a fiend. Haste 'ee back, Chell haste on. Tha' knows where t'find me, an' tha' needs me."

And without another word, off he went, following the little black dog that frisked on ahead, as if this were a pleasure trip, moving so quickly he might have had eyes like an owl. A moment later, and he was lost to the shadows on the moor.

"Is that—" John began.

"Some sort of creature that owes allegiance to Robin?" Sarah finished. "I think so, yes. I think the Gatfer has had his own share of encounters with the Oldest Old One—and Maude and the girls are out of our hands now. Let's get back to Yelverton."

By this time it was so dark that the lights of Yelverton were visible through the trees in the distance, and they were near enough that the horses could smell their stable and were eager to get into it. The stableman looked relieved to see them, but did not make any more fuss about their late return than that.

Wonderful smells as well as light and noise came from the open kitchen door, spilling out into the yard between the kitchen and the stable.

They were all ravenous, but John asked at the bar for a meal of steak and kidney pie to be brought up to the Watsons' room rather than wait for it in the public room; at this point they were all too impatient to dally around where they couldn't speak freely.

They all hurried up the stairs to the second floor and the Watsons' room. But the moment John opened his door, he froze.

"Don't just stand there, Watson," came Holmes' voice from inside. "I think I've found your villain, and mine, and if I am correct, as I deduced, they are one and the same. But before I reveal what I have learned, tell me what you know."

Nan waited somewhat impatiently as the servant who brought up their meal also found another chair for the unexpected visitor, and fussed about laying everything out on the table before she would leave. Nan really wanted to take the girl by the nape and the behind and shove her out the door—but that would have been unpardonably rude, and more important, it would have told her there was something going on that might be worth the risk of listening at the keyhole for.

Finally she left, and they ate—while talking. Holmes listened carefully to everything they had to say, nodding from time to time as he methodically worked his way through his piece of pie and mashed turnips. They each took turns in the telling, and Nan sensed that all of them were paying very little attention to the meal except as fodder, until everything they knew was all laid out in front of Holmes.

And it was at that point that they were all interrupted *again* by the servant coming back for the emptied plates. Nan was about to burst with impatience, when Sarah solved the problem of the girl lingering about—probably hoping to hear some choice gossip she could tell the others in the kitchen—by dropping a substantial tip on her tray. She was in such a hurry then to secure her prize that the dishes clattered as she stacked them hastily, and she fairly flew out the door.

Problem solved. Well done, Sarah.

"I will begin at the beginning," Holmes said. "As you know, I am protecting the reputation of several young ladies. *At least* five, although I only know the identity of one for certain. Now, this is how it began. I am waiting on several schemes for the rounding up of the last of Moriarty's men to come to fruition, and Mycroft knew I was essentially sitting idle. So when I made my usual contact with him, he proposed I take the case of a lady of his acquaintance. She came to him in great distress, and without the knowledge of her husband, to tell him that she had unaccountably fallen prey to a ruffian here in Yelverton. I agreed only to hear her story, before I would commit to helping, partly because I did not know if I could, and partly because I wanted to hear the whole of it from her directly. And, to be honest, partly because I was not in the least interested in helping someone avoid divorce proceedings. Granted, Mycroft is usually very good at sniffing out things that are of no interest to me, but the lady is very fair, and Mycroft is slightly more susceptible to the female sex than I am. So I heard her out myself, and I was immediately both interested and alarmed."

John raised his eyebrow skeptically, but didn't interrupt.

"You know me better than that, John," Holmes chided. "This lady is very much enamored of her husband, and the story she told me was so strange I was certain it had to be true. They were here to take a walking tour of the moors. This unfortunate event occurred on the last night they were to stay, here, at this very hotel. She went out for a breath of air as her husband was entertaining several young Oxford students in the taproom who were here for a walking tour of their own, as he, too, is a Magdalene man. More than a little bored by very old cricket exploits, and not ready to go back to their room alone, she came out to the front to sit and admire the view and the moonlight. And that was when she was accosted by someone she described as 'a very rough fellow.' It began merely as a simple 'wot' 'ee doin' 'ere, miss,' which she rebuffed with, 'I am waiting for my husband.' At least, that was her intention, but what came out was, 'My husband is inside.' And the next thing she knew, she was overcome by what I can only describe as unnatural, inescapable lust for him. She told me that it was as if she was under some evil spell, and her will was not her own. I will not describe what followed, save to say only that not only did she give herself to him, she also gave him every penny she had on her person, and a very valuable necklace, then as if she were sleepwalking, left him, went straight up to the room, undressed and went to bed, and fell instantly asleep. Her husband joined her some time later, none the wiser. She told him later that she had lost the necklace some time that day during their last walk and had not noticed it was gone until morning, but she was so distressed that it and her folly might be traced back to her that she came straight to Mycroft, and then, to me."

"Good Lord, Holmes. . ." Watson said, stunned.

Like Watson, Nan had remained skeptical until she heard the details. What reason would a respectable woman have had to make up such an unbelievable tale? It sounded like the old myth of the incubus, and no one in the modern world would believe her wild tale. They would immediately assume that she'd . . . well . . . that this had been a completely willing and mutual seduction.

No, no one would believe her.

No one, that is, except someone who was a true magician, or knew one. And none of *them* would risk exposure for the sake of helping some foolish wench who'd dared to leave the sacred protection of her husband and wander outside in a strange village alone.

And that made her wonder. Had she and Sarah just escaped the same fate by always being together? Or if Holmes had not approached her that first evening, would she have met this villain?

Holmes tapped one long finger on the table, recapturing her attention. "This was by no means the end of it. I put my ear to the ground, put some discreet advertisements in the Plymouth and London papers, and received four more letters from ladies with identical stories on the condition of anonymity. One such tale is extraordinary. But five? It passes the bounds of reason. And the first thing I thought, now that you have opened my eyes to the world of the supernatural, was—"

"A glamorie," said Watson, interrupting him. "That's the ancient word for it. It's a sort of lust-spell. It clouds the mind of the victim until all she—or he; it can be put on a man as well as a woman— can't think of anything but pleasing the caster. Good Lord!"

Silence reigned for a moment, the muslin curtains stirring in the breeze from the open window, until a nightingale outside the window broke it.

"Indeed," said Holmes, nodding solemnly, his brows slightly creased. "So the first thing that I thought when I heard about your missing children and the fact that there might be magic involved was that it was exceedingly unlikely there were two such practitioners of dark arts in the same area. Although I did not want to think about what use this devil was making of children—"

"It's horrible, but not as horrible as what you are contemplating," Watson said hastily, interrupting him.

Holmes' brow cleared a little. "Well, that is something, at any rate."

"And by Jove, it does sound like your man and ours are one and the same!" John continued. "Because now the reason for taking those children is stunningly clear. He's using them like a battery, Holmes. You remember that blackguard Spencer, who was using spirits for the same purpose? One can use the living as easily as the dead, as long as one can control them. He has not got enough power of his own to enable him to cast the sort of strong glamorie that will completely overpower the will. So he is using the children to give him the power to cast a glamorie over women strong enough to overcome every semblance of sanity and reason they have—and, it sounds like, enrich himself at the same time."

Nan had been thinking quickly. "He has probably been at this for some time. We know, thanks to the chief constable of Yelverton, that more children than usual have gone missing out here for about four years. He probably started longer ago than that, using his abilities to seduce women no one would believe anyway, and who would probably not put up much resistance, since they are—well, accustomed to shabby treatment. Barmaids, scullery maids, servant girls. Then he set his sights higher, and discovered he needed more magical strength in order to overpower a woman who was more likely to resist him. Somehow he learned he could drain this power from others who have the power in them, even though they might not be aware they were magicians, and hit on captive children, unable to resist him, as the perfect—cows, if you will. He must have been collecting them for these past four years, until now he can work his will as fast as they can recharge his powers."

Holmes nodded. "I believe your speculations are correct, Nan. I've laid eyes on the man, Watson. More than that, I've befriended the fiend."

"What?" exclaimed Watson. "How?"

"I've been in disguise, camping rough on the moor in the guise of a tramping fellow, and doing my best to make the close acquaintance of every ne'er-do-well and tramp in and around this village, in hopes of finding him." Holmes traced a little circle on the tabletop with his index finger. "I've bought them drinks, I've listened to their boasts, and I finally came across one 'Ansel Anglin' who swore in his cups that he could have any woman he cared to, no matter her station. In fact, I befriended him so thoroughly that he took me into his confidence. And that was when I got actual proof that he was the man I sought."

They all leaned forward. "Don't keep us in suspense, Sherlock!" exclaimed Sarah.

Sherlock made a little face. "I was winkled, and only the fact that I am not a magician makes this less than an utter shame on my part. He said he needed another set of hands to help him haul some 'supplies' back to his cottage on the moor. And I agreed to help him today, early this morning. And therein lies the problem. I know I did so. I can't remember doing it."

They all stared at Holmes, dumbfounded.

"How is that even possible?" Nan demanded.

"I don't know," Holmes replied, looking exceedingly pained, as if the admission actually hurt him to make. "I can only think that he must have cast another spell to make me forget everything that happened *after* a certain point when I was with him and his ponies, riding out to his home, and *before* I found myself riding my hired nag back, somewhere on the moor near enough to Yelverton to see the smoke from the chimneys in the distance. Everything in between is a blank. I only know I was doing something because of the lapse of time, and the fact that I was outside of the town. *Is* that a spell that is possible?"

"It is," Watson confirmed. "It's another sort of spell that works on the mind like a glamorie. I know how *I* would have done it; as a Master, I could simply control you the moment I cared to, perhaps within sight of my combe, and make you see only what I wanted you to see. In this case, nothing, until I released you within sight of Yelverton. So either the memories never existed at all, or he did something else and the memories vanished, and I very much doubt even Nan can retrieve them."

Sherlock glanced and Nan, who shrugged. "I don't think so," she told him. "If what I am sensing from John is correct, the memories are completely excised, like cutting out a bad piece of ribbon and splicing the ends together. He obviously did this to keep the location of his cot a complete secret."

John nodded. "And if he has a very limited budget of power to draw on, he can probably only cast one strong spell at a time. This would be why he doesn't make the women he abuses forget what happened after he has had his way with them. He'd be much safer if he could do that."

Or he relishes the control it gives him over them even after they are out of his orbit, Nan thought angrily. *He knows that for as long as they live, they will have to live with the memory of him taking liberties with them.*

"Confounded clever," Holmes said sourly. "And if I should confront him about it, he'll likely laugh that I drank too much of his scrumpy to remember what happened. He's getting bolder, Watson. Before, he was hiding. Now, he's counting on his power and the reluctance of the women he despoils to talk to keep from being caught."

It was an angry silence in the room now, and for similar if not identical reasons. Suki was just angry this man was getting away with hurting people. She and Sarah and probably Mary were enraged that this rapist had felt himself absolutely free to do whatever he wanted to any woman he chose, and probably thought it only his due. Holmes—well, Holmes hated injustice more than anything else in the world, and this was a terrible injustice. And Watson—

Watson had been thinking, by the look on his face, and so had Nan, both of them thinking past their rage. She got up first, and got John's map.

She spread it out over the table. "Blue is for the places where we magicians cannot 'see' anything, and Mary's sylphs also cannot see and cannot enter. You'll recall that evil man Spencer had set up exclusionary wards of that sort around his lair. It takes a very powerful magician to do that *for himself*, but lesser magicians can accomplish the same thing by layering protection atop protection over the course of time. We were told by Robin Goodfellow that people have been doing that in isolated spots all over Dartmoor for as long as there have been humans living here. We reckoned that although this man is not strong in himself, he had found one of those places. Not knowing which one he was in, we found and had begun investigating them today."

"And red?" Holmes asked.

"And red is the location of people known to be 'witches' by the locals," Nan finished. "Because we could not be certain that this man had not managed to get himself a reputation as a witch."

Holmes nodded.

John got a pencil and put an "X" through the one in Yelverton itself where Ganmer Dolly lived, the one outside Yelverton where Gaffer Cole lived, both of which were marked by red *and* blue dots, and put a third "X" through the blue dot that represented Maude Rundle's cottage. "As you know, we eliminated these three today, and little Helen Byerly and the girl we only know as 'Rose' is in the third of these locations."

"And those three cannot be the cottage to which I was taken," Holmes noted.

"True. And being the methodical man that you are," Watson continued. "I am certain that you noted the time that you left Yelverton, how fast the horse was traveling, and the time that you found yourself outside of Yelverton again with part of your memory missing. Given that, you can probably give us an arc of the farthest possible point you could have ridden to, assuming that you spent at least half an hour unloading whatever you helped transport."

"What if the fiend took a roundabout way?" Mary objected. "In order to throw off any attempt to backtrack?"

"Given that I know the man fairly well, I think that unlikely," Holmes said. "He is supremely self-confident. He often boasts that he has tricked people 'who think they are smarter than he is.' And he is impatient. He is always in a great hurry to get whatever he has in his head that he wants to do accomplished. I think he would count on his magic to muddle his trail, rather than take a route that would require more time."

Sarah snapped her fingers. "That's *especially* true if he didn't actually have the power to take over your memory when you two rode out!"

"What are you suggesting?" Watson asked.

"That he didn't work his spell the way you thought. He waited until Holmes was in the cottage, and cut out the memories then!" Sarah exclaimed.

"Well," John replied after a long moment to think. "It is true that I have heard Earth Magicians can work the trick that way. Especially if they also have a touch of Psychical abilities like yours, Nan."

"When did you say he came to you and asked for help?" Sarah asked.

"As I said, the night before—early in the evening, just before sundown, in fact," Holmes told her. "Then he said he'd see me in the morning, and left before I could buy him another round—" Holmes' brows rose. "Clever girl. I see where your thoughts are taking you. He surely had a prime plum to pick that night, one that he expected would bring him a pretty piece of money as well as other satisfactions. Plucking that prize would expend all his magical energies, and in addition, he would have to wait till morning in order to buy what he wanted with his stolen money and bring it all back to his lair. And he needed my help because he expected to be able to buy more than he could reasonably transport by himself. That left him a problem—whatever confederate he chose would know where he lived. But he knew that all he had to do was get back to his cot, and he'd be able to restore himself enough to take my memories. Well done! Nan, have you a notion of how long it takes him to recharge from the children's power, based on Helen's memory?"

"Well, she didn't exactly have a watch," Nan replied wryly, "But I can make a good guess. I'd say about half an hour."

Holmes took the pencil from Watson and began scribbling on the edge of the map. "It's like a confounded schoolboy's mathematical problem. If the train starts at the station at 11 o'clock and travels at twenty miles an hour. . . ." he muttered, looking at his sums, then to the map, then erasing a number and substituting another. Finally he got a total he thought he liked. "Have you got a bit of string about you?" he asked, looking from John to Mary and back again—presumably because it was their room.

Mary laughed. "No woman is ever without a bit of string,

Holmes," she chided, and went to her traveling workbox. She brought him a spool of heavy cotton thread of the sort used to mend "cluny" lace.

"Confounded useful creatures, you ladies are," he said, accepting it. "No wonder Watson married one."

"I'll take that as a compliment," all three of the ladies present chorused.

He tied the pencil to the end of it, then measured out a length of the string against the scale on the map and bit it off, put his thumb on the loose end in the center of Yelverton, and drew an arc on the map with the pencil.

"There you are," he said. "Wherever that cottage is, it will be within and probably along that arc."

They all contemplated the result as the nightingale caroled. There was only one blue dot within that arc, lying so close to the penciled sweep that you could not have gotten the edge of a penny between it and the graphite.

"We shouldn't leap into this," Watson said, staring at the map, at Nan's sketches of the cot and the combe, and sometimes into space. "We need a solid plan."

Nan rubbed her temple. Part of her wanted to rush out there and murder the bastard while he slept. Impossible to do, of course, for he surely had protections, if only a locked door—but it was what she wanted to do.

"The obvious, and simplest, approach is to attempt to get to the door unseen, then rush the door and take him by surprise," said Mary, who looked just as impatient to murder him as Nan.

"And what if the door is locked?" said Holmes. "Just because most moorland folk do not leave their doors locked even when they leave their homes, it does not follow that this man will do the same. In fact, I would be extremely surprised if he did *not* keep his door locked except when he is doing something out of doors, or using the earth-closet. He already lost one child; he's unlikely to take that chance again. And he is the sort that would trust no one, especially not now. After all, he stole my memories to keep me from finding him again."

"What if I—" Suki began. Holmes quelled her with a look. "I will not risk your life, Suki, and if he catches a whiff of the rest of us, he will certainly use you as a hostage."

"And therein lies the problem," said Watson. "He has a dozen hostages, all secured in a farther room. If we accost him at his cottage, even with my pistol, he will have the upper hand, and he can and will use any or all of the children as a distraction or a human shield."

Nan's head ached, and that pie was not sitting easily on her stomach.

"Or he can just bolt into that inner room, lock the door, and murder them all to get enough power to make an escape," Nan pointed out. "The only reason they are still alive is because he needs to keep them alive as a constant, reliable source of power. If he's cornered, he has no reason to do that; he can drain them to death while we try to break in, then—could he get enough power to kill *us*?" She looked to Watson.

"Kill all of us? Probably not. A Master could, but he is not a Master, or he wouldn't be using the children as he is, he would be getting power from his Elementals. But he can certainly render all of us unconscious with the power gained by draining a dozen children to death, which would enable his easy escape."

"Oh Lord," Nan moaned, as something else occurred to her. Tomorrow Helen's mother would be expecting a missive, brought by Neville. And what was she going to say? "*What* am I going to send to Maryanne Byerly in the morning? I can't tell her we've found Helen; I can't risk this devil finding out about what I told her! He could come to Maryanne and force her to tell him where Helen is!"

"You'll lie to her," Sherlock said, steadily. "You'll tell her only that you are still certain her children are alive, and that you are slowly eliminating possible miscreants. Tell her any more than that and she'll do what any mother would do—she'll rush into Sheepstor to find someone that knows the way to Maude's cottage and in a few hours all of Sheepstor will know she's found Helen and where Helen is. You'll put Maude, Helen, and Maryanne all in terrible danger."

He was right. Of course he was right. There was absolutely no question that this was exactly what would happen. Gossip flew like the wind, even in a place as isolated as Dartmoor. "I hate this," Nan replied.

"But you'll do it," he countered. "Now, let's find a way to bring this demon to justice."

"Go to the chief constable?" asked Suki. "Bring a whole herd of perlice down on t' bastard?"

There was a certain amount of glee in her voice, and Nan knew why. She'd missed out on the massive raid on Spencer's lair, and desperately wanted to be part of another.

"That would just cause the same problem as before, Suki," Watson said patiently. "You have seen these stone cottages. They have walls like a fortress. The man can just lock himself in with the children, kill them all, and use the power he gains to escape."

"How?" Suki demanded. "He can't put a whole herd of perlice t'sleep!"

"No, but . . . I'm sure he could find another way to escape, like—" John was at a loss for an answer.

But Mary had one that would satisfy Suki. "We already know he can make himself look like a demon. He can use the power to make himself look like a constable. All he needs to do is hide until the police break in, then mingle with them, and escape that way. This won't be a situation where the police all know each other— there are not enough men in Yelverton, the chief constable will want to make a raid in force, and he will take the time to recruit more men from Milton Combe or Tavistock or even Buckfast. It will be easy for this man to hide himself among policemen who do not know each other."

"But—" Suki protested, still wanting to see and be part of a rush of angry, determined police, maybe even with pistols! Nan saw it all in the child's mind, and honestly, Nan couldn't blame her.

"And if he waits to recruit men from outside Yelverton, there is always the chance that someone here will warn him. And if *that* happens, he'll murder the children for their power, call a moor pony, and ride away to freedom with no one the wiser," Holmes added. "When the police raid comes, they will find an empty cottage and eleven dead children."

Crestfallen, Suki subsided. Nan gestured to her to come, and Suki got up off the bed and came to her for a comforting hug.

"I wanta *get* him," she murmured into Nan's side. "Lookit what he done to Helen an' Rose!"

"And we want to get him too. That's why we're working out the perfect plan to do just that, so he can't get away." Nan gave her another squeeze; she sighed, and reluctantly pulled away, going back to the bed to sit.

"Well, let's see if we can eliminate all the other possibilities of taking the monster in its lair," Mary suggested. "No matter how ridiculous they are."

"Get dynamite? Blow 'em up?" Suki suggested hopefully, then sighed. "No, that'd blow up the children."

"What if you approached the cot alone, Holmes, got him to invite you inside, and slipped chloral hydrate into his scrumpy?" Nan asked, thinking of the sort of plot one would find in a penny-dreadful.

"He'll want very much to know how I managed to remember where his cot is," Holmes replied. "And as Watson pointed out, he can probably render me and the rest of you unconscious."

"What if you meet him tonight and—" John looked at his watch. "Hrm. Probably not tonight; if he came here to drink tonight he is probably gone now. Well, tomorrow night, then."

"I could crawl the pubs looking for him, but it's pure luck if I'd find him. I haven't been meeting him every single night," Sherlock replied. "But go on. You were going to suggest?"

"We know he's got jewelry. I don't think he's disposed of it. There's no pawnbroker here in Yelverton," John pointed out. "What if you told him you were making a little trip to Plymouth and suggested that if he had anything he wanted to change for money, you could do that for him? Show some loot of your own; Mary has a couple of pieces of jewelry you could borrow."

"I'd give them to you outright if it would help," Mary encouraged.

"And you can have my watch," Nan offered.

"And then get him to take you back to his cot," John finished. "Then, chloral hydrate in the scrumpy, tie him up and gag him, call the chief constable. A room full of children in chains is going to be hard to explain away, not to mention stolen goods. And I may not be Sherlock Holmes, but I *am* John Watson. Some of your cachet rubs off on me. You disappear after we make him mute and paralyzed even if he wakes from the chloral hydrate, Mary goes for the chief constable, when he gets there I say, 'Look, sir, I have tracked the blackguard to his den, rendered him helpless, and solved the case we have been working on! No, no, sir, I am modest, *you* take all the credit!'"

"That does sound very like you, Watson," Sherlock said dryly. "You gave away all the credit for the Battersea case to Lestrade."

Watson shrugged. "Why not? It does the man good. He's competent on his own ground. And it's not as if I can write about my own cases, only yours."

Sherlock raised an eyebrow at him. "And *do* you have chloral hydrate with you?"

John actually looked a trifle offended. "Even if I didn't take my doctor's bag with me everywhere, and I do, I am *never* without every usual and unusual weapon I have at my disposal when I am on a case."

"But hold that thought about the stolen goods," Holmes said, light suddenly dawning in his eyes. "I think I have a plan. A plan that will not put the children in danger." He glanced over at Suki, and smiled at her. "And will need *all* of us."

19

Nan watched the little cot at the back of the wooded combe through Neville's eyes. He complained a bit—but only a little bit—about having to soar in circles above the general area, but he understood the urgency of their task, and his complaints were, she suspected, more for show than anything else.

Understanding Neville took some sideways thinking. He did not understand altruism except when it pertained to his flock. He didn't care one bit about those eleven children; they weren't in his flock. He didn't care if they were rescued, murdered, or remained enslaved. But the thought of *Suki* being in such a position put him in such a red rage Nan could not control him. The best she could do to keep him interested in this dull task was to remind him that these children were *like* Suki, and she wasn't entirely sure he grasped that idea, but at least he understood that it was important to her, and therefore he should keep doing it.

He'd already delivered a reassuring letter to Maryanne Byerly with a few tidbits of new information, enough to let her know that everyone was still focused on finding her children. He'd delivered a second to Gatfer Cole at Maude's cot, that should get the Gatfer in place by noon. Now he circled over what was a tantalizing blue dot on the map, and had proven to indeed be a wooded combe, with a stone cottage with a slate roof at the rear of it, a garden surrounding it, and what looked like a matching chicken coop, stone walls, slate roof, and all.

And now the door was opening. A black-haired girl, her hair chopped off roughly at chin-level, and dressed only in a man's smock, came out, with a careful look over her shoulder, as if to make certain that she was not going to be interfered with. The glance must have reassured her, because she went around the side of the cottage to open the chicken coop, which disgorged an orderly procession of hens.

Call to her, Neville, Nan said.

Obediently, Neville let out a raucous series of loud *quorks*. The girl looked up, pulling lank-looking black hair out of her eyes.

Deborah, Nan thought with satisfaction, recognizing the girl from Helen's memories. This was the right place.

And that meant that if you drew a straight line from here to Yelverton, Gatfer Cole's cottage would be close enough to that line that someone sitting at the east window with a good pair of binoculars would be able to see anyone heading from the cottage into the village.

All right, Neville. Go to Gatfer Cole's and wait for Mary.

With great relief, the bird stopped circling and headed straight for Gatfer. He liked the old man very much. The old man was *almost* flock. Certainly Neville would have been willing to share a dead sheep with him.

If the situation had not been so serious, Nan would have laughed at that. Instead, she turned to Mary Watson, who stood patiently beside her, wearing her split skirt for riding, watching her with bemusement. "All right, Mary. I have definitely seen and recognized one of the kidnapped girls."

"Time for me to go to Gatfer Cole's, then," Mary said with satisfaction. "There should be enough leeway for me to get something nice for him from the kitchen before I go out there and start making requests of him. It only seems polite."

"Something out of the ordinary—cakes, perhaps?" Nan suggested. "That's the one thing he didn't offer us for nummet. Good luck. You don't think you'll have any difficulty persuading him to come with you?"

"None whatsoever," Mary said firmly. "And good luck to you."

Mary left, and a few moments later, Nan saw her pass beneath the window, riding one of the hotel's horses and leading a moor pony, also saddled and bridled, and bearing two wicker panniers behind the saddle.

Now it was just a matter of waiting.

Waiting was always the hardest part.

Simon had no idea how Deborah and Jess managed to do their work after *two* episodes of the Dark Sleep so close together. But somehow, they'd been working all day, although by common consent the daily sweeping of the prison room had been skipped, and the cleaning of the outer room much skimped. The Dark One didn't seem to care; he was in fine fettle, hadn't even bothered putting his robe and frightening shadow-face on, and indulged himself from cock-crow in quite a few drinks from a tall brown bottle. Whatever was in that—gin, probably—it had made him very confident.

It also made him indulge in something else: petty cruelty. He'd spill things, call one of the girls over to clean it up, then trip them or kick them or slap them with the back of his hand, and laugh uproariously.

Finally he grew bored even of this, and got to his feet. Simon expected him to say something as he moved—his gait only a little unsteady—to the doorway of the prison room. But he didn't. He just stood there, looking at them as if they were all sweeties he was about to eat.

Simon whimpered. He knew it. He could sense it coming. *Three days in a row!* Surely this time the Dark Sleep was going to kill them all, or they'd be like Rose and never come out of it again.

The Dark One surveyed them all with an air of superiority, and despite his scrawny stature, his weak, petulant face, his bald head, with ears like a pair of jug-handles, Simon was even more terrified of him than he had been of the robe-shrouded, shadow-faced thing that had tormented them for so long. This was *worse*, because Simon could see the evil in his eyes—and he looked so *ordinary*!

Every single bad thing he'd done, from throwing stones at birds to spilling the supper milk, had led to this. He was here because he'd been wicked. That was the only explanation. And now he was being tormented by a devil on earth, and when the devil here finished him and he died, he'd be tormented by devils all over again. And he deserved it.

"Right, m'wee bees," the Dark One slurred. "Time t'take tha' 'oney."

This time when Simon crawled out of the horrific embrace of the Dark Sleep, the Dark One was already gone, and Jess was shaking him fearfully by the shoulder. "Simon," she was saying, over and over. "Simon. Tha' gotter wake oop an' et! If tha' don' wake oop, Dark One'll do t' ee what 'd did t'Rose!"

"Wha'?" he managed, thick-tongued and mazed. He tried to sit up, and nothing happened. "Es—ah—"

Jess popped a bull's-eye into his mouth. "Suck on sweetie," she urged. "It'll he'p."

The peppermint seemed to clear his head a bit, and the sugar did seem to help give him strength. She brought him water and another sweetie when the first was gone, and finally he could manage to sit up on his bed and look around, though everything was foggy. Was this how Rose had felt, before she fell into the Dark Sleep and never came out again?

The others didn't seem quite as drained as he was, though no one but Jess and Deborah looked as if they were in any condition to move, even to piss in the bucket. He wasn't sure what time it was, but they were all eating, and their loaves were stuffed with bacon and vegetable stew and sugar-stewed rhubarb. Deborah brought him the latter, put it in his hands, and had to bring it to his mouth before his mazed brain reminded him he had to actually bite into it and chew it before it would do him any good.

He couldn't manage to hold onto any thoughts for long, although a murderous despair gripped him so hard that slow tears fell down his face while he ate. He was so tired he was actually feeling all aquott and sick from the food, which used to give him the only pleasure he had in this place, and from the look of the tear-stained cheeks of the others, he was not alone in this.

When he had finished a second round of bread and rhubarb, urged on him by Deborah with awkward pats and vague murmurs of comfort, he lay back down on his bed, trying to keep something like coherent thoughts in his head.

And that was when the two utter strangers burst in the door.

He didn't even have the strength to feel anything. Not fear, that it was the Dark One back again in a new disguise. Not hope, because that had died. Not—anything.

At least that was true until Deborah suddenly shrieked, "*Gatfer Cole!*" and flung herself into his arms.

And the old man took her and hugged her and called out, "Chillern! Be no afeerd! 'Tis Gatfer Cole an' a bowerly leddy come t' he'p 'ee!"

It was late afternoon, almost dinnertime, when Neville came flying in, the brilliant sun gilding his black feathers, and landed on the windowsill, although he had alerted Nan that he was coming long before he arrived. By this time everyone else in the group had gathered in the girls' room, clad in a bewildering variety of costumes. Nan was dressed in a brown fustian skirt, unbleached linen blouse typical of the area, and white apron, purchased that very morning—to her astonishment—from one of the hotel barmaids. "It's for a costume party when I get back to London," Nan had lied. And since the price Nan had offered was enough to purchase two such outfits, brand new, from the village seamstress—meaning the girl would not even have to sew her own replacement clothing—the bargain had been struck on the spot.

Holmes was wearing the sort of worn-out moleskin trousers, patched boots, faded gray linen shirt, wool waistcoat, and flat cap most workmen around here wore. His shirtsleeves were pushed above his elbows, and his hands looked dirty. They weren't; it was some sort of stain, artfully applied to give the impression of ground-in dirt.

Suki was dressed in one of her Irregulars costumes, as a boy, her curls stuffed into a flat cap of her own. She looked just about as disreputable as Holmes.

In contrast, Sarah wore one of the walking suits that Alderscroft had sent with them in a blue that matched her eyes, a truly stunning new bonnet, and expensive walking boots. Watson was in a good black linen suit, an immaculate white shirt, School Tie, and shining black shoes, with a respectable black Derby, all new, all gifts from Alderscroft.

"He's on the way?" Holmes asked Nan, who nodded. "I'm off, then."

Holmes left the room. Neville joined Grey on his perch, and proceeded to tuck into the food waiting for him there—as a reward, he was getting a mix of hard-boiled egg and cheese, his favorite meal. Their part in this was done.

"Time for us to go as well," John said to Sarah, who nodded. "We should get ourselves dinner and established in place."

"I've been nearly bursting with impatience," Sarah replied. "I have practiced that spell you taught me until I could do it in my sleep! And finally, *finally*, I have a use for all that magic power I've been gathering!"

"Good, because when you need to set it, you may not have much time," Watson told her. He offered her his arm, as she rose. "And off we go to the Drake."

Nan and Suki waited a good ten minutes by her watch. When the last second had ticked by, she got to her feet as well. "Time fer usn's t'flit," she said to Suki, who grinned at her.

They made their way down the back stairs, the ones the hotel servants usually used, and out the back way, through the stableyard. The kitchen was busy preparing supper, and wonderful scents emerged from that door, the stable staff feeding the horses their evening meal with the sound of contented horses whickering, and no one even noticed as they passed out into the street, then headed down the street toward the bridge across the Dart river.

They were headed toward the Drake Manor Inn—technically not *in* Yelverton at all, although whenever anyone in any other village would ask about it, the answer would be, "T' one i' Yelverton, aye?" It was a good two and half miles, so it would be a good brisk walk, but they were wearing the sturdy shoes for it. No one paid them any attention at all, but that was as planned. John had cast a very peculiar illusion spell over both of them—not exactly an *illusion*, but an effect. Anyone who saw them would see two people—a young woman about Nan's age, and a young boy about Suki's age—whom they knew and expected to see together. The illusion would only break if someone tried to stop them and talk to them. But no one would. It was about suppertime, and anyone who wasn't already inside eating or waiting for supper to be ready was hurrying home or to some other place where he or she expected to get a meal. And in fact, it was possible to tell exactly what every family was having by the aromas coming from their open doors.

John had hired a chaise to make the journey; they'd have to walk *back*, of course, but meanwhile the presence of the chaise established him and Sarah as a couple of means. This was very important to their plan.

The Drake Manor Inn was allegedly a very old establishment, dating right back to Tudor times, and supposedly once part of Sir Francis Drake's actual manor. That was all that Nan really knew about it, other than the fact that if the Rock Hotel was at the upper end of the scale of establishments in Yelverton, the Drake was the accommodation of choice for the relatively prosperous farmer. That meant that, unlike the Rock, people of means like John and Sarah would not be out of place, but neither would a working man, provided he established quickly and early that he had the ready cash to pay as he went.

It also had a stable. This part was crucial, because Holmes had met Anglin at a point between Yelverton and the Gatfer's cottage riding a moor pony of his own, as if he had just come from something—what, Nan had no idea, but Holmes was inventive, and his stories were always sound. Whatever that something was, it would have put plenty of shillings, even pounds, in Holmes' pocket, and he would invite his good friend Anglin to share in the bounty. And not at their usual workingman's pub, but at the Drake, which was renowned for its beer, and which also had a stable to house their mounts while they drank.

That was the plan, at any rate. . . .

And about half a mile from the Drake, the sound of hoofbeats behind them prompted Nan and Suki to move off the road. And trotting on past—tall, lanky Holmes looking absurd on the little pony, especially when riding beside the much shorter Anglin.

Nan got a good look at the man as the two passed them while they waited on the verge. And a more pathetic-looking specimen of humanity she could not have imagined. In her mind, he had loomed large: tall, muscular, saturnine, with a roughly hewn face and thick black brows.

In reality he was small, weedy, with narrow, stooped shoulders, a childish, petulant face, prominent ears, and weak eyes and a weaker, pointed chin. He looked like a children's caricature of a brownie or some other, minor elfin creature. Though he was not old, he was already balding, and his attempt to disguise this with a workman's cap was not succeeding. From the thin, ginger-colored fuzz on his chin and upper lip, Nan got the impression that he was trying—and failing—to grow a proper beard and moustache. He and Holmes were talking, and even his voice sounded querulous and petulant. Nan could scarcely believe it. *This* was the monster who had made so many lives a misery?

. . . and rats can bite, and bite hard. Never underestimate a rat.

He was on the pony with no saddle, and just a bit of rope for a bridle, and the pony was foaming with sweat, which told Nan the man was coercing the beast against its will. There was a leather sack slung behind Anglin, with a bit of dark-colored material sticking out of it. And that solved the last mystery of how he maintained his guise as the Dark One without the children discovering his real identity. Anglin would change his clothing and drop the illusion on his face once he was past the forest in front of his cot and out on the moor. Once away from the cottage he'd go from the fearsome Dark One to . . . his true and rather unimpressive self. And then would do the same when he came back.

No wonder he creates a terrifying illusion. Not even children would be afraid of that little weed.

They soon outdistanced Nan and Suki, and as soon as they were out of earshot, Suki looked up at her guardian with a confused face. "'E looks like a sickly monkey," she said, scorn dripping from her voice.

"He does, doesn't he?" Nan replied. "But don't forget, monkeys bite, even sickly ones."

By the time they crossed the bridge over the Dart and reached the Drake, there was no sign of the pair. The Inn was right on the road on the other side of the bridge. Suki ran ahead and dashed inside first, followed by Nan.

It was a whitewashed, two-story building with a slate roof.

There was an imposing church behind it, an interesting neighbor for an inn. The plank door was right on the street, about halfway down the middle of the place. When Nan pushed open the door, she was met with a wave of warmth, the aroma of beer and good, solid food.

The public room was larger than the one at the Rock, but it appeared smaller, because it was long and narrow, and because it was crowded with wooden trestle tables and benches, with a very few smaller tables with proper chairs near the hearth. Sarah was sitting at one of the smaller tables, sipping a glass of what looked like wine, but was probably a local cordial, and picking at the remains of a supper. John was at the bar, and had already made friends with a couple of men who were dressed not dissimilarly from him. Professional men from Plymouth, more likely than not. At the other end of the bar were Anglin and Holmes, already well into what looked like their second or third pints. Pints? No, those were smaller glasses in front of them. Something much stronger than pints. It was a clear liquid . . . gin. *Oh, well done, Holmes. You're getting him drunk, giving him bottle-courage, and making him careless. The more bold and careless he is, the better off we are.*

The bar was about half occupied.

Not crowded enough, Nan decided, and decided to wait until the after-supper crowd came in. She mentally said as much to her co-conspirators, and sensed their agreement.

Meanwhile she seated herself at one of the big tables, right at the door, and near the rack where people could leave their walking sticks. She noted that there were already two in it; good, because she might need one of them. She ordered a pint for herself, and bread and soup. Just enough to justify her staying there, not so much as to be out of place with her costume.

And Suki was ghosting around the place, never getting in the way, like any child who was somewhere he ought not to be, but was not making enough of a nuisance of himself to warrant the adults chasing him out. Suki managed to charm some bread and cheese out of the barmaid for a penny and tucked herself out of the way to bide her time.

Meanwhile, Holmes kept drawing Anglin's attention to Sarah, sitting alone and apparently deserted by her heartless spouse.

Sarah kept consulting her (Nan's) watch, which was Nan's great pride, as it had been a gift, not from Alderscroft, but a Christmas present from Peter, and was a very fine object in a gold case. Peter had given Sarah a lovely cameo brooch just as fine as the watch, and had joked when Nan had opened her present that he wouldn't have *dared* give her anything that wasn't practical *and* pretty.

Sarah looked especially attractive; she'd taken great care with her blond hair, putting it up in a loose pompadour, from which a few charming tendrils escaped. Holmes kept whispering to Anglin, looking first at Sarah, then at John, and probably pointing out the pretty young wife and the older, seemingly neglectful, certainly complacent, older husband with her. Anglin kept nodding and smirking, as the bar and public room filled with what appeared to be mostly locals.

Think the bar is full enough now? Nan thought at Holmes.

My experience would say yes. Find your targets and alert everyone.

Nan eyed the crowd. There was a fat fellow right behind Anglin who was just at the "jolly-tipsy" stage, at which everything had become a bit foggy. He kept addressing the barkeeper as "George," which always elicited a roll of the eyes. He should do nicely.

Get ready, Suki, she told her protégée. *The fat man.*

Sarah, Holmes is ready. The fat man, she told her friend.

She surreptitiously secured a walking stick from the rack. *Now, Suki!* Her heart began to pound and her head to ache with anxiety and nerves. Even drunk as Anglin was, this would have to be timed *perfectly.* No one should have even a moment of suspicion that what they had planned was a ruse and a trap.

Suki squeezed herself through the crowd, right past Sarah. Even though she was watching, Nan didn't see a thing but a small boy squeezing his way past the tables—but now Suki had the gold watch that Sarah had been consulting so frequently. Then, as Sarah got up and moved toward the bar, giving every indication that she was going to speak to John, Suki wriggled her way into a place near enough to Anglin and Holmes to strike.

It all happened in a single moment. Sarah "tripped," and stumbled into the fat man, who was drunk enough not to realize he hadn't been jostled by one of his fellow barflies. He shoved back with a slurred "Watcher self, mate!" and Sarah went stumbling on into Anglin, who "steadied" her, then predictably put his hands where they should not have been.

But instead of the reaction he was probably expecting from a well-bred lady—blushing, shrinking back, and certainly not making a scene, he got something else. A full-armed *slap* across his face that cut through the din of conversation and silenced the entire bar, and a scream of *"How dare you touch me, you dastard!"*

Every head in the place except Nan's and Suki's swiveled in her direction. Those nearest drew back in an automatic reaction of shock.

And then, with the attention of the entire room on them, and a sudden space formed around them, she patted her waist, screamed again, and pointed straight at him. *"My watch! He stole my watch!"*

Suki escaped out the door. She, of course, had taken the moment of the slap to slip the watch into Anglin's back pocket.

The bar erupted with cries of "Thief!" and "Hold him!"

And . . . *something* happened.

Nan did not have enough magic in her to do more than sense it: two spells cast, one after the other. The first was probably Anglin's panic-stricken attempt at . . . well, no telling what, but if it had worked, it probably would have given him a precious few seconds to escape the hue and cry.

But it didn't, because Sarah's counter-spell to dispel *any* magic cast in that moment, learned from John, and fueled by all the hoarded power she had collected from released spirits, shattered his.

Nan would treasure forever the dull look of shock and incomprehension that went over Anglin's face as he turned to flee, and realized he wasn't going to be able to.

Holmes seized Anglin's arm, delaying him just enough for the other bar patrons to surround him.

Stupidly, he fought back.

He might have gotten away with it, if the only patrons were the sort like John. But there were plenty of farmers and working men here now, and they reacted to his aggression by swarming him.

Then it was mere moments before they beat him into near-unconsciousness, searched him, and found Sarah's watch. "Here 'tis!" cried one lad triumphantly, holding it aloft. "'Twas in 'is pocket!"

He looked to Sarah, who cried out, "It says, *To Nan, from*

Peter!" Then she burst into tears. "Nan is my sister! She let me borrow it, and he tried to *steal* it!"

The fellow examined it. "So it do!" and handed it over to her, while half of the rest of the patrons secured Anglin with a rope brought from somewhere behind the bar, and the other half tried to console Sarah with everything from a handkerchief to a beer.

Once Anglin was being pummeled, Holmes slipped out of the scrum and away, leaving Nan to put back the walking stick—no longer needed to trip the bastard in case he had made it to the door, and Sarah and John to wait for the constables to arrive and take Anglin away.

Every constable in Yelverton and the surrounding area seemed to converge on the Drake at once, which was scarcely a surprise, since this was probably the most exciting thing to happen in the village that evening. Every one of them but the two that took Anglin into custody whipped out a little notebook and began taking statements. Nan secured herself an extremely young fellow, who nervously licked the end of his pencil before beginning and looked at her as if he expected to hear a long and rambling tale that would somehow feature her mother, sisters, cousins, and aunts before she got to the point.

But Nan gave him a short and concise account, and finished it with, "An' Es know that aller. Es won't go aneest 'en. A right devil, an' if 'ee was t' go an' search 'is cot, reckon 'ee'd find a mort o' thin's 'e'd got no business 'avin'."

The young constable perked up at that. "Ow'll Es find yon cot, then?" he asked.

"Gatfer Cole," she said promptly. "Ol' Gatfer warnet me 'gainst 'en. Gatfer c'n tell 'ee."

And with that, she left.

It was just sunset, and as she hurried across the bridge, she was met on the other side by Suki, who was dancing from foot to foot with impatience. "It all went to plan," Nan assured her. "Now all we need to do is gather up again and wait."

"Waiting!" Suki exclaimed in tones of complete disgust. "Why do we always have to *wait*?"

* * *

It was almost ten by the time Sarah and John arrived, with a great deal of attention and fanfare, in the chief constable's private chaise. So they hadn't had to walk after all. By this time the entire village was abuzz with the gossip that the young friend of that famous Doctor Watson had been robbed by the ruffian Anglin, and everyone had some sort of story about what a ne'er-do-well he was and always had been, and how the speaker had *always known* he was going to end up at the end of a rope.

Nan and Suki had gotten to the Rock well ahead of the gossip, and slipped inside and changed, and were alerted to it by a servant rapping on their door to tell them "summat 'appened t' tha' friends!" It was all that Nan could do to keep a properly alarmed expression on her face until more accurate word arrived in the person of one of the constables.

And of course, by the time the chaise arrived, their host was waiting impatiently, now thuroughly alarmed at the idea that anything untoward had happened to the Elemental Magicians that Lord Alderscroft himself had placed under his roof.

So the gathering turned out to be—again—in the private parlor of Harold Linwood.

The first thing that John did was beg Linwood for a bowl of water, with which to communicate with his wife. It was enough to make Nan want to scream with impatience to watch him bend over the bowl muttering for what felt like hours (but was probably only minutes) before finally setting the bowl aside with a sigh of relief.

"Linwood, the man who tried to steal Sarah's watch is the same that has been kidnapping children to use as a source of Elemental Power," he said. "We hatched a scheme to get him caught red-handed in theft in order to get him locked up so that the children could be found by the authorities. It's a complicated tale, and I'll tell you as much of it as I can, after I deliver the rest of my information to my friends."

"Eh, *what*?" their host gasped.

And while Linwood was trying to get his mind wrapped around this, John turned to the rest of them. "The children were all there, drained, desperately drained, with two of them missing a fingertip, but otherwise unharmed. Enough of them knew Gatfer

Cole well enough to get the rest to trust him, and he and Mary have got them settled to wait for the police in the morning. The children have been told to tell the police that Anglin was using them as slave labor, hunting for valuable scrap in played-out mines. They have no problem with telling this story. One of them said to Mary that no one would believe them if they told the truth about the witchery anyway. It looks as if two of the girls were made to substitute for Helen Byerly after she escaped, held by the same means as Helen was. Mary found the fingertips and got the girls to knot them into their petticoats until we can figure out how to break the spell. Mary just told them that the police have their captor on a charge of theft, and they all know enough about that to know he is not leaving gaol. Gatfer is going back to his cottage as planned, to lead the police out to the cot in the morning. Mary is on her way back here." He turned back to Linwood. "And now . . . as I promised, the whole of the story."

Leaving out Sherlock's role in it all, in part by making a few things up out of whole cloth, Watson showed why he was such an excellent author by giving Linwood a relatively concise narrative of what they had discovered, and why they had taken the steps to secure Anglin that they had. Linwood was not stupid; though his brow creased many times as he tried to follow the story, by the end, he was nodding, and he heaved an enormous sigh of relief when John was done.

"Eh, well, that's as good a yarn as any that 'ee put i' the Strand, Doctor," he exclaimed.

"Well, you are going to have a part in it as well, Linwood," Watson told him. "I would like you to pop over to the station as soon as you can and tell the chief constable that you've long suspected Ansel Anglin to be pilfering things from the guests at this establishment, and that Gatfer Cole warned you about him. Then add that Gatfer Cole knows where the man's cot is, and that a search of the place will probably turn up a wealth of stolen goods."

"I'll do thet now! Station'll be in a pother anyway till midnight over this row. Make yerselves comfortable 'ere, I'll be back right quick. There's a bit yet I'd like t' have words with ye about." Linwood was as good as his word; he pulled off his apron, grabbed his hat from the hook on the wall, and was off, coatless, with his shirtsleeves still rolled up.

"Well," Nan said into the silence. "Now what?"

John grimaced. "Now comes my least favorite part of a case."

"Which is?" Sarah asked.

"Cleaning up all the loose ends. And this case has a great many loose ends."

20

The first of those loose ends that had to be dealt with was Helen Byerly. While the police were on their way to the cot—and to their credit, after Harold Linwood's statement that added to "Nan Bullen's," the chief constable led a crew of three out there at the crack of dawn—Nan got a horse and headed for Maude Rundle's cottage, while Sarah did the same and headed for Sheepstor.

Poor Maryanne must have been watching for someone to come up the trace every single day since their first visit, as she came running out of their cottage, with hope and fear flickering across her face as soon as Sarah came within view.

"We found them!" Sarah called as soon as she was in earshot, and Maryanne let out a scream, and collapsed on the ground, sobbing. Sarah dismounted and went to the woman, helping her to her feet and leading her and the horse back to the cottage.

Once the horse was tied up, she got Maryanne inside, got her a cup of water, and explained as briefly as possible. "Simon is probably being found by the police at this moment," she said. "Helen is too sick to move, but I can take you to Maude Rundle's cot if you want, as soon as you want."

"But she'll be all right?" Maryanne sobbed.

"She should be fine. Maude is an excellent healer and has some Earth Magic to help her. Helen is an incredibly brave and very smart girl. When the police come to tell you they've found Simon, but not Helen, you are to tell them that Maude came over the moor this very morning to tell you that *she* has Helen and Rose, and that Helen only last night recovered enough to tell her who she and Rose are, and where you live." That was the story the lot of them had worked out last night, and that Nan was riding to Maude's to impart to the reclusive healer even now.

Maryanne nodded, and dried her eyes on her apron. "That is a good, believable story," she said, with a tearful smile. "The dear Lord knows the real one would not be believed. But what about that monster that kidnapped my children?"

"He'll never see the outside of a gaol, unless he's transported," Sarah said grimly. "We can't prove he killed anyone, although I fear he probably has, and we don't hang thieves anymore, but between the stolen goods that Mary found and the evidence of a dozen children kidnapped and chained up, he's never seeing another free day for as long as he lives." She paused. "And John *thinks* I might have blasted his magical abilities badly enough with my counter-spell that he'll never be able to use them again. But even if I didn't succeed in doing that, everything he accomplished relied on his having a secret lair and helpless children. If he's transported, he *might* manage a secret lair again, though I doubt it, but he'll never again have access to children. Probably, though, given what he did here, he will be left to rot in Dartmoor Prison until he dies."

"Then he'll feel what they felt every wretched day of it," Maryanne said fiercely.

"Now—that's something I want to warn you about," Sarah continued. "Your children have endured a time of real horror. They are not going to recover from it quickly. You'll have to be prepared for nightmares, tantrums, and behavior that is unlike anything they have shown before. They may withdraw from everything. They may act manic. I don't know, and I don't know what to advise you. But John Watson *does* know people, doctors, who are Earth Magicians themselves, and can help."

"But we could never afford—" Maryanne began to wail.

Sarah cut her off. "You are now known as Elemental Magicians, and we take care of our own. Don't even think about the cost. Consider instead what the consequences could be if Simon reacted to this by assuming he deserved it all, and had nothing to lose by being even worse than his captor? Mary Watson tells me he has the potential to be even stronger as a magician than his captor."

Maryanne turned shocked eyes on her. "But—"

"It can happen," Sarah said ruthlessly. "And you owe it to everyone around you to see to it that if he needs help, he gets it. Helen will, too, even though she does not have magic herself, because now she knows it exists."

It took over two hours of persuading, but in the end, she convinced Maryanne Byerly, and was able to ride back to Yelverton reasonably sure that the woman would act on her advice.

But just in case, we'll have Linwood, Gatfer Cole, and Maude Rundle keep an eye on things here.

That was the first loose end. There were, however, ten more.

The chief constable of Yelverton was at a complete loss for what to do with the remaining ten children he had found chained up in that little stone cot. "They either got no kin, or their kin are Travelers'r trampin' folk, an' 'ow I'm t'find 'em I dunno!" he told John Watson in despair.

And of course, there was the other aspect that the chief constable was blithely unaware of—the fact that they were all budding magicians, who had suffered the same trauma as Simon, and could have the same emotional troubles because of it. The little healer, Sam, was one that Sarah was particularly concerned about.

But, fortunately, *that* had been what Linwood himself had wanted to talk about the night of the sprung trap. Because he had a plan.

"Or aneest a plan as Es can come," he'd said.

So that was why everyone but Rose—who was now conscious, but still very feeble—was sitting in the sanctuary of the church at Sheepstor. The good Father had promised they could have it as long as they wanted. Standing before them were Mary, Gatfer Cole, Ganmer Dolly, Linwood, and Maude Rundle.

All of the children were looking just about as scared as they must have been when the Gatfer and Mary broke into the cot. Sarah felt terribly sorry for the poor things. They had just endured what would have broken strong adults, and they now faced an uncertain future. Hopefully . . . they had an answer.

"Some uns of 'ee got no kin," she said, bluntly, as all ten pairs of eyes fixed on her. "Some uns got kin, but 'ee don' know where they be. An' some uns got kin as mean as yon barra thet cotched 'ee."

A nervous giggle at calling Anglin a gelded pig, but bobbing heads all around.

"An *all* on 'ee got witchery," she added. "'Ee gotter be taught 'ow t' use 't, or 'ow *not* t'use it. Tis tha' choice, but still means teachin'."

Heads bobbed again.

"So, here's what we bin thinkin'. 'Ee know t'Gatfer. T'Gatfer know Marster Linwood, Maude Rundle what had Helen an' still 'as Rose, an' Ganmer Dolly from Yelverton," she continued, waving at the appropriate people. "T'Gatfer trusts 'em, and they all got witchery an' c'n teach 'ee an' take 'ee in. But 'ee'll have t'earn tha' keep."

"'Ee with Traveler kin, Chell pass word of 'ee, an' when tha' kin come, 'ee c'n stay or go," Gatfer added. "Same for passin' workers. So, no fears, aye?"

Relief from the children of the Travelers.

"So Es got Rose. Es got house-room for twa more," Maude said. "Sam, Es c'n teach 'ee a mort'a healin', but it all be sheep. Naow, sheep don' complain much, so there's that." She raised an eyebrow at Sam, who laughed weakly. "Or t'Gatfer c'n teach 'ee people-healin'. Me, or Gatfer?"

"Pardon, leddy, but Gatfer? Es don' like sheep. 'Cept in mutton stew," said Sam, causing another laugh. "Nay 'arm?"

"Nay taken," Maude said complacently.

And so it went. In the end, Maude got Deborah and Jess along with Rose. Lily and Robbie went with Ganmer Dolly, who took them to her ample bosom as if they were her own grandchildren, and after Sarah learned she'd raised eight children and had nearly twenty grandchildren, she was satisfied Dolly could handle them. The Gatfer got Sam, Mark, and Colin, and after learning that they had a choice of working in the stable or the kitchen, which meant an actual paying *job*, Ben, Stephen, and Bill spoke up immediately for Linwood.

"It's not ideal," John told Sarah, as they rode back with Linwood, Ganmer Dolly, and the inn-wagon full of children to Yelverton. "But it's the best solution I can think of."

"They'll be more or less together, too, which should help," Mary added. She looked over at the children riding in the wagon, looking around with muted excitement. "You hear that? On your half-days and holidays you can always get together with the others. You won't lose your friends."

Bobbing heads, and some relief, especially from the more timid of this lot. Ganmer Dolly reached around and patted Robbie's head fondly. "Es got childer i' Yelverton what's good tradesmen. Oncet 'ee settle, an' 'ee wants a trade, they'll take 'prentices."

"What kinda 'prentices?" Robbie wanted to know, perking up immediately.

"Blacksmith, cooper, millwright, carpenter, farrier," she said proudly. "Good trades all. An' Lily, Es can train 'ee m'self as maid 'r cook, an' send 'ee out as dairymaid t'my eldest gurl, an' 'ee like."

"Any dairy in Yelverton'd take a gurl trained by Dolly'r Daisy," Linwood put in from the driver's box. He seemed fairly content with this arrangement, and Maude's comment about him "feeling he was too good" for the other magicians notwithstanding, he was on easy terms with all of them, and Sarah was inclined to chalk up those comments to Maude's misandry, because it was pretty clear she didn't have a lot of use for men in general.

So much for the children. Sarah was as certain as she could have been that they had done the best they could for them.

And that left—

Ansel Anglin.

While Nan and the rest had been sorting out the problems presented by the children, Holmes had not been idle. Letters had been flying to and from Plymouth and London, and certain advertisements had been placed in papers all over the country.

If any ladies have had valuable jewelry stolen while on holiday in or around the village of Yelverton, Devon, within the last two years, please send a description of said jewelry to Chief Constable Harris of the same village.

There were, of course, plenty of people applying falsely. But the chief constable had managed to find a matching description and a claimant for every piece of jewelry that had been in Ansel

Anglin's possession. Since each piece was a single count of theft, that amounted to quite a hefty number of charges. That, plus eleven charges of false imprisonment and two of kidnapping and false imprisonment. . . .

The trial was a two-day sensation, and even made the London papers. It was short, and brutal. The accused made wild accusations about the ladies who had owned the jewelry, all of which sounded to the jury like nothing more than the ravings of a madman.

They had all either sent testimonies dictated by Holmes, or came in person to present testimonies coached by Holmes. All told similar stories to Sarah's, of being jostled in the public room of the Drake, or the Rock, or one of the Yelverton area pubs, and discovering their jewelry missing afterward. All very credible and believable tales. Who would ever believe a man who claimed they had given him their valuables—and themselves! (sensation!)—freely! A weedy, homely, uncouth bit of moor trash?

All he brought on himself was mockery—and all the ladies got was sympathy for the profound embarrassment of being forced to hear such tripe.

And, of course, what could he possibly claim about the children *found in chains*, Helen and Rose left for dead on the moor, and three of them mutilated girls? No one believed a word he said, and his ravings grew more insane every time he opened his mouth.

When the jury adjourned, they took only ten minutes. Guilty on all counts. Sentenced to life in prison, in conveniently nearby Dartmoor Prison, at hard labor.

Case closed.

Last of all, the unnatural bondage of Jess, Deborah, and Helen to their severed fingers. . . .

The answer to that came, strangely enough, from Anglin himself.

Or rather, from a handwritten grimoire that Mary Watson found when looking for Jess and Deborah's fingers. It had been concealed in a hidden nook above the right-hand oven, along with the finger-ends; a kind of pocket hidden behind a removable stone.

The spell to bind someone or something to their own severed anatomy, and keep them bound to the place where you hid or buried that piece of anatomy, was under the heading of *A Nice and Accurate Spelle To Keepe Chikens And Diverse Kattle From Strayying*. The spell was Earth Magic, and obviously intended only for animals, and it said a great deal about Ansel Anglin that he also used it on people.

And beneath it, *How To Breake Thee Firste Spelle So As To Sell Thee Kattle Again At Market*. Whoever had written this grimoire was a very practical person, in Nan's estimation. But with that in hand, Maude was able to free all three girls.

Not to say that "it was no trouble at all," because it was quite a bit of trouble indeed and took the better part of a day, and involved a number of unpleasant bodily fluids—but it definitely worked, and meant the girls no longer had to keep their mummified and horrific bits of anatomy with them at all times.

But they never did find out what happened to the girl who belonged to the spare finger-end Helen had had with her. The severed finger-ends had never been introduced at the trial, since that would only open things up to questions there was no way of answering easily. In the end, it was concluded that Anglin marked the girls in this way as his servants—and that only Helen had had the courage to run. Deborah and Jess had agreed to this version; at this point the children had only wanted to know what they were to say that ordinary people would believe, so as to lock Anglin up forever. All that Maude could say about the spare finger was—"Reck she was took out t'moor, left like Rose, none found 'er, an she laid a bier. Or mebbe t'barstard droppet 'er down mine. Gi' it a Christian burial."

So in the end, that was what they did. In his younger days, Gatfer Cole had been a sexton, which she reckoned gave him the authority to conduct a burial. And as for "consecrated ground," well, it wasn't hard to bless water, ground, or anything else when you were Spirit Master. They found a pretty place with wildflowers, blessed the ground, and buried the finger with full honors and a cairn and simple cross to mark it.

If the poor thing had left a ghost behind, no amount of searching by Nan and Sarah found her. In the end, they gave up, enjoyed another few days as a pure holiday, actually *did* do some sightseeing on the moor, and came home. And Sarah pocketed the grimoire to add to Alderscroft's library.

* * *

". . . and that's the end of what Watson puckishly refers to as the Case of the Spellbound Child," Nan said, as they all lounged in Alderscroft's bungalow. "I suspect Anglin will be used as a bogeyman to frighten the children of the area for generations to come."

"Very likely," said Alderscroft. "Suki, allow me to commend you in especial in this case for your mature behavior and your ability to follow a plan and orders."

"Thenkee, sir," she said pertly, sticking a finger under her chin, and bobbing in her seat, as if she was curtseying.

"I'm concerned about the Byerlys," Nan continued. "They're desperately poor, unlikely to accept charity, and yet, with only one hand and no skills outside of working in a factory, Roger is unlikely to find work."

"I have been thinking about that," Alderscroft said. "I'm not sure Linwood is the best man to teach Simon, especially as far from Yelverton as their cottage is. I'm going to propose to Memsa'b that she offer places at the school to both children. I can certainly find someone in the Lodge to teach him magic, and I think he'd be better off away from his mother, at least until he has come to terms with everything that has happened to him."

"I was hoping you'd say that, sir," Nan replied. "I'm inclined to agree." She frowned a little, wondering if she should voice her opinion that none of this would have happened if Simon hadn't been as spoiled as it was possible for a child in such poverty to *be* spoiled.

Better not. That's just my opinion, and I've never had a child. Besides, if this hadn't happened, we'd never have found out about Anglin, those children would still be prisoners, and unsuspecting women would still be being raped and robbed.

"As for Maryanne Byerly—would you say that the opinion of the village of Sheepstor has softened toward her?" Alderscroft continued.

"Oh very much so!" Sarah exclaimed. "There is a great deal of sympathy toward her, especially as the fact of *why* the children were out on the moor is only known to us. It's just assumed that they went out foraging for food on their own and got lost, and Anglin came across them and scooped them up."

"Good," said Alderscroft with satisfaction. "I know someone who has decided to endow day schools in small villages the size of Sheepstor. I'll have a word with him, describe the circumstances, and point out that here is a perfectly good teacher being absolutely wasted out in the wilderness. There will be enough money to hire the girl who is already working as a teacher. I'll put him in touch with Father Shaw. The village can use the church as a schoolhouse until a proper building can be erected. We'll have things running in time for Fall Term."

"Given that we know for a fact these people can erect a finished stone building in a day, the church may not be serving as a schoolhouse for very long," Sarah pointed out.

"Well, I think that wraps up all your loose ends, does it not?" Alderscroft said with satisfaction. "Not every case needs to end with saving the world, but then—"

"I'd rather *no* more cases ended with saving the world!" Nan exclaimed with revulsion. "Saving a few people—or one!—is quite enough for us!"

"Well then, in that case, I think we have earned our tea," his Lordship concluded, and looked at the birds. "And what would you like for tea, my feathered friends?"

The birds looked at each other. Neville gave a blood-curdling laugh.

"Ladyfingers?" Grey suggested.

ABOUT THE AUTHOR

Mercedes Lackey is a full-time writer and has published numerous novels and works of short fiction, including the bestselling *Heralds of Valdemar* series. She is also a professional lyricist and licensed wild bird rehabilitator. She lives in Oklahoma with her husband and collaborator, artist Larry Dixon, and their flock of parrots.

www.mercedeslackey.com

For more fantastic fiction, author events, exclusive excerpts,
competitions, limited editions and more

VISIT OUR WEBSITE
titanbooks.com

LIKE US ON FACEBOOK
facebook.com/titanbooks

FOLLOW US ON TWITTER
@TitanBooks

EMAIL US
readerfeedback@titanemail.com